The Story of Old F[...]

Charles Egbert Craddock

Alpha Editions

This edition published in 2024

ISBN : 9789362927071

Design and Setting By
Alpha Editions
www.alphaedis.com
Email - info@alphaedis.com

As per information held with us this book is in Public Domain.
This book is a reproduction of an important historical work. Alpha Editions uses the
best technology to reproduce historical work in the same manner it was first
published to preserve its original nature. Any marks or number seen are left
intentionally to preserve its true form.

Contents

CHAPTER I ....- 1 -

CHAPTER II...- 20 -

CHAPTER III ....- 30 -

CHAPTER IV ....- 45 -

CHAPTER V ....- 63 -

CHAPTER VI..- 82 -

CHAPTER VII...- 95 -

CHAPTER VIII ....- 109 -

CHAPTER IX ....- 122 -

CHAPTER X ....- 133 -

CHAPTER XI ....- 155 -

CHAPTER XII...- 171 -

CHAPTER XIII ....- 187 -

NOTES...- 200 -

CHAPTER I

Along the buffalo paths, from one salt-lick to another, a group of pioneers took a vagrant way through the dense cane-brakes. Never a wheel had then entered the deep forests of this western wilderness; the frontiersman and the packhorse were comrades. Dark, gloomy, with long, level summit-lines, a grim outlier of the mountain range, since known as the Cumberland, stretched from northeast to southwest, seeming as they approached to interpose an insurmountable barrier to further progress, until suddenly, as in the miracle of a dream, the craggy wooded heights showed a gap, cloven to the heart of the steeps, opening out their path as through some splendid gateway, and promising deliverance, a new life, and a new and beautiful land. For beyond the darkling cliffs on either hand an illuminated vista stretched in every lengthening perspective, with softly nestling sheltered valleys, and parallel lines of distant azure mountains, and many a mile of level woodland high on an elevated plateau, all bedight in the lingering flare of the yellow, and deep red, and sere brown of late autumn, and all suffused with an opaline haze and the rich, sweet languors of sunset-tide on an Indian-summer day.

As that enchanted perspective opened to the view, a sudden joyous exclamation rang out on the still air. The next moment a woman, walking beside one of the packhorses, clapped both hands over her lips, and turning looked with apprehensive eyes at the two men who followed her. The one in advance cast at her a glance of keen reproach, and then the whole party paused and with tense attention bent every faculty to listen.

Silence could hardly have been more profound. The regular respiration of the two horses suggested sound. But the wind did not stir; the growths of the limitless cane-brakes in the valley showed no slight quiver in the delicately poised fibers of their brown feathery crests; the haze, all shot through with glimmers of gold in its gauzy gray folds, rested on the mute woods; the suave sky hung above the purple western heights without a breath. No suggestion of motion in all the landscape, save the sudden melting away of a flake of vermilion cloud in a faintly green expanse of the crystal heavens.

The elder man dropped his hand, that had been raised to impose silence, and lifted his eyes from the ground. "I cannot be rid of the idea that we are followed," he said. "But I hear nothing."

Although the eldest of the group, he was still young,—twenty-five, perhaps. He was tall, strong, alert, with a narrow, long face; dark, slow eyes, that had a serious, steadfast expression; dark brown hair, braided in the queue often discarded by the hunters of this day. A certain staid, cautious sobriety of manner hardly assorted with the rough-and-ready import of his garb and the adventurous place and time. Both he and the younger man, who was in fact a mere boy not yet seventeen, but tall, muscular, sinewy,—stringy, one might say,—of build, were dressed alike in loose hunting-shirts of buckskin, heavily fringed, less for the sake of ornament than the handiness of a selection of thongs always ready to be detached for use; for the same reason the deerskin leggings, reaching to the thighs over the knee-breeches and long stockings of that day, were also furnished with these substantial fringes; shot-pouch and powder-horn were suspended from a leather belt, and on the other side a knife-hilt gleamed close to the body. Both wore coonskin caps, but that of the younger preserved the tail to hang down like a plume among his glossy brown tangles of curls, which, but for a bit of restraining ribbon, resisted all semblance to the gentility of a queue. The boy was like his brother in the clear complexion and the color of the dark eyes and hair, but the expression of his eyes was wild, alert, and although fired with the earnest ardor of first youth, they had certain roguish intimations, subdued now since they were still and seriously expectant, but which gave token how acceptably he could play that cherished rôle, to a secluded and isolated fireside, of family buffoon, and make gay mirth for the applause of the chimney-corner. The brothers were both shod with deerskin buskins, but the other two of the party wore the shoe of civilization,—one a brodequin, that despite its rough and substantial materials could but reflect a grace from the dainty foot within it; the other showed the stubby shapes deemed meet for the early stages of the long tramp of life. The little girl's shoes were hardly more in evidence than the mother's, for the skirts of children were worn long, and only now and then was betrayed a facetious skip of some active toes in the blunt foot-gear. Their dresses were of the same material, a heavy gray serge, which fact gave the little one much satisfaction, for she considered that it made them resemble the cow and calf—both great personages in her mind. But she flattered herself; her aspect in the straight, short bodice that enclosed her stout little rotund figure, and the quaint white mob-cap that encircled her chubby, roseate face, all smiles, and indeterminate nose, and expanded, laughing, red mouth, and white, glittering, irregular teeth, had little in common with the mother whom she admired and imitated, and but for the remnant of the elder's stuff gown, of which her own was fashioned, the comparison with the cow and calf would have failed altogether. She was not even a good imitator of the maternal methods. Of course the days of her own infancy, recent though they were, had long been lost to her limited memory, and a token of the length of time that they had dwelt in the wilderness, and the impressions her juvenile faculties had received therefrom might have been given by the fact that her doll was reared after pappoose fashion; on her back was slung a basket in the manner of the peripatetic cradle of the Indian women, and from this protruded the head and the widely open eyes of a cat slightly past kittenhood, that was adapting its preferences to the conditions of the journey with a discretion which might argue an extension of the powers of instinct in pioneer animals,—a claim which has often been advanced.

The cat evidently realized the fact that it was a domesticated creature, that naught was possible for it in these strange woods but speedy destruction by savage beast or man, and that decorous submission became a cat promoted to the estate of a juvenile settler's baby. The cat was as silent and as motionless during the halt as the rest of the party, looking out watchfully over the shoulder of the little three-year-old, who, with perfect and mute trust, and great, serene eyes, gazed up at the face of her father, nothing doubting his infinite puissance and willingness to take care of her. When he spoke and the tension was over, she began to skip once more, the jostled cat putting out her claws to hold to the wicker-work of her basket; the two had ridden most of the day on one of the packhorses, their trifling weight adding but little to the burden of the scanty store of clothing and bedding, the cooking and farming utensils, the precious frying-pan and skillet, the invaluable axe, hand-saw, auger, and hoe,—the lares and penates of the pioneer. There were some surveying-instruments, too, and in the momentary relaxation of suspense the elder of the brothers consulted a compass, as he had done more than once that day.

"I thought I heard something," said the boy, shouldering his rifle and turning westward, "but I couldn't say what."

"Ah, quelle barbarie!" exclaimed the woman, with a sigh, half petulance, half relief.

She seemed less the kind of timber that was to build up the great structure of western civilization than did the others,—all unfitted for its hardships and privation and labor. Her gray serge gown was worn with a sort of subtle elegance hardly discounted by the plainness of the material and make. The long, pointed waist accented the slender grace of her figure; the skirt had folds clustered on the hips that gave a sort of fullness to the drapery and suggested the charm of elaborate costume. She wore a hood on her head,—a large calash, which had a curtain that hung about her shoulders. This was a dark red, of the tint called Indian red, and as she pushed it back and turned her face, realizing that the interval of watching was over, the fairness of her complexion, the beauty of her dark, liquid eyes, the suggestion of her well-ordered, rich brown hair above her high forehead, almost regal in its noble cast, the perfection of the details of her simple dress, all seemed infinitely incongruous with her estate as a poor settler's wife, and the fact that since dawn and for days past she had, with the little all she possessed, fled from the pursuit of savage Indians. She returned with a severe glance the laughing grimace of the boy, with which, despite his own fear but a moment ago, he had, in the mobility of the moods of youth, decorated his countenance.

"If it were not for you, Hamish," she said to him, "I should not be so terrified. I have seen Indians many a time,—yes,—and when they were on the war-path, too. But to add to their fury by an act of defiance on our part! It is fatal—they have only to overtake us."

"What was I to do, Odalie?" said Hamish MacLeod, suddenly grave, and excitedly justifying himself. "There was that red Injun, as still as a stump. I thought he was a stump—it was nearly dark. And I heard the wild turkey gobbling,—you heard it yourself, you sent me out to get it for supper,— you said that one more meal on buffalo meat would be the death of you,— and it was nearly dark,—and—gobble—gobble—gobble—so appetizing. I can hear it yet."

With an expression of terror she caught suddenly at his hand as he walked beside her, but he petulantly pulled away.

"I mean in my mind, Odalie,—I hear it now in my mind. And all of a sudden it came to me that it was that stump up on the slope that was gobbling so cheerful, and gobbling me along into gunshot.[1] And just then I was in rifle range, and I fired at the same minute that the stump fired, or the turkey, whichever you choose to call him—What is the reason, Sandy, that Injuns are so apt to load with too little powder?" he broke off, speaking to his brother. "The turkey shot straight—his ball dropped spent just at my feet."

"Quelle barbarie!" exclaimed Mrs. MacLeod, catching his hand again—this time to give it a little squeeze—impressed with the imminence of the boy's danger and their loss.

But Hamish was quite as independent of caresses and approval as of rebuke, and he carelessly twisted his hand away from his sister-in-law as he cocked his head to one side to hear the more experienced hunter's reply.

"Because their powder is so precious, and scant, and hard to come by, they economize it," said Alexander MacLeod, as he trudged along behind the packhorses, guarding the rear of his little party with his rifle on his shoulder.

"The turkey would better have economized his meat this time," said the boy, swinging round his belt to lift the lid of his powder-horn and peep gloatingly in at the reinforced stores. "He was economical with his powder, but extravagant with his life; for that turkey will gobble no more."

He gobbled a brisk and agitated imitation of the cry of the fowl, and then broke off to exclaim, "Quelle barbarie!—eh, Odalie?"

He looked at his sister-in-law with a roguish eye, as he travestied the tone and manner of her favorite ejaculation, which he was wont to call the "family oath." For indeed they had all come to make use of the phrase, in their varying accent, to express their disaffection with the ordering of events, or the conduct of one another, or the provoking mischance of inanimate objects,—as the gun's hanging fire, or the reluctance of a spark to kindle from flint to make their camp-fire, or the overturning of a pot of buffalo soup, or bear stew, when the famished fugitives were ready to partake in reality of the feast which their olfactory nerves and eyes had already begun. Even the little girl would exclaim, "Quelle barbarie!" when thorns caught her skirts and held her prisoner as she had skipped along so low down among the brambles and dense high cane, that one must needs wonder at the smallness of Empire, as expressed in her personality and funny cap, taking its westward way. "Quelle barbarie!" too, when the cat's culture in elegant manners required of maternal solicitude a smart box on the ear. And if the cat did not say "Quelle barbarie!" with an approved French accent, we all know that she thought it.

"So much better for the soul's health than swearing," Hamish was wont to say, when Odalie showed signs of considering the phrase a bit of ridicule of her and her Frenchy forbears.

Her grandfather had been a Huguenot refugee, driven out of his country by the religious persecution about the time of the Revocation of the Edict of Nantes, seventy odd years previously. Her father had prospered but indifferently in the more civilized section of the New World, and had died early. There his daughter had met her young Scotchman, who was piqued by her dainty disdain of his French accent, which MacLeod had recklessly placed on exhibition, and was always seeking to redeem the impression, finally feeling that he must needs improve it by having a perfect Mentor at hand. He had brought from the land of his birth, which he had quitted in early years, but few distinctive local expressions, yet a certain burr clung to his speech, and combined as incongruously as might be with his French accent. She evidently considered the latter incurable, intolerable, and always eyed him, when he spoke in that language, with ostentatious wonder that such verbal atrocities could be, and murmured gently in lieu of reply— "Quelle barbarie!" He found his revenge in repeating a similar slogan, one that had often been as a supplement to this more usual phrase,—"Partons pour la France aujourd'hui, pour l'amour de Dieu!" It had been urged by her grandmother in moments of depression, and Odalie, born and reared in the royal province of South Carolina, had always the logic and grace to wince at this ungrateful aspiration to return to France,—the dear France that had been so much too hot to hold them. For the family had rejoiced to escape thence with their lives, even at the forfeiture of all that they possessed.

This jesting warfare of words had become established in the MacLeod household, and often recurred, sometimes with a trifle of acrimony. Little they thought how significant it was to be and how it should serve them in their future lives.

The sun was going down. Far, far purple mountains, that they might never have seen but for that great clifty gateway, were bathed in the glory of the last red suffusion of the west; the evening star of an unparalleled whiteness pulsated in the amber-tinted lucidity of the sky. The fragrance of the autumn woods was more marked on the dank night air. One could smell the rich mould along a watercourse near at hand, the branch from a spring bubbling up in the solid rock hard by. Odalie had seated herself on the horizontal ledge at the base of one of the crags and had thrown back her hood, against which her head rested. Her large eyes were soft and lustrous, but pensive and weary.

"Rest, Odalie, while Hamish and I make the fire, and then you can fix the things for supper," her husband admonished her.

It was the first time that they had halted that day, and dinner had been but the fragments of breakfast eaten while on the march. There had been a sudden outbreak of the Cherokee Indians which had driven them from the more frequented way where they feared pursuit,—this, and the fate of the brave who had sought to lure Hamish to his death last night with the mimicry of the gobbler, and was killed in consequence himself. They could not judge whether he had been alone or one of a party; whether his body might be discovered and his death avenged by the death or capture of them all; whether he had been a scout, thrown out to discover the direction they took, and his natural blood-thirstiness had overmastered his instructions, and he must needs seek to kill the boy before his return with his news.

With this more recent fear that they were followed they had not to-day dared to build a fire lest its smoke betray to the crafty observation of the Indians, although at a great distance, their presence in this remote quarter of the wilderness, far even from the Indian war-path, that, striking down the valley between the Cumberland range and the eastern mountains, was then not only the road that the Indians followed to battle, but the highway of traffic and travel, the only recognized and known path leading from the Cherokee settlements south of the Tennessee River through this great uninhabited park or hunting-ground to the regions of other Indian tribes on the Scioto and to Western Virginia. Now, however, rest and refreshment were necessary; even more imperative was the need of a fire as a protection to the camp against the encroachments of wild beasts; for wolves were plentiful and roamed the night-bound earth, and the active panther, the great American cougar, was wont to look down from the branches of overhanging trees. The horses were not safe beyond the flare of the flames, to say nothing of wife and child. Therefore the risk of attracting observation from Indians must be run, especially since it was abated by the descending dusk. The little treacherous smoke escaping from the forest to curl against the blue sky need not be feared at night. The darkness would hide all from a distance; as to foes lurking nearer at hand, why, if any such there were, then their fate was already upon them. With the stout heart of the pioneer, Alexander MacLeod heaped the fagots upon the ground and struck the flint and steel together after giving the officious little Josephine a chance to try her luck with the tinder. Soon the dry dead wood was timidly ablaze, while Hamish led the horses to the water and picketed them out.

Odalie's eyes followed the boy with a sort of belated yet painful anxiety, thinking how near he had been to parting with that stanch young spirit, and what a bereavement would have been the loss of that blithe element from their daily lives.

"Quelle barbarie!" she exclaimed suddenly. "Quelle barbarie!"

Perhaps her husband realized her fatigue and depression and was willing to put his French accent on parade for her amusement; perhaps it was for the sake of the old flouting retort; he theatrically rejoined without looking up, "Partons pour la France aujourd'hui, pour l'amour de Dieu."

And Josephine, taking the cat out of its basket and kissing its whiskers and the top of its head, was condoling with it on its long restraint:—"Quelle barbarie, ma poupée, quelle barbarie, ma douce mignonne," she poutingly babbled.

Alexander MacLeod paused to listen to this affectionate motherly discourse; then glanced up at his wife with a smile, to call her attention to it.

She had not moved. She had turned to stone. It seemed as if she could never move again. A waving blotch of red sumach leaves in a niche in the dark wall of the crag hard by had caught her notice. A waving blotch of red leaves in the autumnal dusk,—what more natural?

What more wonderful? What more fearful?

There was no wind. How could the bough stir? There was no bough. The blotch of color was the red and black of a hideous painted face that in the dusk, the treacherous dusk, had approached very near and struck her dumb and turned her to stone. It had approached so near that she could see its expression change as the sound of the words spoken about the fireside arose on the air. Her mental faculties were rallying from the torpor which still paralyzed her physical being; she understood the reason for this facial change, and by a mighty effort of the will summoned all her powers to avail herself of it.

Alexander MacLeod, glancing up with a casual laugh on his face, was almost stunned to see a full-armed and painted Cherokee rise up suddenly from among the bushes about the foot of the cliff. Standing distinctly outlined against the softly tinted mountain landscape, which was opalescent in its illumined hues, faint and fading, and extending his hand with a motion of inquiry toward Odalie, the savage demanded in a lordly tone,— "Flinch? Flanzy?"

As in a dream MacLeod beheld her, nodding her head in silent acquiescence,—as easily as she might were she humming a tune and hardly cared to desist from melody for words. She could not speak!

The Cherokee, his face smeared with vermilion, with a great white circle around one eye and a great black circle around the other, looked not ill-pleased, yet baffled for a moment. "Me no talk him," he observed.

"What more wonderful? What more fearful?"

He had never heard of Babel, poor soul, but he was as subject to the inconvenience of the confusion of tongues as if he had had an active share in the sacrilegious industry of those ambitious architects who builded in the plains of Shinar.

"But I can speak English too," said Odalie.

"Him?" said the Cherokee, "and him?" pointing at Alexander and then at Hamish—at Hamish, with his recollection of that dead Indian, a Cherokee, lying, face downward, somewhere there to the northward under the dark trees, his blood crying aloud for the ferocious reprisal in which his tribe were wont to glut their vengeance.

"Both speak French," said Odalie.

The Indian gazed upon her doubtfully. He had evidently only a few disconnected sentences of English at command, although he understood far more than he could frame, but he could merely discern and distinguish the sound of the admired "Flanzy." Odalie realized with a shiver that it was only this trifle that had preserved the lives of the whole party. For even previous to the present outbreak and despite the stipulations of their treaties with the English, the Cherokees were known to have hesitated long in taking sides in the struggle between France and Great Britain, still in progress now in 1758, for supremacy in this western country, and many were suspected of yet inclining to the French, who had made great efforts to detach them from the British interest.

"Where go?" demanded the chief, suspiciously.

"To Choté, old town," she averred at haphazard, naming the famous "beloved town, [2]city of refuge," of the Cherokee nation.

He nodded gravely. "I go Choté,—travel with white man," he remarked, still watchful-eyed.

The shadows were deepening; the flames had revealed other dark figures, eight braves at the heels of the spokesman, all painted, all armed, all visibly mollified by the aspect that the dialogue had taken on,—that of an interpreting female for a French husband.

"What do—Choté—old town?" demanded the chief.

"Buy furs," said Odalie at a venture, pointing at her husband.

The Cherokee listened intently, his blanket drawn up close around his ears, as if thus shrouded he took counsel of his own identity. The garment was one of those so curiously woven of the lustrous feathers of wild-fowl that the texture had a rich tufted aspect. This lost manufacture of the Cherokee Indians has been described by a traveler in that region in 1730 as resembling a "fine flowered silk shag."

"Ugh!" muttered the chief. "Ugh!" he said again.

But the tone was one of satisfaction. The buying and shipping of peltry was at that date a most lucrative business, furs bearing a high price in all the markets of the world, and this region bade fair to be one of the large sources of supply. The Indians profited by selling them, and this, too, was the magnet that was beginning to draw the hardy Carolina hunters westward, despite the hazards. At no other industry elsewhere could commensurate sums of money be earned without outlay beyond a rifle and ammunition and a hunter's cheap lodgement and fare. The Indians early developed a dependence on the supplies of civilization,—guns, ammunition, knives, tools, paints, to say nothing of fire-water, quickly demonstrating their superiority to primitive inventions, and this traffic soon took on most prosperous proportions. Thus, although the Cherokees resented the presence of the white man upon their hunting-ground in the capacity of competitor, and still more of colonist, they were very tolerant of his entrance into their towns and peaceful residence there as buyer and shipper—one of the earliest expressions of middleman in the West—of the spoils of the chase, the trophies of the Indian's skill in woodcraft. Although the British government, through treaties with the Cherokees, sought a monopoly of this traffic as a means of controlling them by furnishing or withholding their necessities as their conduct toward the English colonists on the frontier might render judicious, many of the earlier of these traders were French—indeed one of the name of Charleville was engaged in such commerce on the present site of the city of Nashville as early as the year 1714, his base of supplies being in Louisiana, altogether independent of the English, as he was then one of the traders of Antoine Crozat, under the extensive charter of that enterprising speculator.

The French had exerted all their suavest arts of ingratiation with the Cherokees, and as the Indians were now on the point of breaking out into open enmity against the English, the idea of a French trader in furs, which Odalie had suggested, was so acceptable to the Cherokee scheme of things, that for the time all doubt and suspicion vanished from the savage's mind. Vanished so completely, in fact, that within the half-hour the chief was seated with the family-party beside their camp-fire and sharing their supper, and the great Willinawaugh, with every restraint of pride broken down, with characteristic reserve cast to the winds, speaking to the supposed Frenchman, Alexander MacLeod, as to a brother, was detailing with the utmost frankness and ferocity the story of the treatment of the Indians by the Virginians, their allies, in the late expedition against Fort Duquesne. The Cherokees had marched thither to join General Forbes's army, agreeably to their treaty with the English, by which, in consideration of the building of a fort within the domain of their nation to afford them protection against their Indian enemies and the French, now the enemies of their English allies, and to shelter their old men and women and children during such absences of the warriors of the tribe, they had agreed to take up arms under the British flag whenever they were so required. And this the Cherokees had done.

Then his painted, high-cheek-boned face grew rigid with excitement, and the eagle feathers bound to his scalp-lock quivered in the light of the fire as he told of the result. His braves hovered near to hear, now catching the broad flare of the flames on their stalwart, erect forms and flashing fire-locks, now obscured in the fluctuating shadow. The pale-faced group listened, too, scarcely moving a muscle, for by long familiarity with the sound, they understood something of the general drift of the Cherokee language, which, barring a few phrases, they could not speak.

There had been only a very bloody skirmish,—since known as "Grant's defeat,"—but no fight at Fort Duquesne, not even a formal defence of the works. The French had surely forgotten General Braddock! They had forgotten the fleeing red-coated Unaka[A] soldiers who, three years before, had been beaten near there with such terrible slaughter, and their chief warrior, the great Braddock, himself, had been tamed by death—the only foe that could tame him!—and lay now somewhere in those eastern woods. He pointed vaguely with his hand as he spoke, for Braddock's grave had been left unmarked, in the middle of the military road, in order that, passing over it without suspicion, it might not be rifled and desecrated by those savage Indians who had fought with such furious efficiency in the French interest.[3]

Willinawaugh paused, and all his braves muttered in applause "Ugh! Ugh!"

To the warlike Cherokee the event of a battle was not paramount. Victory or defeat they realized was often the result of fortuitous circumstance. Courage was their passion. "We cannot live without war," was their official reply to an effort on the part of the government to mediate between them and another tribe, the Tuscaroras, their hereditary enemies.

But upon this second attempt on Fort Duquesne the British had only to plant their flag, and repair the dismantled works, and change the name to Fort Pitt. For in the night the French had abandoned and fired the stronghold, and finally made their escape down the Ohio River. In all good faith, however, the Cherokees had marched thither to help the Virginians defend their frontier,—far away from home! So far, that the horses of a few of the warriors had given out, and finding some horses running wild as they came on their homeward way through the western region of Virginia, these braves appropriated the animals for the toilsome march of so many hundred miles, meaning no harm; whereupon a band of Virginians fell upon these Cherokees, their allies, and killed them! And his voice trembled with rage as he rehearsed it.

- 11 -

For all her address Odalie could not sustain her rôle. She uttered a low moan and put her hand before her eyes. For he had not entered upon the sequel,—a sequel that she knew well;—the sudden summary retaliation of the Cherokees upon the defenseless settlers in the region contiguous to the line of march of the returning warriors,—blood for blood is the invariable Cherokee rule!

Never, never could she forget the little cabin on the west side of New River where she and her adventurous husband had settled on the Virginia frontier not far from other adventurous and scattered pioneers. They had thought themselves safe enough; many people in these days of the western advance relied on the community strength of a small station, well stockaded, with the few settlers in the cabins surrounded by the palisades; others, and this family of the number, felt it sufficient protection to be within the sound of a signal gun from a neighboring house. But the infuriated homeward-bound Cherokees fell on the first of these cabins that lay in their way, massacred the inmates, and marched on in straggling blood-thirsty bands, burning and slaying as they went. So few were the settlers in that region that there was no hope in uniting for defense. They fled wildly in scattered groups, and this little household found itself in the untried, unfrequented region west of the great Indian trail, meditating here a temporary encampment, until the aggrieved Cherokees on their homeward march should all have passed down the "Warrior's Path" to their far-away settlements south of the Tennessee River. Then, the way being clear, the fugitives hoped to retrace their journey, cross New River and regain the more eastern section of Virginia. Meantime they were slipping like shadows through the dark night into the great unknown realms of this uninhabited southwestern wilderness, itself a land of shadow, of dreams, of the vague unreality of mere rumor. Some intimation of their flight must have been given, for following their trail had skulked the Indian whom Hamish had killed,—a spy doubtless, the forerunner of these Cherokees, who, but for thinking them French, would have let out their spirits into the truly unknown, by way of that great mountain pass opening on an unknown world. If the savages but dreamed of the fate that had befallen their scout!—she hardly dared look at Hamish when she thought of the dead Indian, lest her thought be read.

She wondered what had become of her neighbors; where had they gone, and how had they fared, and where was she herself going in this journey to Choté,—a name, a mere name, heard by chance, and repeated at haphazard, to which she had committed the future.

This fresh anxiety served to renew her attention. Willinawaugh, still rehearsing the griefs of his people, and the perfidy, as he construed it, of the government, was detailing the perverse distortion of the English compliance with their treaty to erect a great defensive work in the Cherokee

- 12 -

nation—the heart of the nation—to aid them in their wars on Indian enemies, and to protect their country and the non-combatants when the warriors should be absent in the service of their allies, the English. Such a work had the government indeed erected, on the south bank of the Tennessee River, mounted with twelve great cannon, not five miles from Choté, old town, and there, one hundred and fifty miles in advance of Anglo-American civilization, lay within it now the garrison of two hundred English soldiers!

Odalie's heart gave a great bound! She felt already safe. To be under the protection of British cannon once more! To listen to an English voice! Her brain was a-whirl. She could hear the drums beat. She could hear the sentry's challenge. She even knew the countersign—"God save the king!"— they were saying that to-night at Fort Loudon as the guard turned out;— she did not know it; she never knew it; she was only sure of it!

Willinawaugh had never heard of the agriculturist who sowed dragon's teeth and whose crop matured into full-armed soldiers. But he acutely realized this plight as he detailed how the Cherokees had protested, and had sent a "talk" (letter) to the Earl of Loudon, who had been at the time commander-in-chief of the British forces in America, setting forth the fact that the Cherokees did not like the presence of so many white people among them as the two hundred soldiers and the settlers that had gathered about the place. The military occupation made the fort a coercion and menace to the Cherokee people, and they requested him to take away the soldiers and relinquish the fort with its twelve great guns and other munitions of war to the Cherokee nation,—to which suggestion the Earl of Loudon had seemed to turn a deaf ear.

Alexander MacLeod, deliberating gravely, realized that under such circumstances the fort would ultimately be used against the English interest that it was designed to foster, by reason of the ever-ready machinations of the French influence among the Cherokees. The fort was evidently intended to afford protection to the Cherokees, but only so long as they were the allies of the English.

Much of the night passed in this discourse, but at length Willinawaugh slept, his feet toward the fire, around which the other Indians, all rolled in their blankets, like the spokes of a wheel about a hub, were already disposed. Alexander MacLeod had been nearly the last man to drop out of the conversation. He glanced up to note that Odalie sat still wide awake with her back against the trunk of a great chestnut-oak, her eyes on the fire, the child in her arms. They exchanged a glance which said as plain as speech that he and Hamish and she would divide the watch. Each would rest for two or three hours and watch while the others slept. It behooved them to be cautious and guard against surprise. The recollection of that dead Indian, lying on his face in the woods miles to the north of them, and the doubt whether or not he belonged to this party, and the sense of vengeance suspended like a sword by a hair,—all impinged very heavily on Hamish's consciousness, and in his own phrase he had to harry himself to sleep. Alexander, realizing that, as the ablest of the family, he was their chief means of defense, betook himself to much-needed repose, and Odalie was the only waking human being in many and many a mile. Now and again she heard far away the hooting of an owl, or the scream of a panther, and once, close at hand, the leaves stirred with a stealthy tread and the horses snorted aloud. She rose and threw more lightwood on the flaring fire, and as the flames leaped up anew two bright green eyes in the dusk on the shadowy side of the circle vanished; she saw the snarl of fierce fangs and no more, for the fire burned brilliantly that night as she fed the flames, and far down the aisles of the primeval forest the protective light was dispensed. Above were the dense boughs of the trees, all red and yellow, but through that great gate, the gap in the mountain wall, she could look out on the stars that she had always known, keeping their steadfast watch above this strange, new land. So accustomed was she to nature that she was not awed by the presence of the somber, wooded, benighted mountain range, rising in infinite gloom, and austere silence, and indefinable extent against the pallid, instarred sky.

She began to think, woman-like, of that home she had left; in her mind it was like a deserted living thing. And the poor sticks of furniture all standing aghast and alone, the door open and flapping in the wind! And when she remembered a blue pitcher,—a squat little blue jug that had come from France,—left on a shelf by the window with some red leaves in it to do duty as a bouquet,—so relieved was she now of her fears for the lives of them all that she must needs shed tears of regret for the little blue pitcher,—the squat little blue jug that came from France. And how had she selected so ill among her belongings as to what she should bring and what leave? Fifine had a better frock than that serge thing; it would not wear so well, but her murrey-colored pelisse trimmed with the sarcenet ribbon would have added warmth enough. If it were not such a waste of goods she would make over her paduasoy coat for Fifine, for she loved to see a small child very fine of attire. But precious little time she would have for remodeling the paduasoy coat,—a primrose-tinted ground with dark red roses, that had been her "grand'maman's" when new. "I wonder if I expected to live always in a hollow tree, that I should have left that pair of sheets, new ten hundred linen, the ones that I have just woven," she arraigned herself indignantly, as she mentally went over the stock in the pack. "And did I think I should be so idle that I must bring instead so much spun-truck so as to weave others. To think of those new linen sheets!

And then too that lovely, quaint little jug—the little squat blue jug that came from France!"

Oh, no; Odalie was not at all lonely during the long watch through the night, and did not lack subjects of meditation. The time did not hang heavily on her hands!

It hardly seemed that an hour had passed when Hamish, in obedience to some inward monition, turned himself suddenly, looked up, stretched himself to a surprising length, then sat up by the fire, motioning to her to close her eyes.

His face was compassionate; perhaps he saw traces of tears about her eyes. He could not know why she had been weeping, or he might have accounted his sympathy wasted. For Hamish looked upon crockery as inanimate and a mere manufacture, yet endowed with a perverse ingenuity in finding occasions to come into disastrous contact with a boy's unsuspecting elbow, and get itself broken and the boy into disgrace. He had his gentle interpretation of her sorrow, and motioned to her, once more, to close her eyes, and pointed up at the skies, where Orion was unsheathing his glittering blade above the eastern mountains—a warning that the night was well-nigh spent and a chill day of early December on the way. And it seemed only an inappreciable interval of time before Odalie opened her eyes again, upon a crimson dawn, with the rime white on the sparse red and brown leaves and bare boughs; to see breakfast cooking under Hamish's ministrations; to see Fifine washing the cat's face with fresh water from the spring—very cold it was, as Fifine herself found it, when it came her turn to try it herself and cry "Quelle barbarie!"—to see the Indians getting a party to horse to go back and search for one of their number, who had become separated in some way; to see poor Hamish's face pale with fear and consciousness, and then harden with resolution to meet the worst like a man.

At length they set forth in the frosty dawn of a new day, changing their route and making their progress further southward along untried ways she had never thought to travel. The sun came grandly up; the mountain range, wooded to the summit, flaunted in splendid array, red, and yellow, and even purple, with the heavy growths of the sweet-gum trees, and their wealth of lingering foliage. Here and there, along the heights, grim crags showed their beetling precipices, and where the leaves had fallen, covering great slopes with russet hues, the bare boles and branches of the forest rose frosted with fine lace-like effects. Sometimes, with a wild woodland call and a flash of white foam, a cataract dashed down the valley. The feeding deer lifted their heads to gaze after the party with evanescent curiosity and then fell to quietly grazing again: they had not known enough of man to acquire a fear of him. Sometimes arose the bellowing of distant herds of buffalo, filling the Cumberland spurs and coves with a wonted sound, to which they have now long been strangers.

Wild turkey, quail, wild duck, wild geese, the latter already beginning their southward migration, were as abundant, one might say, as leaves on the trees or on the ground. There were trout of the finest flavor in these mountain streams, and one might call for what one would for dinner. If one cared for sweets there was honey in the honeycomb in almost any hollow tree, where the wild bees worked and the bear profited; and for fruit and nuts there were the delicious amber persimmons, and the sprightly frost grapes, and walnuts and hickory-nuts and chestnuts galore.

The march was far swifter now than the rate that the settlers had maintained before the Indians had joined the party, and the little girl was added to the burden of one of the packhorses, but Odalie, light, active, with her native energy tense in every nerve, and with every pulse fired by the thought that each moment carried her nearer to the cannon of Fort Loudon and safety, kept step valiantly with the pedestrians. Willinawaugh sat at his ease on his horse, which was somewhat jaded by long and continuous marches, or perhaps his patience would not have sufficed to restrain him to the pace of the pioneers and his own unmounted followers. A grave spirit of amity still pervaded the party, but there was little talk. Odalie relegated herself to the subservient manner and subordinate silence befitting a squaw; MacLeod, restricted to the French language and his bit of Cherokee, feared that his interest might lead him beyond the bounds of the simulation their safety required; Hamish was silent, too, partly tamed by the halt which they now and then made on rising ground, when the chief would turn his keen, high-nosed profile, distinct upon the faint tints of the blue mountains beyond, his eagle feathers on his scalp-lock blowing back against the sky, and cast a sharp-eyed glance over the landscape to discern if perchance the search party, from which they had separated, was now coming to rejoin them. These frequent halts were discontinued after two days, when the Indian saw fit to change his proposed line of march, and the rest of his party, if following, could hardly be expected to also deviate from the agreed plan and overtake them.

They had hitherto proceeded down a valley, between clifty mountain walls on the one hand, and a high, steep, frowning ridge on the other, running with the same trend in unbroken parallelism. Now it suited Willinawaugh to turn his horse's head straight up these seemingly inaccessible slopes; and without exchanging a glance or venturing a comment his fellow-travelers obediently followed his lead, conscious of the sly and furtive observation of his tribesmen and even of Willinawaugh himself, for the suspicion of the Indian never seems quite allayed but only dormant for a time. He noted

- 16 -

naught that could excite it afresh, although it was only by the toil of hours that they could surmount the obstacles of great rocks, could find a deer-path through the dense jungle of the laurel, otherwise impenetrable, could cross foaming mountain torrents so swift and so deep that more than once it seemed that the packhorses, with Odalie also mounted now for the ford, must succumb to the strength of the current.

At length the party stood upon the summit, with a dozen wild outliers of the Cumberland and the intervenient coves below their feet; then came a vast spread of undulating country to the eastward, broken here and there by parallel ridges; and beyond rose mountains brown, and mountains purple, and still further, mountains blue; and still beyond and above, a-glimmering among the clouds, so high and so vague, apparently so like the gossamer texture of the vapor that one could hardly judge whether these congeners of the very heavens were earth or sky, mythical peaks or cloud mountains—the Great Smoky Range. In the wide, wide world below, noble rivers flowed, while aloft, like the gods on Olympus, it seemed the travelers could overlook the universe, so vast as to discount all theories of measurement, and mark its varying mood. So clear and limpid was the air that trivial incidents of that great scene were asserted despite the distance, and easily of note,—a herd of buffalo was distinguishable in an open, trodden space about a salt-lick; a fleet of canoes, like a bevy of swallows, winged along the broad surface of the largest of these splendid streams, called the Tsullakee (Cherokee) as Willinawaugh informed them, for these Indians never used the sound represented by our letter R. In the phonetically spelled words in which it seems to occur the sound is more accurately indicated by the letter L. A notable philological authority states that the English rendering of the word "Cherokee" and others of the language in which the letter R appears is derived from the mistaken pronunciation of neighboring tribes and of the French, who called the Tsullakee[B]—La rivière des Chéraquis.

Odalie could not refrain from asking in what direction was Choté, "beloved town, city of refuge." She had the art to affect to interpret for her husband, but she could not keep the light from her eyes, the scarlet flush of joyful expectation from her cheek, when the savage, with a sweeping wave of his pipe-stem, indicated a region toward the southeast on the banks of a tributary (the Little Tennessee) of that broad and splendid river, which was now running crimson and gold and with a steely glitter, reflecting the sunset, in the midst of the dusky, dull-blue landscape, with the languor of evening slipping down upon it.

There it lay in primeval beauty,—the land of hope. Oh, for the spirit of a soothsayer; for one prophetic moment! What did that land hold,—what days should dawn upon it; what hearthstones should be alight; who should be the victor in the conquests of the future, and what of the victim?

But they loved this country—the Cherokees; their own, they said, for the Great Spirit gave it them. They even sought to associate with those splendid eastern mountains the origin of the Cherokee people by the oft-reiterated claim that the first of their race sprung from the soil of those noble summits or dropped from the clouds that hover about the lofty domes. And now Willinawaugh broke from the silence that the lack of a common tongue had fostered, and despite that embargo on the exchange of ideas he grew fluent and his enthusiasm seemed to whet the understanding of his listeners, who could realize in some sort the language that they could not speak. They caught the names of the great landmarks. The vast range, on an outlier of which they pitched their camp, as insignificant in proportion as an atom to the universe, he called the Wasioto Mountain, and one of the rivers was the Hoho-hebee, and others were the Coot-cla, the Agiqua, the Canot, the Nonachuckeh. Hamish remembered these names long after they were forgotten by others, and the re-christened Clinch and Holston and French Broad flowed as fairly with their uncouth modern nomenclature as when they were identified by as liquid musical syllables as the lapsing of their own currents; for never did he lose the impression of this night;—never faded the mental picture of the Cherokee chief, the war-paint, vermilion and black and white, on his face as he sat before the fire, the waving of the eagle-feathers on his tufted scalp-lock blotting out half the dull-blue landscape below, which had the first hour of the night upon it, and the moon, blooming like a lily, with a fair white chalice reflected in the dark deeps of the Tsullakee River. And in this hour while Odalie reached out with all tender, tremulous hope to the future the savage told of the past.

Of the past,—mysterious, mythical. Of the strange lack of tradition of this new world that was yet so old. For here, in the midst of the Cherokee hunting-ground,—the whole country was but a great uninhabited park heavily stocked with game, the Cherokee settlements being merely a fringe upon its verges,—were vestiges of a previous population; remains of works of defense like forts; fragments of pottery and other manufactures; unfading allegorical paintings high on the face of inaccessible cliffs; curious tiny stone sarcophagi containing pygmy bones, the mysterious evidence of the actual existence of the prehistoric "little people";[4] great burial mounds, with moldering skeletons, and caves entombing mummies of splendid stature and long yellow hair, evidently placed there ages ago, still wearing ornaments of beads and metals, with remnants of strange fabrics of fibers and feathers, and with weapons befitting a high rank and a warlike race. And who were they? And whence did they come? They were always here, said Willinawaugh. So said all the Cherokees. They were always here.

And whither did this unknown people go? The Indian shook his head, the flicker of the fire on his painted face. They were gone, he said, when the Tsullakee came. Long gone—long gone!

And alas, what was their fate? Odalie looked about at the violet night, at the white moon and the dun shadows, with an upbraiding question, and the night was silent with a keen chill fall of a frost. This was no new world into which they were adventuring. It had witnessed tragedies. It held death. It sealed its lips and embodied oblivion. Oh, for the hopes of the future,— and oh, for the hopes of the dead and gone past!

FOOTNOTES:

[A] White.

[B] It is known now as the Tennessee River.

CHAPTER II

The next day when Odalie turned her face once more toward her Mecca of home and peace she felt that she trod on air, although her shoes, ill calculated for hard usage, had given way at last, and suffered the thorns to pierce through the long rifts between sole and upper leather and the stones to still further rend the gaping tatters. MacLeod would not allow himself to comment on it even by a look, lest some uncontrollable sympathy should force him to call a halt, now when he felt that their lives depended on pressing forward and taking advantage of the pacific mood of the Indian and the assumed character of French traders to reach the English fort. Hamish, however, with a dark-eyed, reproachful glance upbraided this apparently callous disregard, and then addressed himself to the task of making light of the matter to Odalie in lieu of other solace.

"Tu ne ought pas l'avoir fait," he gravely admonished her in his queer French. "Tu ought known better, Odalie!"

"Known what better?" demanded Odalie, resenting reprimand in a very un-squawlike fashion.

"Marcher in shoes! Mong Dew! Ces souliers couldn't have been made pour marcher in!" he retorted, with a funny grimace.

The facial contortion seemed suddenly to anger Willinawaugh, who had chanced to observe them; to suggest recollections that he resented, and the reminder shared in his disfavor. He abruptly wreathed his fierce countenance into a simulacrum of Hamish's facetious mug; he shrugged his shoulders with a genuine French twist; and anything more incongruously and grotesquely frightful and less amusing could hardly be imagined.

"Fonny! vely fonny! Flanzy!" he exclaimed harshly. "Balon Des Johnnes!"[5]

His unwilling companions gazed at him with as genuine a terror as if the devil himself had entered into him and thus expressed his presence among them. Willinawaugh abruptly discontinued his "fonny" grimace, that had a very ferocity of rebuke, and leaning from his horse with an expression of repudiation, spat upon the ground. Then he began to talk about Baron Des Johnnes and his sudden disappearance from the Cherokee Nation.

At Choté, it seemed, was this gay and facetious Frenchman, this all-accomplished Baron Des Johnnes, who could speak seven different Indian languages with equal facility, to say nothing of a trifle or two such as English, Spanish, German, and French, of course!—at Choté, City of Refuge, where, if he had shed the blood of the native Cherokee on his own

- 20 -

threshold, his life would have been sacred even from the vengeance of the Indian's brother! And suddenly came the Carolina Colonel Sumter, returning with an Indian delegation that had been to Charlestown, and found the Frenchman here. And with Colonel Sumter was Oconostota, king of the Cherokees, and other head-men, who had just signed a treaty at Charlestown, promising to kill or arrest any Frenchman discovered within the Cherokee Nation. And who so appalled as Oconostota, to see his friend, the gay Baron Des Johnnes, lying on a buffalo skin before the fire, smoking his pipe in the chief's own wigwam. And when Colonel Sumter demanded his arrest Oconostota refused and pleaded the sanctity of the place—the City of Refuge. And Baron Des Johnnes arose very smiling and bland, and bowed very low, and reminded Colonel Sumter that he was in Choté—Old Town!

And what said Colonel Sumter? He spoke in the English, like a wolf might talk—"Old Town—or New Town—I'll take you to Charles Town!"

And what did the Baron Des Johnnes? Not a Cherokee; not bound by the ever-sacred laws of the City of Refuge! Although surrounded by his friends he struck not one blow for his freedom, as man to man. He suffered himself to be arrested, single-handed, by this wolf of a Colonel—Colonel Sumter—saying in gentle protest, "Mais, M'sieur!"

"Mais, M'sieur!" grimaced Willinawaugh, in mimicry. Then "Mais M'sieur!" he threw up both hands. "Mais, M'sieur!" he shrieked in harsh derision to the unresponsive skies.

Alexander knew that the Baron Des Johnnes had been taken to Charlestown and examined, and although nothing could be proved against him, it had been deemed expedient to ship him off to England. Perhaps the authorities were of opinion that a man with such conversational facilities as eight or ten languages had best be kept where "least said, soonest mended."

But for the repeated harsh treatment that the Cherokees sustained from the English settlers, the ingratiating arts of the French might have failed to find so ready a response. Sedate of manner and of a grave cast of mind themselves, the Indians could ill tolerate the levity, the gaieté de cœur, of the French, whom they pronounced "light as a feather, fickle as the wind, and deceitful as serpents."

With this intimation of Willinawaugh's reserves of irritability the pioneers journeyed on, a trifle more ill at ease in mind, which was an added hardship, since their physical sufferings were intensifying with every long mile of continued effort. They began to wonder how they, supposed to be French, would fare when they should meet other Cherokees, perhaps more disposed than Willinawaugh to adhere to the terms of their treaty to kill or make prisoner every Frenchman who should venture into the Cherokee Nation, yet on the other hand perhaps more competent by virtue of a familiarity with the language to detect and resent the fact that they were not of the French nationality. Already Willinawaugh had counseled that they should go further than Choté, to ply their trade in furs, for Choté was dangerously near the English fort for a Frenchman; one of the Tuckaleechee towns on the Canot River was a preferable location, and he promised to contrive to slip them past Fort Loudon without the commandant's knowledge.

They restrained all expression of objection or discomfort and bore their growing distresses with a fortitude that might rival the stoicism of a savage. Only when an aside was possible, MacLeod besought his wife to loose the burden of one of the packhorses and mount the animal herself. She shook her head resolutely. She had already suffered grief enough for the household stores she had left behind. To these precious remaining possessions she clung desperately. "When I can no longer walk," she said, with a flash in her eye which admonished him to desist.

They offered no comment on their route, although it seemed that they had climbed the mountain two days ago for the express purpose of descending it again, but on the eastern side. MacLeod, however, at length realized that the Indian was following some faint trace, well distinguishable to his skilled eye, and the difficulties of the steep descent were rendered more tolerable by his faith in the competence of his guide. The packhorses found it hard work filing down the sharp declivities and sustaining the equilibrium of their burden. The chief, with his lordly impatience and superiority to domestic concerns, evidently fumed because of the delay they occasioned, and had he not supposed that the contents of the bales of goods were merchandise and trinkets to be bartered with the Indians for peltry, instead of Odalie's slim resources of housekeeping wares,—sheets, and table-linen and garments, and frugal supplies of flax and seeds,—he would not have suffered the slow progress.

Through the new country below, that they had watched from the heights, they went now, the mountains standing sentinel all around the horizon— east and west, and north and south, sometimes nearer, sometimes more distant; always mountains in sight, like some everlastingly uplifting thought, luring a life to a higher plane of being. Now and again the way wended along the bank of a river, with the steeps showing in the waters below as well as against the sky above, and one day when they had but recently broken their camp on its shores there shot out from beneath an overhanging boscage of papaw trees a swift, arrowy thing akin to a fish, akin to a bird—an Indian canoe, in which were three braves.

- 22 -

The poor pioneers were exhausted with their long and swift journey; their hearts, which had been stanch within them, could but fail with the failure of physical strength. Their courage only sufficed to hold them to a mute endurance of a dreadful expectation, and a suspense that set every nerve a-quiver. The boatmen had cried out with a wild, fierce note of surprise on perceiving the party, and the canoe was coming straight across to the bank as fast as the winglike paddles could propel it. Willinawaugh rode slowly down to meet them, and in contrast to the usual impassive manners of the Indians he replied to the agitated hail in a tone of tense and eager excitement. There ensued evidently an exchange of news, of a nature which boded little good to the settlers. Dark anger gathered on the brow of the chieftain as he listened when the braves had bounded upon the bank, and more than once he cried out inarticulately like a wild beast in pain and rage. Perhaps it is rare that a man has such a moment in his life as Alexander experienced when one of the savages, a ferocious brute, turned with a wild, untamed, indigenous fury kindling in his eyes, and drawing his tomahawk from his belt smiled fiercely upon the silent, motionless little band, his deadly racial hatred reinforced by a thousand bitter grudges and wrongs.

Hamish's fingers trembled on his gun, but ostensibly no one moved. Willinawaugh hastily interposed, speaking but the magic words—"Flanzy—Flinch!" Then still in English, as if to reassure the pioneers—"Go Choté—Old Town—buy fur!"

The hatred died out of the fierce Indian faces. The French in the South, as has been said, had always used every art to detach the Cherokees from the British interest, and even now the men who had abandoned Fort Duquesne, escaping down the Ohio River, were sending emissaries up the Tsullakee, to the Lower Towns, there finding fruitful soil in which to sow the seeds of dissension against the English. The assertion that these travelers were French, and the fact that by receiving persons of this nation the Cherokees could requite with even a trivial and diplomatic injury some faint degree of the wrong which they considered they had sustained from the Virginians, was more than adequate to nullify for the time the rage they felt against these pioneers as of the white race.

With the instinct of hospitality, which is a very marked element of the Cherokee nature, one of them signed with a free and open gesture to the boat.

"Beaucoup marchez!" he said, smiling with an innocent suavity like a child, "Svim!"

He did not mean literally "swim," and to offer them the facilities of the Tennessee River for that purpose, although this might have been inferred. But the pioneers understood the proffer of the canoe for the remainder of their journey, and a deadly terror seized the heart of Odalie as she marked the demonstrations of the others in pulling Willinawaugh forcibly from his horse in spite of his feigned objections, for the canoe could hold but three persons. Little choice had she, however. Willinawaugh, maintaining the affable demeanor of a guest of conscious distinction, was already seated in the boat, and pointed out Alexander as his preferred companion. For once the Scotchman disregarded the wishes of his guide, philosopher, and friend, and taking his wife by the hand motioned to her to step over the side of the little craft. Odalie could only look reproachfully at him; she could not contend with her lord and master in the presence of savages—such are the privileges of civilization! The Indians, somewhat accustomed by the talk, and on occasion the example, of the French traders, and perhaps by traditions from the white settlements, to the idea of the extreme value that the paleface was wont to place on wife or daughter, scornfully marked the instance, but beyond an expressive "Ugh!" naught was said. The child was lifted to Odalie's arms—the cat strapped pappoose-wise to Josephine's back and accommodating itself quiescently to the situation.

Alexander had never intended to embark Odalie and Josephine alone with the Indians, although his will was but a slight thing, so entirely were they now in the power of the savages; he motioned to Hamish to take the paddle, and with the slight mixture of French and Cherokee at his command, intimated to the apparent owner of the boat that he would rather walk by his side and profit by his converse than to be able to sail at will on the water like the swan there—a large and handsome bird, who was giving the finest exhibition of that method of progression to be easily found anywhere, with her white neck arched, her gliding motion, and snowy breast reflected in the clear water.

And so Odalie had parted from her husband, without so much as a glance of farewell! Perhaps he dared not look at her. So far they had come together, and now in these wild fastnesses, among these blood-loving fiends in the likeness of humanity, they were separated to meet when?— where? Perchance no more. She could not—would not—leave him thus. She would turn back at the last moment! She would go back!

She rose to her feet so precipitately that with the shifting of her weight the canoe careened suddenly and was momentarily in danger of capsizing with all on board. Willinawaugh glanced up with a kindling eye and a ferocious growl. Hamish, throwing himself skillfully on the opposite side, adroitly trimmed the boat. His look of warning, upbraiding and yet sympathizing, steadied Odalie's nerves as she sank back into her place. She tactfully made it appear that she had accidentally come near to dropping the little girl from her grasp and rising to recover her had shaken the poise of the frail craft. Willinawaugh's mutter of dissatisfaction showed that he esteemed the possibility no very great mischance, and set no high store on Josephine. Now and again he eyed the cat, too, malevolently, as if he could ill brook her mannerisms and pampered mien. Hamish had an uncomfortable idea that the Cherokee was not familiar with animals of this kind, and that he harbored a wonder if Kitty would not serve her best and noblest possibilities in a savory stew. But for himself Hamish avoided the Indian's eyes with their curious painted circles of black and white, as much as he might, for whenever their glances met, Willinawaugh's facial contortion to deride the "fonny" disposition he deemed a part of Hamish's supposed French nature so daunted the boy that he bent his head as well as his muscles to the work.

That day was like a dream to Odalie, and, indeed, from the incongruity of her mental images she hardly knew whether she was sleeping or waking. One moment it seemed to her that she was in Carolina, in the new frame mansion that she had always thought so fine, sitting on the arm of her grandmother's chair, with her dark hair against the white locks and the snowy cap, while she babbled, in the sweet household patois of French children that has no lexicon, and no rules, and is handed down from one generation to another, her girlish hopes, and plans, and anxieties, to find the grandmother's fine, old, deft hand smooth all the difficulties away and make life easy, and hope possible, and trouble a mere shadow.

Alas! that brightening perspective of the colonial garden, where the jasmine, gold and white, clung to the tall trellises, and the clove gillyflower, and the lilies and roses grew in the borders in the broad suffusions of the sunshine, was metamorphosed to the wide spread of the Tennessee River, with the noon-day blaze on its burnished expanse of ripples; and grand'maman had long since ceased her ministry of soothing and consolation, and found her own comfort in the peace and quiet of the grave. And ere Odalie could suffer more than a pang to realize that she was so far from that grave, her head drooped once more—she was asleep.

No; she was awake, awake and splendid in a white dress, her beautiful bridal dress in which she had looked a very queen, with her grand'maman's pearl necklace, itself an heirloom, about her white throat. And so, standing at the altar of the little church with Alexander, and much light about her, and a white dress, oh, very white—and suddenly! all the church is stricken to darkness. No; there is light again!

It was a flash from a thunder cloud, reflected in sinister, forked lines in the Tennessee River, so that they seemed in the very midst of the lightning, until it vanished into the darkness of a lowering black sky, that overhung the water and made all the woods appear bleak and leafless, though here and there still a red tree blazed. The world was drearier for these grim portents of storm, for all the way hitherto fair weather had smiled upon their progress. Still she could not heed—she did not care even when the rain came down and pitilessly beat upon her white face; she did not know when Fifine crept under the shawl which Hamish threw around her, and that the frightened little girl held to her tight with both arms around her waist, while the pioneer cat very discreetly nestled down in the basket on Josephine's back. She was not roused even by loud voices when later a pettiaugre, a much larger boat than theirs, pulled alongside with eight or ten warriors and remained in close and unremitting conversation with Willinawaugh for several miles. Poor Hamish could hardly sustain himself. He felt practically alone. Odalie was, he thought, on the verge of death from exhaustion and realized naught of her surroundings. His brother had been left in these wild woods with a party of savages, who were as likely to murder him for a whim or for the treasures of the bales which the packhorses carried, as to respect the safe conduct of Willinawaugh and the supposed character of French traders. This, Hamish was aware, hardly sufficed now, so unrestrained was the ferocity of the glances cast upon them by the Indians in the pettiaugre alongside—so like the glare of a savage catamount, ready to leap upon its prey and yet with a joyance in its ferocity, as if this rage were not the pain of anger but the pleasure of it.

What subtle influence roused Odalie at last she could hardly have said; perhaps the irresistible torpor of exhaustion had in some sort recruited her faculties. The storm was gone, unseasonable and transient, and only a broken remnant of its clouds hung about the western mountains. Toward the east the sky was clear and a dull fluctuation of sunset, alternating with shadow, was on the landscape. As a sudden suffusion of this broad, low, dusky glare lay upon the scene for a moment, she saw against the dark blue Chilhowee Mountain in the middle distance something glimmering and waving, and as she strained her eyes it suddenly floated broadly forth to the breeze,—the blended cross of St. George and St. Andrew blazoned on the British flag.

In one moment she was strong again; alert, watchful, brave, despite that boat close alongside and the alternate questions and remonstrances of the fierce and cruel Indians. One of them, the light of a close and fine discernment in his savage features, was contending that Willinawaugh was deceived; that these were no French people; that the cast of the face of the "young dog" was English; he looked like the Virginia settlers and hunters; even like the men at the fort.

Willinawaugh had the air of deigning much to consider the plea that the other Indians preferred. He only argued astutely that they all spoke French among themselves,—man, boy, squaw, and pappoose. They showed gratitude when he had promised them that they should not be obliged to pass the English fort and risk the chance of detection. He intended to slip them up the Tellico River where it flows into the Tennessee a mile on the hither side of the fort and thence make their way to a remoter Indian town than Choté.

The skeptical Cherokee, Savanukah, immediately asserted boastfully that he spoke "Flinch" himself and would test the nationality of the boy.

Hamish had never had great scholastic advantages and had sturdily resisted those that Odalie would have given him. He remembered with despair the long lines of French verbs in the little dog's-eared green book that all her prettiest sisterly arts could never induce him to learn to conjugate. Why should he ever need more talking appliance than he already possessed, he used to argue. He could tell all he knew, and more besides, in the somewhat limited English vocabulary at his command. "Parlez vous? Parlez, fou!" he was wont to exclaim, feeling very clever. How should he have dreamed that Odalie's little Vocabulaire Français would be more efficacious to save his life than his rifle and his deadly aim?

"The canoe rocked in the swirls."

He looked toward her once more in his despair. The boats were now among a series of obstructions formed by floating débris of a recent storm,—many branches of trees, here and there a bole itself, uprooted and flung into the river by the violence of the tempest,—which necessitated careful steering and paddling and watching the current to take them through safely. It threw the two boats apart for a space, prolonging

Hamish's suspense, yet serving as a reprieve to the ordeal of his examination as to his proficiency in the French language by the erudite Cherokee. The canoe rocked in the swirls, and although Willinawaugh sat still in stately impassiveness, Odalie and Fifine clung to the gunwale. Hamish's eyes met Odalie's, which were clear, liquidly bright, as if fired with some delightful anticipation, and yet weary and feverishly eager. Oh, this was delirium! She did not realize her surroundings; her intelligence was gone! His poor young heart swelled nearly to bursting as he turned back with aching arms and dazzled eyes and throbbing, feverish pulses to the careful balancing of the paddle, for Willinawaugh was an exacting coxswain. Hamish could not know what vision had been vouchsafed to Odalie in the midst of the gloomy woods while the other Indians and Willinawaugh had wrangled and he had hung absorbed upon their words as on the decrees of fate. Even she at first had deemed it but hallucination, the figment of some fever of the brain—this had been a day of dreams! Yet there it had stood on the river bank with the primeval woods around it, with the red sunset amongst the clouds above it, with the sunset below it, reflected in the current of the river, full of sheen and full of shadow,—a figure, a hunter, looking out at the boats; a white man,—a man she had never before seen.

How he stared! She dared make no signal of distress. She only turned her head that she might look back covertly with a face full of meaning. The next moment she saw him mount his horse in the buffalo path in the cane-brake and gallop off at a breakneck speed.

But was she sure—had she seen aught, she asked herself, tremulously. For it had been a day of dreams—it had been a day of dreams! And the confluence of the Tellico River with the Tennessee might be so hopelessly near!

The progress of both boats was very slow now, upstream against the current and the débris of the storm; even the crew of Indian braves needed to pull with vigor to make the clear water again. When this was reached they rested motionless, the duplication of the pettiaugre and the feather headdress of the Cherokees as clearly pictured in the bright, still reaches of the river as above in the medium of the air between sunset and dusk.

They were all looking back, all commenting on Hamish's slow progress. He had the current and his exhaustion both against him, and the most earnest and well-equipped postulant of culture would hardly be eager to go to an examination in the French language when his life was to be the forfeit of failure. The sound of the river was loud on the evening air; a wind was astir on either bank,—a pillaging force, rifling the forest of the few leaves it might still treasure; now and then a scurrying cloud of them fled before the blast against the sky; the evening had grown chill; the boy felt its dank depression in every nerve despite the drops of perspiration that stood upon his brow as he too paddled into the clear water. He held the boat stationary by a great effort.

He had come to the end. He could strive no more. He saw Savanukah rise up in the pettiaugre, looking toward him. The next moment the savage turned his head. There was an alien sound upon the air, so close at hand that despite the fret and turmoil of the water, the blare of the wild wind, the tumultuous clashing together of the bare boughs in the black forest, it arrested the attention. Once more it asserted itself against the tumult, and then Hamish, his head spinning around until he thought that the canoe had broken loose from his mechanical plying of the paddle, recognized the regular rhythmical dash of oars.

CHAPTER III

In the next instant from beyond a curve in the river a boat shot into the current,—a large row-boat, manned by twelve red-coated soldiers, bending to the oars, whose steady strokes sent the craft down the stream with the speed, it seemed, of a meteor.

They were alongside and a non-commissioned officer was in diplomatic converse with Willinawaugh before Hamish had regained possession of his faculties. Very diplomatic was the conference, for the corporal had his pacific orders and Willinawaugh was burdened with the grave anxiety to make the facts conform at once to the probabilities, yet sustain the impeccability of his own conduct. A little network of wrinkles, almost like a visible mesh, gathered at the corners of his eyes and gave token of his grave cogitation.

The corporal, a dark-haired, blue-eyed, florid young Irishman, looking very stanch and direct and steady, but not without a twinkle of humor which betokened some histrionic capacity to support the situation, speaking partly in English and partly, glibly enough, in very tolerable Cherokee, although incongruously embellished with an Irish brogue, detailed that Captain Stuart had been apprised that there was a band of Indians on the river who had some white people with them, and he wished to know if these white people were French, in which case, according to the treaty made with the Cherokees, they must be arrested and delivered up to the commandant of the fort, or if English, he wished to be assured that they were at liberty to go where they pleased, and were under no restraint.

As the officer concluded, having bowed to Odalie with much politeness, considering he was not yet informed as to whether she were of a party of French emissaries, forever sowing dissension amongst the Cherokee allies of the English, he drew himself up very erect, with a complacent mien. He was conscious of being a fine-looking fellow, and he had not seen so handsome a young woman of her evident position in life for a month of Sundays. Nevertheless he kept one eye on Willinawaugh, who was also eminently worthy of his respectful attention.

"Ingliss—all Ingliss," said the chief, unexpectedly.

The Indians in the pettiaugre, listening attentively, gave no sign of surprise upon this statement, so at variance with the warrior's previous representations. His ruse to shield the travelers now by declaring them English shielded himself as well, for being a chief and head-man he could hardly find a plausible subterfuge to cloak his playing the rôle of guide,

- 30 -

philosopher, and friend to people of a nation so obnoxious to his English allies, and establishing them in the very heart of the Cherokee nation, contrary to its many solemn obligations and treaties.

After a moment's further reflection, Willinawaugh said again with emphasis, "Ingliss, Ingliss." Perhaps he did not desire to avail himself of the added fluency of explanation which the Cherokee language would have afforded him, and which Corporal O'Flynn evidently understood. "Go Choté—Old Town. Buy fur—man—packhorse," he added, pointing across the woods in the direction in which Alexander MacLeod was presumably still wearily tramping.

The corporal for the moment forgot how good-looking he was. He concentrated his whole attention on Willinawaugh's disingenuous countenance, and then turned and cast a long, searching look upon Odalie. The eyes that met his own were swimming in tears, and with an expression of pleading insistence that fairly wrung his heart, although he hardly understood it. If she were English, why then she was free as the air. If French—well, bedad, thin, Corporal O'Flynn wished himself at the bottom of the Tennessee River, for a French lady in grief and under arrest had no right to be so good-looking at all, at all. Here was something wrong, he could but perceive, and yet because of Willinawaugh's diplomacy he could not fix upon it.

"What's your name, my lad?" he said abruptly to Hamish.

Hamish had his eyes on the water. His fortitude, too, had given way in the sudden relaxation of the strain of suspense. He could not, would not, lift his face and let that boat's crew of stalwart soldiers resting on their oars, the two ranks gazing at him, see the tears in his eyes.

"Hamish MacLeod," he made shift to say, and could say no more.

"A good English name, bedad, for a Scotch one, and an English accent," Corporal O'Flynn mentally commented, as he looked curiously at the boy, standing with downcast face, mechanically handling the paddle.

"Now by the powers," said the young soldier to himself with sudden resolution, "Captain Stuart may undertake the unraveling o' this tangle himself."

"English!" he exclaimed aloud. Then with much courtesy of manner, "Captain Stuart desires his compliments, and begs the English party to do him the honor to lie at Fort Loudon to-night and pursue their journey at their convanience." He glanced up at the sky. "It grows late and there are catamounts out, an' other bletherin' bastes, an' their howlin' might frighten the leddy."

Odalie, remembering the real dangers that had beset her and catching his serious, unconscious glance as he animadverted on the possibly terrifying vocalizations, burst into momentary laughter, and then into a torrent of tears.

At which the corporal, the boat's crew, and the Indian braves gazed at her in blank astonishment. Hysterics were a new importation on the frontier. She controlled with an effort her tendency to laugh, but still wept with the profusion of exhaustion and nervous tension.

Willinawaugh's eyes were fixed on her with deep displeasure. "Ugh!" he grunted from time to time. "Ugh!"

"Oh, there's bloody murder here, if one could but chance upon the carpse," said the corporal to himself, looking bewildered from her to the boy.

And now was demonstrated the fact that although the corporal had but the slightest bit of a brogue in the world, there was a twist in his tongue which showed that he had at some time in his career made a practice of kissing the "Blarney Stone" and was as Irish as County Clare.

"Of course Captain Stuart couldn't have known that his valued friend, the great chief, Willinawaugh, was to be passing with the English party, but, sure, he would take it mighty ill if the chief did not stop over, too, and lie at the fort to-night,—an' he so seldom up from Toquoe! Captain Demeré, too, will expect the great chief. My word on't, he will."

Now Willinawaugh, an epitome of craft, had no idea of adventuring with his supposed French friends, whom he had endeavored to pass off as English, into the British stronghold, for he doubted their capacity to sustain their character of compatriots; he had no means of judging of their knowledge of the English language and how soon their ignorance might betray them. Since the ruse he had adopted had evidently not sufficed to evade the enforced stoppage at Fort Loudon, he had relinquished the intention to take them on past Choté to some other of the Overhill towns, and let them establish themselves as French traders. He feared that were they once inside the walls of Fort Loudon this design against the agreement with his allies would become transparent. To be sure, it must be soon elucidated, but Willinawaugh was determined to be far away by that time, and, moreover, he could send a "talk" (letter) to Captain Stuart, whose good opinion he greatly coveted, to say that the French trader had deceived him and made him believe that the party was English. At the same time he was too wary to venture into his valued friend's power with this fresh grievance and with stormy times for the two peoples evidently in prospect.

But he was flattered, infinitely flattered, as indeed who would not have been, by Corporal O'Flynn's tone and expression of ingenuous eyes and respectful word of mouth. Willinawaugh was glad to have these Choté Cherokees see how highly he was esteemed—he was indeed a great warrior and a "Big Injun" of exclusive privilege. The invitation in no wise was to be extended to the others to pass the night at Fort Loudon—not even to Savanukah, a chief himself, who spoke French!

Corporal O'Flynn was now going over in his mind how Willinawaugh might best be insulated, so to speak, that he might not have means to fire the barracks, should that enterprise suggest itself to his fertile brain, or find a way to open the gates, or otherwise afford ingress to confederates without; how to lock him in, and yet not seem to treat him as a prisoner; to leave him at liberty, and yet free to do nothing but that which his hosts should please. All such complicated and contradictory details did Corporal O'Flynn deem himself capable of reconciling—but one such subject was enough. Unfortunately for the triumphant elucidation of these puzzling problems, Willinawaugh, with dignity and a certain gruffness; yet now and again a flicker of covert smile as if to himself, declined to partake of Captain Stuart's hospitality. He had a mission to the head-men of Choté which would not brook delay. Yet he had a message to leave for the English officer. He desired to tell Captain Stuart that he often thought of him! Whenever he heard tales of famous warriors, of British generals, he thought of him! He considered these fighting men brave and noble, when he learned of their splendid deeds in battle; and then again, they were as naught in his mind,—for he had once more thought of the great Captain Stuart!

The corporal, listening attentively to pick out the meaning of Cherokee and English, made a low bow in behalf of Captain Stuart, with a flourishing wave of his hat.

"I'll bear yer message, sir, and a proud man Captain Stuart ought to be the day! An those jontlemen,"—he glanced at the pettiaugre full of Indians,— "be so good as to ask them to lead the way."

Then he added in an undertone to his own men, "I am glad on't. I don't want the responsibility of takin' care of the baste. I might be accused of kidnapin' the craythure if anythin' was to happen to 'm,—though as to kids, he's more like the old original Billy-goat o' the whole worruld!"

Corporal O'Flynn cast the eye of a disciplinarian about him. It was one of the rules of the tyranny he practiced, thus remote from civilization, that however jocose he might be not a trace of responsive merriment must decorate the faces of the men. They were all now, as was meet, grave and wooden. At the orders in his clear, ringing voice—"Let fall!" and the oars struck the water with emphasis, "Give way!"—Odalie's tears must needs flow anew. She gazed at the dozen fresh, florid young faces, as the boat swung round and they came once more near the canoe, as if they were a vision of saints vouchsafed to some poor groping, distraught spirit,—when they were far indeed from being saints, though good enough in their way, too! They all looked with unconscious sympathy at her as she sat and wept and looked at them, and Corporal O'Flynn, moved by the tears, exclaimed below his breath, "But, be jabbers, afther all, what's the good of 'em now— better have been cryin' yesterday, or mebbe the day before. Back oars! Now—now! Give way!"

He was the last in the little fleet, and Hamish paddled briskly now to keep ahead, as he was evidently expected to do, for Corporal O'Flynn intended that his own boat should bring up the rear. As they fared thus along, Odalie noted the inflowing of that tributary, the Tellico River—how solitary, how remote, how possible its loneliness had rendered the scheme of Willinawaugh. Some distance beyond appeared a settler's cabin in an oasis of cultivated land in the midst of the dense cane-brake; then others, now dull and dusky in the blue twilight, with the afterglow of the sunset redly aflare above in the amber sky and below in the gray and glimmering water; now with a lucent yellow flicker from the wide-open door gemming the night with the scintillations of the hearthstone, set like a jewel in the center of the wilderness; now sending forth a babbling of childish voices where the roof-tree had been planted close by the river-side and the passing of the boats had drawn all the household to the brink. How many they seemed— these cabins of the adventurous pioneers! How many happy homes—alas, that there should ever be cause to cry it were better for them had they never been!

Odalie began to realize that she owed her liberty and perhaps her life to the first of these settlers who had espied the craft upon the river; as she marked the many windings and tortuous curves of the stream she understood that he must have galloped along some straight, direct route to the fort to acquaint the officers with the suspicious aspect of the Indian party and their white captives. As to the tremendous speed the commandant's boat had made to their rescue,—she blessed anew those reckless young saints who had plied the oars with such fervent effort, which, however, could hardly have effected such speed had it not been too for the swift current running in their favor.

Suddenly the fort came into view—stanch, grim, massive, with the great red-clay exterior slopes and the sharp points of the high palisades on the rampart distinct in the blue twilight. It was very different from the stockaded stations of the early settlers with which she had been familiar. This fort had been erected by the British government, and was a work of very considerable strength and admirably calculated for defensive purposes, not only against the subtle designs of the Indians but against possible artillery attacks of the French. There were heavy bastions at the angles and within each a substantial block-house, the upper story built with projections beyond the lower, that would not only aid the advantage which the bastions gave of a flanking fire upon an assailant, but enable a watch to be maintained at all times and from all quarters upon the base of the wooden stockade on the rampart lest an enemy passing the glacis should seek to fire the palisades. But this was in itself well-nigh impracticable. Strong fraises, defending both scarp and counterscarp, prevented approach. The whole was guarded by twelve cannon, grimly pointed from embrasures, and very reassuring their black muzzles looked to one who hoped to ply the arts of peace beneath the protection of their threat of war. Even the great gates were defended, being so thickly studded with iron spikes that not an inch of the wood was left uncovered. They were broadly aflare now, and a trifle in advance of the sentry at the entrance two officers were standing, brilliant with their red coats and cocked hats. They were gazing with a certain curiosity at the boats on the river, for Corporal O'Flynn, having pressed forward and landed first, had left his men resting on their oars and taken his way into the presence of his superior officers to make his report. He had paused for half a dozen words with Hamish MacLeod as the boat passed the canoe, and when Odalie and the boy, with a couple of soldiers at either side maintaining the aspect of a guard, came up the gentle ascent at a slower pace, Captain Stuart was already fully apprised of their long and perilous flight from Virginia. He stood awaiting their approach,—a tall man of about twenty-eight years of age, bluff and smiling, with dense light-brown hair braided in a broad, heavy queue and tied with a black ribbon. He had a fair complexion, considerably sun-burned, strong white teeth with a wide arch of the jaw, and he regarded her with keen steel-blue eyes, steady and unfathomable, yet withal pleasant. He took off his hat and cordially held out his hand. Odalie could do naught but clasp it in both her cold hands and shed tears over it, mute and trembling.

With that ready tact which always distinguished him, Captain Stuart broke the tension of the situation.

"Do you wish to enlist, Mrs. MacLeod?" he said, his smile showing a glimpse of his white teeth. "His majesty, the king, has need of stout-hearted soldiers. And I will take my oath I never saw a braver one!"

And Odalie broke into laughter to blend with her tears, because she divined that it was with the intention of passing on a difficulty that he not ungracefully transferred her hands to the officer standing near with the words, "I have the pleasure of presenting Captain Demeré." However capable Captain Stuart might be of dealing with savages, he evidently shrank from the ordeal of being wept over and thanked by a woman.

- 35 -

He has been described by a contemporary historian as "an officer of great address and sagacity," and although he may have demonstrated these qualities on more conspicuous occasions, they were never more definite than in thus securing his escape from feminine tearfulness.

Captain Demeré was of a graver aspect. He heard without impatience her wild insistence that the whole available force of the fort should turn out and scour the wilderness for her husband—he even argued the matter. It would be impossible to find Mr. MacLeod at night and the effort might cost him his life. "So marked a demonstration of a military nature would alarm the Indians and precipitate an outbreak which we have some reason to expect. If he does not appear by daylight, the hunters of the fort who always go out shall take that direction and scout the woods. Rest assured everything shall be done which is possible."

She felt that she must needs be content with this, and as it had been through the intervention of the officers that she and Hamish and Fifine were set free, it did not lie in her mouth to doubt their wisdom in such matters, or their capacity to save her husband. Looking back to the river, as upon a phase of her life already terminated, she saw the canoe in which she had spent this troublous day already beginning to push out upon the broad current. Willinawaugh, with an Indian from the other crew to paddle the craft, had eluded Captain Stuart, who had reached the water's edge too late for a word with him, and who stood upon the bank, an effective martial figure, and blandly waved his hand in farewell, with a jovial outcry, "Canawlla! Canawlla!"[C]

The features of the chief were slightly corrugated with those fine lines of diplomatic thought, and even at this distance he muttered the last word he had spoken to the corporal as he swiftly got away from him—"Ingliss!" he said again. "All Ingliss!"

As Odalie turned, the interior of the fort was before her; the broad parade, the lines of barracks, the heavy, looming block-houses, the great red-clay wall encircling all, and the high, strong palisades that even surmounted the rampart. It gave her momentarily the sensation, as she stood in its shadow, of being down in a populous and very secure well. There was a pervasive sentiment of good cheer; here and there the flicker of firelight fluctuated from an open door. Supper was either in progress or just over, and savory odors gushed out into the air. The champing of horses and now and then a glad whinny betokened that the corn-bin was open in the stables somewhere in the dusk. She felt as if the wilderness was a dream, for surely all this cordial scene of warmth, and light, and cheer, and activity, could not have existed while she wandered yonder, so forlorn, and desolate, and endangered; in pity of it,—surely it was a dream! Now and again groups of fresh-faced soldiers passed, most of them in full uniform, for there had been a great dress parade during the afternoon, perhaps to impress the Indians with the resources and military strength of the fort; perhaps to attach them by affording that spectacular display, so new to all their experience, so imposing and splendid. Some of the savage visitors lingered, wistful, loath to depart, and were being hustled carefully out of the place by a very vigilant guard, who had kept them under surveillance as a special charge all the afternoon. A few soldiers of the post coming in laden with game wore the buckskin leggings, shirt, and coonskin cap usual among the settlers, for it had been bitterly demonstrated that the thorns of the trackless wilderness had no sort of reverence for the texture of the king's red coat.

Even the cat realized the transition to the demesne of civilization and in some sort the wonted domestic atmosphere. She suddenly gave an able-bodied wriggle in the basket on Josephine's back where she had journeyed, pappoose-wise, sprang alertly out, and scampered, tail up and waving aloft, across the parade. Josephine's shriek of despair rang shrilly on the air, and Captain Demeré himself made a lunge at the animal, as she sped swiftly past, with a seductive cry of "Puss! puss!" A young soldier hard by faced about alertly and gave nimble chase; the cry of "Puss! puss!" going up on all sides brought out half a dozen supple young runners from every direction, but Kitty, having lost none of the elasticity of her muscles during her late inaction, darted hither and thither amongst her military pursuers, eluded them all, and scampering up the rampart, thence scaled the stockade and there began to walk coolly along the pointed eminence of this lofty structure as if it were a backyard fence, while the soldier boys cheered her from below. In this jovial demonstration poor Josephine's wailing whimper of despair and desertion was overborne, and with that juvenile disposition to force the recognition and a share of her woe on her elders she forthwith lost the use of her feet, and was half dragged, rather than led, by poor Odalie, who surely was not calculated to support any added burden. She herself, with halting step, followed Captain Demeré across the parade to a salient angle of the enclosure, wherein stood one of the block-houses, very secure of aspect, the formidable, beetling upper story jutting out above the open door, from which flowed into the dusky parade a great gush of golden light. Josephine's whimper was suddenly strangled in her throat and the tears stood still on her cheeks, for as Captain Demeré stepped aside at the door with a recollection of polite society, yielding precedence to the ladies, which formality Odalie marveled to find surviving in these rude times so far on the frontier, Josephine seemed resolved into a stare of dumb amazement, for she had never seen a room half so fine. Be it remembered she was born in the backwoods and had no faint recollection of such refinement and elegances as the colonial civilization had attained on the

Carolina coast, and which her father and mother had relinquished to follow their fortunes to the West. And in truth the officers' mess-hall presented a brave barbaric effect that had a sort of splendor all its own. It was a large room, entered through the gorge of the bastion, and its deep chimney-place, in the recesses of which a great fire burned with a searchingly illuminating flare, was ample enough to afford a substantial settee on either hand without impinging on the roomy hearth of flagstones that joined the puncheons of the floor. Around the log walls the suffusion of light revealed a projecting line of deer antlers and the horns of buffalo and elk, partly intended as decoration and trophies of the chase, and partly for utilitarian purposes. Here and there a firelock lay from one to another, or a powder-horn or brace of pistols swung. A glittering knife and now and again a tomahawk caught the reflection of the fire and bespoke trophies of less peaceful pursuit. Over the mantel-shelf a spreading pair of gigantic antlers held suspended a memento evidently more highly cherished,—a sword in its sheath, but showing a richly chased hilt, which Odalie divined was a presentation in recognition of special service. Other and humbler gifts were suggested in the long Indian pipes, with bowls of deftly wrought stone; and tobacco-bags and shot-pouches beaded with intricate patterns; and belts of wampum and gorgeous moccasons; and bows and arrows with finely chiseled flint-heads winged with gayly colored feathers—all hanging from antlers on either side, which, though smaller than the central pair, were still large enough to have stretched with surprise more sophisticated eyes than Fifine's. The variegated tints of the stained quills and shells with which a splendid curious scarlet quiver was embroidered, caught Odalie's attention, and reminded her of what she had heard in Carolina of the great influence which this Captain Stuart had acquired among the Indians, and the extraordinary admiration that they entertained for him. These tokens of Aboriginal art were all, she doubted not, little offerings of the chieftains to attest good-will, for if they had been merely bought with money they would not have been so proudly displayed.

There was a continual fluttering movement in the draught from the loop-holes and open door, and lifting her eyes she noted the swaying folds of several banners against the wall, carrying the flare of color to the ceiling, which was formed only by the rude floor of the room above.

But in all the medley her feminine eye did not fail to perceive high up and withdrawn from ordinary notice, a lady's silk riding-mask such as was used in sophisticated regions at the period to protect the complexion on a journey,—dainty, fresh, of a garnet hue with a black lace frill, evidently treasured, yet expressively null. And this was doubtless all that was left of some spent romance, a mere memory in the rude military life on the far frontier, barely suggesting a fair and distant face and eyes that looked forth on scenes more suave.

With a sentiment of deep respect Odalie observed the six or eight arm-chairs of a rude and untoward manufacture, which were ranged about the hearth, draped, however, to real luxury by wolfskins, for the early settlers chiefly affected rough stools or billets of wood as seats, or benches made of puncheons with a couple of auger-holes at each end, through which four stout sticks were adjusted for legs, which were indeed often of unequal length and gave the unquiet juvenile pioneer of that day a peculiarly acceptable opportunity for cheerily jouncing to and fro. There were several of these benches, too, but placed back against the walls, for the purpose she supposed of affording seats when the festive board was spread at length. An absolute board, this figurative expression implied, for the stern fact set forth a half dozen puncheons secured together with cleats and laid across trestles when in use, but at other times placed against the wall beside the ladder which gave access to the room above. The table was now in the center of the floor, spread with some hasty refreshments, of which Captain Demeré invited the forlorn travelers to partake. At the other end lay a draughtsman's board, a Gunter's scale, a pair of dividers and other materials, where he had been trying to reduce to paper and topographical decorum for transference to an official report a map of the region which Rayetaeh, a chief from Toquoe, who had visited the fort that afternoon, had drawn on the sand of the parade ground with a flint-headed arrow. The officer had found this no slight task, for Rayetaeh was prone to measure distance by the time required to traverse it—"two warriors, a canoe, and one moon" very definitely meaning a month's journey by watercourse, but requiring some actively minute calculation to bring the space in question to the proportional scale. Rayetaeh might be considered the earliest cartographer of this region, and some of his maps, copied from the sand, are extant to this day. Captain Demeré laid the papers of this unfinished task carefully aside, and by way of giving his hospitality more grace took the head of the table himself.

But Odalie could not eat, and wept steadily on as if for the purpose of salting her food with tears, and Fifine's hunger seemed appeased by the feast of her eyes. Now and again her head in its little white mob-cap turned actively about, and she seemed as if she might have entered upon a series of questions save for the multiplicity of objects that enthralled her attention at once. Captain Demeré desisted from insistence after one or two well-meant efforts, and the man who had served the table waited in doubt and indecision.

"It's a hard life for women on the frontier," the officer observed as if in polite excuse for Odalie's ill-mannered tears that she could not control.

"And for men," she sobbed, thinking of Alexander and marveling if the Indians would carry him on without resistance to Choté,—for he could not know she had found lodgement in the fort,—or further still and enslave him—many captives had lived for years in Indian tribes—she had heard of this even in Carolina; or would they murder him in some trifling quarrel or on the discovery of his nationality or to make easier the robbery of the packhorses. Ah, why had she brought so much; why had she hampered their flight and risked their lives for these paltry belongings, treasures to the Indians, worth the shedding of much blood? How could she have sacrificed to these bits of household gear even her own comfort! She remembered, with an infinite yet futile wish to recall the moment, how eagerly Sandy had urged the abandonment of these poor possessions, that she might herself mount the horse and ease her bleeding and torn feet. Is every woman an idolater at heart, Odalie wondered. Do they all bow down, in the verity of their inner worship, to a few fibers of woven stuff and some poor fashioning of potter's clay, and make these feeble, trivial things their gods? It seemed so to her. She had bled for the things she had brought through the wilderness. She had wept for others that she had left. And if for such gear Sandy had come to grief—"I wonder—I wonder if I could find a pretext to care for them still!"

But she only said aloud, with a strong effort to control her attention, "And for men, too."

"Men must needs follow when duty leads the way," said Captain Demeré, a trifle priggishly.

Odalie, trying to seem interested, demanded, lifting her eyes, "And what do women follow?"

If Captain Demeré had said what he truly thought, he would have answered:—

"Folly! their own and that of their husbands!"

He had had close observation of the fact that the pioneers gave heavy hostages to fate in their wives and children, and a terrible advantage to a savage foe, and the very bravery of so many of these noble helpmeets only proved the value of all they risked. He could not elaborate, however, any scheme by which a new country should be entered first by the settlers aided by a strong occupancy of soldiery, and only when the lands should be cleared and the savages expelled the women and children venture forth. So he said:—

"They follow their destiny."

He had a smile in his eyes as if appealing to her clemency not to tax him with ascribing a humbler motive to the women than to the men, as he was only making talk and spoke from a natural deprecation of dangers to non-combatants who of right should be exempt from peril. His eyes, which were large, were of a color between gray and brown—darker than the one and lighter than the other. His hair was brown and smooth; he was slender and tall; his aquiline nose and finely cut lips gave a certain cast of distinction to his face, although the temples were slightly sunken and the thinness of his cheek revealed the outline of the jaw and chin which showed determination and force, despite his mild expression at present. Josephine fixed an amazed stare upon his polished shoes as he crossed his legs, never having seen any men's foot-gear save a buskin of deer hide.

"The men have a natural interest in warfare," suggested Odalie, forlornly, seeking to be responsive to his conversational efforts.

"Warfare!" exclaimed Captain Demeré, with sudden animation. "Contention with savages is not warfare! It cannot be conducted on a single recognized military principle." He went on to say that all military tactics counted for naught; the merely mechanical methods of moving bodies of troops were unavailable. Discipline, the dexterities of strategy, an enlightened courage, and the tremendous force of esprit de corps were alike nullified.

The problem of Indian fighting in America was then far greater than it has been since the scene has shifted to the plains, the densely wooded character of the tangled wilderness affording peculiar advantage to the skulking individual methods of the savage and embarrassing inconceivably the more cumbrous evolutions of organized bodies. But long before Captain Demeré's time, and often since, the futility of opposing regular scientific tactics to the alert wiles of the savage native in his own difficult country has been commented upon by observers of military methods, and doubtless recognized in the hard knocks of experience by those whose fate it has been to try again the experiment.[6]

"As to military ethics," he added, "to induce the Indian to accept and abide by the principles governing civilized warfare seems an impossibility. He cannot be constrained for a pledge of honor to forego an advantage. He will not respect his parole. He continually violates and sets at naught the provisions of his solemn treaty."

Odalie would not ask if the white man never broke faith with the red—if the Indian had not been taught by example near at hand of what brittle stuff a treaty was made. It was not worth while to reason logically with a mere man, she said to herself, with a little secret sentiment of derision, which served to lighten a trifle the gloom of her mental atmosphere, and since she could not eat and little backwoods Fifine's eyes had absorbed her appetite, it was just as well that Hamish, who had been greatly interested in being shown over the fort by the jolly Corporal O'Flynn, appeared at the door with the intelligence that their quarters were assigned them. The courteous Captain Demeré handed her to the door, and she stepped out from the bizarre decorated mess-hall into the dark night, with the stars showing a chill scintillation as of the approach of winter in their white glitter high in the sky, and the looming bastion close at hand. The barracks were silent; "tattoo" had just sounded; the great gates were closed, and the high walls shut off the world from the deserted parade.

Naught was audible in all the night save the measured tread of a sentry walking his beat, and further away, seeming an echo, the step of another sentinel, while out in the wilderness the scream of a wildcat came shrilly on the wind from the darkness where Alexander roamed with savage beasts and still more savage men far from the sweet security so trebly protected here.

Not even the flare of another big homelike fire in the cabin assigned to her could efface the impression of the bleak and dark loneliness outside the walls of the fort, and when the three were together, untrammeled by the presence of others, they were free to indulge their grief and their awful terror for husband and brother and father. They could not speak of it, but they sat down on a buffalo rug spread before the fire, and all three wept for the unuttered thought. The suspense, the separation of the little party, seemed unbearable. They felt that they might better have endured anything had they been together. Perhaps it was well for the elder two that their attention was diverted now and again by the effort to console Fifine in a minor distress, for with the ill-adjusted sense of proportion peculiar to childhood she had begun to clamor loudly too for her cat—her mignonne, her douce fillette that she had brought so far in her arms or on her back.

Alas, poor Fifine! to learn thus early how sharper than a serpent's tooth it is to have a thankless child! For indeed Kitty might have seemed to lie under the imputation of having merely "played baby" in order to secure free transportation. At all events, she was a cat now, the only one in the fort, and for all she knew in the settlement. The douce mignonne was in high elation, now walking the palisades, now peeping in at a loop-hole in the upper story of one of the block-houses where a sentinel was regularly on guard, being able to scan from the jutting outlook not only the exterior of the fort on two sides, but a vast extent of darkling country. In his measured tramp to and fro in the shadowy apartment lighted only by the glimmer of the night without, he suddenly saw a flicker at the loop-hole he was approaching, caught a transient glimpse of a face, the gleam of a fiery eye, and he nearly dropped his loaded firelock in amazement.

- 42 -

"By George!" he exclaimed, "I thought that was a blarsted cat!"

He had not seen one since he left Charlestown a year before.

He walked to the loop-hole and looked far down from the projecting wall and along the parapet of the curtain and the scarp to the opposite bastion with its tower-like block-house.

Nothing—all quiet as the grave or the desert. He could hear the river sing; he could see in the light of the stars, and a mere flinder of a moon, the clods of earth on the ground below,—naught else. For the douce mignonne, with her back all handsomely humped, had suddenly sprung aside and fled down the interior slope of the rampart into the parade and over to the cook's quarters neighboring the kitchen. She nosed gleefully about among pots and kettles, feeling very much at home and civilized to the verge of luxury; she pried stealthily, every inch a cat, into the arrangements for to-morrow's breakfast, with a noiseless step and a breathless purr, until suddenly a tin pan containing beans was tumultuously overturned, being within the line of an active spring. For the douce fillette had caught a mouse, which few sweet little girls are capable of doing;—a regular domestic fireside mouse, a thing which the douce fillette had not seen in many weeks.

The stir in the neighboring cabin did not affright Kitty, and when the officers' cook, a veritable African negro, suddenly appeared with an ebony face and the rolling whites of astonished eyes, she exhibited her capture and was rewarded by a word of commendation which she quite understood, although it was as outlandish as the gutturals of Willinawaugh.

When the night was nearly spent, a great star, splendidly blazing in the sorceries of a roseate haze, seemed to conjure into the blackness a cold glimmer of gray light above the high, bleak, serrated summit line of the mountains of the eastern horizon, showing here and there white blank intervals, that presently were revealed as stark snowy domes rising into the wintry silence of a new day. The resonant bugle suddenly sounded the reveillé along the far winding curves of the river, rousing greetings of morning from many a mountain crag, and before the responsive echoes of the forest were once more mute the parade was full of the commotion elicited by the beating of the drums; shadowy military figures were falling in line, and the brisk authoritative ringing voice of the first sergeant was calling the roll in each company.

And on the doorstep of Odalie's cabin, when Josephine opened the door, sat the douce mignonne with her most babified expression on her face, now and again mewing noiselessly, going through the motions of grief, and cuddling down in infantile style when with wild babbling cries of endearment the little girl swooped up maternally the renegade cat.

FOOTNOTES:

[C] Friendship! Friendship!

CHAPTER IV

With the earliest flush of dawn Hamish MacLeod was seeking one of the officers in order to solicit a guide to enable him to go in search of his brother with some chance of success.

Captain Stuart, whom he finally found at the block-house in the northwestern bastion, was standing on the broad hearth of the great hall, where the fire was so brightly aflare that although it was day the place had all the illuminated effect of its aspect of last night. The officer's fresh face was florid and tingling from a recent plunge in the cold waters of the Tennessee River. He looked at Hamish with an unchanged expression of his steady blue eye, and drawing the watch from his fob consulted it minutely.

"The hunters of the post," he said, still regarding it, "have been gone for more than half an hour. There is no use in trying to overtake them. They have their orders as to what kind of game they are to bring in."

He smiled slightly, with the air of a man who in indulgent condescension would humor natural anxiety and overlook the effort of intermeddling, and as he returned the watch to his pocket, Hamish felt dismissed from the presence. The sun was well over the great range of purple bronze mountains in the east, their snowy domes a-glister in the brilliance between the dark slopes below and the blue sky above, and the fort, as he came forth, was a scene of brisk activity. The parade ground had already been swept like a floor, and groups of soldiers were gathered about the barracks busily burnishing and cleaning their arms, pipe-claying belts and rotten-stoning buckles and buttons, and at the further end near the stables horses were in process of being groomed and fed; one of them, young and wild, broke away, and in a mad scamper, with tossing mane and tail, and head erect and hoofs scattering the gravel, plunged around and around the enclosure, baffling his groom. A drill-sergeant was busy with an awkward squad; another squad without arms, in charge of a corporal, was marching and marching, making no progress, but vigorously marking time, whether for exercise or discipline Hamish could hardly determine, for he began to have a very awesome perception of the rigor of authority maintained in this frontier post. He had noticed—and the gorge of a freeman had risen at the sight—a soldier mounted high upon a trestle, facetiously called a horse, and he was well aware that this was by no means a new and a merry game. Hamish wavered a little in his mental revolt against the powers that be, as he noticed the reckless devil-may-care look of the man. He was a ruddy young fellow; he had a broad visage, with a wide, facetious red-lipped mouth, a quick, blithe, brown eye, and a broad, blunt nose. Hamish knew intuitively that this was the typical inhabitant, the native, so to speak, of the guard-house; his sort had ridden the wooden-horse, for many a weary hour in every country under the sun, and when an Indian's tomahawk or a Frenchman's bullet should clear the ranks of him, the gap would be filled by a successor so like him in spirit that he might seem a lineal descendant instead of a mere successor in the line. He had long ago been dubbed the "Devil's Dragoon," and he looked down with a good-humored glance at a bevy of his comrades, who from the door of the nearest log-cabin covertly cast gibes at him, calling out sotto voce, "Right about wheel—Trot!—March!"

In another quarter of the parade the regular exercise was in progress, and Hamish listened with interest to the voice of the officer as it rang out crisp and clear on the frosty air.

"Poise—Firelock!"

A short interval while the sun glanced down the gleaming barrels of the muskets.

"Cock—Firelock!"

A sharp metallic click as of many sounds blent into one.

"Take—Aim!"

A moment of suspense.

"Fire!"

A resonant detonation of blank cartridges—and all the live echoes leaped in the woods, while the smoke drifted about the parade and glimmered prismatic in the sun, and then cleared away, escaping over the ramparts and blending with the timorous dissolving mists of the morning.

Several Indians had come in through the open gate, some arrayed in feather or fur match-coats and others in buckskin shirt and leggings, with their blankets purchased from the traders drawn up about their ears; they were standing near the walls of one of the block-houses to see the drill. A certain expectancy hung upon this group as they watched the movements of the men now loading anew.

"Half-cock—Firelock!" came the order in the peremptory voice of the officer.

Once more that sharp, metallic, unnerving click.

"Handle—Cartridge!"

A sudden swift facial expression went along the line with a formidable effect. With the simultaneous show of strong teeth it was as if each soldier had fiercely snarled like a wild beast. But each had only bitten the end of the cartridge.

"Prime!"

The eyes of the Indians followed with an unwinking, fascinated stare the swift, simultaneous movement of the rank as of one man, every muscle animated by the same impulse.

"Shut—Pan!"

Once more the single sound as of many sounds.

"Charge with—Cartridge!"

The watchful eyes of the Indians narrowed.

"Draw—Rammer!"

Once more the loud, sharp, clash of metal rising to a menace of emphasis with the succeeding,—

"Ram down—Cartridge!"

"Return—Rammer!"

And as hard upon the clatter of the ramrods, slipping back into their grooves, came the orders—

"Shoulder—Firelock!"

"Advance—Arms!" the Cherokees drew a long breath as of the relief from the tension of suspense. They were evidently seeking to discern the utility of these strange military gyrations. This the Indians, although always alert to perceive and adopt any advantage in arms or military method, despite their characteristic tenacity to their ancient customs in other matters, could not descry. They had, even at this early day, almost discarded the bow and arrow for the firelock, wherever or however it could be procured, but the elaborate details of the drill baffled them, and they regarded it as in some sort a mystery. Their own discipline had always sufficed, and their military manœuvres, their march in single file or widely extended lines, their skulking approach, stalking under cover from tree to tree, were better suited, as even some of their enemies thought, for military movements, than tactical precision, to the broken character of the country and the dense forest of the trackless wilderness.

They noticed with kindling eyes a brisk reprimand administered to Corporal O'Flynn, when Lieutenant Gilmore called attention to the fact that one of the men had used three motions instead of the prescribed two motions in charging with cartridge, and two motions, instead of one, in ramming down cartridge. Corporal O'Flynn's mortification was painted in a lively red on his fresh Irish cheek, for this soldier was of a squad whose tuition in the manual exercise had been superintended by no less a tactician than himself.

"Faith, sir," he said to his superior officer, "I don't know what ails that man. He has motion without intelligence. Like thim windmills, ye'll remember, sir, we seen so much on the Continent. He minds me o' thim in the way he whur-r-ls his ar-rms."

The lieutenant—they had served together in foreign countries—laughed a trifle, his wrath diverted by the farcical suggestion, and the instant the command to break ranks had been given, Corporal O'Flynn, with the delinquent under close guard, convoyed him to the scene of the exploits of the awkward squad, where he might best learn to discard the free gestures of the windmills of the Continent of Europe.

"To disgrace me afore the officers," said Corporal O'Flynn, "and I fairly responsible for ye! I larned ye all ye know—and for ye to show the leftenant how little 'tis! Ye've got to quit that way of loading with ca'tridge with as many motions as an old jontleman feeling for his snuff-box! I'm fairly responsible for yez. I'm yer sponsor in this business. I feel like yer godfathers, an' yer godmothers, an' yer maiden aunt. I never seen a man so supple! Ye have as much use of yer hands as if ye was a centipede!"

The matter and manner of this discourse tried the gravity of the awkward squad, but no one dared to laugh, and Corporal O'Flynn himself was as grave as if it were a question of the weightiest importance involved, as he stood by and watched for a time the drill of the men.

The Indians turned their attentive eyes to Captain Stuart and Captain Demeré, who were both upon the terre-pleine at the shoulder-point of a bastion where one of the twelve cannon, mounted en barbette, looked grimly forth over the parapet. The gunners were receiving some instructions which Stuart was giving in reference to serving the piece; now and again it was pointed anew; he handled the heavy sponge-staff as if in illustration; then stepped swiftly back, and lifted the match, as if about to fire the gun. The Indians loitering in the shade watched the martial figure, the sun striking full on the red coat and cocked hat, and long, heavy queue of fair hair hanging on his shoulders, and as he stood erect, with the sponge-staff held horizontally in both hands, they turned and looked with a common impulse at one another and suddenly spat upon the ground. The sentry in a sort of cabin above the gate—a gate-house, so to speak— maintained a guard within as well as without, for an outer sentinel was posted on the crest of the counterscarp beyond the bridge; he kept his eye on the Cherokees, but he did not note their look. He was not skilled in deciphering facial expression, nor did he conceive himself deputed to construe the grimaces of savages. Gazing without for a moment, he turned back and cast a glance of kindly concern on Hamish MacLeod, who was disconsolately strolling about, not daring to go back and encounter the reproaches of Odalie, who doubtless thought him even now in the wilderness with a searching party, too urgent to admit of the time to acquaint her with so hasty a departure—and yet striving against his eagerness to go on this very errand, relying on the superior wisdom of the officers even while rebelling against it. All that he observed tended to confirm this reliance. How safe it was here! How trebly guarded! Even to his callow experience it was most obvious that whatever fate held in store for this garrison, whose lives were intrusted to the wisdom and precaution of the commandant, surprise was not among the possibilities. He remembered anew poor Sandy, far from these stanch walls, the very citadel of security, within which he felt so recreant; and as he thought again of the perils to which his brother was exposed, and a possibly impending hideous fate, he felt a constriction about his throat like the clutch of a hand. The tears rose to his eyes—and through them as he looked toward the gate he saw Sandy coming into the fort! In the extremity of the revulsion of feeling Hamish gave a sudden shrill yell that rang through the woods like a war-whoop. Even the Indians, still loitering in the diminishing shadow of the block-house, started at the sound and gazed at him amazed, as he dashed across the parade and flung his arms around his brother. Sandy, who had had his own terrors to endure concerning the fate of his family, was not altogether appreciative of their terrors for his sake. He felt amply capable of taking care of himself, and if he were not—why, his scalp was not worth saving! He extricated himself with unflattered surprise from Hamish's frantic embrace that was like the frenzied hug of a young bear and made his ribs crack.

"That's enough, Hamish; that's enough!" he said. "Of course I'm safe, all right. That's enough."

He advanced with what grace he could command after such an exhibition to shake hands with the two officers near the sally-port and thank them for the shelter the fort had afforded his family.

And here was Odalie,—for a good-natured soldier, one of the boat's crew of the previous evening, had instantly run to her cabin with the news of the arrival—restored to her normal poise in an instant, in the twinkling of an eye, by the shattering of her dismal forebodings in the glad reality of MacLeod's safety. So composed was her manner, so calmly happy, that Captain Stuart could not forbear to unmask the sham, and let the poor man know how he had been bewept yesterday at even.

"We were very glad to take in the wanderers, although I cannot say it was a cheerful scene. I never realized until Mrs. MacLeod reached the gate here the meaning of the phrase 'dissolved in tears.'"

Alexander looked anxiously at his wife—had she found the journey, then, so vexatious?

"I was tired and dusty," she said demurely, as if in explanation. "My shoes—one of them was in tatters; and, Sandy, I was so ashamed."

Captain Stuart stared at her for a moment and broke into a laugh. "That's putting the shoe on the other foot, at all events," he said.

He and Captain Demeré, accompanied by the newcomer, turned into the block-house, in order to question Sandy as to any information he might have been able to acquire concerning French emissaries, the disposition of the Cherokees, the devastation of the Virginia settlements, and any further news of General Forbes and the fall of Fort Duquesne now called Fort Pitt. However, Sandy had naught to report, save the angry threat with the tomahawk which gave way upon the assurance that the party was French. In the solitary journey with those who had resigned their boat to Willinawaugh, he had experienced no worse treatment than the destruction of his pocket compass. With this at first they had been highly delighted, but some ten miles from the fort they had been joined by an Indian who declared he had seen such things in Carolina, doubtless among land-surveyors, and who stigmatized it as a "land-stealer," forthwith crushing it with his tomahawk. MacLeod had expected this revelation to bring about ill-feeling, but the party shortly met the hunters of the post, who had insisted on conducting him to the fort on suspicion of being a Frenchman.

These pioneers never forgot that day, a rich, languid day of the lingering St. Martin's summer-tide. What though in the early morn the frost had lain in rime as white as snow on the bare branches of the great trees where now the yellow sunshine dripped in liquid light! A tender haze like that of spring suffused the depths of the forest, the gleaming, glancing reaches of the river, the level summit-lines of the great massive purple mountains of the west, and half concealed, and shifting half revealed, always elusively, the fine azure snow-capped domes against the pearl-tinted eastern sky. What though the flowers were dead, the leaves had fled, the woods were bare and rifled,—when the necromancy of the powers of the air filled all the winter day with sweet, subtle odors that excelled the fragrance of summer, as a memory might outvie the value of the reality, seeming to exhale now from the forest, and again from the river, and anon from some quality of the beneficent sunshine, or to exist in ethereal suspension in the charmed atmosphere. Nature was in such blessed harmony, full of graceful analogy; a bird would wing his way aloft, his shadow careering through the sun-painted woods below; a canoe with its swift duplication in the water would fly with its paddles like unfeathered wings down the currents of the river; those exquisite traceries of the wintry woods, the shadows of the leafless trees, would lie on a sandy stretch like some keen etching, as if to illustrate the perfection of the lovely dendroidal design and proportion of the growth it imaged; now and again the voice of herds of buffalo rose thunderously, muffled by distance; a deer splashed into the river a little above the fort, and gallantly breasting the current, swam to the other side, while a group of soldiers standing on the bank watched his progress and commented on his prowess. No shot followed him; the larders were filled, and orders had been given to waste no powder and ball.

The newcomers were made most heartily welcome in the settlement near the fort, as newcomers were apt to be in every pioneer hamlet, whatever their quality; for the frontiersmen, in their exposed situation, earnestly appreciated the strength in numbers. But this gratulation was of course infinitely increased when the arrivals were, like these, people of character, evidently so valuable an addition to the community. Finally several of the settlers persisted in carrying off Sandy to look at a fertile nook where the river swung round in a bend, earnestly recommending the rich bottom lands for the growth of corn, and the crest of the hill with a clear free-stone spring for that home he sought to plant in the far west. Hamish went too,—he could not bear Sandy to be out of his sight and was "tagging" after him as resolutely and as unshake-off-ably as when he was four and Sandy was twelve years of age.

In their absence Odalie and Josephine and the douce mignonne sat on the doorstep of their latest entertainer, and watched the shadows and sunshine shift in the woods, and listened to the talk of their hostess. And here was where the trail of the serpent began to be manifest; for this old woman was a professed gossip, and Odalie speedily learned the points of view from which the settlement about Fort Loudon ceased to present the aspect of the earlier Paradisaic era.

Mrs. Halsing had a hard, set visage, and was very shrewd,—none the worse gossip for that,—and went straight to the weak point, and unraveled the tangle of mystery in any subject that presented itself for discussion. She was thin and angular and uncultivated, and had evidently come of people who had been used to small advantages in education and breeding. Equally humble of origin was another of Odalie's future neighbors, with a sort of homespun dress made after the fashion called a "short gown," a red petticoat, and a pair of moccasons in lieu of shoes. Her face was as broad as the moon, and as bland. Much smiling had worn dimples around her mouth instead of wrinkles in her forehead. She, too, had a keen gleam of discernment in her eyes, but tempered with a perception of the sweetly ludicrous in life, which converted folly into the semblance of fun. She seemed to love her comfort, to judge by her leisurely motions and the way her arms fell into easy foldings, but the wife of a pioneer could never have lived at ease in those days. She sat opposite Mrs. Halsing, by the cabin door, on a bench which the hostess had vacated in her favor, adopting instead an inverted tub, and although admitting as true much that was said, Mrs. Beedie advanced palliating theories which, paradoxically enough, while they did not contradict the main statement, had all the effect of denial.

For her part, said Mrs. Halsing, she did not see what anybody who was safe in Virginia or Carolina, or anywhere else, would come to this country for. She wouldn't, except that her husband was possessed! The sight of a road put him into a "trembly fit." He was moving west to get rid of civilization, and he was as uncivilized as a "bar himself, or an Injun."

Odalie learned that a number of the men were wild, roving, roaring fellows, who came here because they hated law and order; then, without contradiction, Mrs. Beedie's exposition tended to show that it was a new country with splendid prospects and they desired to take advantage of its opening opportunities; some of them being already poor, sought here cheaper homes, with more chance for development.

And, pursuing the interpretation of her side of the shield, Mrs. Halsing detailed the fact that some people love change and adventure, because no matter what the Lord gave 'em they wouldn't fold their hands and be thankful. Were the Rush people poor and oppressed in Carolina? Mighty well off, they seemed to her—had cows, if the wolves hadn't got 'em, and had owned property and held their heads mighty high where they came from, and claimed kin with well-to-do people in England. People said Captain Stuart said he knew who they were—but the Lord only knew what Captain Stuart knew! Then Mrs. Halsing further unfolded the fact that Mrs Rush's husband had been the son of a bishop, but had got among the dissenters, and had been cast out like a prodigal, because he took to preaching.

"Preachin' being in the blood, I reckon," Mrs. Beedie palliated.

Thereupon he emigrated to America and was seized with a mission to the Indians, that fastened upon him like a plague; and he lost his scalp and his life—not even a red Indian would tolerate the doctrine he set up as the Word! And Mrs. Halsing pursed her lips with a truly orthodox fixity. And now we have no religion at the fort and the settlement.

But here Mrs. Beedie took up her testimony with unction and emphasis. We had Captain Stuart!

Mrs. Halsing gave a sudden cry of derision like the abrupt squawk of a jay-bird. Captain Stuart was not a humble man. That back of his was never bent! She wondered if his heart had ever felt the need of aught.

"Yes," Mrs. Beedie affirmed. "When one of the soldiers died of the pleurisy last winter in the fort and Captain Demeré was ill himself, Captain Stuart read the service all solemn and proper, and had men to march with arms reversed and fire a volley over the grave."

Mrs. Halsing rose to the occasion by demanding what good such evidences of religion might do in such a lot as there was at the fort. Forgetting her scorn of the bishop's son, who had taken to Methodism and Indians, she set forth the fact that the whole settlement was given to dances—that the settlers with their wives and daughters, not content with dances at home, must needs go to the fort on state and special occasions, such as Christmas, and there participate in the ball, as they called it, given in the officers mess-hall. They went in daylight, and did not return till daylight, and the fiddle it sang the whole night through! And cards—the soldiers played cards, and the settlers too; and the officers, they played "loo," as they called it, as if that made it any better. Even Captain Demeré! This latter phrase occurred so frequently in Mrs. Halsing's prelection that it created a sort of mitigating effect, and made the enormity it qualified gain a trifle of respectability from the fact that Captain Demeré countenanced it. Odalie knew already that he was the commandant, and it was plain to be seen that Captain Demeré stood first in Mrs. Halsing's estimation. And the officers all, she declared, the captains, the frisky lieutenants, and the ensigns, all drank tafia.

"When they can git it," interpolated Mrs. Beedie, with twinkling eyes.

"They are deprived, I will say, by the slowness and seldomness of the express from over the mountains. But if they are a sober set, it is against their will, and that I do maintain," Mrs. Halsing added, turning an unflinching front toward Mrs. Beedie. Then resuming her dissertation to Odalie:—

"But there's one thing that rests on my mind. I can't decide which one it belongs to, Captain Stuart or Captain Demeré. Did ye see—I know ye did—a lady's little riding-mask on the shelf of the great hall. Ye must have seen it,"—lowering her voice,—"a love token?"

"Oh," said Odalie, in a casual tone and with a slight shrug of the shoulders, not relishing the intrusive turn of the disquisition, "a souvenir, perhaps, from the colonies or over seas."

"La, now!" cried Mrs. Halsing, baffled and disconcerted, "you're as French as a frog!"

- 53 -

Recovering herself, she resumed quickly. "It's the deceitfulness of Captain Stuart that sets me agin him. Ye must be obleeged to know he can't abide the Injuns. He keeps watch day and night agin 'em. Yet they think everything o' Captain Stuart! They all prize him. Now don't ye know such wiles as he hev got for them must be deceit?"

Odalie made an effort to say something about magnetism, but it seemed inadequate to express the officer's bonhomie, when Mrs. Halsing continued:

"Ye never know how to take Captain Stuart," she objected. "Before folks he'll behave to Captain Demeré as ceremonious and polite as if they had just met yesterday; but if you hear them talking off together, in another minute he'll be rollicking around as wild as a buck, and calling him 'Quawl—I say Quawl!'"

She evidently resented this familiarity to the dignified officer, and Odalie pondered fruitlessly on the possible ridicule involved in being called "Quawl."

In this remote frontier fort a strong personal friendship had sprung up between the two senior officers which not only promoted harmony in their own relations, but a unanimity of sentiment in the exertion of authority that redoubled its force, for the garrison was thus debarred from the support on a vexed question of the suspicion of a dissentient mind in high quarters. Stuart had chanced to address his friend as "Paul," in a fraternal aside on an unofficial occasion, and one or two of the Indians overhearing it, and unaccustomed to the ceremony of a surname, had thus accosted him,—to Stuart's delight in the incongruity that this familiarity should be offered to the unapproachable Demeré, rather than to himself, whose jovial methods might better warrant the slack use of a Christian name. Moreover, "Paul" was transmogrified as "Quawl," the Cherokees never definitely pronouncing the letter P; and thereafter in moments of expansive jollity Stuart permitted himself the liberty of imitation in saying "Quawl," and sometimes "Captain Quawl."

As Odalie puzzled over this enigma, Mrs. Halsing became more personal still, having noticed during the pause the crystal clearness of her visitor's eyes, the fairness of her complexion, the delicacy of her beauty, her refinement, and the subtle suggestion of elegance that appertained to her manner, and—

"How old be you?" asked Mrs. Halsing, bluntly.

"Twenty-one," replied Odalie, feeling very responsible and matronly.

"Child," said Mrs. Halsing, solemnly, "why did you ever come to the frontier?"

"We were lacking somewhat in this world's goods. And we wish to make a provision for our little girl. We are young and don't care for privation."

"You ain't fitten for the frontier."

"I walked all the way here from New River," cried Odalie, "and not by the direct route, either—not by the old 'Warrior's Path.' We came by way of the setting sun, as Willinawaugh has it."

"You can't work," Mrs. Halsing's eyes narrowed as she measured the figure, slight and delicate despite its erect alertness.

"I can spin two hanks of yarn a day, six cuts to the hank," boasted Odalie. "I can weave seven yards of woolen cloth a day—my linen is all ten hundred. And I can hoe corn like a squaw."

"That's what you'll be in this country—a squaw! All women are. You'll have to hoe all the corn you can plant." Mrs. Halsing shook her head mournfully from side to side. "I'd like to see the coast towns agin. If I was as young as you I'd not tarry, I'd not tarry in the wilderness."

Odalie was all unaffected by her arguments, but this talk, so deadly to the progressive spirit of the pioneer settlements, and so rife then and later, was, she knew, inimical to content. The disaffection of those who remained to complain wrought more evil against the permanence of the settlements than the desertion of the few who quitted the frontier to return to the towns of the provinces. She welcomed, therefore, with ardor the reappearance of Sandy and Hamish from their tour of investigation of the site of their new home, and her eyes sparkled responsively as she noted their enthusiasm. She was glad to be again hanging on Sandy's right arm, while Hamish hung on his left, and Fifine, with her fillette toute chérie, toddled on in front.

Very cheerful the fort looked to Odalie as they approached. The afternoon dress-parade was on. The men were once more in full uniform, instead of the pioneer garb of buckskin shirt and leggings and moccasons which had won such universal approval, and was so appropriate to general use that it was almost recognized as a fatigue uniform. The sun was reddening upon the still redder ranks of scarlet coats that took even a higher grade of color from the effect of the white belts and the burnished metallic glitter of the gun-barrels. A different effect was afforded by the dress of a small body of militia from the provinces that had recently reinforced the garrison, whose dark blue had a rich but subsidiary tone and abated the glare of the ranks of scarlet, even while heightening the contrast. The Indians, always gathering from their towns up the river to revel in this feast of color and spectacle of military pomp, so calculated to impress them with the superior capacity and knowledge of the arts of warfare possessed by the white race, had mustered in stronger numbers than usual and stood in rows about the walls of the block-houses or along the interior slopes of the rampart.

In groups near the gate were some of the Cherokee women, huddled in blankets, although one wore a civilized "short gown" that had a curiously unrelated look to her physiognomy and form. Their countenances were dull and lack-luster, and the elder hag-like and hideous, but as the new settlers passed the group of squaws a broadside of bright black eyes, a fresh, richly tinted, expressionless, young face, and a string of red beads above a buckskin garb that was a sort of tunic, half shirt, half skirt, only partly revealed by the strait folds of a red blanket girt about a slender, erect figure, reminded the observant Odalie of the claim to a certain sort of beauty arrogated for the youthful among these denizens of the woods—a short-lived beauty, certainly.

Fifine had caught sight of other children, the families of the settlers having gathered here to witness the parade. Here, too, were many of the men; now a hunter, leaning on his rifle, with a string of quail, which he called "pat-ridges," tied to one another with thongs detached from the fringes of his buckskin shirt and looking themselves like some sort of feathered ornament, as they hung over his shoulder and almost to his knee, and a brace of wild turkeys, young and tender, at his belt; another, attracted from the field by the military music and the prospect of the rendezvous of the whole settlement, still carried a long sharp knife over his shoulder, with which he had been cutting cane, clearing new ground. A powerful fellow leaning on an ax was exhibiting to another and an older settler a fragment of wood he had brought, and both examined with interest the fiber; this was evidently a discovery, the tree being unknown in the eastern section, for these people were as if transplanted to a new world.

Odalie's attention was suddenly arrested by a man of gigantic build, wearing the usual buckskin garb, and with a hard, stern, fierce face, that seemed somehow peculiarly bare; he wore no queue, it is true, for at this period many of the hunters cut their hair for convenience, and only the conservative retained that expression of civilization. Under his coonskin cap his head was tied up in a red cotton handkerchief, and as he stood leaning against the red-clay wall of the rampart, talking gravely to another settler, the children swarmed up the steep interior slope of the fortifications behind him and from this coign of vantage busied themselves, without let or hindrance, in pulling off his cap, untying the handkerchief, and with shrill cries of excitement and interest exposing to view the bare poll. For the man had been scalped and yet had escaped with his life.

"Quelle barbarie! Oh, quelle barbarie!" murmured Odalie, wincing at the sight.

Years ago it must have chanced, for the wounds had healed; but it had left terrible scars which the juvenile element of the settlement prized and loved to trace as one might the map of the promised land, were such charts known to mere earthly map-makers. A frequent ceremony, this, evidently, for the shrill cries were of recognition rather than discovery, and when the unknown became a feature it was as a matter of speculation.

"Here! here!" exclaimed one wiry being of ten,—his limited corporeal structure, too, was incased in buckskin, the pioneer mother, like other mothers, feeling no vocation toward works of supererogation in the way of patching, and having discovered that skins of beasts resist the clutch of briers and the destructive propensities characteristic of callow humanity better than cloth, even of the stoutest homespun weave,—"here's where the tomahawk knocked him senseless!"

"Here's where the scalping-knife began!" cried a snaggle-toothed worthy, from the half-bent posture in which he had been surveying the forlorn cicatrices of the bare poll, and digging his heels into the red-clay slope to sustain his weight.

"No, no—here!" advanced another theorist.

Odalie turned her head away; it was too horrible!—or she would have seen the tugging climb of Josephine and her triumphant emergence on the slope amongst the boys. They looked at her in surprise for a moment, but without resentment, for it was too good an opportunity to rehearse the history that so enchanted them.

"Here, here," the shrill voices began anew. "Here's where the tomahawk hit him a clip!" "An' here," shrieked out another, seizing upon Fifine's chubby little hand that her own soft finger might have the privilege of exploring the wound, "here's where the scalping-knife circled him round!"

"The Injun begun here first, but his knife was dull, an' he had to mend his holt!" screeched a third.

"An',—an', 'n," vociferated another, almost speechless in the contemplation of so bloody a deed, "ter git a full purchase onto it the Injun held him down by putting a foot on his breast!" He lifted his own bare foot, itself a cruel and savage sight, scarred with the scratching of briers and stone-bruises and the results of what is known as dew-poison—he called it "jew-pizen," and so do those of his ilk to this good day,—and aped the gesture so present to his imagination.

Fifine knew only too well what it all meant, as her soft infantile face, incongruously maternal with compassion, bent above the hideous record of a hideous deed.

"All this here," cried the first expositor, sparing a sustaining hand to hold her by the elbow,—for her weight not being sufficient to drive her heels into the clay slope, she had given imminent signs of slipping down the incline,—"all this here top of his 'ead ain't the sure enough top; the Injuns scalped that off. This is just sich top as growed since; he ain't got no real top to his 'ead."

Fifine's baby hands traveled around this substitute top; her mouth quivered pitifully; then she bent down and kissed the grim wounds in several places with a sputter of babbling commiseration. At this moment Hamish caught sight of her and advanced in great contrition. He flushed to the roots of his hair as he spoke to the man, for as a rule those few fortunate yet unfortunate persons who had chanced to survive the cruel disaster of being scalped were exceedingly sensitive on the subject of their disfigurement—it was usually a subject not to be mentioned. But this settler looked at Hamish in surprise as the boy said, "Pray excuse the little girl, sir. I had lost sight of her and didn't know she was so vexatious with her curiosity."

"No, no," returned the stalwart giant, in a singularly languid voice, mild and deep and pacific to the last degree. "It pleases the chil'n, an' don't hurt me."

He was busying himself in tying up the horrible exhibition in his red handkerchief preparatory to putting on his coonskin cap, for the brisk interest the children took in disrobing, so to speak, his scalpless head, did not extend to the task of properly accoutering it again, and repairing the disarray they themselves had made, for they had scampered off through the great gate of the fort. His voice gave Hamish a sort of intimation how they had had the hardihood to venture on these familiarities with one so formidable of aspect. Hamish learned afterward that he had lost his scalp rather through this quality of quiet indulgence, so open to treachery, than to inability to keep it. A terrible fighter he was when he was roused, though even then his utmost prowess was exerted without anger. In the Indian fights his friends had often exhorted him to scalp the wretches he slew, as he had been scalped, and thus complete his revenge, for the Indians believed that a scalpless person would be excluded from the happy hunting-grounds of heaven, their fury thus following their foes from this world into the next.

"Let 'em have all the heaven they can git," he would remark, wiping his bloody knife upon the mane of his horse. "I expec' to smoke the pipe o' peace with all I meet on Canaan's shore,—Cherokees, Creeks, or Chickasaws,—Reg'lars, Millish, or Settlers."

For he was intensely religious and had a queer conglomeration of doctrines that he had picked up here and there in his rambles through this western world. He embraced alike the theory of purgatory and the Presbyterian tenets of predestination and justification. He had acquired the words of "Hail Mary!" from a French Catholic with whom he had hunted on the banks of the Sewanee, as the Indians called it, and Chauvanon, as the Gallic tongue metamorphosed the name,—perhaps these two were the first white men that ever trod those bosky ways,—and he believed faithfully in total immersion as promulgated by the Baptists. He was all for peace, like the Quakers,—peace at any price; and yet when for the entertainment of the boys at a friendly fireside he was urged to recount how many men he had fought and killed, the long list failed only from failure of memory.

Hamish expected to hear no more of him after they parted, and he experienced a sort of repulsion which found an echo in Odalie's exclamation, when Captain Demeré proposed that Gilfillan should live with them. "I should recommend a strong stockade if you go as far from the fort as the bend of the river," the officer commented, when the spot they had selected was made known to him. "And with only two gun men," he cogitated, as he paused. "It would not be safe." Then brightening,—for the officers of the post sought to facilitate in every way the prospects of the settlers and the extension of the settlement,—"Take Gilfillan with you; he's an odd fish, but he is equal to any four men, and he has never quite settled down since the massacre on the Yadkin where he lost his wife and children. Take Gilfillan."

A group from the fort strolled along the river-bank, and the ripples were red under the red sunset sky, and the eastern mountains were blue and misty, and the western were purple and massive and distinct, and though sedges were sere and the birds gone, summer was in the air, and they talked of hope and home.

Captain Demeré's suggestion broke discordantly on the serenity of the hour and the theme.

"Oh! oh!" cried Odalie, "and have Fifine forever tracing the map of anguish all around that terrible head, never tiring of 'Here's where the tomahawk hit him a clip!' and 'Here's where the scalping-knife began!'"

"What a consideration!" exclaimed the officer, with some asperity. "And if you will excuse me, how very French! The man's rifle—the finest marksman I ever saw—is the point for your consideration. And you find his looks not convenable."

"Fifine, herself, will be less likely to have a head like his, perhaps, if he will come and strengthen our station," suggested Alexander MacLeod, astutely.

"Oh,—yes, yes!" assented Odalie, with a sudden expression of fright.

"Besides," said Captain Stuart, with his bluff nonchalance, "the river-bend will be so easily famous for the good looks of the stationers that a trifle of discount upon Gilfillan will not mar the sum total."

"And then," said Captain Demeré, "he is a very exceptional kind of man—you are fortunate to find such a man—for a single man, in the settlements. You would not like it if he were one of the rattling, roaring blades that such irresponsible single fellows are here, usually."

"Mighty sprightly company, some of these rufflers," remarked Captain Stuart, with a twinkling eye. "Rarely good company," he averred.

"And besides," added Captain Demeré, whose extreme sensitiveness enabled him better to appreciate her sentiment than the others, despite his rebuke, "you need not have him in the same house with you; you can have two cabins within the stockade and connected by the palisades from one house to the other. Otherwise, in the present state of feeling among the Cherokees it would hardly be safe so far from the fort."

It had been explained that Alexander was especially solicitous concerning the choice of his location, since the quality of the land had not been well selected in his former home on New River. Here he had found in a comparatively small compass the ideal conjuncture for those growths so essential to the pioneer who must needs subsist on the produce of his own land. In that day and with the extremely limited and difficult means of transportation, no deficit could be filled from the base of a larger supply. The projected station, he thought, would be as safe as any other place outside the range of the guns of the fort, but he welcomed the idea of numbering among its denizens the hardy hunter, Gilfillan, and cared no more for his bald head than he did for the broad, smooth, handsome plait of Captain Stuart's fair hair. MacLeod had all the desperate energy of one who seeks to retrieve good fortune, although no great deal of money was involved in his earlier disasters. His father had had shipping interests, and the loss of a barque and her cargo at sea had sufficed to swamp the young man's financial craft on shore. As to the possessions of his wife's family—they were a few inconsiderable heirlooms, some fine traditions, growing now a trifle stale and moldy with age, and a brave, proud spirit in facing the world, the result of the consciousness of having a fine old record to sustain; her forefathers had been of that class of refugees from religious persecution whose property was of such a character and whose emergency was so imminent that they had fled from France with little else than the garments in which they stood. They had not prospered since, nor multiplied, and Odalie was nearly the last of the family. A certain innate refinement in both, MacLeod's gravity and dignity of carriage and the distinction of Odalie's

- 60 -

manner, notwithstanding its simplicity, marked their exceptional quality to a discerning judgment, despite their precarious plight. The two officers had grave doubts as to the wisdom of their adventuring so boldly in the quest of fortune in these savage wildernesses, but both felt that it was well for the community that harbored them, and each knew of isolated instances elsewhere when such folly had been transmuted into a potent sapience by the bounty of uncovenanted good luck. They had experienced a sort of pleasure in the advent of the newcomers, for Sandy's intelligence and information were far above the average, and they were more or less isolated in this remote frontier post from those dainty charms of toilette and manner which Odalie would have found means to practice were she cast away on a desert island, all the more marked, perhaps, from their demure simplicity and a sort of unstudied elegance.

It was only a serge gown she wore, of the darkest red hue,—murrey-colored, she called it,—but all faint vestige of the journey had vanished, and over the long, straight bodice of those days was a cape or fichu of fine white cambric, embellished with a delicate tambour, one of those graceful accomplishments which her "grand'maman" had brought from France, and transmitted to a docile pupil as among the arts which should adorn a woman. The deep red and the vivid white of this costume comported well with her fine dark-brown hair, rising straight from her forehead in a heavy lustrous undulation, and drawn back to be gathered into a dense knot, her fair smooth complexion, the contemplative yet suave expression of her large dark eyes, and their heavy, almost diplomatic eyelashes,—for they implied so much that they did not say, and were altogether the most effective feature of that most effective face. Often Sandy, who had taken more notice of those eyes and eyelashes than any one else in the world,— although they had not been unremarked in general,—could not decipher what she meant by them, and at other times he marveled why she should say so much with them instead of with the means which Nature had bestowed for the expression of her views,—of which, too, she made ample use. Those eyelashes, for instance, indicated disdain, reproof, reproach, and yet a repudiation of comprehension when Captain Stuart said significantly that he hoped she found her footing quite satisfactory to-day—she was wearing a spruce pair of prunella brodequins which had come in the pack. With his bluff raillery he inquired of her how she had the conscience to grudge her husband the triumph of knowing that she had shed a tun of tears for his absence yesterday and had demanded of the commandant of the post that the whole strength of the garrison should instantly take the field to search for him.

"For discipline," she answered, with placid solemnity. "If he knew that I care enough to weep for him instead of for my shabby shoes, my authority would be shattered. And a mutiny, under any circumstances, is not pretty."

The river carried the officer's jovial laughter far along the lapsing current that was growing steely now, reflecting a pale gray sky of very luminous tone, beneath which the primeval woods were dark and gloomy, and the mountains on the east loomed but dimly through the gray mists, while on the west the summit-line was hard and darkly distinct. It was winter, for all the still air; no sound of bird, no chirring of cicada, no rustle of leaf. The voice of the river rose quite alone in the silence, and a single star seemed to palpitate in a white agitation as it listened.

And when the party sat down on the rocky ledges of the river-bank, Captain Demeré was beside Odalie, and they talked not of this new country lying before them, with the unread, unrecorded mystery of its past, and the unsolved, impenetrable question of its future, but of his own people. With her delicate tact she had evaded the continual occupation of the general attention with her experiences and expectations, and the details of her new home, and led him to speak of himself and his own interests, which he was insensibly brought to do with little disguise, so potent were the reminiscent effects of the murrey-colored gown, and the dainty freshness of the cambric fichu, and the delicate feminine attraction that hung about her like an exquisite fragrance, and seemed, because of her lack of arrogation, less peculiar to herself than some sweet quality appertaining to the whole species of womankind.

She noted how the future of men like these is not with the future of the country. They were not to participate in the prosperity which their presence here might foster. While all the others looked forward they looked backward, or perhaps aside, as at a separate life. Such is the part a garrison must always play. She doubted if many felt it. With Mrs. Halsing, she, too, marveled if Captain Stuart felt the need of aught.

But Demeré, looking into the past as the tide of reminiscence rose, said to a sympathetic heart a thousand things of home. Trifles came back, hitherto forgotten; sorrows seared over by time; old jests that had outworn the too frequent laugh at last; resolutions failing midway, half-hearted; friends heretofore dead even to memory; old adventures conjured up anew; affections lingering about an old home, like the scent of roses when the fallen petals have left but the bare stalk; vanished joys, reviviscent with a new throb that was more like pain than pleasure. And if he did not look to the future that sweet December night of Saint Martin's summer by the placid Tennessee River, perhaps it was as well,—oh, poor Captain Demeré!

CHAPTER V

The next day ushered in a crisis in the affairs of the would-be stationers—the house-raising began. All the men of the settlement gathered to the fore, and the cabins—a substantial double-cabin the larger was, and the other, one room and a loft—went up as if by magic. The stockade, boles of stout young trees sawed off in lengths of twenty feet and sharply pointed at the upper end, the other end deeply sunken into the ground, began to grow apace. The spring was within the enclosure—a point of vast importance in that day, since in times of danger from the Indians it was not necessary to sally forth from the protection of the stockade for the indispensable water-supply for household and cattle. The prospects of many an early station were blighted by overlooking in a period of comparative peace and comfort this urgent advantage, and many a life was taken during some desperate sortie with piggins and pails by the defenders of the stockade, who could have held out valiantly against the savage except for the menace of death by thirst. The officers had urged this point upon the pioneers.

"Of course in any emergency," Demeré argued, "the forces at the fort would relieve you at once. But the true military principle ought to govern even in such a minor stronghold. An unfailing water-supply ought to be a definitely recognized necessity in every military post subject to beleaguerment. Otherwise the station can be held only very temporarily; one can lay in provisions and stand a siege, but drouth means death, for surrender is massacre."

Nevertheless, eastward at the time, and later in westward settlements, this obvious precaution was often neglected and the obvious disaster as often ensued.

The woodland spring within the stockade was a charming and rocky spot with no suggestion of flowing water till one might notice that the moss and mint beneath a gigantic tree were moist; then looking under a broad, flat, slab-like ledge might be descried a deep basin four feet in diameter filled with water, crystal, clear, and brown in the deep shadow—brown and liquid as the eyes of some water-nymph hidden among the rocks and the evergreen laurel.

And, oh joy! the day when Odalie kindled her own fire once more on her own hearth-stone—good, substantial flagging; when traversing the passage from one room to another she could look down through the open gate of the stockade at the silvery rushing of the Tennessee in its broad expanse under the blue sky, giving, as it swirled around, a long perspective, down the straight and gleaming reach before it curved anew. And oh, the moment of housewifely pride when the slender stock of goods was unpacked and once more the familiar articles adjusted in their places, her flax wheel in the chimney corner, her china ranged to its best advantage on the shelf; and often did she think about the little blue jug that came from France and marvel what had been its fate! All her linen that was saved, the pride of her heart, made, too, its brave show. She had a white cloth on her table, albeit the table seemed to have much ado to stand alone since its legs were of unequal length, and white counterpanes on her beds, and gay curtains at the windows opening within the stockade—the other side had but loop-holes—on which birds of splendid plumage, cut from East Indian chintz, had been overcast on the white dimity, and which looked when the wind stirred them, for there was no glass and only a batten shutter, as if all the winged denizens of the brilliant tropics were seeking entrance to this happy bower; the room had an added woodland suggestion because of the bark adhering to the logs of the walls, for the timbers of these primitive houses were unhewn, although the daubing and the chinking were stout and close, and with the aid of the great flaring fires stood off Jack Frost with a very valiant bluff.

So many things had she brought in small compass. When the fire was a-flicker on a dull wintry afternoon, and the snow a-whirl outside, and the tropical birds quite still on their shadowy perches against the closed batten shutters, Odalie, Hamish, Fifine, and the cat were wont to congregate together and sit on the buffalo rug spread on the puncheon floor beside the hearth, and explore sundry horns of buffalo or elk in which many small articles of varying degrees of value had been compactly packed. They all seemed of an age—and this a young age—when the joyous exclamations arose upon the recognition of sundry treasured trifles whose utility had begun to be missed.

"My emery bag!" her eyes dewy with delight, "and oh, my cake of wax!"

"And Lord!" exclaimed Hamish, "there's my bullet-mould—whoever would have thought of that!"

"And your new ribbon; 'tis a very pretty piece," and Odalie let the lustrous undulations catch the firelight as she reeled it out. "The best taffeta to tie up your queue."

"And oh, the moment of housewifely pride!"

"I don't intend to plait my hair in a queue any more," Hamish declared contemptuously. "The men in this country," he continued with a lofty air, "have too much men's work to do to busy themselves with plaiting hair and wearing a bobbing pig-tail at their ears." He shook his own dangling curls as he spoke.

Fifine babbled out an assortment of words with many an ellipsis and many a breathy aspiration which even those accustomed to the infant infirmities of her tongue could with difficulty interpret. Both Odalie and Hamish, bending attentive eyes upon her, discerned at last the words to mean that Mr. Gilfillan had no hair to plait. At this Hamish looked blank for a moment and in consternation; Odalie exclaimed, "Oh, oh!" but Fifine infinitely admired Mr. Gilfillan, and nothing doubted him worthy of imitation.

"I'll have none, but for a different reason. I'll cut my lovely locks close with Odalie's shears as soon as she finds them," Hamish declared.

He did not dream that they were already found and bestowed in a safe nook in a crevice between the chinking where they would not be again discovered in a hurry, for he had earlier expressed his determination to forsake the gentility of long hair in emulation of sundry young wights, the roaring blades of single men about the settlement.

Odalie was too tactful to remonstrate. "And oh!" she exclaimed with a sort of ecstasy. "My pouncet-box! how sweet! delicieux!" She presented the gold filigree at the noses successively of Hamish and Fifine and the cat, all of whom sniffed in polite ecstasy, but Kitty suddenly wiped her nose with her paw several times and then began to wash her face.

"My poppet! my poppet!" cried Fifine, ecstatically, as a quaint and tiny wooden doll of a somewhat Dutch build and with both arms stretched out straight was fished out. She snuggled it up to her lips in rapture, then showed it to the cat, who evidently recognized it, and as it was danced seductively before her on the buffalo rug, put out her paw and with a delicate tentative gesture and intent brow was about to play with it after her fashion of toying with a mouse, when one of her claws caught in a mesh of the doll's bobinet skirt. Now the doll's finery, while limited in compass to minuteness, was very fine, and as Josephine's short shriek of indignation, "Quelle barbarie!" arose on the air, the cat turned around carrying the splendidly arrayed poppet off on her unwilling claw—to be lost, who knew where, in the wilderness! The frantic little owner seized the tail of the mignonne toute chérie, which sent up a wail of poignant discordance; the romping Hamish, with a wicked mimicry of the infantile babbling cry, "Quelle barbarie!" impeded the progress of Fifine by catching the skirt of her little jacket, called a josie; whereupon Odalie, imitating his dislocated French accent and boyish hoarseness in the exclamation, "Quelle barbarie!" laid hold upon his long curly hair, held together by a ribbon as an apology for a pig-tail. There ensued an excited scramble around on the buffalo rug before the fire, during which the horn was turned over and some of its small treasures escaped amidst the long fur. This brought Odalie to a pause, for the lost articles were buttons of French gilt, and they must be found in the fur and counted; for did they not belong to Sandy's best blue coat, and could not be dispensed with? In the course of the merry-go-round the cat's claw had become disentangled from the doll's frock. Fifine had released the clutch of reprisal on the cat's tail. Hamish had been visited with a fear that the end of Fifine's josie might give way in rents before her obstinacy would relax; and Odalie had not the heart to pull his hair with more cruelty than she had heretofore indulged. So the magic circle gave way by its own impulse as it had formed, and all the heads were once more bent together in earnest absorption in the search and the subsequent disclosures of the buffalo horn. Such choice symposia as these were usually reserved for the dusk of the afternoon in bad weather when the outdoor work was done, and Odalie—her house all in order—needed more light for her other vocations. It was quite incredible how soon a loom was set up and warping-bars constructed, and all the details in motion of that pioneer home life, which added the labor and interests of domestic manufacture to the other absorbing duties of the housewife that have survived in these times of machinery and delegated responsibility.

These were the holiday moments of the day, but once when the mother and the little girl and the cat sat intent upon the rug, their treasures spread before them, Odalie's face paled and her heart almost sprang into her mouth as she heard Hamish's step outside, quick and disordered. As he burst into the room she knew by his eyes that something of grave import had happened. And yet, as she faced him speechless, he said nothing. She noted his uncaring casual glance at that potent fascinator, the buffalo horn, and his hasty, unsettled gesture. He seemed resolved not to speak—then he suddenly exclaimed solemnly:—

"Odalie, there is the prettiest creature in this settlement that you ever saw in your life—and—the gracefullest!"

"A fawn?" said the mercurial Odalie, who recovered her poise as suddenly as it was shaken.

He looked at her in a daze for a moment.

"A fawn? What absurdity!"

"Nothing less than a dear, I must needs be sure."

He apprehended her sarcasm. Then, too absorbed to be angry, he reverted to himself.

"Oh," he cried with bitterness, "why do you let me go about in worshipful company with my hair like this?—" he clutched at his tousled locks.

"Yes—yes, I see. It always goes to the head," said Odalie, demurely.

"Don't laugh at me," he exclaimed, "but how had you the heart—and Sandy's hair always in such trim-wise, and you and Fifine like people of fashion."

Odalie could but laugh in truth; she had known such splendors as colonial life at that day could present and she was well aware how the ill-equipped wife of a pioneer on the furthest frontier failed of that choice aspect.

"I thought," she said, still laughing, "that you were ambitious of the fashion of such coiffure as Mr. Gilfillan affects—oh, poor man!—and had made up your mind to plait your hair no more."

Hamish took this very ill, and in dudgeon would not divulge the name and quality of the fair maiden the sight of whom had so gone to his head. But it was the next evening only that they were to attend a ball in the officers' mess-hall at the fort, in celebration of the joys of Christmastide, and Odalie perceived the rancor of resentment gradually departing when he came and begged—not her pardon—but that she would do him the infinite favor to plait his hair. Try as he would, and he had tried for an hour, he could not achieve a coiffure that seemed satisfactory to him in the solicitous state of his feelings. This ceremony she performed, perched upon what she called a tabouret, which was nothing but a stout, square billet of wood with a cover and valance of a dull blue fustian, while he sat at her feet, and Sandy looked on with outward gravity, but with a twinkle in his sober eyes that made Hamish's blood boil to realize that she had told his brother of the sudden reason for a change of heart touching the mode of wearing his hair, and that they had quietly laughed at him about it. Nevertheless, now he valued every strand of it as if it were spun gold, and would have parted with it as hardly.

The Christmas ball was indeed an affair of much splendor. Profuse wreaths of holly, with berries all aflame, decorated the walls of the great hall, and among them the lines of buffalo horns and the antlers of deer and the waving banners showed with enhanced effect. From the centre of the ceiling the mystic mistletoe depended with such suggestively wide-spreading boughs that it might seem that no fair guest could hope to escape the penalty; this was the broad jest of the masculine entertainers. The hosts, all the commissioned officers being present, were in full uniform, seeming brilliant against the decorated walls and in the great flare of the fire; even lace ruffles were to be seen and many a queue was braided and tied as fairly as Hamish's own. A huge Yule log, such as could not be discredited by any that had ever sent up sparks and flame at this sacred season, made the great chimney place one vast scarlet glow; the door of necessity stood open, although the snow was on the ground, and the dark, bare branches of the rows of trees left in military alignment, down the centre of the parade, whitely glimmered with frost and ice akin to the chilly glitter of the wintry stars which they seemed to touch with their topmost boughs.

The garrison had been surprised on the previous midnight by the sudden outbreak of the sound on the icy air of certain familiar old Christmas carols sung by a few of the soldiers, who had the memory and the voice to compass the feat, and who had been wont for a time to steal off to the woods to rehearse in secret, in order to bring to the Yule-tide, so surely coming, even to these far-away fastnesses, something of the blithe association and yet the spirit of sanctity of the old remembered Yule-tides of long distances agone both of time and place. The enthusiasm that this reminder awakened nullified all thought of the breach of discipline. The singers were summoned into the hall by the commandant, and the embers stirred up, and they drank his health and the king's as long as he dared let them have the liquor. And now, all unseen in the darkness, the waits were stationed at a little distance to mellow the sound, and were singing these old Christmas carols while the guests gathered. The rough martial voices rang out with a sort of jubilant solemnity and a strongly defined tempo giusto, very natural to men who "mark time" for their sins, and whose progress through life is to the sound of the drum.

The iterative beat pulsed through the open doors to the groups about the big Yule-tide fires and those coming in out of the dark wilderness, not daring to stir without firelock, knife, and pistol, for fear of a treacherous foe. And in the hearts and minds of the full-armed guests was roused a sentiment not new but half-forgotten, to hear in those confident, mellow, assured tones—

"God rest ye, merry gentlemen,
Let nothing ye dismay;
For Jesus Christ our Saviour
Was born upon this day."

Between each stanza when silence came unwelcome to the ear and the chatter of tongues seemed dull and trivial a bugle sang out suddenly, its golden-sweet notes vibrating and ringing in the air in the intervals of this sweet old hymning theme.

After this tribute, such as they could pay to the holier character of the day and the reminder of home, the festivity and jollity began. The introduction was auspicious and touched the sense of the picturesque of those to whom life was wont to show but a sordid aspect. The settlers were pleased with the pomp and ceremony of their reception, genuinely delighted with the effect of the carols and the summoning up of old memories and homing thoughts so tenderly stirred, satisfied with themselves and disposed to admire each other.

One would hardly have believed that there was so much finery in the settlement—of different dates and fashions, it is true, and various nationalities. The wife of one settler wore a good gown of brocade, although her husband seemed quite assured in his buckskins. Two or three heads were held the higher from a proud consciousness of periwigs[7] and powder. Mrs. Halsing had a tall, curious comb of filigree silver and great silver ear-rings, a sad-colored stuff gown, but a queer foreign apron across which were two straight bands of embroidery of a pattern and style that might have graced a museum; Odalie, the expert, determined that the day was not far distant when she should sue for the privilege of examining the stitch. She herself was clad in the primrose-flowered paduasoy, with a petticoat of dark red satin and all her Mechlin lace for a fichu, while pearls—her grand'maman's necklace—were in her dark hair. Mrs. Beedie had woven her own frock with her own sturdy hands, and with a fresh mob-cap on her head and a very fresh rose on her cheek actively danced the whole night through.

The widow of the man who had come hither to forward his passion for the ministry to the Indian savages, and who had lost his life in the fruitless effort, now probably deemed dissent a grievous folly and had returned to earlier ways of thinking and conventional standards. She wore no weeds— one could not here alter the fashion of one's dress, the immutable thing, for so transitory a matter as grief. She regarded the scene with the face of one who has little share, although she wore a puce-colored satin with some fine lace frills and a modish cap on her thin hair.

But the daughter! With a lordly carriage of her delicate head that might have been reminiscent of her grandfather, the bishop, and yet joyous girlish red lips, full and smiling and set about with deep dimples; with her hair of red-gold, and sapphire eyes, she was eminently calculated to shatter what poor remnant of peace of mind the young ensign and two young lieutenants who clustered about her had been able to keep in this desert place—the more precarious since it was well understood that the fair Belinda had high expectations, and as to matrimonial bait hoped for the opportunity to "bob for whale." This gay exile herself, born and reared in the provinces and surrounded always by the little court her beauty summoned about her, did not look forward to a life on the frontier. She anticipated at some time an invasion of England and a life worthy the brilliance of her aspect, and occasionally when her interlocutors were such as could attribute to her no braggart pride, she would mention that she had relatives there—of good quality—who would doubtless be glad to receive her. The mother, poor sad-visaged martyr of deceit, would only draw her thin wrinkled collapsed lips the closer, holding hard hidden the fact that the girl's father had been looked upon by these relatives "of good quality" as a monster of ingratitude, and at the same time as a candidate for a strait waist-coat, whose apostasy and voluntary exile had hastened the good bishop's old age and broken his heart; that the children of the ingrate would be avoided by this conventional clique, like the leprosy, and esteemed sure to develop sooner or later terrible and infinitely inconvenient heresies, and occasion heaven only knew what bouleversement in any comely and orthodox and reasonable method of life. She had not much vigor of sentiment, but such flicker of hatred as could burn among the ashes of her nature glowed toward those who had cut her husband off and ostracized him, and made of his earnest sacrificial effort to do his duty, as it was revealed to him, a scoff, a burlesque, a reproach, and a bitter caricature. She knew, too, how much of money, of dress, and of connections it would require to return to that country where they would have no base from which to organize the brave campaign that the brilliantly equipped daughter contemplated with such gay and confident courage.

The girl's brother, however, Hamilton Rush, five years her senior, forgetting that he was the grandson of a prelate and the son of a martyr by election, bent all the energies he had inherited from both in the effort to build up home and wealth and a fair future in this rich land, which held out such bounties to the strong hand and the brave heart. He was here to-night, looking on at the scene of pleasure with as absent and absorbed a face as a London stockbroker might have worn in the midst of a financial crisis.

The brilliant mirage before the shining anticipative eyes of the fair Belinda did not preclude her from entering with youthful ardor into these festivities now faute de mieux garbed in a canary-colored tabby, of which the moiré effect, as we should say nowadays, glistened and shoaled in the light and the luster of the silk. It was worn opening over a skirt of white satin with yellow stripes, enclosing in each a delicate pattern of a vine of roses in several natural tints from pink to a deep purplish red, all having that sere sort of freshness which comes from solicitous preservation rather than newness—like a pressed flower; one might imagine that garbed thus the galvanized widow had captured the affections of the bishop's son, not then perhaps so severely ascetic of outlook. But Miss Belinda danced as graciously with the ensign as if she had no splendid ulterior views, and graced the minuet which Odalie and Captain Demeré led. Hamish looking at them thought that though she was as unlike Odalie as a splendid tulip differs from the stately, tender sweetness of the aspect of a white rose, they both adorned the dance like flowers in a parterre. He resolved with a glow of fraternal pride that he would tell Odalie how beautiful she was in her primrose-tinted gown and deep red jupon with her dark hair rolled high, and its string of white pearls, her step so deliberate and smooth with its precision of grace as with uplifted clasped hands she and the officer opened the dance.

This minuet was a splendid maze to Hamish's limited experience, as the firelight glowed and flashed on the scarlet uniforms and the delicate, dainty tints of the gowns of the ladies, giving out the gloss of satin and now and again showing the soft whiteness of a bare arm held upward to the clasp of a partner's hand in a lace ruffle and a red sleeve in the graceful attitudes prescribed by the dance. The measured and stately step, the slow, smooth whirl, the swinging changing postures, the fair smiling faces and shining eyes, all seemed curiously enhanced by the environment—the background of boughs of holly on the walls, and the military suggestions of the metallic flashing of the arms resting on the line of deer antlers that encircled the room—it was like a bird singing its roundelay perched in a cannon's mouth.

Hamish himself stood against the wall, and for a time it may be doubted if any one saw how very handsomely his "lovely locks" were plaited, so did he court the shadows. Sandy noted with secret amusement how persistently the boy's eyes followed the beautiful Miss Rush, for it was evident that she was nineteen or twenty years of age, at least three years older than her latest admirer.

Despite his sudden infatuation, however, Hamish was a person of excellent good sense, and he soon saw the fatuity of this worship from afar. "Let the ensign and the lieutenants pine to death," he thought—then with the rough old frontier joke, "I'm saving my scalp for the Injuns." Nevertheless he was acutely glad that his hair was like a gentleman's, and when he finally ventured out of the crowd he secured, to his great elation, a partner for one of the contra-dances that succeeded the minuet, for the men so greatly outnumbered the women that this argued considerable enterprise on a newcomer's part. Hamish had determined to dance, if with nobody but Mrs. Halsing; but there were other girlish flowers, somewhat overshadowed by the queens of the parterre, whom he found when his eyes had lost their dazing gloat upon the beauty of the belle of the settlement—mere little daisies or violets, as near half wild as himself, knowing hardly more of civilized society than he did. Most of these were clad in bright homespun; one or two were so very young that they found it amazing sport, and in truth so did he, although he had the style of patronizing the enterprise, to plunge out of the great hall and scamper across the snowy parade to a room, emptied by the gradual exhaustion of the munitions it had contained, and now devoted to the entertainment of the children of the settlers, who it is needless to say had come necessarily with the elder members of the pioneer families to participate in the gayeties of the fort. It was a danger not to be contemplated to leave them in the wholly deserted settlement; so, sequestered here in this big room, bare of all but holly boughs upon the wall and a great fire and a bench or two about the chimney corner, they added éclat to the occasion of the officers' ball by reason of the enthusiastic spirit that pervaded the Christmas games under the direction of Corporal O'Flynn. He had been delegated to supervise and control the juvenile contingent, being constituted master of the revels. With his wild Irish spirit aflame he was in his element. A finer looking Bruin than he was when enveloped in a great bearskin never came out of the woods, and certainly none more active as he chased the youthful pioneers, who were screaming shrilly, from one side of the hall to the other. As "Poor Puss" he struggled frantically for a corner, failing, however, when a settler of the advanced age of four, but mighty enterprising, made in swiftly between his knees, gave him a tremendous fall, and gained the coveted goal. "Mily, mily bright" was infinitely enlivened by the presence of the recruits from the ball-room, and the romp became tumultuous when Hamish undertook the rôle of one of the witches that waited by the way to intercept those—among whom was the corporal—who sought to get there by "candle-light," and who were assured that they could do this if their "legs were long enough." When he pursued the soldier and his juvenile party from one side of the room to the other, winding and doubling and almost tumbling into the fire, the delighted screams of the children were as loud and shrill as if they were all being scalped, and caused the sentries in the block-house towers to look in surprise and doubt in that direction more than once, and finally brought Captain Stuart from the officers' quarters to see for himself what was going on. As he stood in the door with his imperious face, his bluff manner, his military dress, and his great muscular height, the children, inspired by that love of the incongruous which always characterizes childhood, swarmed about him with the insistence that he should be blindfolded in Blindman's Buff. And surely he proved the champion blind man of the world! After one benighted stumbling rush half across the room, amidst a storm of squealing ecstasy, he plunged among his pygmy enemies with such startling success as to have caught two or three by the hair of their heads with one hand, while with the other he was laying about him with such discrimination that his craft became apparent. He was not playing fair!—he could see!—he peeped! he peeped! and his laugh being much resented, he was put to the door by his small enemies, who evidently expected him to feel such repentance as he might experience if he were to be court-martialed.

O'Flynn, watching him go off across the snowy shadowy parade, noticed that he did not at once return to the open door of the great hall where the swirl of the dance could be seen in a kaleidoscopic glow of color, and whence the glad music came forth in a mellow gush of sound; but stood at some little distance watching the progress of the corporal of the guard, who with the relief was on his way to the posts of the sentinels; then Stuart disappeared within one of the block-houses, evidently ascending to the tower; after an interval he came out and again traversed the parade, going diagonally across the whole enclosure without doubt to the block-house at the further bastion; thus from these two coigns of vantage he could survey the whole of the region on the four sides of the fort.

"I'll go bail, ould Foxy," said Corporal O'Flynn, apostrophizing his superior officer under his breath, "that there's nothin' that your sharp eyes doesn't see—if it's just a snake takin' advantage o' the privacy o' the dark hour to slough his skin. But I'd give ye," he hesitated, "me blessin', if you'd tell me what 'tis ye're lookin' for. I want to know, not from a meddlesome sphirit, but jist from sheer curiosity—because my mother was a woman an' not a witch."

For Captain Stuart had encountered a difficulty in these simple backwoods Christmas festivities which was altogether unexpected. He had diligently considered the odds against success, in which, however, the chief seemed the lack of appropriate refreshment, for one could not serve venison and buffalo and wild fowl to hunters as luxuries, and the limited compass and utilitarian character of the goods sent from the base of supplies over the mountains rendered even the accumulation of the requisite materials for the punch-bowl a matter of forethought and skilled strategy. After the wheat-bread had been secured to make the ramequins this feature came near to being dropped because of the difficulty of obtaining the simple ingredients of eggs and cheese to compound the farce wherewith they should be spread. But this too had been accomplished. The method of providing for the safety and entertainment of the children of the settlers, without whom they could not leave home yet whose presence would have hindered if not destroyed the enjoyment of the elders, seemed a stroke of genius. The soldiers and non-commissioned officers were satisfactorily assigned a share in the entertainment appropriate to their military rank and in consonance with their taste, and were even now carousing gayly in their quarters, where there was more Christmas spirit in circulation than spirituous liquor, for the commandant's orders were niggardly indeed as to serving out the portions of tafia, not in the interests of temperance so much as of discipline in view of their perilous situation so far from help, so alone in the midst of hordes of inimical savages; his parsimony in this regard passed with them as necessity, since they knew that rum was hard to come by, and even this meager dole was infrequent and a luxury. Therefore they drank their thimbleful with warm hearts and cool heads; the riotous roared out wild songs and vied with one another in wrestling matches or boxing encounters; the more sedate played cards or dominoes close in to the light of the flaring fire, or listened with ever fresh interest to the great stories often told by the gray-headed drum-major who had served under the Duke of Cumberland in foreign lands, and promptly smote upon the mouth any man who spoke of his royal highness as "Billy the Butcher";[8] for there were Scotchmen in the garrison intolerant of the title of "Hero of Culloden," having more or less remote associations with an experience delicately mentioned in Scotland as "being out in the Forty-five." With each fresh narration the drum-major produced new historical details of the duke's famous fields and added a few to the sum of the enemies killed and wounded, till it seemed that if the years should spare him, it would one day be demonstrated that the warlike William Augustus had in any specified battle slain more men by sword and bayonet and good leaden ball than were ever mustered into any army on the face of the earth. All the soldiers were in their spruce parade trim, and every man had a bunch of holly in his hat.

Even the Indians had been considered. In response to the invitation, they had sent the previous day their symbolic white swan's wings painted with streaks of white clay, and these were conspicuously placed in the decorated hall. The gates of the fort that morning had been flung wide open to all who would come. Tafia—in judiciously small quantities, it is true—was served to the tribesmen about the parade, but the head-men, Atta-Kulla-Kulla, Willinawaugh, Rayetaeh, Otacite, more than all, Oconostota, the king of the Cherokee nation, were escorted to the great hall of the officers' quarters, the latter on the arm of Captain Stuart himself; the Indian king, being a trifle lame of one leg,—he was known among the soldiers as "Old Hop,"—was evidently pleased by the exceptional attention and made the most of his infirmity, leaning heavily on the officer's arm. Arrayed in their finest fur robes with beautiful broad collars of white swan's down about their necks, with their faces mild and devoid of paint, seated in state before the great fire, the head-men were regaled with French brandy, duly diluted, and the best Virginia tobacco, offered in very curious pipes, which, with some medals and gorgets imported for the purpose, were presented as gifts when the ceremony was concluded, and which the Cherokees accepted with a show of much pleasure; indeed, they conducted themselves always under such circumstances with a very good grace and a certain dignity and propriety of feeling which almost amounted to good breeding.

This was maintained when, invited by the commandant, they witnessed the dress parade, especially elaborate in honor of the occasion, and they listened attentively when Captain Stuart made a short address to the troops on the subject of the sacred character of the day and adjured them in a frank and soldierly fashion to have a care that they maintained the moral discipline in which they had all been drilled and gave no advantage to the Enemy because they were here, cut off from the main body of Christianity, so far from the ministrations of a chaplain and the beneficent usages of civilization. "Every soldier learns command from obedience," he said. "And if I should send a detail from the ranks on some special duty, the file-leader would know how to command it, although he had never given an order in his life. You are each, with all your spiritual forces, detached on special duty. You are veteran soldiers of the Cross and under marching orders!"

Oconostota, with a kingly gesture, signified that the interpreter should repeat in his ear this discourse, and now and again nodded his head during its translation with cogitation and interest, and as if he understood and approved it. He watched too, as if with sympathy, the ranks go suddenly down upon their knees, as the commandant read the collect for the day followed by the unanimous delivery of the Lord's prayer, in their hearty, martial voices.

After the tap of the drum had given a resonant "Amen!" they marched off upon the word and broke ranks; and such little observance as the fort could offer in commemoration of the event was over.

The Indians all realized this, and were soon loitering out of the great gate, the commandant receiving their compliments upon the good behavior of his "young men" and their fine appearance, an elaborate and flowery speech of farewell. Then Oconostota took his presents, by far the largest and most elaborate of the collection, and, leaning on Stuart's arm, left the fort, the officer attending him in this fashion down to the river-bank, where his pettiaugre awaited him. Stuart evolved, apparently without effort, a felicitous phrase of farewell and esteem, graded carefully to suit the rank of the other head-men who followed with Captain Demeré and several lieutenants. These words, Atta-Kulla-Kulla, a Cherokee of an intelligent, spirited countenance, either had the good feeling or the art to seem to especially value.

"Such smoke as goes up from this pipe between my face and your face, my friend," he said through the interpreter, "shall never come between you and me. I shall always see you very clear, for I know your heart. Your ways are strange; you come from a far place; but I know you well, for I know your heart."

He laid his hand for a moment on the broad chest of the red coat of the tall, blond officer, then stepped into the canoe, and the little craft shoved off to join a very fleet of canoes, so full was the shining surface of the river of Indians who had come from the towns above to the celebration of the "big Sunday"[D] at the fort.

Captain Stuart felt relieved that all had gone off so well and that they were rid of the Cherokees for the day.

But now the unforeseen was upon him, the fatally uncovenanted event for which none can prepare. An express had come after nightfall from over the mountains, bringing, besides the mail, rumors of another Indian outbreak on the South Carolina frontier. A number of settlers had been massacred, and the perpetrators of the deed had escaped unpunished. Stuart, charging the man to say nothing of his news to blight the Christmas festivities— since the reports might not be true—sent him to make merry among the soldiers. Anxiety had taken possession of that stout heart of Stuart's. When the settlers had begun to gather to the ball, the earliest arrivals brought no suggestion of difficulty. The next comers, however, had seen straggling bands of Indians across the river, but they were mentioned casually and with no sense of premonition. The guests to enter last had been somewhat surprised to notice numbers of canoes at the landing-place, and presently Captain Stuart was called aside by the officer of the day, who stated that in making the rounds he had learned that the sentinel at the gate had reported having observed bands of Indians lurking about on the edge of the woods, and that quite a number had come, singly and in groups, to the gate to demand admission. The gathering of the white people had roused their attention evidently. They had always held the cannon-mounted fort and the presence of the soldiery as a menace, and they now sought to discern what this unprecedented assemblage might portend. If their entrance were resisted, they who so often frequented the place, it was obviously inimical to them. They had heard—for the transmission of news among the Indians was incredibly swift—of the massacres on the frontier and feared some effort at reprisal. The scanty numbers of the garrison invited their blood-thirsty rapacity, but they were awed by the cannon, and although entertaining vague ideas concerning the management and scope of artillery, realized its terrible potencies.

Perhaps it was with some idea of forcing an entrance by surprise—that they might be within the walls of the fort and out of the range of the guns at this critical juncture of the massing of the forces of the settlers and the garrison—that a party of thirty or forty Cherokees suddenly rushed past the sentinel on the counterscarp, who had hardly time to level his firelock and to call lustily on the guard. The guard at once turning out, the soldiers met the onset of the savages at the gate and bore them back with the bayonet. There was the sudden, quick iterative tramp on the frozen ground of a man running at full speed, and as Stuart dashed through the sally-port he called out "Bar the gates! Bar the gates!" in a wild, imperative voice.

In another moment he was standing outside among the savages, saying blandly in Cherokee, of which he had mastered sundry phrases—"How now, my friends,—my best friends!" and holding out his hand with his frank, genial manner first to one of the Indians, then to another.

They looked upon his hand in disdain and spat upon the ground.

The sentry in the gate-house above, his firelock ready leveled to his shoulder, gazed down at the officer, as he stood with his back to the heavy iron-spiked oaken gates; there was light enough in the reflection of the snow, that made a yellow moon, rising higher and higher into the blue night and above the brown, shadowy woods, seem strangely intense of color, and in the melancholy radiation from its weird, gibbous disk to show the officer's calm, impassive face; his attitude, with his arms folded, the rejected hand withdrawn; even the gold lace on his red coat and the color of his hair in the thick braid that hung down under his cocked hat. Even the latent expectation might be discerned in his eyes that the interval of silence would prove too irksome to the hot impulse, which had nerved the rush on the gates, to be long continued, and that the moment would reveal the leader and the purpose of the demonstration.

A Cherokee stepped suddenly forward—a man with a tuft of eagle feathers on his scalp-lock quivering with angry agitation, his face smeared with

- 77 -

vermilion, clad in the buckskin shirt and leggings that the settlers had copied from the Indians, with pistols at his belt as well as a firelock in one hand—the barrel sawed off short to aid its efficacy. The air was bitterly cold, but the blood blazed hot in his face; in Cherokee he spoke and he paused for no interpreter; if the unaka Captain did not understand him, so much the worse for the unaka Captain. Through his teeth the tense swift utterances came in half-suppressed breathless tones, save when a sudden loud exclamation now and again whizzed out on the air like the ascent of a bursting rocket. His fury was such that even without the disguise of the paint on his face, Stuart might hardly have recognized him were it not for his peculiarly sinewy, slight elegance of shape. He had advanced one foot and he brandished his tomahawk—a furious gesture, but without immediate intention, for now and again he thrust the weapon into his belt.

"The white captain calls on his friends—and where are they? Not on the outside of these great guns that bar us from our own. The fort is ours! To-e-u-hah! It is our own. To-e-u-hah![E] Did we not bargain for it in solemn treaty! Did we not make our peace and smoke our pipe and give our belts of white wampum and sign names to the treaty we made with the white English? Wahkane?[F] Did we not join his cause and fight his battles and shed our blood in his wars against the French? Wahkane, John Stuart, wahkane? And for what? That the great King George should build us some forts in our nation to protect our women and children, our old men and our young boys while the Cherokee braves are away fighting the battles of this great King George against the French—yes, and to make strong the arm of our warriors should the French come here with the great guns like these, that make naught of the small gun,"—he looked scornfully at the firelock and shook it in his left hand—"and the bow and arrows—"he spat upon the ground. "And what does the great Earl of Loudon? He builds this fort for which we have paid with our blood! blood! blood!—these guns bought with long marches and burnt towns and the despiteful usage of the Virginians"—once more he spat upon the ground. "And then he sends his redcoat soldiers to hold our fort from us and man our great guns and be a threat and a danger forever to our peace and make us slaves to the fear of the great cannon! Yo-he-wah! Yo-he-wah![G] And when we send a talk to tell him this, he sends more soldiers! And the white men gather together for grief to the red man, and take the Indians' fort paid for with the Indians' blood and turn the great cannon against him who bought them with a dear price, and bar out his entrance from his own"—the foam flew from his lips. "You call on your friend—where?"

He turned a scornful fiery face to look at the scornful fiery faces about him. "Where?"

"Here!" Captain Stuart's calm, full voice struck the vibrating air at least an octave lower than the keen, high vociferation of the Cherokee. "Here is my friend! That is the moon, Atta-Kulla-Kulla, neus-se a-nan-to-ge"[H]—he lifted his arm and with his debonair, free gesture pointed at it. "Another sun has not risen. And yet this day, and before the sun was high, you told me that naught should come between you and me. You told me that even a cloud coming between you and me could not separate us because you knew my heart—and my heart swelled with pride at your words."

He hesitated for a moment; he detected a sudden change in the Indian's face. "My heart swelled with pride," he went on, firmly, "for I believed you! And I believe you still, for"—he laid his hand on the Cherokee's breast in imitation of the gesture of Atta-Kulla-Kulla as he repeated Atta-Kulla-Kulla's words—"for I know your heart."

There was a moment of tense silence. Then not waiting for the dramatic effect to be lost, he continued: "And now, if you say it is not well to shut the gates on this array of braves, I open them! I come here because I am sent—a unaka soldier has no will of his own. He is held to a strict law, and has no liberty such as your young fighting men, who sometimes grow rash, however, and make the wisdom of the plans of your 'beloved men,' your sage councils, mere folly. The Earl of Loudon sent the garrison here. Perhaps if you send a 'talk' to the new head-man, General Amherst, he will take the soldiers away. I go or stay according to orders—I march at a word. But to-night the children of the settlers make merry. I told you this morning of our religion. This day is the festival of the Child. So the children make merry—you can hear them now at their play." And indeed there was a sharp, wild squealing upon the air, and Stuart hoped that the beat of the dancing feet might be supposed to be of their making and the sound of the music for their behoof—for the dance of the Indians often heralds war and is not for sheer joy. "The parents bring them here and share their mirth. For this is the festival of the Child. Now your warriors are brave and splendid and terrible to look upon. If they go through the gates, the little children would be smitten with fear; the heart of a little child is like a leaf in the wind—so moved by fear. Do not the Cherokee children flee from me—who am not a great warrior and have not even paint for my face—when I come to visit you at Nachey Creek. Say the word—and I open the gates."

There was something in this Cherokee which Stuart saw both then and afterward, and which also attracted the attention of others, that indicated not only an acute and subtle intelligence and a natural benignity, but a wide and varied scope of emotion, truly remarkable in a savage without education, of course, and without even the opportunity of observing those of a higher culture and exercising sentiments esteemed of value and grace in a civilized appraisement. Yet he was experiencing as poignant a humiliation to be convicted of an ungenerous attitude of mind and upbraided with a protest belied as if he had been a Knight of the Round Table, bred to noble thoughts as well as to chivalrous deeds of arms, and had never taken the scalp of a child or treacherously slain a sleeping enemy.

Stuart could feel the Cherokee's heart beat fast under his hand. Atta-Kulla-Kulla grasped it suddenly in his own, gripping it hard for a moment, while with his other hand he waved a command for his men to retire, which they did, slowly, with lowering, surprised eyes and clouded brows.

"Go back!" he said to Stuart. "Hold the gate fast. You make your feast. Keep it. I believe your words. And because—" there was a slight convulsion of his features—"of the wicked ways of the wicked Earl Loudon I have forgot to-night my words I said to-day, I say them again—and I do not always forget!"

He turned suddenly and went down toward the river, the sad, yellow moon sending his brown, elongated shadow with its quivering tuft of feathers far along the stretches of white snow. Captain Stuart paused for a moment, leaning heavily against the gate; then as he slipped within it and into the shadow of the wall, he was full glad to hear the dancing feet, all unconscious of the danger that had been so near, and the childish treble scream of the unscalped children.

"A little more, and there would have been another massacre of the innocents," he said, walking slowly across the parade; he had hardly the strength for a speedier gait. He rescinded the order concerning the hour at which "tattoo" and "lights out" should sound. "For," he thought, noticing the cheerful groups in the soldiers' quarters, "I could get them under arms much more quickly if awake than by drumming them up out of their beds in barracks."

He carried no sign of the agitation and the significance of the interview just past when he returned to the prismatic tinted swirl of the dancing figures in the flaring light of the great fire, made more brilliant by the glow of the holly boughs and the flutter of banners and the flash of steel from the decorated walls about them. He, too, trod a gay measure with the fair Belinda Rush, and never looked more at ease and care-free and jovially imperious than in the character of gallant host. Even in the gray dawn as he stood at the sally-port of the fort and there took leave of the guests, as group by group departed, he was as debonair and smiling throughout the handshaking as though the revels were yet to begin.

FOOTNOTES:

[D] The Indians in North Carolina called the Christmas holidays Winick-kesbuse, or "the Englishman's God's moon."

[E] It is most true.

[F] Is it not so?

[G] It has been maintained that this exclamation constantly used by the Cherokees in solemn adjuration signified "Jehovah."

[H] Literally "the sun of the night."

CHAPTER VI

Breakfast, the rigorous cleaning of the quarters, guard mounting, and inspection, followed in their usual sequence, but the morning drills were omitted to give the opportunity to recruit from the vigils of the previous night, protracted, as the soldiers began to suspect, that they might be in readiness to respond to an onslaught of the savages. For Captain Stuart made no effort to restrain the story of the scene at the gate, since the sentries were already cognizant of it; he always saw fit to maintain before the troops an attitude of extreme frankness, as if the officers suppressed no intelligence, whatever its character, even with the intention of conducing to the public good.

In the great hall in the block-house of the northwestern bastion, when the officers were congregated about the fire, in the rude arm-chairs, and their pipes lighted, he divulged without reserve the news which the express had brought. In an instant all the garnered sweetness of the retrospect of the little holiday they had made for themselves and their co-exiles was turned to gall. It even held bitter dregs of remorse.

"And we were dancing all the night through while you knew this horrible thing!" exclaimed Captain Demeré, his voice tense with reproach.

"Lord!—it happened three weeks ago, Paul," returned Stuart, "if it happened at all! Some of the settlers had already come. I did not feel qualified to balk the children and the young people of their enjoyment—or the elders, either. The world will go on after such tragedies. It must, you know." He pulled at his pipe, meditatively. "To have called a halt could have done those poor fellows no good," he nodded toward the south, "and might have done us incalculable harm. There had already been a demonstration of the Indians, before the express came in, because they had noticed the gathering of the guests, and I thought the settlers safer congregated in the fort until daybreak than going home scattered through the night. This is no time or place to give ceremonious deference to questions of feeling."

"Was there a demonstration of the Indians last night, Captain?" asked Lieutenant Gilmore.

Stuart detailed both occurrences at the gate. "Without the chief's guaranty I don't see how we could have let the settlers go this morning," he concluded.

Demeré frowned deeply as he sat upright in his chair and gazed at the fire.

"You have great presence of mind in these queer emergencies, John," he said. "For my life I could not have thought how to get rid of them peaceably—to offer to open the gates!"

"I can't soothe the Indians," said Ensign Whitson, with a quick flush. "My gorge rises at the very sight of them."

"If a dog licks my hand, I must needs pat him on the head," said Stuart, lounging easily among the soft rugs that covered the chair.

"But if a wolf licks your hand, sir, would you pat him on the head?" asked the ensign.

"A wolf will not lick my hand," retorted the superior officer. "Besides, my young friend, bear this in mind,—if this dog is not patted on the head, he will fly not only at my throat, but at the throat of the garrison and of the settlement as well."

There was silence for a time, while the flames of the great fire sprang elastically upward in the strong draught with an impetuous roar. The holly boughs and the banners stirred fitfully on the wall. The men's heads were surrounded by tobacco smoke. Demeré sat upright, meditative, with one elbow on the table. Stuart was lolling far back in the soft fur rugs that covered the great chair, his hat on the floor behind him, where it had fallen off his dense, blond hair, which so much attracted the curiosity and admiration of the swarthy Indians.

"And then," he said suddenly, drawing some official letter-books and files from the table, and fluttering the pages with one hand while he held the pipe-stem with the other, "were we not admonished to be diplomatic in such matters? We had our orders to cultivate the graces of our manners! The Earl of Loudon desired that we should," and he began to read aloud, "'You can best retain our confidence by promoting, in every way in your power, the preservation of peace with the Cherokees.'"

He shoved the papers away on the table, and laughing, put the stem of his pipe between his teeth.

"Now," he said, "I am as much disposed toward peace as a man of war may decently be. I only wish my lord could have won Oconostota to his lordship's pacific way of thinking. A garrison of two hundred soldiers is not likely to prove very overbearing to a neighbor who can muster three thousand fighting men armed with British muskets. My lord's advice was timely."

He glanced with raillery at Demeré, and laughed again.

While the individual soldier is but a factor in a great machine, and moves only as one motor element acts and reacts on another, making naught of his own volition or intelligence, it being his "to do and die," the courage and strength of character which make this abnegation of will and mind possible are the greater from the fact that the reasoning faculties cannot by the same process be annulled. He sees the convergence of the circumstances drawing to the event; whether consciously or not he deliberates upon the validity of the policy unfolded; he often goes to meet disaster, perceiving its undisguised approach from afar off. And yet he goes unfalteringly.

"When our government armed these savage fiends against the French,— civilized men and 'palefaces' like ourselves," said Captain Demeré, "and the American colonists fought with them as allies, side by side, despite their hideous barbarities, we fell upon our own sword."

"Honors are easy," returned Captain Stuart, lightly. "Have the French armed no Indian allies? Did they not do it first?"

"We are not wont to look so far afield for our warrant," Demeré retorted testily. Then resuming: "These barbarous beasts are no fit allies for English arms. They degrade our spirit, and destroy our discipline, and disgrace our victories. I would rather suffer any honorable defeat than win through their savageries."

He was unconsciously the advance guard of that sentiment which caused the Earl of Chatham, nearly twenty years afterward, to declare in the House of Lords that it was a reflection on the honor of the nation that the scalping-knife and the tomahawk should be the aids of the British firelock and sword, and wreak their savage deeds under the sanction of the same brave banner; but even then Lord Gower was able to retort that, when still Mr. Pitt the "great Commoner," and the ruling spirit of the ministry, he, himself, had without scruple employed American savages in warfare. As yet, however, this objection was but a sensitive protest in the heart and mind of an obscure officer, the commandant of a merely temporary post on the furthest western frontier.[9]

The papers had been pushed near Demeré's elbow, and he began to look over them disaffectedly.

"Hear Governor Lyttleton," he said, and read in a tone that was itself a commentary: "'Use all means you think proper to induce our Indians to take up the hatchet. Promise a reward to every man who shall bring in the scalp of a Frenchman or a French Indian.'"

"As if one could be sure of a dead man's nationality or allegiance by seeing the hair on his scalp," said Whitson, as ever readily disgusted.

Stuart sought to take an unprejudiced view. "I never looked upon war as a pastime or an elegant accomplishment," he declared, watching the wreaths rise from the deep bowl of his long pipe. "War is war, and when we call it civilized we only mean that invention has multiplied and elaborated our methods of taking life. A commander can but use the surest means to his end against his enemy that the circumstances afford. A soldier is at best but the instrument of the times."

"And what of the torture, the knife, the fagot?" demanded Demeré, excitedly. "What do you think of them?"

"I never, dear Captain Demeré, think of them, in a garrison of two hundred men in a little mud fort on the frontier, with the Cherokees three thousand strong just outside, toward whom I have been admonished to mind my pretty manners. But since you are so keen to reason it out, I will remind you that until comparatively recently the torture was one of our own methods of punishment, or coercion, tending to the disclosure of secret conspiracies or any other little matter that the government might want to know and could not otherwise find out, and was practiced, thumb-screws, iron-boot, and all, in the worshipful presence of men of high estate— councils, commissions, and what not! Men and women—women, too!— have been burned alive in England under due authority because their style of piety was not acceptable. They were Christians, to be sure, but not exactly the highest fashion of Christian. You will say all this was long ago. Granted! but if such practices still obtain in such an oligarchy as Oconostota's realm,—the frontier being, paradoxically, a little in the rear of the times,—should we be surprised? No! I don't think of such things. I keep my mind on the discipline of the garrison, and control my temper very nicely when in the presence of the Cherokee kings, and bless God and the Earl of Loudon for the cannon at the embrasures and the powder and ball in the magazine."

He leaned forward suddenly to examine with momentary interest the sole of his boot as he sat with his leg crossed, then with a bantering "Eh, Captain Quawl?" he glanced up with a smile of camaraderie at Captain Demeré as if to test the effect of his argument, and finally laughed outright at his friend's silent gravity.

Such arguments were the ordinary incidents in the great hall of the block-house of the northwest bastion. The time hung heavily on the hands of the officers of the garrison. For beyond the military routine, a little hunting and fishing, a little card and domino playing, a little bout now and again of fencing, there was naught to relieve the monotony, for books were few and the express with mail from over the mountains infrequent, and therefore discussions in familiar conclave on abstract subjects, protracted sometimes for hours, filled the breach. Often these questions developed on paper, for a continual correspondence, as regular as might be compassed, was maintained with the officers of Fort Prince George, another frontier post, estimated as three hundred miles distant from Charlestown, yet still two hundred miles from Fort Loudon. As a matter of public policy it was deemed expedient that the commandants of the two posts should keep each other informed as to the state of the country about their respective strongholds, of the condition of the settlers, the temper of the Indians, the masked movements of French emissaries. In dearth of official intelligence, as the express necessarily went back and forth with mail and dispatches from Charlestown, the correspondence sympathetically expanded into personal interests, for the conditions surrounding both posts were in many respects similar. Fort Prince George also was a work designed with special reference to the military needs of that region and the character of its possible assailants. The defenses consisted of a rampart of clay, eight feet high, surmounted by a strong stockade, forming a square with a bastion at each angle; four small cannon were mounted on each bastion, and a deep ditch surrounded the whole; there was a natural glacis where the ground fell away on two sides of the quadrangle and on the others a strong abatis had been constructed at a short distance from the crest of the counterscarp. Within the fort were two block-houses and barracks for a garrison of one hundred men.

The sequestered, remote situation of each post developed a certain mutual interest and the exchange of much soldierly chaff; the names and disposition of even the subalterns were elicited in this transmitted gossip of the forts; in default of news, details of trivial happenings were given, unconsciously fertile in character-drawing; jokes, caricatures, good stories,—and thus at arm's length sprung up a friendship between men who had never seen one another and who were possibly destined never to meet. Of course all this gayety of heart vanished from the paper when serious tidings or despondent prospects were at hand, but even in the succinct official statements an undertone of sympathy was perceptible, and the slightest nerve of thought, of danger, of joy, of dissatisfaction touched at Fort Loudon thrilled in kind at Fort Prince George.

The attention of the group about the fire of the officers' mess-hall had seldom been brought to themes so grave as the news of the recent massacre, holding so definite and possible a personal concern, and after the evening of the Christmas ball life at Fort Loudon began to seem more serious and the current event to be scanned and questioned as to a probable bearing on the future.

Even Odalie's optimistic mind, forever alert to hope and fair presage, felt the influence of the atmospheric change of the moral conditions. But the fact was revealed to her in an incident sufficiently startling.

That morning after the festivity, when gayly rowing down the bleak river to MacLeod's Station, as the bend had begun to be called, she looked blithely enough over the stream's gray stretches of ruffled steel to the snowy slopes of the banks, and to the brown woods, and beyond to the dark bronze and dusky blue mountains as they stretched away in varying distance. The dull suffusive flare of carmine beginning to show above them seemed a spell to drive the day-star out of the sky, to bid the weird mists hie home with the fancies of the night, to set a wind keenly astir in a new dawn. All this she watched with eyes as clear, as soft, as confiding as if it were a May morning coming over the mountains, scattering the largesse of the spring—new life, new hopes, new strength, and all the glad inspiration of success that has a rarer, finer flavor than the actual consummation of the triumph.

The stationers landed at the bend, and she was glad of her home as she took her way within the enclosure of the high stockade. She looked around at it, still leading the sleepy Fifine by one hand and only half hearing Hamish's enthusiastic sketches of the boys and girls in the settlement, with whom he had made fast friends. The snow was heavy on the roofs of the two log cabins and the shanty of poles that served as a barn, and lay in fluffy masses between the sharp points of the palisades and on the bare boughs of sundry great trees that Odalie had insisted should not be cut away with the rest in the enclosure or "girdled" like those outside in the field. The smoke still curled up lazily from the chimneys, and after she had uncovered the embers and donned her rough homespun dress and housewifely apron and cap, and had the preparations for breakfast well under way, she went to the door and called aloud in the crisp, chill air to "Dill," as Gilfillan was christened by Fifine,—the name being adopted by all the family,—insisting that he should not cook his own breakfast but join them.

"There are going to be 'flim-flams,'" she shouted triumphantly. Then with a toss of the head—"Short eating!"

It had chanced that one day when the lonely pioneer had dined with his fellow-stationers he had remarked approvingly of certain dishes of French cookery acquired from her Grand'maman's receipts—"I dunno what ye might call them flim-flams, Mrs. MacLeod, but they make powerful short eatin'."

He and she and Fifine had become fast friends, and it was indeed a happy chance that had thrown the lonely man into this cordial and welcoming atmosphere of home. Even his terribly ghastly head Odalie had begun to forget, so deeply did she pity him for other things,—for the loss of wife and children and friends in the terrible Yadkin massacre; for the near approach of age,—and stalwart as he was, it was surely coming on; for the distortions of his queer religion, which was so uncouth as to be rendered hardly the comfort it might have been otherwise.

"I can't see how you can mention it," she said one day, with wincing eyes, when he was telling Hamish, who manifested that blood-thirsty imagination peculiar to boys, how he was conscious throughout the whole ordeal of scalping; how the tomahawk hit him a clip; how the Indian, one whom he had trusted, put his foot on his breast for a better purchase on the knife.

"Why, Mrs. MacLeod," Dill replied, "it makes me thankful to think he took nothing but the scalp. If he had mended his holt a little he could have took my whole head, and where would I have been now!"

"By the grace of God you would be a saint in Paradise," said Odalie, presenting the orthodox view.

"Yes," he admitted, "I've always feared there might be more in that notion of the Injuns about the scalpless being shut out of heaven than we know about—revelation, mebbe."

"No, no!" and horrified at this interpretation she made her meaning clear.

After that she undertook the rôle of missionary in some sort, and in quiet unobtrusive ways suggested bits of orthodox doctrine of much solace to his ruminating spirit, and sometimes on dreary, icebound days he and she and Fifine sat on the crudely fashioned benches before the fire and sang psalms and hymns together till the station rang with the solemn choiring.

"Dill" came in now, bringing his own knife for breakfast, and a very cheery face under his coonskin cap and red handkerchief, and when the "short eating" was disposed of all three men took their axes to chop up a tree for fuel, close outside the stockade, for the great chimney-places had capacious maws, and the weather was fast hardening to a freeze.

Presently Odalie heard the quick strokes of their axes, alternating with sharp clangs, the blows ringing out briskly on the icy air. The house was very still. Fifine had fallen asleep on the rug before the fire, having peevishly declined the folly of being disrobed and put to bed in the daytime, to recuperate from the exhaustion attendant upon her first ball. As she could not stay awake without whimpering, Odalie saw with satisfaction her little distorted countenance, round head, and chubby body collapse on the opposite side of the fireplace. Odalie herself sat down to rest for one moment on the befrilled block of wood which she complimented by calling a tabouret. Once she roused herself, smoothed out the expanse of her white apron over her blue homespun dress, then careful to permit the attitude to foster no crumple in her stiff, sheer, white mob-cap on the lustrous folds of dark hair, she leaned her head against the rude chimney.

How long she sat there she did not know. While sleeping she saw the faces of Indians, and when she gradually woke she thought she still slept. For there beside the fire were the Indian faces of her dream! She was stifled and dumbly sought to cry out, for this was surely some terror of the nightmare. But no! without was the light of the wan wintry day, showing in a vague blear at the half-open door, and within, the dull glow of the fire, sunken now to a vermilion mass of embers. On the opposite side of the hearth lay Fifine on the rug, sleeping still, with the sleeping cat in her arms—and between were Indian faces, the Indian faces of her dream!

Odalie breathed more freely, for they were women's faces—two women, muffled to the ears in red blankets, were calmly seated on the rug before the fire as if they had long been there gazing at her with blank, expressionless faces. She still heard the regular strokes of the axes of the men of the station, as just outside the stockade they resolutely pursued the chopping of the tree. She could not understand how the two women, unobserved by them, had slipped in at the open gate; Odalie was able to smile faintly at a prevision of Sandy's amazement at his own negligence.

One of the Indian women smiled in return, a bright-eyed demonstration, and suddenly Odalie remembered the young Cherokee beauty she had noted at the sally-port, watching the parade, the day after her arrival at Fort Loudon. The other, encouraged, began to speak, and to speak in French—a curious, dislocated patter. Asking how she had acquired the language, Odalie was informed that this was the squaw of Savanukah, and that he had journeyed as guide and hunted much with a French trader who had formerly dwelt at Choté, and hearing them talk the squaw, too, had learned.

"And how did you know that I speak French?" asked Odalie.

The elder woman pointed at the girl, who laughed and tucked down her head like a child. She was obviously solicitous that Odalie should observe the many strings of red beads about her neck; these she now and again caught in her fingers and drew forward, and then looked down at them with her head askew like a bird's. Odalie, with ready tact, let her eyes rest attentively on them, and smiled again. Her instinct of hospitality was so strong that it was no effort to simulate the gracious hostess. It was one of Hamish's stock complaints, often preferred in their former home when visitors were an intrusion and their long lingering a bore, that if the Enemy of Mankind himself should call, Odalie would be able to muster a smile, and request him to be seated, and offer him a fan of her best turkey feathers, and civilly hope that the climate of his residence was not oppressive to him!

"And how do you know that I am French?" she asked, with a delightful expression of her fascinating eyes.

The soldier had told her,—the handsome young brave who talked to her one day at Choté,—the girl said in fairly good English. Odalie asked her name, and, as it was given, exclaimed that it was a whole sentence. Both the Cherokee women laughed at this in the pleasure of camaraderie, and the elder translated the name as the "Wing of the flying Whip-poor-will." The young Indian girl came to be known afterward at MacLeod's Station as Choo-qualee-qualoo, the Cherokee word which imitates the note of the bird. Recurring to the subject, she attempted to describe the soldier, by way of identification, as having hair the color of the lace on the Captain's red coat. Odalie was able to recollect a certain smart young soldier, who as orderly had one day accompanied Captain Stuart on a visit of ceremony to Oconostota, at his seat of government at Choté—old town. While the young orderly had led the horse of the English Captain up and down before the door of the chief's great council-house, Choo-qualee-qualoo had been set to ask him some questions, and as she told this the little minx laughed with her sharp white teeth shining, and looked like some sly little animal, malevolent, yet merry, and of much grace. Willinawaugh, she continued, believed that he had been duped by MacLeod into affording him and his family safe conduct on his journey hither, under the pretext that he was French, and therefore an enemy to the English, whom Willinawaugh hated; for the newcomer, MacLeod, and his brother, had been suffered to build a house and settle here among the English, while if Frenchmen they would have been hung as spies at the great gate of the fort or sent direct to Charlestown as prisoners. So Willinawaugh had set her to weave her toils about the young soldier and discover the truth from him, as he walked the officer's fine horse up and down, and the tall English Captain and the great warrior, Oconostota, smoked their pipes in the council chamber. Thus it had chanced that the unsuspicious orderly, free with his tongue, as a young man is apt to be in the presence of a pretty girl, told all that Choo-qualee-qualoo asked to know, as far as he knew it himself, and sooth to say, a trifle further. He gave forth the fact that MacLeod was English—that is Scotch, which he made as one of the same tribe, and so was the brother. But the wife was French—he himself had overheard her talking the frog-eaters' lingo—and, by George, she was a stunner! The baby was hers, and thus a mixture of English and French; as for the cat, he could not undertake to pronounce upon the animal's nationality, for he had not the pleasure of the acquaintance of its parents.

Choo-qualee-qualoo laid down this last proposition with a doubting gravity, for the young man had promulgated it as if with a sense of its importance and a weighty soberness, although he laughed at most that he said himself and at everything that any one else said.

He saw fit to remark that he did not understand how that sober-minded Sawney—meaning the Scotchman—had ever contrived to capture such a fine woman, but that was always the way with these dull prigs. Now as for such rattling blades as himself and his Captain—who would have been disposed to lay the flat of his sword smartly across the shoulders of the orderly, could he have dreamed of mention in such irreverent fellowship— they had no chance with the women, and for his own part this made him very sad. And he contrived to look so for about a minute, as he led the Captain's horse up and down before the door of the council-house, while Choo-qualee-qualoo, at one end of his beat, stood among a clump of laurel and talked to him as he came and went, and Willinawaugh, in the shadowy recesses of a neighboring hut, watched through the open door how his scheme took effect.

It made him very sad, the soldier said, mournfully, for the girls to like other fellows better than him—as they generally did!

And Choo-qualee-qualoo broke off to say here that she did not discern why such preference should be, for this soldier's hair was the color of the Captain's gold lace on his red coat (the orderly was called "Carrots" by his comrades), and he had a face with—and at a loss she dabbled the tips of her fingers delicately about the bridge of her nose and her eyes to intimate the freckles on his fair skin, which beauty-spots she evidently admired.

The Scotchman's French wife was a stunner, the orderly was good enough to declare again, and everybody else thought so too. But he had overheard Captain Demeré say to Captain Stuart that her husband had no right to bring her to this western wilderness, and that that terrible journey of so many hundred miles, keeping up on foot with men, was enough to have killed her; and Captain Stuart had replied that she would make a fine pace-setter for infantry in heavy marching order. The orderly protested that for his part, if he were a condemned fine woman like that, he wouldn't live in a wilderness—he would run away from the Scotchman and go back to wherever she came from. Handsomest eyes he ever saw—except two eyes!

Here Choo-qualee-qualoo gave Odalie a broadside glance which left no doubt as to whose eyes this exception was supposed to refer, and put two or three strands of the red beads into her mouth, showing her narrow sharp teeth as she laughed with pleasure and pride.

Thus it was that Odalie was apprised of the fact that she was regarded by the Indians as a French prisoner in the hands of the English, and that the young soldier's use of the idea of capture by her husband, figuratively, as in the toils of matrimony, was literally construed. Her first impulse was to repudiate this suggestion of captivity, of detention against her will. Then her strong instinct of wisdom,—for she had no foresight in the matter,— that made Hamish sometimes charge her with being as politic as Captain Stuart himself, moved her to reserve this detail for the consideration of the commandant of the fort, as every matter, however trivial, that bore upon the growing enmity of the Cherokees toward the English amongst them, and their disposition to fraternize with the French, was important.

The two captains listened with serious attention when she detailed this conversation to them, having repaired to the fort for the purpose, and being received as a guest of much distinction in the great hall, summarily cleared of the junior officers, and, not so summarily, of the clouds of tobacco smoke. They both instantly commended her course in leaving the impression on the minds of the Indian women as it had chanced to be made, and in dismissing them in unimpaired good humor with some little presents—a tiny mirror set locket-wise and an ivory bobbin wound around with red thread. The women had evidently derived special pleasure from the slyness and presumable secrecy of their interview, skulking out with a craft of concealment that completely eluded the notice of Sandy and "Dill," and this had given Odalie a sense of disapprobation and repulsion.

"Why should you care?" demanded Demeré, always sympathetic with a woman's whim-whams, even when he could not feel with them. "No amount of explanation could enable the Indian women to comprehend the situation from your standpoint."

And Captain Stuart could not restrain his laughter at her discomfiture.

"Do you consider yourself so free, then? Do you call it freedom—in the holy bonds of matrimony? I had no idea how much you object to hear the clanking of your chains!"

As he noted her long-lashed glance of disdain,—"Doesn't the holy Scripture call it a 'yoke,'" he persisted, bursting out laughing afresh.

She would not reply but sat listening to Captain Demeré, who began to reason,—"This impression on the part of the Cherokee women might afford us—I don't know how—some means of learning and frustrating the treacherous plans of the savages. It gives us a source of information through you that we can trust."

"I don't relish the deceitful part assigned to me," she protested.

"What would we do with any information, Mrs. MacLeod, supposing we gain aught of value," returned Demeré with some haughtiness, "except to use it for the defense of the fort, and your own outlying station? Are we here to wage war or to maintain peace?"

She was silent, a trifle mortified because of her own mortification to be supposed a mere captive.

"Everybody else knows that you are the commanding officer at MacLeod's Station," said Stuart in pretended consolation, only half smothering a laugh.

"Besides," Demeré argued, gravely, "you will never be able to convince them of the facts. Of course you know I intend no disparagement to you when I say they will believe that young soldier's rodomontade in preference to your word—being women of such extreme ignorance."

"Why, the man ought to be gagged!" exclaimed Stuart, in delight at her seriousness.

The color mounted to Odalie's cheek. She had but entered her twenties, and despite her matronly arrogations she felt very young, now and then. Notwithstanding her humble pioneer status, she retained much of the aristocratic traditions inherited from her "Grand'maman"; she was beginning to feel it a great liberty that the young orderly should have expressed his admiration of her, although of course he was not aware that it would be repeated. She objected that he should know that she knew of it.

"I hope you will not acquaint him with the circumstances," she said, stiffly.

"By no means," said Demeré, appreciating her scruples. "That sort of thing is beyond discipline. The men in a garrison will tell everything they know or think they know."

Odalie sat for a moment longer. "I think," she said, recovering her equanimity after a fashion, "that since I immediately placed the information of this ludicrous contretemps at your disposal, for whatever you may make it worth, I should be promised exemption from the kind of raillery—and jokes—which Captain Stuart—frequent mention of chains, and bond-slave, and matrimonial noose and—such things," she paused, rising and looking at Stuart, wistfully remonstrant, for she could but notice how her chagrin ministered to his mischievous delight.

"How can you, Mrs. MacLeod!" he cried. "Captain 'Quawl' will have me clapped into irons at the first offence! And this is the vaunted tender-heartedness of women!"

Even Captain Demeré joined in the laugh at her, only becoming grave to insist that she should not, without notice to him, divulge the fact that she

- 93 -

was not French, but of Carolinian birth and parentage, and the further fact—and his serious face relaxed—that she, herself, was the commandant at MacLeod's Station, and that Sandy and Hamish, Fifine and "Dill," were the mere minions of her power.

She found discretion the better part of valor, and thought it wise to laugh a little at herself and her own pride, although the dimples came and went in very red cheeks, and her eyes were so bright as they rested on the merry face of the big blond officer that they might be said to flash. She diverted with difficulty Hamish's attention from Captain Demeré's half-finished map on the table at the other end of the room, over which the boy had been poring during the entire interview, and then they took their leave.

Little did any of the party realize how important the mistaken impression of the Cherokee women was to prove!

CHAPTER VII

The winter wore gradually away. While the snows were still on the ground, and the eastern mountain domes were glittering white against a pale blue sky, all adown the nearer slopes the dense forests showed a clear garnet hue, that betokened the swelling of congregated masses of myriads of budding boughs. Even the aspect of more distant ranges bespoke a change, in the dull soft blue which replaced the hard lapis-lazuli tint that the chill, sharp weather had known. For the cold had now a reviviscent tang—not the bleak, benumbing, icy deadness of the winter's thrall. And while the flames still flared on the hearth, and the thumping of the batten and the creak of the treadle resounded most of the day from the little shed-room where Odalie worked at her loom, and the musical whir of her spinning-wheel enlivened all the fire-lit evenings as she sat in the chimney corner, the thaws came on, and brought the mountain snows down the Tennessee River with a great rushing turbulence, and it lifted a wild, imperious, chanting voice into the primeval stillness. A delicate vernal haze began to pervade the air, and a sweet placidity, as if all nature were in a dream, not dead,—an expectant moment, the crisis of development. Now and again Odalie and Fifine would come to the door, summoned by a loud crackling sound, as of a terrible potency, and watch wincingly the pervasive flare of the great elastic yellow and vermilion flames springing into the air from the bonfires of the piles of cane as the cleared land was transformed from the cane-brake into fields. And soon the ploughs were running. Oh, it was spring in this loveliest of regions, in this climate of garnered delights! As the silvery sycamore trees, leaning over the glittering reaches of the slate-blue river, put forth the first green leaves, of the daintiest vernal hue, Odalie loved to gaze through them from the door of the cabin, perchance to note an eagle wing its splendid flight above the long, rippling white flashes of the current; or a canoe, as swift, as light, cleave the denser medium of the water; or in the stillness of the noon a deer lead down a fawn to drink. She was wont to hear the mocking-bird pour forth his thrilling ecstasy of song, the wild bee drone, and in the distance the muffled booming thunder of the herds of buffalo. Who so quick to see the moon, this vernal moon,—surely not some old dead world of lost history, and burnt-out hopes, and destroyed utilities, but fair of face, virginal and fresh as the spring itself,— come down the river in the sweet dusk, slowly, softly, pace by pace, ethereally refulgent, throwing sparse shadows of the newly leaved sycamore boughs far up the slope, across the threshold that she loved, with the delicate traceries of this similitude of the roof-tree.

"Oh, this is home! home!" she often exclaimed, clasping her hands, and looking out in a sort of solemn delight.

"Why don't you say that in French, Odalie?" Hamish would mischievously ask. For his researches into the mysteries of the French language, although not extensive, had sufficed to acquaint him with the fact that the tongue has no equivalent for this word, and to furnish him with this home-thrust, as it were. Odalie, always rising with spirit to the occasion, would immediately inquire if he had seen or heard of Savanukah lately, and affect to be reminded to urge him to put himself in preparation to be able to stand an examination in French by that linguistic authority by conjugating the reflective verb S'amuser. "So much you might, Hamish, amuse yourself with Savanukah."

"I am not disturbed, now," Hamish would declare, "since we have made interest with the family. I'd just get your friend, Mrs. Savanukah, to intercede for me."

For Odalie had to run the gauntlet of a good deal of merriment in the family circle because of her close acquaintance with the Indian women. Their visits annoyed her extremely. If she went for an afternoon's talk with Belinda Rush,—the two had become fast friends,—she deprecated leaving her scanty store of possessions lest their dainty order be disturbed by the Indian intruders in her absence. She dared not quit Fifine, whom it was sometimes inconvenient to take, even though the child's father was inside the stockade, lest she be kidnapped, so covert and sly was their slipping in and out, for somehow they were never discovered at the moment of entrance. Nevertheless, she treated her Cherokee callers with such sweet patient courtesy that it is not to be wondered that they came again and again. She gave them trifles that she could spare, and a share of the seeds of vegetables which she had brought with her, and this they received with real and unfeigned gratitude, for the women were the gardeners among the Cherokees and the tillers of the soil.

Odalie herself had that strong nerve of sympathy with the springing growths of the earth that made every turned furrow of the rich mould a delight to her. It was not work—it partook of the nature of a pastime, wrought for the love of it, when following her husband's plough she dropped the Indian corn and covered it with her hoe. She loved the soft, tender, sprouting blades, as they put strongly forth; she loved hardly less the quickly springing weeds even as she cut them mercilessly away with her hoe. She loved the hot sun, and the clear, fresh wind that came rushing down the rushing river, and the delicious delicate perfume of its waterside ferns, and the cool, sleeping shadows in the dark mysteries of the woods, and the solemnity of the great mountains on the eastern horizon, and the song of a thrush in mid-air above it all. And when the clouds gathered and came the soft, soft falling of the steady spring rain, she loved the interval it afforded for the setting of things in order within, and once more she and Hamish and Fifine and the cat were congregated on the buffalo rug in front of the fire, which had dwindled to an ember kept from meal to meal, to sort treasures brought with them in the small compass of a buffalo horn,— seeds now, the seeds of certain simple flowers, a bulb and a root or two,— the precious roots of an eglantine and a clematis vine. And now that the chance of killing frosts was overpast, Odalie and Fifine were grubbing much of the time in the ground and Hamish often came and grubbed too. The seeds were sown and grew apace; the bulbs and roots throve; the vines began to clamber over the support of a rude bower of saplings built above the door; and soon when Odalie sat here beside her spinning-wheel, in her white linen dress with its broad collar of her own hand-wrought lace, to enjoy the cool air from the mountains, and the color of the red sunset on the river, she had a canopy of vines above her head, and between her upward glance and the sky, a blooming rose, faintly pink, and a bird's nest with four blue eggs.

Captain Demeré, coming in at the gate of the stockade one afternoon, exclaimed in surprise and pleasure at the prettiness and the completeness of this rude comfort. There was but one room in the house with a floor; the seats were only puncheon benches with rough staves for legs thrust through auger-holes and one or two of her befrilled "tabourets"; the table was of like manufacture; the beds and pillows were mere sacks filled with dried balsam fringes from the great fir-trees, and supported on the rudest frames; but the fresh aromatic fragrance the fir dispensed, the snow-white linen the couches displayed, the flutter of the quaint bird-decorated curtains at the windows, the array of the few bits of treasured old china, the shelf of precious old books, the cluster of purple and white violets arranged in a great opaline pearly mussel-shell from the river, in default of vase, in the center of the wabbly table, the dainty freshness and neatness of the whole—"This is home!" he declared. "I accept a new anthropological dogma. Man is only the fort-builder—woman is the home-maker!"

"Yes," said Odalie in content and pride, surveying her treasures, as she conducted him about the place, for he had not been here since the completion of the improvements; "I often say that this is home!"

"But never in French," put in Hamish at her elbow.

Nevertheless, this did not contribute to alter Captain Demeré's opinion that the frontier was no place for women, though that would imply, with his later conclusions, no place for home. He went away wearing in his buttonhole a sprig of sweetbrier, which he declared again reminded him so of home. He had not thought to find it here, and memory fell upon him unprepared and at a disadvantage. The moon was up when he stepped into his boat, and the orderly, bending to the oars, shot straight out into the river. Long, burnished white lines lay upon its gleaming surface, and looking back Demeré could see beyond the shadow and sheen of the sloping bank the cleared space, where the moonbeams fell in unbroken splendor before the stockade, and through its open gate the log-cabin with its primitive porch, where, young and beautiful, she sat in her white dress in the bright light beside the silent little flax-wheel. Home undoubtedly! As the boat headed up the river he looked moodily at the ripples, glancing in the moonbeams, and noted with a keen new sensitiveness the fragrance of the eglantine, reminiscent of summers dead and gone, and life as fleeting and frail as the transitory flower.

For the news that came in these days from over the mountains was always heavy news,—rumors of massacres, now of a single individual in some exposed and dangerous situation, and again of settlers surprised and overcome by numbers within the defenses of their own stanch stockade.

All along the frontier the spirit seemed to extend, first toward the north and then southward, and it was apparently only a question of time when the quiet and peace that encircled Fort Loudon should be summarily broken. Many of the pioneers, could they now have returned to Virginia or the Carolinas without danger, would have forever relinquished their new homes, and have set forth on their long journey without delay. But the Cherokees about them, personally known to them and apparently without individual animosity, seemed a slighter menace than the probable encounter with wild wandering bands, glutted with blood yet thirsting still for vengeance. In one of Demeré's reports about this time, early in the year 1759, he says: "We are living in great harmony here—no 'bad talks' at all."

Again and again he and Captain Stuart, accompanied only by an orderly to mark their sense of confidence, went to Choté to confer in a friendly way with the king and half-king, and seek to induce them to take some order with these depredators, and restore the peace of the border.

The great council-house at Choté was a curious circular structure, formed of withes and willows and wand-like timbers, woven together in a dome-like shape to the height of twenty feet, with a diameter of thirty feet at the base; the whole was covered over with a thick coating within and without of the deeply and richly tinted red clay of that region, and pierced by no window or chimney or other outlet than the tall and narrow doorway. The last time the two officers together sought the presence of the kings in the Ottare district, as the mountainous region was called,—the towns designated as the Ayrate settlements signified the lower country,—they were received here, and Stuart, from the moment of their entrance, knew that their mission was hopeless.

They had recently been ordered to demand the surrender to them of certain notable Cherokees, for having been concerned in the distant border murders, and who lived in the towns of Citico and Tellico hard by, close at hand to both Choté and Fort Loudon. They realized that this measure was at once displeasing and impracticable to the kings, whose authority could not compass the surrender of their tribesmen to the justice of the gibbet, after the expiatory methods of the English, and who foresaw that such compliance would but provoke reprisal on the paleface and further outbreaks.

Sitting motionless on buffalo rugs, a number of which were spread over the floor of the room, on which the two officers were also invited to be seated, the Indians advanced none of the equivocal statements and doubtful promises and fallacious expectations of peace as heretofore, but kept their eyes fixed upon the ground, while the officers once more expressed their earnest remonstrances and made their summary demand, implicitly obeying their orders, although this extreme and impolitic measure was secretly deprecated by both.

The "talk" was conducted by means of the services of an interpreter, an Indian, who stood behind the great chiefs and recited, now in Cherokee and now in English, and always with a wooden, expressionless accent, as if he were a talking machine and understood not a word for which he furnished the equivalent, in deference to the great company not permitting his mind to take part in the deeper significance of the ideas they interchanged. He kept his eyes fixed upon the blank wall opposite, and effaced his individuality as far as possible. But after the first sentences of merely formal greeting, the wooden clapper of the interpreter's tongue vibrated back and forth with Cherokee only, for the Indian chiefs said nothing to be rendered into English. Silent and stony they sat, looking neither to the right nor left, unmoved by urgency, stolid to remonstrance, and only when Demeré with a flash of fire suggested that Governor Lyttleton of South Carolina, or General Amherst the new "head-man," who was now commander-in-chief of the army, would soon take fierce measures to retaliate these enormities, there was a momentary twinkle in the crafty eyes of Oconostota, and he spoke briefly. The interpreter woodenly repeated:—

"I can well believe you, for after an English treaty we have fraud and then force and at last bloodshed."

Stuart, the sombre red shadow of the terra-cotta walls hardly dulling the glare of his red uniform, sat looking out, quite placid and self-poised, through the open portal at the scattered huts of the town, at the occasional passing of an Indian's figure, at Chilhowee Mountain in the middle distance, densely green with the dark lush growths of summer, and beyond at the domes of the Great Smoky range, a soft velvet blue against the hard turquoise blue of the sky. The object, however, on which his eyes fixed most intently was the bright spot of color of the orderly's red coat, like a buoy, one might say, against the glimmering river, in the foreground, as he rested on his oars in the glow of the sunset, while the little boat swung idly in the shallows.

Not again did either of the chiefs speak. Demeré flushed with anger as sentence after sentence rang out in English, now from Stuart's lips, now from his own,—cogent, persuasive, flattering, fruitless; repeated by the interpreter in Cherokee, and followed by a blank pause. Finally Demeré rose, and with a curt phrase of formal farewell, to which neither of the chiefs responded, bowed angrily, and walked out, pausing near the entrance to wait for Stuart, who with blandest ceremony was taking his leave,— saying how much he hoped there would be no interruption to the kind friendship with which the great men had personally favored them, and which they so highly valued; and how earnestly he desired to express their thanks for the interview, although it grieved him to perceive that the chiefs felt they could say so little on the subject that had brought him hither. He could not have bowed with more respectful formality if he were quitting the presence of General Amherst himself, the cocked hat in his right hand sweeping low as he made his obeisance; but he could detect in both faces no change of expression, except that the eye of Oconostota twinkled with derision or anger or pleasure—who can say? He left them sitting motionless there in the deep red dusk reflected down from the terra-cotta walls, and the interpreter, looking as wooden as his voice sounded, standing bolt upright behind them.

Stuart did not comment on the character of the audience vouchsafed as, shoulder to shoulder, he and Demeré took their way down to the boat, where the young soldier awaited them. He only said, "I have been uneasy about that orderly all the time for fear our presence here did not protect him, as he was not on the ever-sacred soil of the 'beloved city of refuge'— Choté—old town. I wished we had taken the precaution of ordering him ashore. Affairs are near the crisis, Paul."

They seated themselves, and the young soldier pulled out from the shore, Demeré, both angry and cast down, realizing as he had not heretofore the imminence of the peril to the settlement.

Dusk was upon the river; stars began to palpitate elusively in the pallid sky; shadows mustered thick along the bank. Suddenly a sound, sharp, discordant, split the air, and a rifle-ball whizzed past between the two officers and struck the water on the further side of the boat. The unarmed orderly seemed for a moment as if he would plunge into the river.

"Steady—steady—give way," said Stuart. Then to Demeré, who had his hand on his pistol, and was casting a keen glance along the shore preparatory to taking aim,—"Why do you return the fire, Paul? To make our fate certain? We should be riddled in a moment. I have counted nearly fifty red rascals in those laurel bushes."

Why the menace was not repeated, whether the skulking braves feared the displeasure of their own authorities, or the coolness of the little group extorted their admiration, so quick to respond to an exhibition of stoical courage, no further demonstration was offered, and the boat was pulled down the five miles from Choté to Fort Loudon in better time perhaps than was ever made with the same weight on that river. The landing was reached, to the relief even of the phlegmatic-seeming Stuart.

"So ends so much," he said, as he stepped out of the boat. "And I go to Choté—old town—no more."

But he was destined one day to retrace his way, and, sooth to say, with a heavier heart.

The season waxed to ripeness. The opulent beauty of the early summer-tide was on this charmed land. Along the heavily-wooded mountain sides the prodigal profusion of the blooming rhododendron glowed with a splendor in these savage solitudes which might discredit the treasures of all the royal gardens of Europe. Vast lengths of cabling grape-vines hung now and again from the summit of one gigantic tree to the ground, and thence climbed upward a hundred feet to the topmost boughs of another, affording ambush for Indians, and these darkling coverts began to be craftily eyed by the soldiers, whose daily hunt for the provisions of the post carried them through many dense jungles. Everywhere the exquisite mountain azalea was abloom, its delicate, subtle fragrance pervading the air as the appreciation of some noble virtue penetrates and possesses the soul, so intimate, so indissoluble, so potent of cognition. It seemed the essential element of the atmosphere one breathed. And this atmosphere—how light—how pure! sheer existence was a cherished privilege. And always on this fine ethereal medium came the echo of woe; blended with the incense of the blooming wild grape seemed the smell of blood; the rare variety of flame-tinted azaleas flaring on some high, secluded slope showed a color reminiscent only of the burning roof-trees and stockades of destroyed homes. Peace upon the august mountains to the east, veiling their peaks and domes in stillness and with diaphanous cloud; peace upon the flashing rivers, infinitely clear and deep in their cliff-bound channels; and peace upon all the heavily-leaved shadowy forests to the massive westward range, level of summit, stern and military of aspect, like some gigantic rampart! But the mind was continually preëmpted by the knowledge that in the south were murder and despair, in the east were massacre and pillage, that rapine was loosed upon the land, and that this external fixity of calm was as unstable as the crystalline sphere of a bubble to collapse at a touch. Every ear was strained to a whisper; the express from over the mountain was met afar off by stragglers from the settlement, and came, delivering by word of mouth such news as he personally possessed, before his package was rendered up to the officers at the fort. Every heart seemed subject to the tension of suspense except such organ as might serve Captain Stuart for the cardiacal functions. He appeared wholly engrossed in perfecting the details of battalion drill, and the attention of the garrison was concentrated on these military maneuvers; even the men of the settlement, especially the rattling single men, were drawn into these ranks, the garrison not being strong enough to furnish the complement desired. In their buckskin hunting-shirts and leggings, with their muscular, keen activity, their ready practice, and their suppleness in handling their rifles, the pioneers made what he was pleased to call "a very pretty body of fencibles." His praise and their evident advance in proficiency gratified them, although the tactical arts of war in the heavy growths of this wild and rocky country were at a discount, since the defeat of that martinet and military precisian, General Braddock. Thus the afternoon drill at the fort became of increasing public interest, and afforded the social opportunity of a rendezvous for the whole settlement; and despite the growing disaffection of the Cherokees, now and again groups of Indian spectators appeared at the gate.

Stuart's tact never deserted him; one day when ordering a knot of pioneers near the sally-port to "fall in"—for he himself drilled the fencibles—he motioned too, with his imperious gesture, to half a dozen braves who were standing hard by, as if he made no difference between them and the other civilian neighbors. One moment of astounded doubt, then they "fell in" as front-rank men, evidently infinitely flattered and marvelously quick in adapting the manual exercise they had often witnessed. Now and again there was an expression of keen interest on their stolid faces, and more than once when woe befell the effort to ploy the battalion into double column to form square and the movement became a contortion, they laughed out gutturally—that rare Indian mirth not altogether pleasant to hear. And as they went home in the red sunset to Citico, and Great Tellico, and Tennessee Town and Choté, from along the river banks came their harsh cries—"Shoulder firelock!" or "Fa'lock," as they rehearsed it. "Feex Bay'net! Pleasant A'hms!"

- 102 -

It became evident that they rehearsed their learning, suiting the action to the word, once too often,—for they returned no more. Whatever might have been the advantage of their acquiring the secret of the military maneuvers from so competent and patient an instructor as the condescending Captain Stuart, the powers that were at Choté had no mind to expose their stalwart young braves to the winning wiles of that magnetic commander, and permitting them to acquire among the troops, perchance, a personal regard for the officer and an esprit de corps in addition to a more available military spirit. If he had had a scheme and the scheme had failed there was no intimation to that effect on the imperturbable exterior he maintained.

It had always been known that Captain Stuart was somewhat fond of the pleasures of the table, and he suddenly developed a certain domesticity in this regard. He desired to experiment on the preserving of some "neat's tongues,"—as he politely called those of the buffalo,—and for the sake of this delicacy utilized a floorless hut, otherwise unoccupied, at the further end of the whole enclosure, as a smokehouse. Often smoke was seen issuing thence, but with this understanding it created no surprise. Sometimes the quartermaster-sergeant and two or three other non-commissioned officers were seen pottering about it. Now and again Captain Demeré stood at the door and looked in. One day it chanced that Hamish, who had secured two tongues, desiring to offer them as a small tribute, came up close to him, in his deft, noiseless deerskin buskins, before Captain Demeré was aware. As he turned and saw the boy, he instantly let the door in his hand fly back—not, however, before the quick young fellow had had a dissolving view of the interior. A fire smoked in the center of the chimneyless place, half smothered with stones that constituted at once a hearth and protection from the blaze, but one flickering shred of flame revealed not only the tongues which Captain Stuart coveted, but rows of haunches and saddles of venison and bear hams, and great sections of buffalo meat, as well as pork and beef.

The boy understood in an instant, for the hunters from the fort provided day by day for the wants of the garrison from the infinite reserves of game in the vast wilderness without; these were preparations against a state of siege, kept secret that the garrison might not be dispirited by so gloomy a prospect, possibly groundless, and the settlement with its women and children affrighted. Hamish, with a caution beyond his years, affected to see naught, made his little offering, and took his way and his speculations homeward. There he was admonished to say nothing of the discovery; it was very proper, Sandy thought, for the garrison to be prepared even against remote contingencies.

Hamish dutifully acquiesced, although he could but feel very wise to know the secret workings of Captain Stuart's subtle mind and divine his hidden plans, when that officer seemed to grow gravely interested in the development and resources of the country, in which he had no share save the minimum of space that the ramparts enclosed. He speculated adroitly about mineral wealth in gossiping with the groups of settlers at the gates after the drill. He told some strange stories that Atta-Kulla-Kulla had recounted of the vestiges of previous vanished inhabitants of this country—of certain evidences of ancient mining ventures where still lay curious outlandish tools; he felt certain of the existence of copper and lead, and he believed most faithfully too in the proximity of gold; for his own part, he declared, he thought the geological formation indicated its presence. These themes, transferred to the great hall, served to fill it with eager discussions and clouds of tobacco smoke, and to detain the settlers as long as the regulations would admit of the presence of visitors. As to iron and other minerals, the springs indicated iron ore beyond a doubt, and he inquired earnestly had any one ever tried to obtain salt by the usual primitive process of boiling and evaporation at the big salt-lick down the river? Thus nobody was surprised when Captain Stuart and the quartermaster and a detail of soldiers and a lot of big cauldrons were reported to be actively engaged in the effort to manufacture salt down at the lick. No necessary connection was apprehended between the circumstances when four packhorses came over the mountain laden with salt, for even after that event Captain Stuart continued the boiling and stirring that went on down at the lick.

Hamish wondered how long he would care to keep up the blind, for the need of salt for the preservation of more meat had by this last importation been satisfied. Perhaps Stuart himself felt it a relief when one day it chanced that some buffalo bulls met at the salt-lick,—as if by appointment,—and the battle that ensued among them was loud and long and stormy. So numerous were the contestants, and so fiercely did the conflict wage, that the officer and his force were compelled to climb to a scaffold built in one of the gigantic trees, used by the settlers who were wont to wait here for the big game and fire down upon them without the danger of being trampled to death.

This battle had other observers: a great panther in the same tree crouched on a limb not far above the soldiers, and sly and cowardly as the creature is, gazed at them with a snarling fierce distention of jaws, plainly unaware of any weapons that could obviate the distance, and counting on a lingering remnant of the party as evidently as on the slain bison to be left on the ground when the battle should be over. Now and again came a glimpse of the stealthy approach of wolves, which the tumult of the conflict had lured to the great carcass of the defeated. Although the salt-makers waited in much impatience through several hours for the dispersal of the combatants, and were constrained to fire their pistols almost in the faces of the wolves and panthers, Captain Stuart's chief emotions seemed expressed in admiring the prowess of a champion in the fight, whom he identified as the "big yanasa[1] that was the pivot man of the wheeling flank," and, on his return, in guying the quartermaster on the loss of the great cauldrons, for their trampled remains were unrecognizable; but indeed, this worthy's countenance was lugubrious enough to grace the appellation of chief mourner, when he was apprised of the sad ending of the salt-making episode, for he loved a big kettle, as only a quartermaster or a cook can, in a country in which utensils are small and few and not to be replaced.

That Stuart felt more than he seemed to feel was suspected by Demeré, who was cognizant of how the tension gave way with a snap one day in the autumn of that year of wearing suspense. Demeré looked up with a changed face from the dispatches just received—the first express that had come across the mountains for a month, having dodged and eluded bands of wandering Indian marauders all the way.

"Governor Lyttleton has taken the field," he said.

"At last!" cried Stuart, as in the extremity of impatience.

For upon the massacre of all the inmates of a strong station, carried by storm, in addition to other isolated murders up and down the frontier, the royal governor of South Carolina had initiated a series of aggressive measures; asked aid of North Carolina, urged Virginia to send reënforcements and provisions to Fort Loudon (it being a place which from its remote situation was very difficult at all times to victual, but in the event of a Cherokee war entirely cut off from means of supply), and by great exertions succeeded in mustering a force of eight hundred militia and three hundred regulars to advance into the Indian country from the south. The vigor and proportions of this demonstration alarmed the Cherokees, grown accustomed to mere remonstrance and bootless threats. They had realized, with their predominant military craft, the most strongly developed of their mental traits, that the occupation of all the available forces of the government in Canada and on the northwestern frontiers crippled the capacity to make these threats good. Thus they had reveled in a luxury of fancied impunity and a turbulent sense of power. Now they were smitten with consternation to perceive the cloud upon the horizon. Suddenly the privileges of trade which they had forfeited,—for they had become dependent on the supplies of civilization, such as ammunition, guns, tools, blankets, etc., and certain stores in transit to them had been, by Governor Lyttleton's instructions, intercepted by Captain Coytmore, the commandant at Fort Prince George;—the opportunities of a strong alliance that they had discarded; the advantageous stipulations of the treaties they had annulled; all seemed precious when annihilated by their own act.

The Upper towns and the Lower towns—the Ottare and the Ayrate—met in solemn conclave at Choté to consider the situation.

Fort Loudon, hard by, maintained quiet and keen watch and strict discipline. The drums beat, the bugles sounded for the measured routine. The flag waved in the sunshine, slipping up to meet the dawn, fluttering down as the last segment of the vermilion disk slipped behind the dark, level, rampart-like summit of the distant Cumberland range, and the sunset-gun boomed till the echoes blared faintly even about the council-chamber at Choté, where the warriors were gathered in state. Whether the distant thunderous tone of that potent force which the Indians admired, and feared, and sought to comprehend beyond all other arms of the service, the artillery, suggested anew the untried menace of Lyttleton's invasion of their country with a massed and adequate strength; whether they had become desirous now to regain those values of trade and alliance that they had thrown away in haste; whether their repeated reprisals had satiated their greed of vengeance for their comrades, slain on the return march from aiding the defense of the Virginia frontier; whether they were inspired only by their veiled deceit and savage craft, in which they excelled and delighted, and which we now call diplomacy, exercised between the enlightened statesmen of conferring and Christian nations,—whatever motive urged their decision, no gun barrel was sawed off, an unfailing preparation for battle, no corn pounded, no knife whetted, no face painted, no bow strung, no mysterious scalp-dance celebrated—the Cherokees were not upon the war-path!

A deputation of their "beloved men" went to forestall the martial advance of the Carolinians—Oconostota, the "great warrior," with his many wrinkles, and his crafty eye, and his port of meaning that heralded events; and Atta-Kulla-Kulla, of whom all had heard, whose courage was first of the brain and then of the hand, whose savage instincts were disciplined by a sort of right judgment, an intelligence all independent of education, or even of that superficial culture which comes of the observation of those of a higher and trained intellect; and also Willinawaugh, fierce, intractable, willing to treat for peace, to be sure, but with a mental reservation as to how far it might serve his purposes. Savanukah was of the delegation, doubtful, denying, with a dozen devices of duplicity; he could not at times understand the English he spoke fairly well, and the French, in which he could chaffer smartly and drive a bargain, nor even the Cherokee, for which he kept a deaf ear to hinder a settlement he deprecated with the hated English—invaluable at a council was Savanukah! Of the number, too, was

Tennessee Warrior, who fought, and did nothing but fight, and was ready and willing to fight again, and yet again, and to-morrow! He was always silent during the conferences, studying with successive scowls the faces of the white men. He knew nothing about numbers, and did not yearn to handle the match, and make the big gun howl; he had but to paint his face, and whet his scalp-knife, and load his firelock, and blaze away with as deadly an aim as a pioneer's. What need had the Tennessee Warrior for diplomacy? If there was to be any fighting the Tennessee Warrior would rejoice in going along to partake. If there was to be only diplomacy, and diplomacy were long continued with peace unbroken, then the white men and the red men might be sure of one thing—of hearing the Tennessee Warrior snore! He was an excellent selection to go to a council. Then there was Bloody Fellow, Eskaqua, who had scant need of vermilion, so sure he was to paint himself red in another way. And Tus-ka-sah, the Terrapin of Chiletooch, and old Abram, Ooskuah, of Chilhowee, and Otassite, the Man-Killer of Hiwassee, and old Tassel, Rayetaeh of Toquoe,—about thirty-five in all,—went in a body to Charlestown to negotiate for peace, and some of them signed. These chiefs who signed were Oconostota, Atta-Kulla-Kulla, Otassite, Kitagusta, Oconnocca, and Killcannokea. The day on which they set forth Captain Stuart and Captain Demeré, themselves in council in the great hall at Fort Loudon, heard the news of the departure of the delegation on this errand, looked at each other in amazement, and fell into bursts of laughter. Had their sense of triumph been such as to find joy in reprisal they might have relished the fact that the anxieties, the secret fear, the turmoil of doubt, which Oconostota had occasioned to them, were returned to him in plenitude on his arrival in Charlestown. Governor Lyttleton had not yet set out, but the military forces summoned forth were already entered upon their long and toilsome march from various distant districts to the appointed rendezvous at Congaree, and thither the commander of the expedition felt that he must needs forthwith repair to meet them. "I did not invite you to come here," he said to Oconostota, and despite the remonstrance of the delegation, and doubtless thinking he could treat with the savages to more effect at the head of an armed force invading their country, he postponed hearing their "talk" till he should have joined his little army, but offered them safe-conduct in accompanying his march. "Not a hair of your head shall be touched," he declared. Returning thus, however, almost in the humiliated guise of prisoners, in fact under a strong guard, accompanying a military force that was invading Cherokee soil, comported little indeed with Oconostota's pride and his sense of the yet unbroken power of his nation. The coercions of this virtual captivity extended to the stipulations of the treaty presently formulated. While ratifying previous pledges on the part of the Indians to renounce the French interest, and providing for the renewal to them of the privileges of trade, this treaty required of them the surrender of the murderers concerned in the massacres along the frontier; pending the delivery of these miscreants to the commandant at Fort Prince George, and as a guarantee of the full and faithful performance of this compact, the terms dictated the detention at the fort, as hostages, of twenty-two of the Cherokee delegation now present.[10]Oconostota himself was numbered among the hostages to be detained at Fort Prince George until the surrender of the Cherokee murderers, but the representations of Atta-Kulla-Kulla, who was at liberty, compassed the king's release, urging his influence with his nation and the value of his counsels in the British interest for the restoration of peace. The little band of Cherokees, helpless among overwhelming numbers, was hardly in a position to openly withstand these severe measures proposed, and consequently the treaty thus signed on the 26th day of December, 1759, might have been expected to prove of but slight cohesive properties. The hostages remained of necessity at Fort Prince George; the few Indians of the unfortunate embassy who retained their freedom began to scatter, sullen, fierce, disconsolate, to their towns; the army, already discontented, mutinous, and eager to be gone because of the devastations of the smallpox in a neighboring Indian village, and the appearance of that disease among a few of the volunteers, set out upon its homeward march, without striking a blow, from an expedition that cost the province the sum of twenty-five thousand pounds sterling.Oconostota and Willinawaugh, sitting together on the ground, in the flickering sunlight and the sparse wintry shadows of the leafless woods, looking like two large rabbits of some strange and very savage variety, watched the rear-guard file over the hill in the narrow blazed way that seemed a very tolerable road in that day. When the last man had vanished, they listened for a long time to the throb of the drum—then the sound was lost in the distance; a mere pulsing in the air continued, discriminated by the keen discernment of the Indians. At last, when not even a faint ripple of sound-waves could be felt in the still atmosphere, Oconostota keeled over suddenly and laid his ear to the ground. No vague reverberation, no electrical thrill, no stir of atom of earth striking against atom; nothing! The army was gone! The two savage old rabbits squatted again upright and seemed to ruminate on the situation. Then, as if with a single impulse, they looked at each other and broke into sudden harsh gutturals of triumphant laughter.

FOOTNOTES:

[1] Buffalo.

CHAPTER VIII

Peace was welcome—so welcome. Hence the turning of the soil by the pioneers commenced betimes in the chill spring with heartfelt thankfulness to be anew between the stilts of a plow. The sap was rising; the winter had gone like a quiet sleep ensuing on the heavy tumults of troubled dreams.

One day a wren came and perched in a loop-hole of the block-house of the northwestern bastion and sang very loud and sweet and clear, till all the men sitting about the fire turned to look at it, amazed at its temerity, and enjoying in a lazy, sensuous way the jubilance and thrilling crystalline purity of its tone. Two of the youngsters, Lieutenant Gilmore and Ensign Whitson, ready to wager anything on anything, disputed as to the size of the creature,—if it had on no feathers,—one maintaining that it was two inches long, the other, an inch and a half. The bird brought a straw and arranged it carefully in place in the loop-hole, and then singing, flew away, and came back with a feather. His intention was evident.

"My young friend," said Stuart, carelessly eyeing him, "you are a fine figure of a settler, but that loop-hole is ours!"

"Let him have it," said Demeré. "We shall never need it."

The door opened suddenly, and the orderly, saluting, announced the express from over the mountains. At once there ensued a great stir of the tobacco smoke, and a laying aside of pipes in any coign of vantage to better handle the mail from home, as soon as the official dispatches should be read. And then, "Here's something from Fort Prince George," said Demeré, from where he sat at the rude table with the papers scattered before him. "A goodly packet," he continued, as he broke the seal, in the expectant, pleased silence of the others. "Ensign Milne is writing—both the official communication and a long personal letter," noting the signature.

At the first glance along the lines his face fell.

"Captain Coytmore is dead," he said in a low voice.

Murdered by the Indians he had been, in front of the fort, in the presence of the officers of his own command! As the news was unfolded, startled, amazed glances were exchanged; no word was spoken; the silence was only broken by the low, tense voice as Demeré read, and now and again the wren's clear, sweet, reedy note, full of joyance, of life, as the bird fluttered in and out and builded his nest in the loop-hole.

- 109 -

Without warning the blow had fallen. One morning it happened, the 16th of February, when naught of moment seemed to impend. On the bank of the Keowee River opposite to Fort Prince George, two Indian women appeared, and as they loitered, seeming to have something in hand, the sentinel called the attention of an officer of the fort,—Doharty it was,— who at once went out to speak to them, thinking they might have some news. He called out to them, having a trifle of Cherokee at command, but before they could answer they were joined by Oconostota, the king of the Indian tribe, arrayed in his buckskin shirt and leggings, and mounted upon a very excellent chestnut horse. He told Doharty that he desired to speak to the commandant of the fort. Doharty, thinking it a matter of importance, and possibly having reference to the surrender of some of the murderers of the settlers in exchange for the hostages, went in great haste and summoned Captain Coytmore, who instantly came, accompanied by Lieutenant Bell with Foster, the interpreter, following. The writer detailed that he himself was within, engaged in inspection duty as officer of the day, or his interest and curiosity would have carried him in their company. In expectation of developments they all went down to the water's edge, and Coytmore asked the chief if he would not ford the stream and come over. But Oconostota stated that he was in haste touching matters of great moment which he wished to impart to the royal governor of South Carolina. It was imperative that he should treat of the subject in person, and thus he would go to Charlestown to see Governor Lyttleton if Captain Coytmore would send a white man to accompany him as a safeguard in the white settlements. Captain Coytmore seemed to consider for a moment whom he could send; and then, evidently desirous of furthering any pacific negotiation, said that he could detail a man for that duty. Oconostota replied that that courtesy was all he would ask of the commandant—a white man as a safeguard. He himself would furnish a horse for the man to ride. He had come prepared for the purpose, and he lifted a bridle, which he had brought over one arm, to show it. He then remarked that he would get the horse, which he had left a little distance back, while Captain Coytmore gave the man his instructions. So saying, he lifted up the bridle in his hand, whirling it three times around his head, and wheeling his horse, galloped off, while from an ambush amongst the trees and underbrush a fire of twenty or thirty muskets was poured upon the little group at the river bank. Captain Coytmore was shot through the left breast and died that day. Bell and Foster were each wounded in the leg. Doharty and the sentinel had much ado to get them into the fort with Coytmore's help, for the commandant was able to run to shelter with the rest through the sally-port, and until Parker, who the writer said had had considerable experience as a chirurgeon, examined Coytmore's wound, neither he nor the others knew that it was mortal. Milne, being now the officer in command, thought it fit to order the hostages into irons, fearing some outbreak within the fort as well as an attack from without. One and twenty stalwart savages were dangerous inmates at large, with the freedom of the parade as they had had much of the time. They resisted; one of the soldiers was killed in the effort to shackle them, for arms appeared among them, evidently brought and secreted by their friends who had been permitted to visit them, much leniency having been accorded them, being hostages and not themselves criminals. Another soldier was wounded in the head with a tomahawk. Upon the death of their comrade, and the announcement that the commandant was dying, the garrison was seized with an uncontrollable frenzy, fell upon the hostages, and within five minutes had slaughtered the last man of them.

"I know you will feel for me," Milne wrote. "I dared scarce reprimand the men, for they were full of fury. I see here and there signs of sullenness. They watch me—their way of showing regret. I can scarcely blame—yet the Cherokees were hostages and I am sorry; I was much alone, with the temper of the soldiers to consider. Coytmore dead, and Bell gone into a delirium with the fever—his wound bled very little—the ball is near the bone. Doharty had been ill of a pleurisy and seems to relapse. On the night after, I sat for a time in the block-house where we had laid the commandant, feeling very low in my mind. There is one of the men a bit of a joiner, and a great billet of the red cedar, used in building the fort, being left over, he made a decent coffin, the wood working easily and with a fine grain and gloss. I could hear as I sat there the tapping of his mallet and chisel as he worked on the coffin, while Coytmore lay with the flag over him, his sword and hat by his side—there was no fire, because of him, and only a candle at his head, or I think the savages would have seen the light. But the work being finished and everything still, they supposed all asleep. I cannot think why they did not smell the blood—for the ground of the room where the hostages lay reeked of it. Twenty-one!—I could not think how I could bury them inside the fort and I dared not send out a detail, nor do I think the men would obey—the barracks seemed steeped in the smell, though none there. Of a sudden, the night being fine and chill as I sat there with Coytmore, a sentry outside the door, I heard a great voice like a wind rushing. I thought I had been sleeping. And again I heard it—words in Cherokee. O-se-skinnea co-tan-co-nee! I slipped outside the block-house where was the sentinel, much startled, and bade him fetch the interpreter, alive or dead. He came limping—not greatly hurt. The words he said meant, "Good tidings for the unhappy." Then as we stood there other words sounded signifying 'Fight manfully and you will be assisted!' They were spoken to the hostages and close to the rampart hard by their hut, unknowing their—I cannot think how they should not smell the blood! Then from a greater distance came the "Whoo-whoop!" and a thick hail of musketry. The men got under arms very quick and tractable, and I think wished to atone. The fire of the savages had no effect, the balls being buried in the earth of the escarp, or falling spent within the fort. But we were kept at it all night, the men tireless and dutiful. The savages now and then paused at first, expecting some token from the hostages. Then they fought with great persistence—realizing. With what loss we do not know, since they carried off their dead. Sure, how strange 'tis to be fighting all night, firing through the loop-holes of the block-house around Coytmore, with never a word from him, an order, or a sign. I miss him more since he is out of sight. I am afraid to speak of burying the savages inside the fort, along with the commandant and Private Mahone—and yet I must get rid of them. Twenty-one!—in so narrow an enclosure——

"Much gratified by a deputation of Indians, realizing at last, and asking for bodies. Would not open gates for fear of surprise. Had each hoisted up and slipped out of embrasure; could hardly force men to touch them. I said, 'You were too quick once!'—drew my pistol. The Indians seemed mighty glad to get them, yet women went off howling. Soldiers seemed relieved to find in the hut tomahawks buried in ground, and a phial of liquid, which they think was poison for well. I poured this out on the earth, and broke bottle. Men's spirits improve—quite cheerful. Hope you have better luck at Ft. Loudon. Pray some one of you write to me! Bell and the others too ill to send remembrances—doubtless would."

The circle listened in appalled silence, and when the reading was concluded, except here and there a murmur of commiseration, or a deep imprecation, hardly a stir was in the room until the joyous notes of the building wren arose, so clear that they had a suggestion of glitter, if the quality of light can ever be an attribute of sound. Then Captain Stuart asked for the letter and silently read it from end to end, while a fragmentary conversation concerning the personality of the slain hostages, all men of great note in their respective towns, began to be prosecuted by the others.

That evil days were upon the land hardly admitted of a doubt, and they fell to discussing the improbability of measures of relief and reprisal being undertaken so early after the bootless return of Governor Lyttleton's troops without striking a blow. The Cherokees, too, were surely cognizant of the fact that it was scarcely possible in view of the great expense of mustering and sending forth this force that such an expedition would again be soon set on foot. Acting upon this theory, and always instigated by the subtle French, their demonstration probably heralded a systematic and vigorous outbreak all along the frontier, to exterminate the settlers and free their land forever from the encroachments of the hated English. This view was confirmed by an attack which presently ensued on Fort Ninety-six, and being without effect, the repulsed Indian forces drew off and fell upon the more defenseless settlements, ravaging the frontier throughout the borders of the two Carolinas and Virginia and practicing all the horrible atrocities of savage warfare. The settlers about Fort Loudon quaked in their little log-cabins and looked upon their limited clearings in the wilderness and their meager beginnings of a home, and wondered if it were worth coming so far and risking so much to attain so little. As yet, save for glances of a flashing ire and sullen silence, the Indians had made no demonstration, but it was a period of poignant doubt, like waiting for the falling of a sword suspended by a hair.

One day Odalie was startled by seeing Fifine, seated on the threshold, persistently wreathing her countenance into a grimace, which, despite the infantile softness of her face and the harsh savagery of the one she imitated, was so singularly recognizable that the mother took her hands from the bread-trough where she was mixing the pounded corn meal and went near to hear what the child was saying:—

"Fonny! Fonny!" with the terrible look of malevolent ridicule with which Willinawaugh had rebuked Hamish's poor pleasantries on that heart-breaking journey hither.

Odalie's pulses seemed to cease to beat. The child could hardly have remembered an incident of so long ago without some recent reminder.

"Where, Josephine? Where did you see Willinawaugh?"

But Fifine had no mind to answer, apprehending the agitation in the sharp tones, and translating it as displeasure. She drew her countenance straight in short order, and put a meditative forefinger in her mouth as she looked up doubtfully at her mother.

Odalie changed her tone; she laughed out gayly.

"Fonny! Fonny!" and she too imitated the Indian. Then exclaimed—"Oh, isn't it droll, Fifine?"

And Fifine, deceived, banged her heels hilariously against the door-step, laughing widely and damply, and crying, "Fonny! Fonny!" in infantile derision.

"You didn't see 'Fonny' yesterday. No, Fifine! No!" Odalie had the air of detracting from some merit on Fifine's part, and as she played her little rôle she trembled so with a realization of terror that she could scarcely stand.

Yes, Fifine protested with pouts and anger. She had seen him; she had seen him, only yesterday.

"Where, Fifine, where?" cried Odalie bewildered, for the child sat upon the threshold all the day long, while the mother spun and wove and cooked within the sound of the babble of her voice, the gates of the stockade being closed in these troublous times, and always one or more of the men at work hard by in the fields without.

The mystery was too fraught with menace to be disregarded, but Odalie hesitated, doubting the policy of this direct question. Fifine's interest, however, was suddenly renewed and her importance expanded.

"Him wasn't all in," she explained. "Him top-feathers—him head—an' him ugly mouf!" She looked expectantly and half doubtfully at her mother, remembering her seeming anger.

"Oh, how droll! One might perish with laughter!" screamed Odalie, with a piercing affectation of merriment, and once more Fifine banged her heels hilariously against the door-step, as she sat on the threshold, and cried in derision, "Fonny! Fonny!"

"Where, Fifine? At the stockade? Some hole?"

Fifine became angry at this suggestion, for had not "Dill" built the stockade, and would he build a stockade so Indians might get through and cut off her curls—she bounced them about her head—that Dill said were "'andsomer than any queen's."

But Odalie knew she had seen "Fonny" at the stockade, and Fifine contradicted, and after a spirited passage of "Did!" "Didn't!" "Did!" "Didn't!" Fifine arose to go and prove her proposition.

There at the little spring, so sylvan sweet, so full, yet with the merest trickle of a branch that hardly wet the mint, so shyly hidden amongst its rocks, was a fissure. Odalie had often noted it; dark it was, for the shadows fell on it, and it might be deep; limited—it would but hold her piggin, should she thrust it there, or admit a man's head, yet not his shoulders—and this was what it had done yesterday, for protruding thence Fifine maintained she had seen Willinawaugh's face with "him top-feathers, him head, an' him ugly mouf!"

Odalie laid her ear to the ground to listen; smooth, quiet, full, she heard the flow of water, doubtless the branch from the little spring always brimming, yet seeming to send so tiny a rill over the slopes of the mint. There was evidently a cave beneath, and they had never dreamed of it! She began to search about for fissures, finding here and there in the deep herbage and the cleft rocks one that might admit the passage of a man's body. She remembered the first sudden strange appearance of the Cherokee women at her fireside, and afterward, and that Sandy and Hamish and Dill often declared that watch the gate as they might they never saw the squaws enter the stockade nor issue therefrom. Doubtless they had come through the cave, that had a hidden exit.

Her heart throbbed, her eyes filled; "I ought to be so thankful to discover it in time—to think how safe we felt here when the gates were locked! But, oh, my home! my sweet, sweet home!"

The way the men's faces fell when they were summoned, and stood and looked at the slope, might make one pity them. It represented the hard labor of nearly two years—and it was all to begin anew.

When Sandy, with the vigorous Scotch thrift, began to show how easily the stockade might be moved to exclude the spring, Gilfillan shook his head warningly. A station should never be without water. Sooner or later its days were numbered. As to the stockade, it was futile. Twenty—nay, fifty men might be surprised and massacred here. For the ordinary purposes of life the place was useless.

Hamish, after the first sharp pang, was resolved into curiosity; he must needs slip through the fissure and into the cave below. When Odalie ceased her tears to remonstrate, he declared that he could get out of any cave that Willinawaugh or Choo-qualee-qualoo could, and then demanded to be tied to her apron-string to be drawn up again in case he should prove unable to take care of himself. He went down with a whoop, somewhat like Willinawaugh's own war-cry, then called out that the coast was clear, and asked for his rifle to be handed to him.

Following the wall with his hand and the sound of the water he took his way through a narrow subterranean passage, so densely black that it seemed he had never before known what darkness was. He could hear naught but the wide, hollow echo of the flow of the stream, but never did it touch his feet; and after he had progressed, as he judged, including the windings of his way, some five or six miles, he began to recollect a little, meager stream, yet flowing with a good force for its compass, that made a play in the current not a quarter of a mile, not more than one thousand feet, from the fort. So well founded was his judgment of locality that when the light first appeared, a pale glimmer at the end of a long tunnel, growing broader and clearer on approach, and he reached an archway with a sudden turn, seeming from without a mere "rock-house"—as a grotto formed by the beetling ledges of a cliff is called in that region—and with no further cavernous suggestion, the first thing that caught his eye was the English flag flying above the primitive block-houses and bastions and out-works of Fort Loudon, while the little stream gathered all its strength and hied down through the thick underbrush to join the Tennessee River.

The officers heard with evident concern of the disaster that had befallen MacLeod Station, and immediately sent a runner to bid the stationers come to the fort, pending their selection of a new site and the raising of new houses. So Odalie, with such few belongings as could be hastily collected once more loaded on a packhorse, again entered the gates of Fort Loudon with a heavy heart.

But it was a cheery group she encountered. The soldiers were swaggering about the parade in fine form, the picture of military jollity, and the great hall was full of the officers and settlers. An express had come in with news of a different complexion. Long delayed the bearer had been; tempted to turn back here, waiting an opportunity there, now assisted on his backward journey by a friendly Indian, and again seeing a dodging chance of making through to Loudon, he had traveled his two hundred miles so slowly that the expedition he heralded came hard on the announcement of its approach. While the tidings raised the spirits of the officers and the garrison, it was evident that the movement added elements of danger and developed the crisis. Still they consisted with hope, and with that sentiment of good cheer and jovial courage which succeeded the reading of the brief dispatch from Fort Prince George.

> Advices just received from Charles Town. General Amherst detaches Colonel Montgomery with adequate force to chastise Indians.

Discussions of the situation were rife everywhere. There was much talk of the officer in command of the expedition, a man of distinguished ability and tried courage, and the contradictory Gilmore and Whitson found themselves in case to argue with great vivacity, offering large wagers of untransferable commodities,—such as one's head, one's eyes, one's life,— on the minor point, impossible to be settled at the moment, as to whether or not he spelled his name with a final "y," one maintaining this to be a fact, the other denying it, since he was a younger brother (afterward succeeding to the title) of the Earl of Eglinton, who always spelled his name Montgomerie. It might have afforded them further subject for discussion, and enlarged their appreciation of the caricature of incongruity, could they have known that some two years later three of these savage Cherokee chiefs would be presented to His Majesty King George in London by the Earl of Eglinton, where they were said to have conducted themselves with great dignity and propriety. Horace Walpole in one of his letters chronicles them as the lions of the hour, dining with peers, and having a vocal celebrity, Mrs. Clive, to sing on one of these occasions in her best style for their pleasure. In fact, such was the grace of their deportment, that several of the newspapers seemed to deduce therefrom the failure of civilization, since the aboriginal state of man could show forth these flowers of decorum, a point of view that offends to the quick a learned historian, who argues astutely throughout a precious half-page of a compendious work that the refinements of spiritual culture are still worth consideration, seeming to imply that although we cannot all be Cherokee chieftains, and take London by storm,—in a manner different, let us say in passing, from their previous reduction of smaller cities,—it is quite advisable for us to mind our curriculum and our catechism, and be as wise and good as we may, if not distinguished.

Perhaps the Cherokees acted upon the intuitive perception of the value of doing in Rome as the Romans do. And that rule of conduct seems earlier to have been applied by Colonel Montgomery. However he spelled his name, he was sufficiently identifiable. He came northward like an avenging fury. Advancing swiftly with a battalion of Highlanders and four companies of the Royal Scots,[11] some militia and volunteers, through that wild and tangled country, he fell on Little Keowee Town, where with a small detachment he put every man to the sword, and, by making a night march with the main body of his force, almost simultaneously destroyed Estatoe, taking the inhabitants so by surprise that the beds were warm, the food was cooking, loaded guns exploded in the flames, for the town was promptly fired, and many perished thus, the soldiers having become almost uncontrollable on discovering the body of an Englishman who had only that morning suffered death by torture at the hands of the savages. Sugaw Town next met this fate—in fact, almost every one of the Ayrate towns of the Cherokee nation, before Colonel Montgomery wiped his bloody sword, and sheathed it at the gates of Fort Prince George, having personally made several narrow escapes.

These details, however, were to Fort Loudon like the flashes of lightning of a storm still below the horizon, and of which one is only made aware by the portentous conditions of the atmosphere. The senior officers of the post began to look grave. The idea occurred to them with such force that they scarcely dared to mention it one to the other, lest it be developed by some obscure electrical transmission in the brain of Oconostota, that Fort Loudon would offer great strategic value in the possession of the Indians. The artillery, managed by French officers, who, doubtless, would appear at their appeal, might well suffice to check the English advance. The fort itself would afford impregnable shelter to the braves, their French allies and non-combatants. Always they had coveted it, always they claimed that it had been built for them, here in the heart of their nation. Stuart was not surprised by the event. He only wondered that it had not chanced earlier.

That night the enmity of the Indians was prefigured by a great glare suddenly springing into the sky. It rose above the forests, and from the open spaces about Fort Loudon, whence the woods had been cleared away, one could see it fluctuate and flush more deeply, and expand along the horizon like some flickering mystery of the aurora borealis. But this baleful glare admitted of no doubt. One needed not to speculate on unexplained possibilities of electrical currents, and resultant thrills of light. It only epitomized and materialized the kindling of the fires of hate.

It was Odalie's little home; much that she valued still remained there—left to be quietly fetched to the fort next day. Their flitting had taken place at dusk, with but a load of wearing apparel, and it was supposed that the rest was quite safe, as the Cherokees were not presumed to be apprised of their absence. The spinning-wheel and the loom; her laborious treasures of home-woven linen for bed and table; the fine curtains on which the birds flickered for the last time; the beds and pillows, adding pounds on pounds of dry balsam needles to the fire; the flaunting, disguised tabourets, showing themselves now at their true value, and burning stolidly like the chunks of wood they were; the unsteady tables and puncheon benches; all the uncouth, forlorn little makeshifts of her humble housekeeping, that her embellishing touch had rendered so pretty, added their fuel to the flames which cast long-glancing lines of light up and down the silvery reaches of the river she had loved.

Captain Stuart and Captain Demeré, who had gone instantly to the tower in the block-house by the gate, on the report of a strange, distant light, saw her as they came down, and both paused, Demeré wincing a trifle, preferring not to meet her. She was standing beside one of the great guns and had been looking out through the embrasure. The moon was directly overhead above the parade, and the shadows of the palisades fell outward. The officers could not avoid her; their way led them down near at hand and they needs must pass her. She turned, and as she stood with one hand on the big cannon, her white dress richly a-gleam in the moonlight, she looked at them with a smile, something of the saddest, in her eyes.

"If I wanted to scream, Mrs. MacLeod, I should scream," exclaimed Demeré, impulsively.

She laughed a little, realizing how he would have upbraided the futility of tears had she shed them—he was always so ready with his staid, kind, undeniably reasonable rebukes.

"No," she said, "I am trying to remember that home is not in a house, but in the heart."

"I think you are trying to show us the mettle of a soldier," said Demeré, admiringly.

"Mrs. MacLeod would like the king's commission!" cried Stuart, breaking the tension with his bluff raillery, striking the cannon a smart tap with the butt of the pistol he carried in his hand, while the metal gave out a deep, hollow resonance. "Her unbridled ambition was always to be the commanding officer!"

Both Stuart and Demeré thought more seriously of the demonstration as affecting the public weal than did the pioneers of the settlement. Still hoping for the best, it seemed to them not unnatural that an abandoned station should be fired as merely wanton mischief, and not necessarily with the knowledge or connivance of the head-men of the Cherokees.

The next day, the hunters of the fort went out betimes as usual, and Hamish found it agreeable to make one of the party. Corporal O'Flynn was among the number, and several horses were taken to bring in the game; a bright, clear day it was, of that sweet season when the spring blooms gradually into the richness of summer. The wind was fresh; the river sang; the clouds of a glittering whiteness, a flocculent lightness, floated high in the blue sky. Suddenly the sentry at the gate called out sharply for the corporal of the guard. The men, lounging about the parade, turned to look and listen.

"Plunging through the gate and half across the parade ground."

The hoof-beats of a horse coming at frantic speed smote first upon the ear; then across the open space to which the glacis sloped, with snorting head and flying mane and tail, the frightened creature galloped, plunging through the gate and half across the parade ground; a soldier was on his back, leaning forward upon the animal's neck, his arms clasped about it, the stirrups and his position alone retaining him in the saddle; for he was dead—quite dead. Too dead to answer any of the dozen questions hurled at him as the soldiers caught the bridle; when the horse whirled he reeled out of the saddle, so hopelessly dead that they asked him no more. The good sorrel would have told much, if he might, as he stood, snorting and tossing his head, and trembling in every fiber, his eyes starting out of their sockets, yet, conscious he was among his friends, looking from one to another of the soldiers as they handled him, with an earnest appeal for sympathy and consolation which implied some terrible ordeal. Before an order could be given the crack of rifles came from the woods, and a few of the hunters were seen bursting from the forest, one by one, and coming at a double-quick up the slope of the glacis.

Hamish and O'Flynn were the last. They had been together a little distant from the others. Now and again they had heard the report of firearms, multiplied into something like a volley.

"Listen at them spalpeens wastin' powdher," the corporal exclaimed once, wroth at this unsoldierly practice. "Must they have twenty thrys to hit a big black buffalo? Just lemme git 'em into the gyard house wunst agin—time they git out they'll be fit to worship the outside o' the dure; it'll look so strange an' good to 'm."

It was a wolf-trap which he was exploiting at the moment, made of logs cumbrously adjusted and baited with buffalo meat, and within it now were two large, handsome specimens whose skins were of value, and who had evidently resolved to part with those ornamental integuments as reluctantly as might be; they were growling and plunging at the timbers with a most ferocious show of fangs and the foam flying from their snarling jaws.

The sun sifted down through the great trees and the soft green shadows on the man and boy, both clad in the hunter's buckskin shirt and leggings. Corporal O'Flynn had knelt down outside the pen the better to see in the shadow the two plunging wild beasts.

"I'm afeared to shoot so close lest I might singe yer hair, but I can't stand on ceremony, me dears," he said, addressing the wolves, as he drew his pistol. "Bedad, I must go and stop that wastin' o' powdher!"

The next moment something suddenly sang aloud in the wilderness—a wild, strange, sibilant strain. It seemed materialized as it whizzed past Hamish's ear, and so long had it been since he had heard the flight of the almost discarded arrow that he did not recognize the sound till he heard a sharp exclamation of pain and saw the shaft sticking in O'Flynn's right arm, pinning it to the logs of the wolf-trap. The claws of the wild beasts, reaching through, tore now the buckskin and now the flesh from his chest, as he pluckily struggled to free himself; the pistol went off in his grasp and one of the wolves fell in convulsive agonies; the other, dismayed, shrank back. Hamish caught up O'Flynn's loaded gun, looking about warily for Indians, and prudently reserving his fire. He saw naught, and the next moment he realized that O'Flynn was fainting from the pain. He knew that the straggler who had shot the arrow had sped swiftly away to summon other Cherokees, or to secure a gun or more arrows. He risked his life in waiting only a moment, but with the fellow-feeling which was so strong among the pioneers of the Tennessee Valley that it would induce two men at parting, having but one knife between them, to break and share the blade, to divide the powder that meant life in that wild country equally to the last grain. Hamish did not for one instant contemplate any other course. He rushed to O'Flynn and sought to release him, but the flint of the arrow that had gone through the heavy muscular tissues of the arm still stuck fast in the strong fiber of the logs of the trap, and the blood was streaming, and once more the wolf was angrily plunging against the side of the pen. Suddenly the boy remembered the juvenile account of the scalping of "Dill." Calling piteously to O'Flynn not to mind, if he could help it, Hamish placed one firm foot against the straight back of the soldier, and bracing himself with his left arm around a stanch young tree, he pulled at the arrow with all his might. There was a ripping sound of flesh, a human scream, a creak of riving wood, and Corporal O'Flynn lay face downward on the ground, freed, but with the shaft still in his arm, the blood spurting from it, and the wolf plunging and snarling unheeded at the very hair of his head.

CHAPTER IX

With a great effort Hamish dragged O'Flynn, who was a heavy, muscular fellow, out of the reach of the wolf. Fortunately there chanced to be a spring branch near at hand, and the ice-cold water hurriedly dashed into the corporal's face, together with an earnest reminder of the hideous danger of death and torture by the Indians, and a sense of the possibility of escape, served to sufficiently restore him to enable him to get upon his feet, unsteadily enough, however, and with Hamish's help make his way toward the fort at a pretty fair speed. He fainted after they crossed the ditch, and the great gates closed. These two were the last of the hunters who found rescue; the others who had straggled in previously, reported having been fired upon by Indians, and that several dead soldiers were left upon the ground.

The parade was a scene of wild turmoil, far different from its usual orderly military aspect. The settlers and their families, alarmed at last, had fled for refuge to the fort, bringing only a small portion of their scanty possessions. Women were weeping in agitation and terror of the dangers passed, and in despair because of the loss of their little homes, which the Indians were even now pillaging; children were clinging about their mothers and peevishly plaining, their nerves unstrung by the rush and commotion, and the unaccustomed aspect of the place; bundles of clothing and bedding lay about on the ground; the pioneers moved hither and thither, now seeking to adjust discomforts and clear the domestic atmosphere, now aiding in the preparations for an expected attack.

Odalie, who had braced up her heart, found little to encourage her as she went from one to another of the matrons and sought to comfort them with the reflection that it might have been worse. "For my own part," she declared, "I think of what might have been. If my household gear were not sacrificed we should have been at home last night when the Indians came and found us gone and sacked and fired the house. And such a little thing to save us—Fifine's talk of seeing Willinawaugh."

"Him top-feathers, him head, an' him ugly mouf," reiterated Fifine, who had become impressed with the belief that she had done something very clever indeed, and was enchanted to hear it celebrated.

Odalie's exertions were more appreciated at the hospital, where she assisted in dressing the wounds and caring for the comfort of the soldiers who had been shot. Afterward, still determined to make the best of things and to help all she could, she discovered a mission to tax her powers in offering to assist in what manner she might the quarter-master-sergeant. That functionary looked as if the conundrum of the created world had suddenly been propounded to him. He was a short, square, red-faced man, with light, staring, gray eyes, and they seemed about to pop out of his head whenever the finding of quarters for another family was required of him.

"Why couldn't they have brought some conveniences, such as knives and forks and cups and platters, instead of fool trifles?" he demanded fiercely, aside, as he turned away from one group who were as destitute of all appliances as if they had expected to peck off the ground, or drink out of the bubbles of the spring branch. "I have got none to spare except those of the poor fellows who were killed and Corporal O'Flynn's, for he will be equal to nothing but spoon-meat for one while."

"Oh, the poor settlers,—I pity them,—and poor Mr. Green,—I feel very guilty, for I came here just such a charge on the resources of the fort, myself."

He paused pudgily, as if he were mentally in full run and had brought up with a short stop.

"Oh, you—" he exclaimed, in the tone of making an exception, "you are you."

He felt equal to any arrangements for merely military mortals, but the "squaw question," as he mentally called it, overwhelmed him. With a lot of anxious, troubled, houseless women and querulous, distraught, frightened children, and difficult half-grown boys,—and the commandant's general orders to quarter them all to their satisfaction and to furnish whatever was necessary,—the strain might have proved too great for the old bustling sergeant, and like undue pressure on the boiler of one of our modern locomotives, which he much resembled, as he went back and forth puffingly, might have exploded his valuable faculties, but for Odalie's well-meant hints.

"I should give Mrs. Halsing the larger room if I were you," she suggested. "Mrs. Beedie is a friend of mine and I will answer for it that she won't mind." Or—"If I might suggest, I wouldn't put Mrs. Dean and the twin babies next to Mrs. Rush. Nervous headaches and other people's twin babies won't keep step—not one bit. Put them next to me. I am conveniently deaf at times."

And Mrs. Halsing said, "That French thing flirts with every man in the fort, from the commandant down to Mrs. Dean's one-year-old boy twin!" For Odalie was presently conveying this juvenile personage about in her arms, and he left off a whimper, characteristic of no particular age or sex, to exhibit a truly masculine interest in the big soldiers with their bright uniforms and clanking accouterments, and although constrained by the force of the concussion to blink and close his eyes whenever the great guns were fired, he fairly wheezed and squealed with manly ecstasy in the sound—for a cannonade had begun, seeking to deter the plunder of the deserted houses in the settlement.

The din suddenly ceased; the active military figures paused in the swift preparations that were in progress to meet the expected attack; the confusion and stir of the groups of settlers' families in the parade were petrified in a sort of aghast disarray; amongst them appeared half a dozen stalwart fellows bearing a stretcher, on which lay the body of the dead soldier whom the horse had brought into the fort, his young boyish face all smooth again and serenely upturned to the serene sky. He was dressed in his uniform, with his belt and gloves freshly pipeclayed and glittering white. His melancholy progress from the crowded barracks to a vacant building where were kept the spare arms,—called the armory,—there to wait the few remaining hours of his sojourn in these familiar scenes, served to deepen the gloom with the thought of the others of the little band, lying out in the woods, who would not receive even such simple honors of sepulture as the fort could bestow.

But after the next day, when the poor young soldier was buried (the children wept dreadfully at the sound of the muffled drum, the troops being touched by their sympathetic tears, and Captain Demeré read the burial service and alluded feelingly to the other dead of the garrison, to whom they could only do reverence in the heart and keep their memory green)—after all this the place took on an air of brisk cheerfulness and the parade ground presented somewhat the appearance of the esplanade of a watering-place, minus the wealth and show and fashion.

In the evenings after the dress-parade and the boom of the sunset-gun, the elder women sat about in the doors and porches, and knitted and gossiped, and the men walked up and down and discussed the stale war news from Europe—for the triumphs of British arms were then rife in all the world—or sat upon the grass and played dominoes or cards; the soldiers near the barracks threw horseshoes for quoits; the children rollicked about, shrill but joyous; Odalie and Belinda Rush in their cool fresh linen dresses, arm in arm, the admiration of all beholders, strolled up and down with measured step and lissome grace; and the flag would slip down, and the twilight come on, and a star tremble in the blue summer sky; and the sweet fern that overhung the deep clear spring, always in the shadow of the oaks near one of the block-houses, would give out a fresh, pungent fragrance. Presently the moon would shed her bland benediction over all the scene, and the palisades would draw sharp-pointed shadows on the dark interior slope, and beside each cannon the similitude of another great gun would be mounted; a pearly glister would intimate where the river ran between the dense glossy foliage of the primeval woods, and only the voice of the chanting cicada, or the long dull drone of the frogs, or the hooting of an owl, would come from the deserted village, lying there so still and silent, guarded by the guns of the fort.

And after a little Odalie would be strolling on her husband's arm in the moonlight, and would silently gaze about with long, doubting, diplomatic eyelashes and inquiring eyes when asked where was Belinda Rush,—which conduct induced Mrs. Halsing's comment as to Mrs. MacLeod's proclivity toward matchmaking. For in the neighborhood of the northwestern bastion one might see, if one were very keen, sitting in the moonlight on the tread of the banquette, Belinda Rush and Ensign Whitson—talking and talking—of what?—so much!—in fact so much that at other times Ensign Whitson had little to say, and Lieutenant Gilmore pined for lack of contradiction, and his powers of argument fell away.

Captain Demeré and Captain Stuart, on their way to a post of observation in the block-house tower, came near running over these young people seated thus one moonlight night—to Captain Demeré's manifest confusion and Captain Stuart's bluff delight, although both passed with serious mien, doffing their hats with some casual words of salutation. Despite his relish of the episode, Stuart glanced down at them afterward from the block-house tower and said, in a tone of commiseration, "Poor little love-story!"

"Why preëmpt ill-fortune for them, John?" broke out Demeré, irritably.

"Bless you, my boy, I'm no prophet!" exclaimed Stuart easily.

Belinda and the Ensign on the moonlit rampart.

The expected attack by the Indians took place one night late, in the dead hour, after the sinking of the moon, and with all the cunning of a designed surprise. The shadowy figures, that one might imagine would be indistinguishable from the darkness, had crept forward, encompassing the fort, approaching nearly to the glacis, when the crack of a sentry's firelock rang out, splitting the dead silence, and every cannon of the twelve roared in hideous unison, for the gunners throughout the night lay ready beside the pieces. A fusillade ill-directed upon the works, for the besiegers encountered the recoil of the surprise they had planned, met a furious response from the loop-holes where the firelocks of the garrison were reënforced by the rifles of the backwoodsmen. Every man had been assigned his post, and it seemed that the wild alarum of the drum had hardly begun to vibrate on the thrilling air when each, standing aside from the loop-hole according to orders, leveled his weapon without sighting and fired. Wild screams from without, now and again, attested the execution of these blind volleys into the black night, and the anguish that overcame the stoical fortitude of the warlike Cherokee. The crashing of the trees, as the cannon on all sides sent the heavy balls thundering beyond the open space into the forest, seemed to indicate that the retreat of the assailants was cut off, or that it must needs be made under the open fire of the artillery.

How the movement fared the defenders could ill judge, because of the tumult of their own rapidly delivered volleys—all firing to the word, the "fencibles" adopting the tactics of the garrison in which they had been so well drilled—and the regular reverberations of the rapidly served cannon.

They only knew when the ineffectual fire of the assailants slackened, then ceased; the crash of riving timber, and now and again a hideous yell from the forest, told of the grim deed wrought beyond the range of the firelock by the far-reaching great guns.

It was soon over, and although the garrison stood ready at their posts for an hour or more afterward, till the night was wearing into dawn, no further demonstration was made.

"Vastly fine! They will not return to the attack,—the fun's over," Captain Stuart cried hilariously;—his face and hands were as black with powder "as if he had been rubbing noses with the cannon," Corporal O'Flynn said, having crawled out of the hospital on his hands and knees to participate in the fight in some wise, if only as spectator.

"They have had a lesson," said Demeré, with grim triumph, "how severe, we can't judge till we see the ground."

This satisfaction, however, was to be denied them, for the corporal of the guard presently brought the report of a sentinel whose sharp eyes had descried, in the first faint gray siftings of the dawn through the black night, parties of Indians, chiefly women, carrying off the dead and disabled, and now and then a wild, shuddering groan or a half-smothered cry of the wounded attested their errand of mercy.

"They ought to show a white flag," said Demeré, exactingly, like the martinet he was.

"And they ought to wear top-boots on their feet, and Steinkirks around their gullets, and say their prayers, but they don't," retorted Stuart in high good humor, for his rigorous discipline and persistent formality were exerted only on his own forces; he cared not to require such punctiliousness of the enemy since it did not serve his interest. "Let them take the carrion away. We don't want to play scavenger for them—from an ambuscade they could make it mighty hot for us! And we should be compelled to do it for sanitary reasons—too close to the fort to let the bodies lie there and rot."

And with this prosaic reminder Captain Demeré was content to dispense with the polite formality of a flag of truce. They never knew what the loss might be on the Indian side, nor did the braves again venture within gunshot. Now and then the cannon sought to search the woods and locate the line, but no sound followed the deep-voiced roar, save the heavy reverberations of the echo from up and down the river and the sullen response of the craggy hills. The cannonade had served to acquaint the Cherokees with an accurate estimate of the range of the guns. The fact that a strong cordon was maintained just beyond this, was discovered when the post hunters were again sent out, on the theory that the repulse of the Indians had been sufficiently decisive to induce a suspension of hostilities and a relinquishment of their designs to capture the fort, if not a relapse into the former pacific relations. The hunters were driven back by a smart fire, returning with one man shot through the leg, brought in by a comrade on horseback, and four others riding double, leaving their slain horses on the ground. It became very evident that the Cherokees intended to maintain a blockade, since the fort obviously could not be carried by storm, and the commandant was proof against surprise. To send the hunters out again was but to incur the futile loss of life and thus weaken the garrison. The supply of fresh game already in the fort being exhausted, the few head of cattle and the reserves of the smoke-house came into use.

The very fact that such reserves had been provided put new heart into the soldiers and roused afresh the confidence of the settlers, who had begun to quake at the idea of standing a siege so suddenly begun, without warning or preparation, save indeed for the forethought for all emergencies manifested by the senior officers. Both Demeré and Stuart became doubly popular, and when there was a call for volunteers to run the blockade and severally carry dispatches to Colonel Montgomery, they had but to choose among all the men in the fort. The tenor of these dispatches was to apprise Colonel Montgomery of the blockade of Fort Loudon and ask relief, urging him to push forward at once and attack the Ottare towns, when valuable assistance could be rendered him by the ordnance of the fort, as well as by a detachment of infantry from the forces of the garrison attacking the Indians on the flank in support of the aggressions of his vanguard.

Gilfillan was selected as the earliest express sent out, and loud and woeful was Fifine's outcry when she discovered that her precious "Dill" was to be withdrawn from her sight. But when he declared that he needs must go to keep the Indians from cutting off her curls and starving out the garrison— Mrs. Dean's twin babies were represented as the most imminent victims, so much more precious than one, "being philopenas" as O'Flynn admonished her—she consented, and tearfully bade him adieu. And he kissed her very gravely, and very gravely at her request kissed the cat. So with these manifestations of his simple affection he goes out of these pages beyond all human ken, and into the great unknown. For Dill returned no more.

His long backwoods experience, his knowledge of Indian character, his wide familiarity with the face of the country, and many by-ways and unfrequented routes, his capacity to speak the Cherokee language, all combined to suggest his special fitness for the dangerous part he had undertaken to play.

The next express, going two days later and following the beaten track, was a man who had frequently served in this capacity and knew half the Indians of the Lower Towns and Middle Settlements by name—a quick-witted pioneer, "half-trader, half-hunter, and half-packman," as he often described himself, and he had been in the country, he boasted, "ever since it was built."

The choice of these two men was evidently specially judicious, and after the mysterious disappearance of each, being smuggled out of the fort in dead silence and the darkest hour of the deep night, the garrison settled down to a regular routine, to wear away the time till they might wake some morning to hear the crack of Montgomery's musketry on the horizon, or the hissing of his grenades burning out their fuses and bursting among the dense jungles, where the Cherokees lay in ambush and blockaded Fort Loudon.

The military precision and order maintained continued as strict as heretofore. It argued no slight attention to detail and adroit handling of small opportunities that the comfort of the soldiers was in no wise reduced by the intrusion into their restricted domain of so considerable a number of people, many unprovided with the most ordinary conveniences of life. Even in such a matter as table and cooking utensils the food of the companies was served as heretofore, and only after the military had breakfasted or dined, or supped, could their precious pewter platters and cups be borrowed by the families, to be rigorously cleaned and restored before the preparations began for the next meal. Every utensil in the place did double duty, yet not one failed to be ready for service when required. Mrs. Halsing ventured to cavil, and suggested that she had always heard elsewhere that it was polite to serve ladies and children first, instead of giving a lot of hulking soldiers precedence.

"Why, madam," Demeré said, with rebuking severity, "the men are the muscles of our defense, and must be kept in the best possible physical condition."

Nothing was allowed to interfere with the regular hours of the troops or break their rest. Tattoo and "lights out" had the same meaning for the women and children and wild young boys as for the soldiery; no boisterous callow cries and juvenile racing and chasing were permitted on the parade; no belated groups of gossipers; no nocturnal wailing of wickedly wakeful infants in earshot.

"A-body would think the men was cherubim or seraphim the way the commandant cares for them," plained Mrs. Halsing.

The supplies were regulated by the same careful supervision and served out duly by weight and allowance. Somewhat frugal seemed this dole, especially to those who had lived on the unlimited profusion of the woodland game, yet it was sufficient. No violent exercise, to which the men had been accustomed, required now the restoring of exhausted tissues by a generous food supply. There was ample provision, too, made for the occupation of the men's attention and their amusement. The regular cleaning of quarters, inspection, drill and guard duties, and dress-parades went on as heretofore, with the "fencibles" as an auxiliary body. The rude games of ball, ring toss, leap-frog were varied sometimes by an exhibition, given under the auspices of the officers, of feats of strength; certain martial Samsons lifted great weights, made astonishing leaps, ran like greyhounds competing with one another in a marked-off course, or engaged in wrestling-matches—to the unbounded applause of the audience, except the compassionate Fifine, who wept loudly and inconsolably whenever a stalwart fellow caught a fall. One rainy evening, in the officers' mess-hall, the society of the fort was invited to hear the performance of a clever but rascally fellow, more used to ride the wooden horse than to any other occupation, who was a bit of a ventriloquist. Among other feats he made Fifine's cat talk, and tell about Willinawaugh with "him top-feathers, him head, an' him ugly mouf," to the great relish of his comrades (who resented the fact that the Indians, exceedingly vain of their own personal appearance,[12] were accustomed to speak of the paleface as the "ugly white people"); to the intense, shrieking delight of the elder children; and to the amazement of Fifine, who could not understand afterward why the douce mignonne would not talk to her. When the pretended conversation of the cat grew funnily profane, Captain Demeré only called out "Time's up," from the back of the hall, and the fellow came sheepishly down from the platform, holding the borrowed kitty by the nape of the neck, and half the audience did not catch the funny swear that he attributed to the exemplary feline. Then there was a shadow-pantomime, where immaterial roisterers "played Injun," and went through the horrid details of scalping and murders, with grotesque concomitant circumstances,—such as the terrifying ricochet effects on an unsophisticated red-man of riving a buzz-wig from the head of his victim in lieu of a real scalp, and the consequent sudden exchange of the characters of pursued and pursuer,—all of which, oddly enough, the people who stood in imminent danger of a horrible fate thought very funny indeed.

One evening the commandant devised a new plan to pass the time. All were summoned to the parade ground to share in an entertainment designated as "Songs of all nations."

"An' I could find it in my stommick to wish it was to share in 'Soups of all nations,'" said Corporal O'Flynn to a comrade. For it seemed that the quartermaster-sergeant had docked his rations by an ounce or two, a difference that made itself noted in so slender a dole and a convalescent's appetite.

It was a night long to be remembered. The great coils of Scorpio seemed covered with scintillating scales, so brilliant were the stars. No cloud was in the sky, unless one might so call that seeming glittering vapor, the resplendent nebulose clusters of the Galaxy. A wind was moving through the upper atmosphere, for the air was fresh and cool, but below was the soft, sweet stillness of the summer night, full of fragrant odors from the woods, the sound of the swift-flowing river, the outpour of the melody of a mocking-bird that had alighted on the tip of the great flagstaff, and seemed to contribute thence his share to the songs of all nations. He caught upon his white wing and tail-feathers, as he flirted them, the clear radiance of the moon,—not a great orb, but sending forth a light fair enough to be felt in all that sidereal glitter of the cloudless sky, to show the faces of Odalie and Belinda and others less comely, as the ladies sat in chairs under the line of trees on one side of the parade with a group of officers near them, and the soldiers and "single men" and children of the settlers filling the benches of the post which were brought out for the occasion. So they all sang, beginning with a great chorus of "Rule Britannia," into which they threw more force and patriotism than melody. Then came certain solo performances, some of which were curious enough. Odalie's French chansonnettes acquired from her grand'maman, drifting out in a mellow contralto voice, and a big booming proclamation concerning the "Vaterland," by the drum-major, were the least queerly foreign. Mrs. Halsing, after much pressing, sang an outlandish, repetitious melody that was like an intricate wooden recitative, and the words were suspected of being Icelandic,—though she averred they were High Dutch, to the secret indignation of the drum-major, who, as O'Flynn afterward remarked, when discussing the details of the evening, felt himself qualified by descent to judge, his own father-in-law having been a German. The men who had sung in the Christmas carols remembered old English ditties,—

"How now, shepherd, what means that,
Why that willow in thy hat?"

and "Barbara Allen." Corporal O'Flynn, in the most incongruously sentimental and melancholy of tenors, sang "Savourneen Deelish eileen ogg." The sober Sandy gave a rollicking Scotch drinking-song that seemed to show the very bead on the liquor, "Hey the browst, and hey the quaigh!". The officers' cook, a quaint old African, seated cross-legged on the ground, on the outskirts of the crowd, piped up at the commandant's bidding, and half sang, half recited, in a wide, deep, musical voice, and an unheard-of language that excited great interest for a time; but interpreting certain manifestations of applause among the soldiers as guying, he took himself and his ear-rings and a gay kerchief, which he wore, to the intense delight of the garrison, as a belt around the waistband of his knee-breeches, to his kitchen, replying with cavalier insubordination,—pioneer of the domestic manners of these days,—to Captain Stuart's remonstrances by the assertion that he had to wash his kettle.

There were even cradle songs, for Mrs. Dean, who certainly had ample field for efforts in that line, sang a sweet little theme, saying she knew nothing else, and a big grenadier, whose hair was touched with gray, and who spoke in a deep sonorous voice (the Cherokees had always called him Kanoona, "the bull-frog"), respectfully requested to know of the lady if she could sing one that he had not heard for forty years, in fact, not since his mother sang it to him. One or two of the settlers, hailing originally from England, remembered it too, and some discussion ensued touching the words and the exact turn of the tune. In the midst of this a wag among the younger pioneers mischievously suggested that the grenadier should favor them with a rendition of his version, and the big soldier, in the simplicity of his heart and his fond old memories, in a great bass voice that fairly trembled with its own weight, began "Bye-low, bye-low"; and the ventriloquist who had made the cat swear, and who so often rode the wooden horse, was compelled during the performance to wear his hat adjusted over his face, for his grin was of a distention not to be tolerated in polite society.

Perhaps because of the several contradictory phases of interest involved in this contribution to the entertainment, it held the general attention more definitely than worthier vocal efforts that had preceded it, and the incident passed altogether unnoticed, except by Captain Stuart, when the corporal of the guard appeared in the distance, his metal buttons glimmering from afar in the dusk as he approached, and Captain Demeré softly signaled to him to pause, and rising quietly vanished in the shadow of the block-house. He encountered Stuart at the door, for he had also slipped away from the crowd, himself, like a shadow.

"Dispatches?" he asked.

"The express from Fort Prince George," Demeré replied, his voice tense, excited, with the realization of an impending crisis.

CHAPTER X

Demeré was not a man to consider an omen and attach weight to trifling chances, yet he was in some sort prepared for disaster. Within the hall a pair of candles stood on the table where it was the habit to transact official business,—to write letters; to construct maps of the country from the resources of the information of the officers and the descriptions of the Indians; to make out reports and the accounts of the post. Writing materials were kept in readiness here for these purposes—a due array of quills, paper, inkhorn, wafers, sealing-wax, sand-box, and lights. As the door was opened the candles flickered in the sudden draught, bowed to the wicks grown long and unsnuffed, and in another moment were extinguished, leaving the place in total darkness, with the papers on which hung such weighty interests of life and death, of rescue or despair, unread in his hand.

"The tinder-box—the flint—where are they? Cannot you strike a spark?" he demanded, in agitated suspense, of Stuart, who made more than one fruitless effort before the timorous flame was started anew on the old and drooping wicks, which had to be smartly snuffed before they would afford sufficient light to discern the hasty characters, that looked as if they might have been written on a drumhead—as in fact they were.

"Here—read them, John—I can't," said Demeré, handing the package to Stuart, and throwing himself into a chair to listen.

Although the suspense had been of the kind that does not usually herald surcease of anxiety, he was not prepared for the face of consternation with which Stuart silently perused the scrawled lines.

"From Montgomery!" he exclaimed. "But our dispatches evidently have never reached him."

For in the bold strain of triumph Colonel Montgomery acquainted the commandant of Fort Loudon with the successful issue of his campaign, having lost only four men, although he had burned a number of Indian towns, destroyed incalculable quantities of provisions, killed and wounded many braves, and was carrying with him a train of prisoners, men, women, and children. He was now on the march to the relief of Fort Prince George, which the savages had invested, where the garrison was in much distress, not for the want of provisions but for fuel to cook food, since the enemy was in such force that no sortie could be made to the woods to procure a supply. Two of his prisoners he had set at liberty, Fiftoe, and the old warrior of Estatoe, that they might acquaint the nation of his further

- 133 -

intentions, for, if the Indians did not immediately sue for peace and deliver up the principal transgressors to justice, he would sally forth from Fort Prince George on another foray, and he would not hold his hand till he had burned every Cherokee town of the whole nation. He deputed Captain Stuart and Captain Demeré to offer these terms to the Upper towns, and let them know that they were admitted to this clemency solely in consideration of the regard of the government for Atta-Kulla-Kulla. This chieftain, the half-king of the Cherokee tribe, had deprecated, it was understood, the renewal of the war, since he had signed the last treaty at the Congarees, and having shown himself friendly on several occasions to the British people his majesty's government esteemed him as he deserved.

The two officers gazed silently at one another. Montgomery was obviously entirely unaware of their situation. Here they were, penned up in this restricted compass, besieged by an enemy so furious that even a hat showing but for one moment above the palisades,—for the soldiers had tried the experiment of poising an old busby on the point of a bayonet,— would be riddled in an instant. Often a well-directed bullet would enter the small loop-holes for musketry, and thus, firing from ambush, endanger the sentinel as he stood within the strong defenses. More than once arrows, freighted with inflammable substances, all ablaze, had been shot into the fort with the effort to fire the houses; it was dry weather mostly, with a prospect of a long drought, and the flames thus started threatened a conflagration, and required the exertions of the entire garrison to extinguish them. This proclivity necessitated eternal vigilance. Ever and anon it was requisite that the cannon should renew their strong, surly note of menace, and again send the balls crashing through the forest, and about the ears of the persistent besiegers. Only the strength of the primitive work saved the garrison from instant massacre, with the women and children and the settlers who had sought safety behind those sturdy ramparts. Of the ultimate danger of starvation the officers did not dare to think. And from this situation to be summoned to send forth threats of sword and fire, and to offer arrogant terms of peace, and to demand the surrender, to the justice of the gibbet, of the principal transgressors in the violation of the treaty!

There were no words that could express what they felt. They could only look at one another, each conscious of the other's sympathy, and say nothing.

Outside, Odalie, Belinda, and Ensign Whitson were singing a trio, the parts somewhat at haphazard, the fugue-like effects coming in like the cadences of the wind, now high, now low, and in varying strength. The stars still glittered down into the parade; the moon cast a gentle shadow along the palisades; the sentries in the block-house towers, the gunners lying flat beneath their great cannon, feeling the dew on their faces, looking toward the moon, the guard ready to turn out at the word,—all listened languorously, and drank in the sweets of the summer night with the music. A scene almost peaceful, despite the guarded walls, and the savage hordes outside, balked, and furious, and thirsting for blood.

"Let us see the express, Paul," said Stuart at last.

The express had repeatedly served as a means of communication between Fort Loudon and Fort Prince George, and as he came in he cautiously closed the door. He was a man of war, himself, in some sort, and was aware that a garrison is hardly to be included in the conference between commanders of a frontier force and their chosen emissary. With the inside of his packet his brain was presumed to have no concern, but in such a time and such a country his eyes and ears, on his missions to and fro, did such stalwart service in the interests of his own safety that he was often able to give the officers at the end of his route far more important news, the fruits of his observation, than his dispatches were likely to unfold. He was of stalwart build, and clad in the fringed buckskin shirt and leggings of the hunter, and holding his coonskin cap in his hand. He had saluted after the military fashion, and had evidently been enough the inmate of frontier posts to have some regard for military rank. He waited, despite his look of having much of moment to communicate, until the question had been casually propounded by Stuart: "Well, what can you tell us of the state of the country?" then in disconnected sentences the details came in torrents.

Montgomery's campaign had been something unheard of. His "feet were winged with fire and destruction,"—that was what Oconostota said. Oh, yes, the express had seen Oconostota. But for Oconostota he could not have made Fort Loudon. He had let him come with the two warriors, set free by Montgomery to suggest terms of peace and spread the news of the devastation, as a safe-guard against any straggling white people they might chance to meet, and in return they afforded him safe-conduct from the Cherokees. The devastation was beyond belief,—dead and dying Indians lying all around the lower country, and many were burned alive in their houses when the towns were fired. Many were now pitifully destitute. As the fugitives stood on the summits of distant hills and watched their blazing homes and great granaries of corn—"I could but be sorry for them a little," declared Major Grant of Montgomery's command.

But the result was not to be what Montgomery hoped. The Cherokees were arming anew everywhere. They would fight now to the death, to extermination,—even Atta-Kulla-Kulla, who had been opposed to breaking the treaty. Oh, yes, he had seen Atta-Kulla-Kulla. The chief said he would not strike a blow with a feather to break a treaty and his solemn word. But to avenge the blood of his kindred that cried out from the ground he would give his life, if he had as many years to live as there were hairs on his head! The express added that Atta-Kulla-Kulla had been sitting on the ground in his old blanket, with ashes on his head, after the council agreed to break the treaty. But now he was going round with his scalp-lock dressed out with fresh eagle-feathers, and armed with his gun, and tomahawk, and scalp-knife, and wearing his finest gear, and with all his war-paint on—one side of his face red, and the other black, with big white circles around his eyes,—"looks mighty keen," the man exclaimed with a sort of relish of the fine barbaric effect of the fighting trim of the great warrior.

Then his face fell.

"And I told Oconostota that I would not deliver his message to you, Captain Stuart and Captain Demeré, sir," he hesitated; "it was not fit for your worshipful presence; and he said that the deed might go before the word, then."

"What message did he send?" asked Demeré, with flashing eyes.

"Well, sir, he said Fort Loudon was theirs,—that it was built for the Cherokees, and they had paid the English nation for it in the blood they had shed in helping the Virginians defend their frontier against the French and their Indian allies. But you English had possessed the fort; you had claimed it; and now he would say that it was yours,—yours to be burnt in,—to be starved in,—to die in,—to leave your bones in, till they are thrust forth by the rightful owner to be gnawed by the wolf of the wilderness."

There was a momentary silence.

"Vastly polite!" exclaimed Captain Stuart, with a rollicking laugh.

"Lord, sir," said the man, as if the sound grated upon him, "they are a dreadful people. I wouldn't go through again what I have had to risk to get here for—any money! It has been full three weeks since I left Oconostota's camp. He is with the Lower towns—him and Atta-Kulla-Kulla, but Willinawaugh is the head-man of the force out here. They seemed to think I was spying,—but they have got so many men that I just doubts but what they want you should know their strength."

"You will go back to Colonel Montgomery at Fort Prince George with dispatches?" said Demeré.

The man's expression hardened. "Captain Demeré," he said, "and Captain Stuart, sir, I have served you long and faithful. You know I bean't no coward. But it is certain death for me to go out of that sally-port. I couldn't have got in except for that message from Oconostota. He wanted you to

- 136 -

hear that. I believe 'Old Hop' thinks Willinawaugh can terrify you out of this place if they can't carry it by storm. I misdoubts but they expects Frenchmen to join them. They talk so sweet on the French! Every other word is Louis Latinac! That French officer has made them believe that the English intend to exterminate the Cherokees from off the face of the earth."

He paused a moment in rising discontent,—to have done so much, yet refuse aught! "I wouldn't have undertook to bring that message from Oconostota except I thought it was important for you to have your dispatches; it ain't my fault if they ain't satisfactory." He cast a glance of the keenest curiosity at the papers, and Captain Stuart, lazily filling his pipe, took one of the candles in his hand and kindled the tobacco at the blaze.

"Nothing is satisfactory that is one-sided," he said easily. "We don't want Colonel Montgomery to do all the talking, and to have to receive his letters as orders. We propose to say a word ourselves."

A gleam of intelligence was in the scout's eyes. It was a time when there was much professional jealousy rife in the various branches of the service, and he had been cleverly induced to fancy that here was a case in point. These men had a command altogether independent of Colonel Montgomery, it was true, but he was of so much higher rank that doubtless this galled them, and rendered them prone to assert their own position. He bent his energies now, however, to a question touching his pay, and answering a seemingly casual inquiry relative to the fact that he had heard naught of Gilfillan and the other express, was dismissed without being subjected to greater urgency.

The two maintained silence for a time, the coal dying in Captain Stuart's pipe as he absently contemplated the fireless chimney-place filled now with boughs of green pine.

Demeré spoke first. "If we can get no communication with Colonel Montgomery it means certain death to all the garrison."

"Sooner or later," assented Stuart.

The problem stayed with them all that night. They were forced to maintain a cheerful casual guise in the presence of their little public, and the appearance of the express put great heart into the soldiery. The fact that the commandant was in the immediate receipt of advices from Colonel Montgomery and his victorious army seemed itself a pledge of safety. The express was turned loose among them to rehearse the exploits of Montgomery's troops,—the splendid forced marches they made; the execution of their marksmanship; the terror that the Cherokees manifested of their sputtering grenades, hurled exploding into the ambuscades by the

- 137 -

stalwart grenadiers at the word,—"Fall on"; the interest of the Indians in the sound of the bagpipes and in the national dress, the plaid and philibeg, of the Highlanders, which, although now generally proscribed by law, was continued as a privilege granted to those enlisted in regiments in the British army. He told of the delight of the Highlanders in the sight of the Great Smoky Mountains, how they rejoiced to climb the crags and steep ravines even of the foothills. He repeated jokes and gibes of the camp outside Fort Prince George, for Montgomery had overtaken him and raised the siege before he reached the fort, so difficult was the slow progress of the express among the inimical Cherokees. He detailed Colonel Montgomery's relish of the sight of a piece of field artillery which Ensign Milne showed him; that officer had mounted it one day before the siege when he was with a detail that he had ordered into the woods to get fuel for the post, and a band of Cherokees had descended upon him,—"a Quaker," he called it; you might have heard Colonel Montgomery laugh two hundred miles to Fort Loudon, for of course it wouldn't fight,—a very powerful Friend, indeed,—only a black log mounted between two wheels, which the soldiers had been in the habit of using to ease up the loads of wood. But the Indians were deceived, and with their terror of artillery got out of range in short order, and the soldiers made their way back into the fort under the protection of their "little Quaker."

When the barracks were lost in slumber, and the parade was deserted but for the moon, and the soft wind, and the echo of the tramp of the sentry, Captain Stuart went over to Captain Demeré's house, and there until late the two discussed the practicabilities, that each, like a blind trail, promised thoroughfare and led but to confusion. The officers did not dare to call for volunteers to carry dispatches to Montgomery, in the face of the fact that the express just arrived could not be prevailed on to return. Without, moreover, some assurance of the safety of the messengers previously sent out, no man would now so lightly venture his life as to seek to slip through the vigilant savage hordes. To explain the terrors of the crisis to the garrison would be to have the ferocious Cherokees without, and panic, mutiny, and violence within. Yet a man must go; a man who would return; a man who would risk torture and death twice. "For we must have some assurance of the delivery of our dispatches," Stuart argued. "I am anxious as to the homing qualities of our dove that we are about to send out of this ark of ours," he said, as he lay stretched out at full length on the buffalo rug on the floor, in the moonlight that fell so peacefully in at the window of his friend's bedroom. Demeré was recumbent on his narrow camp-bed, so still, so silent, that more than once Stuart asked him if he slept.

"How can I sleep,—with this sense of responsibility?" Demeré returned, reproachfully.

- 138 -

But Stuart slept presently, waking once to reply to Demeré's remark that a married man would have the homing quality desired, the fort holding his family; Stuart declared that no one would be willing to leave wife and children to such protection as other men might have presence of mind to give them in a desperate crisis. The mere communication might create a panic.

"Of all things," said Stuart, as he lay at his stalwart length, his long, fair hair blowsing in the wind over the rug, "I am most afraid of fear."

When Demeré presently asked him if he were quite comfortable down there, his unceremonious presence placing him somewhat in the position of guest, his silence answered for him, and he did not again speak or stir until the drums were sounding without and the troops were falling in line for roll-call.

Neither gave sign of their vigil; they both were exceedingly spruce, and fresh, and well set up, to sustain the covert scrutiny of the garrison, who regarded them as a sort of moral barometer of the situation, and sought to discern in their appearance the tenor of Montgomery's official dispatches.

That morning, when Stuart went with his spy-glass to reconnoiter from the tower of one of the block-houses, he noted, always keenly observant, a trifle of confusion, as he entered, in the manner of the sentinel,—the smart, fair-haired, freckled-faced young soldier whose services were sometimes used as orderly, and whose name was Daniel Eske. The boy immediately sought to appear unconcerned. The officer asked no question. He raised the glass to his eye and in one moment discerned, amongst the laurel jungles close to the river, an Indian, a young girl, who suddenly lifted her arm and gracefully waved her hand toward the bastion. Stuart lowered the glass and gravely looked a grim inquiry at the young soldier.

Daniel Eske answered precipitately: "For God's sake, sir, don't let this go against me. I'm not holding any communication with the enemy,—the red devils. That baggage, sir, has been twice a-waving her hand to me when I have been on guard here. I never took no notice, so help me God,— Captain,—I—"

The distance being minimized by the lens, Stuart could discern all the coquettish details of the apparition; the garb of white dressed doe skin—a fabric as soft and flexible, the writers of that day tell us, as "velvet cloth"— the fringed borders of which were hung with shells and bits of tinkling metal; the hair, duly anointed, black and lustrous, dressed high on the head and decorated with small wings of the red bird; many strings of red beads dangled about the neck, and the moccasons were those so highly valued by the Indians, painted an indelible red. With a definite realization of the

- 139 -

menace of treachery in her presence, Stuart's face was stern indeed as he looked at her. All at once his expression changed.

"Do as I bid you," he said to the sentry, suddenly remembering "Wing-of-the-Flying-Whip-poor-will," and her talk of the handsome young orderly with his gold hair and freckles, and his gossip touching the Scotchman's beautiful French wife, whom she regarded merely as a captive. "Wait till she waves again. But no,—she is going,—show yourself at the window,—must risk a shot now and then."

The loop-hole here attained the size of a small window, being commanded only by the river, which would expose any marksman to a direct return fire.

"Now, she sees you," exclaimed Stuart, as the young fellow's face appeared in the aperture, gruff, sheepish, consciously punished and ridiculous,—how could he dream of Stuart's scheme! "Take off your hat. Wave it to her. Wave it with a will, man! There,—she responds. That will do." Then, with a change of tone, "I advise you, for your own good, to stay away from that window, for if any man in this garrison is detected in engaging in sign language with the enemy he will certainly be court-martialed and shot."

"Captain," protested the boy, with tears in his eyes, "I'd as lieve be shot now, sir, as to have you think I would hold any communication with the enemy,—the warriors. As to that girl,—the forward hussy came there herself. I took no notice of her waving her hand. I'd—"

But Captain Stuart was half down the ladder, and, despite young Eske's red coat, and the fact that he smelled powder with more satisfaction than perfume, and could hear bullets whizzing about his head without dodging, and had made forced marches without flinching, when he could scarce bear his sore feet to the ground, the tears in his eyes overflowed upon the admired freckles on his cheek, and he shed them for the imputation of Captain Stuart's warning as to communicating with the enemy.

That officer had forgotten him utterly, except as a factor in his plan. He sat so jocund and cheerful beside the table in the great hall that Odalie, summoned thither, looked at him in surprise, thinking he must have received some good news,—a theory corrected in another moment by the downcast, remonstrant, doubtful expression on Demeré's face. He rose to offer her a chair, and Stuart, closing the door behind her, replied to something he had already said:—

"At all events it is perfectly safe to lay the matter before Mrs. MacLeod."

To this Demeré responded disaffectedly, "Oh, certainly, beyond a doubt."

"Mrs. MacLeod," said Stuart deliberately, and growing very grave, as he sat opposite to her with one hand on the table, "we are trusting very deeply to your courage and discretion when I tell you that our situation here is very dangerous, and the prospect nearly desperate."

She looked at him silently in startled dismay. She thought of her own, of all that she loved. And for a moment her heart stood still.

"You know that all received methods, all military usages, fail as applied to Indian warfare. You can be of the greatest service to us in this emergency. Will you volunteer?" There was a little smile at the corner of Stuart's lip as he looked at her steadily.

"No, no, I protest," cried Demeré. "Tell her first what she is to do."

"No," said Stuart, "when you agreed to the plan you expressly stipulated that you were to have no responsibility. Now if Mrs. MacLeod volunteers it is as a soldier and unquestioningly under orders."

"It is sudden," hesitated Odalie. "May I tell my husband?"

"Would he allow you to risk yourself?" asked Stuart. "And yet it is for yourself, your husband, your child, the garrison,—to save all our lives, God willing."

Odalie's color rose, her eyes grew bright. "I know I can trust you to make the risk as slight as it may be,—to place me in no useless danger. I volunteer."

The two men looked at her for one moment, their hearts in their eyes.

Then Captain Stuart broke out with his reassuring raillery. "I always knew it,—such a proclivity for the military life! In the king's service at last."

Odalie laughed, but Captain Demeré could not compass a smile.

Stuart's next question she thought a bit of his fun. "Have you here," he said, with deep gravity, "some stout gown, fashioned with plaits and fullness in the skirt, and a cape or fichu,—is that what you call it,—about the shoulders? And, yes,—that large red hood, calash, that you wore the first day you arrived at the fort,"—his ready smile flickered,—"on an understanding so little pleasing to your taste. Go get them on, and meet me at the northwestern bastion."

The young soldier, Daniel Eske, still standing guard in the block-house tower, looked out on a scene without incident. The river shone in the clear June daylight; the woods were dark, and fresh with dew and deeply green, and so dense that they showed no token of broken boughs and riven hole, results of the cannonade they had sustained, which still served to keep at a distance, beyond the range of the guns, the beleaguering cordon of savages, and thus prevent surprise or storm. Nevertheless there were occasional

- 141 -

lurking Indians, spies, or stragglers from the main line, amongst the dense boughs of the blooming rhododendron; he saw from time to time skulking painted faces and feathers fluttering from lordly scalp-locks, which rendered so much the more serious and probable the imputation of communicating with the enemy that the presence and gestures of Choo-qualee-qualoo, still lingering there, had contrived to throw upon him. Her folly might have cost him his life. He might have been sentenced to be shot by his own comrades, discovered to be holding communication with the enemy, and that enemy the Cherokees,—good sooth!

Suddenly rampant in his mind was a wild strange suspicion of treachery. His abrupt cry, "Halt, or I fire!" rang sharply on the air, and his musket was thrust through the window, aiming in intimidation down alongside the parapet, where upon the exterior slope of the rampart the beautiful Carolina girl, the French wife of the Scotch settler, had contrived to creep through the embrasure below the muzzle of the cannon, for the ground had sunk a trifle there with the weight of the piece or through some defect of the gabions that helped build up the "cheek," and she now stood at full height on the berm, above the red clay slope of the scarp, signing to Choo-qualee-qualoo with one hand, and with the other motioning toward the muzzle of his firelock, mutely imploring him to desist.

How did she dare! The light tint of her gray gown rendered her distinct against the deep rich color of the red clay slope; her calash, of a different, denser red, was a mark for a rifle that clear day a long way off. He was acutely conscious of those skulking braves in the woods, all mute and motionless now, watching with keen eyes the altercation with the sentry, and he shuddered at her possible fate, even while, with an unrealized mental process, doubts arose of her loyalty to the interests of the garrison, which her French extraction aided her strange, suspicious demonstration to foster. He flushed with a violent rush of resentment when he became aware that Choo-qualee-qualoo was signing to him also, with entreating gestures, and so keen-eyed had the Indian warfare rendered him that he perceived that she was prompted to this action by a brave,—he half fancied him Willinawaugh,—who knelt in the pawpaw bushes a short distance from the Cherokee girl and spoke to her ever and anon.

"One step further and I fire!" he called out to Odalie, flinching nevertheless, as he looked down into her clear, hazel, upturned eyes. Then overwhelmed by a sense of responsibility he raised the weapon to fire into the air and lifted the first note of a wild hoarse cry for "Corporal of the guard,"—and suddenly heard O'Flynn's voice behind him:—

"Shet up, ye blethering bull-calf! The leddy's actin' under orders."

And not only was O'Flynn behind him but Stuart.

- 142 -

"Sign to Mrs. MacLeod that she may go," said that officer, "but not for long. Shake your head,—seem doubtful. Then take your hat and wave it to the Cherokee wench, as if you relent for her sake!"

"Oh, sir,—I can't," exclaimed the young soldier even while he obeyed, expressing the revolt in his mind against the action of his muscles.

"It's mighty hard to kape the girls away from ye, but we will lend ye a stick nex' time," said Corporal O'Flynn, in scornful ridicule of his reluctance, not aware of the imputation of colloguing with the enemy to which the long-range flirtation with Choo-qualee-qualoo had seemed to expose him in Captain Stuart's mind.

Captain Stuart had placed in a loop-hole the muzzle of a firelock, which he sighted himself. O'Flynn leveled another, both men being of course invisible from without; as the young sentinel obeyed the order to openly lounge in the window and look toward Choo-qualee-qualoo he could see within the parapet that the gunners of the battery were standing to their shotted pieces, Captain Demeré, himself, in command. With this provision against capture, or for revenge, one might fear, rather than protection, Odalie took her way down the steep slope amongst the impeding stakes of the fraises, thickly sown, and looking, it might seem, like dragons' teeth in process of sprouting. More than once she paused and glanced up at the sentinel leaning in the window with his firelock and entreated by signs his forbearance, which he seemed to accord qualified, doubtful, and limited. She soon crossed the ditch, the glacis, so swift she was, so sure and free of step, and paused in the open space beyond; then Choo-qualee-qualoo, too, began to advance. Better protected was the Cherokee girl, for she carried in her hand, and now and again waved, laughingly, as if for jest, a white flag, a length of fluttering cambric and lace.

"By the howly poker!" exclaimed Corporal O'Flynn, beneath his breath, "that is the cravat of a man of quality,—some British officer of rank, belike."

He glanced with anxiety at Captain Stuart, whose every faculty seemed concentrated on the matter in hand.

"The Cherokees know that a white flag is a sign which we respect, and that that squaw is as safe with it as if she were the commandant of the post. I only wish Mrs. MacLeod could have a like security." This aspiration had the effect of fastening O'Flynn's eye and mind to the sighting of his firelock and obliterating his speculations concerning the cravat as spoil stripped from some slain officer of rank.

The two women met in the open space, with the rifles of how many keen-sighted, capricious savages leveled toward the spot Demeré hardly dared to think, as he watched Odalie in a sort of agony of terror that he might have felt had she been a cherished sister. They stood talking for a time in the attitudes and the manner of their age, which was near the same, swinging a little apart now and then, and coming together with suddenly renewed interest, and again, with free, casual gestures, and graceful, unconstrained pose, they both laughed, and seemed to take a congenial pleasure in their meeting. They sat down for a time on a bit of grass,—the sward springing anew, since it was so little trodden in these days, and with a richness that blood might have added to its vigor. Odalie answered, with apparent unsuspiciousness, certain shrewd questions concerning the armament of the fort, the store of ammunition, the quantity of provisions, the manner in which Stuart and Demeré continued to bear themselves, the expectation held out to the garrison of relief from any quarter,—questions which she was sure had never originated in the brain of Choo-qualee-qualoo, but had been prompted by the craft of Willinawaugh. Odalie, too, had been carefully prompted, and Stuart's anticipatory answers were very definitely delivered, as of her own volition. Then they passed to casual chatting, to the presentation of a bauble which Odalie had brought, and which seemed to touch Choo-qualee-qualoo to the point of detailing as gossip the fact that the attack on the white people had been intended to begin at MacLeod Station, Willinawaugh retaining so much resentment against the Scotchman to whom he had granted safe-conduct, thinking him French, when he only had a French squaw as a captive. Savanukah, who really spoke French, had made capital of it, and had rendered Willinawaugh's pretensions ridiculous in the eyes of the nation, for Willinawaugh had always boasted, to Savanukah at least, that he understood French, although it was beneath his dignity to speak it. This was done to reduce Savanukah's linguistic achievements, and to put him in the position of a mere interpreter of such people, when Savanukah was a great warrior, and yet could speak many languages, like the famous Baron Des Johnnes. And what was there now at MacLeod Station? Nothing: stockade, houses, fields, all burnt! Great was the wrath of Willinawaugh!

This talk, however, was less to the taste of Choo-qualee-qualoo than questions and answers concerning the young sentinel, whom the Cherokees had named Sekakee, "the grasshopper," as he was so loquacious; she often paused to put the strings of red beads into her mouth, and to gaze away at the glittering reaches of the river with large liquid eyes, sending now and then a glance at the window where that gruff young person leaned on his firelock. Savanukah's wife said Sekakee must be hungry, Choo-qualee-qualoo told Odalie. Was Sekakee hungry? She would bring him some beans. Savanukah said they would all be hungry soon. And the fort would be the Indians', and there would be nobody in the land but the Cherokees, and the French to carry on trade with them—was Odalie not glad that she was

French?—for there had been great fighting with the English colonel's men, and Willinawaugh had told her to tell the captains English both that fact: much blood did they shed of their own blood, as red as their own red coats!

Odalie regarded this merely as an empty boast, the triumphs of Montgomery's campaign rife this day in the garrison, but it made her tremble to listen. Nevertheless, she had the nerve to walk with Choo-qualee-qualoo almost to the water-side, near the shadowy covert of the dense woods. Nothing lurked there now,—no flickering feather, no fiercely gay painted face. Her confidence seemed the ally of the Indians. The French captive of the Carolina Scotchman would be to them like a spy in the enemy's camp!

Perhaps the ordeal made the greater draughts on the courage of the men who stood in the shelter of the works and sighted the guns. The tension grew so great as she lingered there in the shadows that cold drops stood on Demeré's face, and the hand with which Stuart held the firelock trembled.

"It's a woman that can't get enough of anything," O'Flynn muttered to himself. "I'll have the lockjaw in me lungs, for I'm gittin' so as I can't move me chist to catch me breath."

But Odalie turned at last, and still signaling anxiously to the sentry, as if to implore silence and forbearance, she crossed the open space with her swift, swinging step, climbed the red clay slope among the spiked staves of the fraises, knelt down, slipped through the embrasure, and was lifted to her feet by Demeré, while the gunners stood by looking on, and smiling and ready to cry over her.

Twice afterward, the same detail, all enjoined to secrecy, loaded their cannon, and stood with burning matches ready to fire at the word, while the maneuver was repeated; an interval of a day or so was allowed to elapse on each occasion, and the hour was variously chosen—when it was possible for the French woman to escape, as Choo-qualee-qualoo was given to understand. Both times Demeré protested, although he had accorded the plan his countenance, urging the capricious temper of the Indians, who might permit Mrs. MacLeod's exit from the fort one day, and the next, for a whim, or for revenge toward her husband, who had incurred their special enmity for outwitting them on his journey hither, shoot her through the heart as she stood on the crest of the counterscarp. And of what avail then the shotted cannon, the firelocks in the loop-holes!

"You know they are for our own protection," he argued. "Otherwise we could not endure to see the risk. The utmost we can do for her is to prevent capture, or if she is shot to take quick vengeance. Loading the cannon only saves our nerves."

"I admit it," declared Stuart,—"a species of military sal-volatile. I never pretended to her that she was protected at all, or safe in any way,—she volunteered for a duty of great hazard."

Demeré, although appreciating the inestimable value to the garrison of the opportunity, was relieved after the third occasion, when Alexander MacLeod, by an accident, discovered the fact of these dangerous sorties in the face of a savage enemy, no less capriciously wicked and mischievous than furious and blood-thirsty. His astonished rage precluded speech for a moment, and the two officers found an opportunity to get him inside the great hall, and turning the key Stuart put it in his pocket.

"Now, before you expend your wrath in words that we may all regret," he said, sternly, "you had best understand the situation. Your wife is not a woman to play the fool under any circumstances, and for ourselves we are not in heart for practical jokes. Mr. MacLeod, we have here more than three hundred mouths to feed daily, nearly three hundred the mouths of hearty, hungry men, and we have exhausted our supply of corn and have in the smoke-house barely enough salted meat to sustain us for another fortnight. Then we shall begin to eat the few horses. We are so closely beleaguered that it has proved impossible to get an express through that cordon of savages to the country beyond. To communicate with Colonel Montgomery as early as practicable is the only hope of saving our lives. Mrs. MacLeod's sorties from the fort are a part of our scheme—the essential part. You may yet come to think the dearest boon that fate could have given her would have been a ball through her brain as she stood on the escarp—so little her chances are worth!"

This plain disclosure staggered MacLeod. He had thought the place amply victualed. A rising doubt of the officers' capacity to manage the situation showed in his face.

Stuart interpreted the expression. "You see,—the instant disaster is suggested you can't rely on us,—even you! And if that spirit were abroad in the garrison and among the settlers, we should have a thousand schemes in progress, manipulated by people not so experienced as we, to save themselves first and—perhaps the others. The ammunition might be traded to the Cherokees for a promise of individual security. The gates might be opened and the garrison delivered into the enemy's hands by two or three as the price of their own lives. Such a panic or mutiny might arise as would render a defense of the place impracticable, and the fort be taken by storm and all put to the sword, or death by torture. We are keeping our secret as well as we can, hoping for relief from Montgomery, and scheming to receive assurance of it. We asked Mrs. MacLeod's help, and she gave it!"

The logic of this appeal left MacLeod no reply. "How could you!" he only exclaimed, glancing reproachfully at his wife.

"That is what I have always said," cried Stuart, gayly, perceiving that the crisis was overpast. "How could she!"

There was no more that Odalie could do, and that fact partially reconciled the shuddering MacLeod to the past, although he felt he could hardly face the ghastly front of the future. And he drew back wincingly from the unfolding plans. As for Odalie, the next day she spent in her room, the door barred, her hair tossed out of its wonted perfection of array, her dress disordered, her face and eyes swollen with weeping, and when she heard the great guns of the fort begin to send forth their thunder, and the heavy shot crashing among the boughs of the forest beyond, she fell upon her knees, then rose, wild and agitated, springing to the door, yet no sooner letting down the bar than again replacing it, to fall anew upon her knees and rise once more, too distraught for the framing of a prayer.

Yet at this same moment Mrs. MacLeod, in her familiar gray serge gown and red calash, was seen, calm and decorous, walking slowly across the parade in the direction of the great hall of the northwest bastion. The soldiers who met her doffed their hats with looks of deep respect. Now and again she bowed to a settler with her pretty, stately grace,—somewhat too pronounced an elegance for the wife of so poor a man as MacLeod, it was thought, he being of less ornamental clay. She hesitated at the door of the block-house, with a little air of diffidence, as might befit a lady breaking in upon the time of men presumed to be officially busy. The door opened, and with a bow of mingled dignity and deprecation she entered, and as the door closed, Hamish dropped the imitation of her manner, and bounded into the middle of the room with a great gush of boyish laughter, holding out both arms and crying, "Don't I look enticing! To see the fellows salaaming to the very ground as I came across the parade!—what are you doing to my frock, Captain Demeré?" he broke off, suddenly. "It's just right. Odalie fixed it herself."

"Don't scuffle up these frills so," Captain Demeré objected. "Mrs. MacLeod is wont to wear her frock precisely."

"Did O'Flynn mistake you for Mrs. MacLeod?" asked Stuart, relishing the situation despite his anxiety.

"I wish you could have seen the way he drew down that red Irish mouth of his," said Hamish, with a guffaw, "looking so genteel and pious!"

"I think it passes," said Demeré, who was not optimistic; but now he too was smiling a little.

"It passes!" cried Stuart, triumphantly.

For the height of Odalie and Hamish was exactly the same—five feet eight inches. Hamish, destined to attain upward of six feet, had not yet all his growth. The full pleated skirt with the upper portion drawn up at the hips, and the cape about the shoulders, obviated the difference between Odalie's delicately rounded slenderness and Hamish's lank angularity. The cape of the calash, too, was thrown around the throat and about the chin and mouth, and as she was wont to hold her head down and look up at you from out the dusky red tunnel of its depths the difference in the complexion and the expression of the hazel eyes of each was hardly to be noticed in passing. To speak would have been fatal, but Hamish had been charged not to speak. His chestnut curls, brushed into a glossy similarity, crept out and lay on the folds of the red cape of the calash with a verisimilitude that seemed almost profane.

Admonished by Stuart to have heed of long steps, and the dashing swing of his habitual gait, he was leaning on Sandy's arm, as they went out, in an imitation of Odalie's graceful manner. The young sentry, Daniel Eske,—no one else was permitted at these times to stand guard in this block-house tower,—noted this, with the usual maneuver of Mrs. MacLeod's escape through the embrasure, and he was filled with ire. He had fancied that her husband did not know of this recklessness, as he was half inclined to think it, although evidently some fine-spun scheme of Captain Stuart's; it seemed especially futile this evening, so near sunset, and the odd circumstance of the cannonade having sufficed to clear every Indian out of the forest and the range of the guns. Mrs. MacLeod could not speak to Choo-qualee-qualoo now, he argued within himself; the girl would not be there in the face of this hot fire! How rapidly Mrs. MacLeod walked; only once she paused and glanced about her as if looking for the Cherokee girl,—what folly!—for with a flash of fire and a puff of white smoke, and a great sweeping curve too swift to follow with the eye, each successive ball flew from the cannon's mouth over her head and into the woods beyond.

From the opposite bank of the river an Indian, crouched in the cleft of a rock, yet consciously out of the range, watched her progress for one moment, then suddenly set off at a swift pace, doubtless to fetch the young squaw, so that when the firing should cease she could ascertain from the French woman what the unusual demonstration of the cannonade might signify.

It was only for a moment that the sentry's attention was thus diverted, but when he looked again the gray gown, the red calash, the swiftly moving figure had disappeared. The gunners had been ordered to cease firing, and the usual commotion of sponging out the bore, and reloading the guns, and replacing all the appliances of their service, was interrupted now and again by the men looking anxiously through the embrasure for Mrs. MacLeod's return. They presently called up an inquiry to the sentinel in the tower, presuming upon the utility of the secret service to excuse this breach of discipline. "Why," said the soldier, "I took my eye off her for one minute and she disappeared."

"You mean you shut your eyes for five minutes," said Corporal O'Flynn, gruffly, having just entered. "Captain Stuart told me that he himself opened the little gate and let her in by the sally-port. And there she is now, all dressed out fresh again, walking with her husband on the parade under the trees. An' yonder is the Injun colleen,—got here too late! Answer her, man, according to your orders."

Against his will the young sentinel leaned out of the window with a made-to-order smile, and as Choo-qualee-qualoo waved her hand and pointed to the empty path along which Odalie was wont to come, he intimated by signs that she had waited but was obliged to return to the fort and was now within, and he pointed down to the gorge of the bastion. To-morrow when there should be an eastern sky she would come out, and Choo-qualee-qualoo signed that she would meet her. Then she lingered, waving her hand now and again on her own account, and he dutifully flourished his hat.

"Gosh," he exclaimed, "if treachery sticks in the gizzard like this pretense there is no use in cord or shot,—the fellow does for himself!"

He was glad when the lingering twilight slipped down at last and put an end to the long-range flirtation, for however alert an interest he might have developed, were it voluntary, its utility as a military maneuver blunted its zest. Choo-qualee-qualoo had sped away to her home up the river; the stars were in the sky, and in broken glimmers reflected in the ripples of the current. The head-men among the cordon, drawn around Fort Loudon, sat in circles and discussed the possible reasons of the sudden furious cannonade, and the others of minor tribal importance listened and adjusted their own theories to the views advanced; the only stragglers were the spies whom the cannonade had driven from the woods that afternoon, now venturing back into the neighborhood, looking at the lights of the fort, hearing often hilarious voices full of the triumph of Montgomery's foray, and sometimes finding on the ground the spent balls of the cannonade.

It had so cleared the nearer spaces that it had enabled Hamish, in a guise become familiar to them, to gain the little thicket where Choo-qualee-qualoo and Odalie were wont to conclude their talks. Close by was the mouth of the cavernous passage that led to MacLeod's Station, which no Indians knew the white people had discovered. With a sudden plunge the boy was lost to sight in its labyrinthine darkness, and when Hamish

MacLeod emerged at the further end five miles away, in his own garb, which he had worn beneath the prim feminine attire,—this he had carefully rolled into a bundle and stowed in a cleft in the rocks of the underground passage,—he issued into a night as sweet, as lonely, and as still, in that vast woodland, as if there were no wars or rumors of wars in all the earth. But, alas! for the sight of Odalie's home that she had loved and made so happy, and where he had been as cherished as Fifine herself,—all grim, charred ashes; and poor Dill's cabin!—he knew by this time that Dill was dead, very dead, or he would have come back to them. The fields, too, that they had sown, and that none would reap, trampled and torn, and singed and burnt! Hamish gave but one sigh, bursting from an overcharged heart; then he was away at full speed in the darkness that was good to him, and the only friend he had in the world with the power to help him and his.

Captain Demeré that night was more truly cheerful than he had been for a long time, despite his usual port of serene, although somewhat austere, dignity.

"The boy has all the homing qualities you desired in an express," he said to Stuart. "He will come back to his brother's family as certainly as a man with wife and children, and yet in quitting them he leaves no duty to devolve on others."

"Moreover," said Stuart, "we have the satisfaction of knowing that he safely reached the mouth of the underground passage without detection. He could not have found the place in a dark night. In the moonlight he would have been seen, and even if we had protected his entrance by a cannonade, and cleared the woods, his exit at the other end of the passage would have been intercepted. Disguised as Mrs. MacLeod, seeking to meet Choo-qualee-qualoo in bold daylight, he passed without a suspicion on the part of the Indians. And we know that the exit of the passage at MacLeod Station is fully three miles in the rear of the Indian line. I feel sure that the other two expresses never got beyond the Indian line. This is the best chance we have had."

"And a very good chance," said Demeré.

Stuart could but laugh a little, remembering that Demeré had thought the plan impracticable, and, although there was no other opportunity possible, had protested against it on the point of danger involved to Mrs. MacLeod. Stuart, himself, had quaked on this score, and had seized on this ingenious device only as a last resort.

"Mrs. MacLeod is fine timber for a forlorn hope," he said reflectively.

The matter had been so sedulously guarded from the knowledge of the garrison, save such share as was of necessity divulged to the men who fired the guns, the young sentinel, and Corporal O'Flynn,—and even they were not aware that there had been a sortie of any other person than Mrs. MacLeod,—that Hamish's absence passed unnoticed for several days, and when it was announced that he had been smuggled out of the fort, charged with dispatches to Colonel Montgomery, no one dreamed of identifying him with the apparition in the gray gown whom the gunners had seen to issue forth and return no more. Even Corporal O'Flynn accepted the statement, without suspicion, that Captain Stuart had let Mrs. MacLeod in at the sally-port. These excursions, he imagined, were to secure information from Choo-qualee-qualoo.

The announcement that an express was now on the way was made to encourage the men, for the daily ration had dwindled to a most meager portion, and complaints were rife on every hand both among the soldiery and the families of the settlers. A wild, startled look appeared in many eyes, as if some ghastly possibility had come within the range of vision, undreamed-of before. The facts, however, that the commandant was able to still maintain a connection beyond the line of blockading Cherokees, that Hamish had been gone for more than a week, that decisive developments of some sort must shortly ensue, that the officers themselves kept a cheerful countenance, served to stimulate an effort to sustain the suspense and the gnawing privation. Continual exertions were made in this direction.

"Try to keep up the spirits of the men," said Demeré to O'Flynn one day.

"I do, sor," returned O'Flynn, his cheek a trifle pale and sunken. "I offer meself to 'm as an example. I says to the guard only to-day, sor, says I,— 'Now in affliction ye see the difference betune a person of quality, and a common spalpeen.' An' they wants to know who is this person of quality, sor. And I names meself, sor, being descended from kings of Oirland. An', would ye belave me, sor, not one of them bog-trotting teagues but what was kings of Oirland, too, sor."

Corporal O'Flynn might have thought his superior officer needed cheering too, for the twinkle in his eye had lost none of its alluring Celtic quality.

The distressing element of internecine strife and bickerings was presently added to the difficulties of the officers, who evidently faced a situation grievous enough in itself without these auxiliary troubles. Certain turbulent spirits opined loudly that they, the humbler people, had advantage taken of them,—that the officers' mess was served in a profusion never abated, while the rest starved. Captain Stuart and Captain Demeré would not notice this report, but the junior officers were vehement in their protestations that they and their superiors had had from the beginning of the scarcity the identical rations served out to the others, and that their gluttony had not reduced the general supply. The quartermaster-sergeant confirmed this, yet

- 151 -

who believed him, as Mrs. Halsing said, for he carried the keys and could favor whom he would. That he did not favor himself was obvious from the fact that his once red face had grown an ashen gray, and the cheeks hung in visible cords and ligaments under the thrice-folded skin, the flesh between having gradually vanished. The African cook felt his honor so touched by this aspersion on his master's methods that he carried his kettles and pans out into the center of the parade one day and there, in insubordinate disregard of orders, cooked in public the scanty materials of the officers' dinner. And having thus expressed his indignant rage he sat down on the ground among his kettles and pans and wept aloud in a long lugubrious howl, thus giving vent to his grief, and requiring the kind offices of every friend he had in the fort to pacify him and induce him to remove himself, his pans, and his kettles from this unseemly conspicuousness.

At the height of the trouble, when Stuart and Demeré, themselves anxious and nervous, and greatly reduced by the poor quality and scarcity of food, sat together and speculated on the problem of Montgomery's silence, and the continued absence of the express, and wondered how long this state of things could be maintained, yearning for, yet fearing the end,—talking as they dared not talk to any human being but each to the other,—Ensign Whitson burst into the room with an excited face and the news that there had been a fight over in the northeast bastion at the further side of the terrepleine.

Captain Stuart rose, bracing his nerves for the endurance of still more.

"A food riot? I have expected it. Have they broken into the smoke-house?"

Whitson looked wild for one moment. "Oh, no, sir,—not that!—not that! Two Irishmen at fisticuffs,—about the Battle of the Boyne!—Corporal O'Flynn and a settler."

For the first time in a week Stuart laughed with genuine hilarity. "Mighty well!" he exclaimed. "Let us settle the important questions between the Irish Catholics and the Irish Protestants before we go a step further!"

But Demeré was writhing under the realization of a relaxed discipline, although when O'Flynn presented himself in response to summons he was so crest-fallen and woe-begone and reduced, that Demeré had not the heart to take summary measures with the half-famished boxer.

"O'Flynn," he said, "do you deem this a fitting time to set the example of broils between the settlers and soldiers? Truly, I think we need but this to precipitate our ruin."

Stuart hastily checked the effect of this imprudent phrase by breaking in upon a statement of Corporal O'Flynn's, which seemed to represent his right arm as in some sort a free agent, mechanically impelled through the air, the hand in a clinched posture, in disastrous juxtaposition with the skulls of other people, and that he was not thinking, and would not have had it happen for nothing, and—

"But is the man an Irishman?" asked Stuart. "He has no brogue."

"Faith, sor," said the repentant O'Flynn, glad of the diversion, "he hits loike an Oirishman,—I don't think he is an impostor. My nose feels rather limber."

O'Flynn having been of great service in the crisis, they were both glad to pass over his breach of discipline as lightly as they might; and he doubtless reaped the benefit of their relief that the matter was less serious than they had feared.

The next day, however, the expected happened. The unruly element, partly of soldiers with a few of the settlers, broke into the smoke-house and discovered there what the commandant was sedulously trying to conceal,—nothing!

It stunned them for the moment. It tamed them. The more prudential souls began now to fear the attitude of the officers, to turn to them, to rely again upon their experience and capacity.

When the two captains came upon the scene, Demeré wearing the affronted, averse, dangerous aspect which he always bore upon any breach of discipline, and Stuart his usual cool, off-hand look as if the matter did not greatly concern him, they listened in silence to the clamor of explanations and expostulations, of criminations and recriminations which greeted them. Only a single sentence was spoken by either of them,—a terse low-toned order. Upon the word, Corporal O'Flynn with a squad of soldiers rushed briskly into the crowd, and in less than two minutes the rioters were in irons.

"Jedburgh justice!" said Stuart aside to Demeré, as they took their way back across the parade. "Hang 'em first, and try 'em afterward."

The bystanders might argue little from Demeré's reticent soldierly dignity, but Stuart's ringing laugh, as he spoke aside to his brother officer, his cheerful, buoyant, composed mien, restored confidence as naught less than the sound of Montgomery's bugles outside the works might have done. Doubtless he was apprised of early relief. Surely he did not look like a man who expected to live on horse-flesh in the midst of a mutinous garrison, with the wild savages outside, and within that terrible strain upon the courage,—the contemplation of the sufferings of non-combatants, the women and children, who had entered into no covenant and received no compensation to endure the varying chances of war.

Yet this prospect seemed close upon him before that day was done. The orderly routine had slipped again into its grooves. The hungry men, brisk, spruce, were going about their various military duties with an alacrity incongruous with their cadaverous aspect. The sentinels were posted as usual, and Captain Stuart, repairing according to his wont to a post of observation in the block-house tower of the northwest bastion, turned his glass upon the country beyond, lowered it suddenly, looking keenly at the lens, as if he could not believe his eyes, and again lifted it. There was no mistake. On the opposite side of the river, looking like some gigantic monkey capering along on a pair of thin bare legs, was a stalwart Indian, arrayed for the upper part of his person in a fine scarlet coat, richly laced, evidently the spoil from some British officer of high rank. Perhaps no apparition so grotesque ever sent a chill to so stout a heart. Stuart was no prophet, quotha. But he could see the worst when it came and stared him in the eyes.

CHAPTER XI

Stuart and Demeré argued the matter in their secret conclaves. Both admitted that although Montgomery had had only four or five men killed, among them no officers, on his first expedition, he might have again taken the field, and this was as they hoped. He was advancing; he must be near. The trophy of the fine red coat meant probably that he had lost an officer of value;—perhaps meant less—the personal disaster of the capture of baggage or the necessity of throwing it away. Montgomery had advanced,—that was indubitable. Nevertheless,—and perhaps it was the lowering influence of the scanty fare on which they had so long subsisted,—both officers dreaded the suspense less than the coming disclosure.

Stuart felt all his nerves grow tense late one day in the red July sunset, when there emerged from the copse of pawpaw bushes, close to the river where Odalie had once been wont to repair to talk to Choo-qualee-qualoo, a tall form, arrayed in a gray gown, a trifle ill-adjusted, with a big red calash drawn forward on the head, that walked at a somewhat slashing gait across the open space toward the glacis. He thanked heaven that Mrs. MacLeod was ill in her bed, although he had some twenty minutes ago been sending to her through her husband expressions of polite and heartfelt regret and sympathy.

"Why, I hardly thought Mrs. MacLeod was well enough to take a walk," he observed to the sentry. Daniel Eske naturally supposed that Mrs. MacLeod had slipped out before he had gone on duty, having just been sent to the relief of the previous sentinel. Stuart went down to the embrasure, assisted the supposed lady to her feet as she slipped through, and ceremoniously offered her his arm as she was about to plunge down the steep interior slope in a very boyish fashion. They found Demeré in the great hall, and both officers read the brief official dispatch with countenances of dismay.

"This says that you can explain the details," said Demeré, with dry lips and brightly gleaming eyes.

"Oh, yes," said Hamish. "All the time that I was at Fort Prince George the commandant was writing letters to Governor Bull—for Lyttleton has been appointed to Jamaica—and hustling off his expresses to South Carolina. He sent three, and said if he heard from none by return he would send more."

For this was the appalling fact that had fallen like a thunderbolt,—Colonel Montgomery had with his command quitted the country and sailed for New York. His orders were to strike a sudden blow for the relief of Carolina and return to head-quarters at Albany at the earliest possible moment. No word of the grievous straits of the garrison of Fort Loudon had reached him. He had, indeed, advanced from Fort Prince George, which he had made the base of his aggressive operations against the Cherokees, but not for the relief of Fort Loudon, for neither he nor the commandant of Fort Prince George knew that that post was in danger. The overtures to the Cherokees for peace having proved fruitless, Colonel Montgomery had sought to make peace by force. In pursuance of this further effort he pushed forward with great energy and spirit, but encountered throughout disasters so serious as to cripple his enterprise, culminating finally in a result equivalent to a repulse. The Indians, in the skulking methods peculiar to their warfare, harassed his march, hanging upon the flanks of the main body, and firing in detail from behind trees and rocks, from the depths of ravines and the summits of hills of the broken, rugged wilderness. Never did they present any front that it was possible to charge and turn. The advance-guard, approaching through a narrow valley, the town of Etchoee, which the Indians had abandoned, fell into an ambuscade of considerable strength, and there he lost Captain Morrison of the Rangers, and ten or twelve men who fell at the first fire. The vanguard, discouraged, began to give way, when the light infantry and grenadiers were detached for its support. They succeeded in locating the chief strength of the Cherokees sufficiently to drive the savages back, despite the disastrous results of their scattered fire. The main body, coming up, encamped near Etchoee, on a level space which proved, however, to be commanded by eminences in the vicinity. Thence the Indians poured destructive volleys into the British ranks, and only after repeated charges the soldiers succeeded in dislodging them. Impetuously attacked on the flank, the Cherokees suffered severely at the hands of the Royal Scots before being able to get out of their reach. The terrible aspect of the painted savages, and their nerve-thrilling whoops with which the woods resounded, failed also to affect the courage of the wild Highlanders, and all the troops fought with great ardor. But Colonel Montgomery deemed it impossible to penetrate further through the wilderness, hampered as he was by seventy wounded men whom he could not leave to the mercies of so savage an enemy, by the loss of many horses, by the necessity—which was yet almost an impossibility—of carrying a train of cattle and other provisions with him in so rugged, trackless, and heavily wooded a region, and relinquished the attempt, thinking the terrible losses which the Indians had sustained would prove sufficient punishment and dispose them to peace. He was even compelled to sacrifice a considerable portion of his stores, throwing away bags of flour in large numbers in order to effect the release of the packhorses to transport his wounded. His dead he sunk heavily weighted into the rivers, that the bodies might not be dragged from their graves and scalped by the Indians. His return march of sixty miles to Fort Prince

George, which was accomplished with great regularity, was marked by the same incidents that had characterized his advance,—the nettling fire of the masked enemy, the futile response, and the constant loss of men and horses.

And so he was gone, and all the hopes that had clustered about his advance had gone with him! To Fort Loudon remained only two remote chances,—that Governor Bull of South Carolina might be able to act on the belated information and send out an expedition of relief; yet this was to the last degree improbable, since the province, after its first expensive expedition against the Cherokees, had been compelled to appeal for its own protection to the British commander-in-chief, the militia being practically disabled by the ravages of smallpox. But even at the best could such an expedition reach them in time? The other possibility of succor lay in Virginia, and it was obvious wisdom to embrace both chances. Stuart knew that Demeré's quill, scraping over the paper, was fashioning the appeal to the royal governor of that province, even while Hamish was still speaking, and he, himself, wrote supplemental letters to other persons of note, that the news of their desolation, failing to carry in one direction, might be spread in another.

"Now, Hamish," he said, smiling behind the candle as he held the wax in it for the seal, "can you do as much again?"

"Where? When?" demanded Hamish, in surprise.

"To Virginia. To-night."

Hamish's eyes stretched very wide. "You won't wait for Governor Bull? The officers at Fort Prince George said they would lay their lives that Governor Bull would respond."

"We must try Virginia, too. My boy, we are starving. To-morrow we begin to eat the horses,—then there may be a dog or two."

Hamish rose precipitately. "Where is Sandy? Where is Odalie?"

Stuart pushed him back into his chair, sternly giving him to understand that the only possible hope of saving their lives was to get away as quickly as might be with the dispatches for Virginia.

"Without seeing Sandy and Odalie?" said Hamish, his lip quivering.

"We have not the time to spare. Besides, would they let you risk it again, even for them?"

And Hamish was suddenly diverted to telling of his risks, of all the escapes, by flood and fell, that he had made;—how often he had been shot at from ambush; how he had swum rivers; how he had repeatedly hidden from the

- 157 -

Indians by dropping himself down into the hollows of trees, and once how nearly he had come to getting out no more, the place being so strait that he could scarcely use his constricted muscles to climb up to the cavity that had let him in. He had not so much trouble on the return trip; Ensign Milne had procured for him a good horse, and a rifle—he had had a brace of pistols—the horse was a free goer—as fresh now as if he had not been a mile to-day.

"And where is he now?" asked Demeré, a look of anxiety on his face.

"At MacLeod Station, hitched there with a good saddle on him and saddle-bags half full of corn."

"Come, Hamish," said Stuart, rising, "you must be off; some Indian might find the horse."

Hamish's eyes filled with tears,—to leave Odalie and Sandy without a word! He could not endure for the men to see these tears, although they thought none the less well of him for them.

"Let me drop a tear in farewell for Odalie," he said, trying to be very funny, brushing his right eye with his right hand. "And for Sandy," his left eye with his left hand. "And Fifine," his right eye with his right hand. "And the cat," his left eye with his left hand.

There could be nothing unmanly or girlish in this jovial demonstration!

"Come, you zany!" exclaimed Stuart, affecting to think these tremulous farewells very jocose.

"Yes," said Demeré, seriously, "we do not know how soon the Indians may discover our use of that passage,—up to this time it has been our only hope."

Hamish gathered up his calash, and the precise Demeré assisted him to adjust it and his disordered dress more after the manner in which Odalie wore it. Hamish, as directed, took Stuart's arm as they went out, his eyes still full of tears, and for his life he could not control the tremor of emotion, not of fear, in the fibers of his hand, which he was sure the officer must note. But Stuart's attention was fixed on the skies. It was later than in those days when Odalie was wont to keep tryst with Choo-qualee-qualoo, now nearly a month ago. Still he fancied that in the afterglow of the sunset the Indians might discern the color and the style of the costume. Now and then a ball flew from the cannon to the woods, to clear the forest of too close observers,—whatever risk there was must needs be dared. The cannoneers summoned to this queer duty looked at "Mrs. MacLeod" curiously, as she slipped through the embrasure and made her way with a swinging agility down the slope amongst the fraises and then off through the gloaming at a fresh, firm pace. Then they gazed at Stuart, who presently bade them cease firing, and they had no excuse to wait to see her return. A queer move, they thought it, a very queer move!

Hope had grown so inelastic because of the taut tension to which its fine fibers had been subjected, that Stuart felt a thrill of merely mechanical apprehension when the next day Daniel Eske, the young soldier, came in, desiring to make a special report to him. While on guard duty he had heard a deep subterranean explosion, which had been reported to the officer of the day. Later, Choo-qualee-qualoo had come, waving her flag of truce, and after waiting vainly for Mrs. MacLeod, she had ventured up the slope of the scarp, knowing full well that she was safe under that white flag. She had brought a bag of beans, which she had given him,—he bit his lip and colored with vexation, consciously ridiculous in speaking of his feminine admirer to his superior officer,—and he had taken the opportunity to ask some questions about affairs outside the fort, upon which she detailed that an Indian—it was Savanukah—had seen Mrs. MacLeod, as he thought, enter the subterranean passage that used to lead to MacLeod Station. At first he had considered it a slight matter, since the Carolinian's French wife had come so often to talk to Choo-qualee-qualoo. But it somehow flashed into his mind how this woman had walked,—with what a long stride, with what strength, and how fast! And suddenly he realized that it was a man, despite the full skirts and flutterings of capes and calash. So Savanukah ran swiftly to his boat and pulled down the river, and made MacLeod Station just in time to see a youth, arrayed in buckskins, issue from the cave and mount a tethered horse. Savanukah fired at him, but without effect, and the young man wheeled in his saddle and returned the fire with such accuracy that even at the distance and in the twilight the ball, although nearly spent, struck Savanukah in the mouth with such force as to knock out a tooth. Then the boy made off with a tremendous burst of speed. And the gray gown and the calash which the youth had worn were found inside the passage. And great was the wrath of Willinawaugh! He had blown up with powder both ends of the passage,—like thunder, een-ta-qua ros-ke,—use could no more be made of it. But some were sorry, wishing the paleface to return by that way, so that he might be stabbed in the dark windings of the passage. This was impossible now, Choo-qualee-qualoo said, for the spring had burst forth, forced in a new direction, and was flooding all that part of the slope, flowing outside instead of within, and Willinawaugh could not now change its disposition if he would.

Stuart breathed more freely. If Hamish should return alone, which God forbid, and not with an armed force, the external changes wrought at MacLeod Station would preclude his effort to enter into the cavern, and force him to devise some other method of approach. He wondered at

Willinawaugh—to destroy so promising a trap! But rage may overpower at times the most foxy craft.

The dull days, dragging on, seemed each interminable while the beleaguered garrison watched the impassive horizon and awaited developments, and hoped against hope. The wonted routine came to be abridged of necessity; the men on their reduced fare were incapable of drill duty; the best hope was that they might make shift to stand to their arms should a sudden attack require the exertion of all their reserve force in the imminent peril of their lives. The diet of horse-flesh proved not only unpalatable but insanitary, perhaps because the animals had thus far shared the physical distresses of the siege, and were in miserable plight, and there were as many men on the sick list as the hospital could accommodate; this misfortune was mitigated to a degree when Choo-qualee-qualoo brought another bag of beans to the hero of the long-range flirtation, and he generously offered to share the food with his fellow-sufferers. Odalie suggested its devotion to hospital uses; and a few days of a certain potage which she compounded of the beans and her economic French skill, and administered with her own hands to the invalids, with her own compassionate smiles, and with a sauce of cheering words, put a number of the stouter fellows on their feet again.

The efforts to amuse and entertain had given way under the stress of a misery that could form no compact with mirth, but from time to time the officers made short spirited addresses to the troops to animate and encourage their hope, and continue to the utmost their power of resistance. And the exhalation of every sigh was with a thought of South Carolina, and the respiration of every breath was with a prayer toward Virginia.

As the number of horses had greatly diminished, and the discovery was made that certain lean dogs had gone to the kitchen on an errand far different from the one that used to lure them to the pots, about which they had been wont to greedily and piteously snuff and whine, the quiescent waiting and reliance on the judgment and the capacity of the commandant to extricate the garrison from this perilous plight gave way anew. Criticisms of the management grew rife. The return of Hamish MacLeod, at the moment when starvation seemed imminent, and his instant departure at so great a peril, for the circumstances of his escape had been learned by the soldiers from the confidences of Choo-qualee-qualoo to young Eske, who was always free with his tongue, implied that Hamish's earlier mission had failed, and that no troops were now on the march to their succor. They, too, had seen the capering Indian in the red coat of an officer of rank, the lace cravat of a man of quality which Choo-qualee-qualoo flourished, and they deduced a shrewd surmise of Montgomery's repulse. The men who had earliest revolted against the hardships now entertained rebellious sentiments and sought to foster them in others. Although, as ringleaders in the food riot, they had been summarily placed in irons, their punishment had been too brief perhaps for a salutary moral effect. Demeré's severity was always theoretical,—a mental attitude one might say. The hardship of adding shackles to the agonies of slow starvation so preyed upon his heart that he had ordered the prisoners released before a sober reflection had done its full work. The exemplary conduct, for a time, of the culprits had no sufficient counterpart in chastened hearts, for they nourished bitterness and secretly agitated mutiny.

The crisis came one morning when the meager supply of repulsive food had shrunken to the scope of a few days' rations, the quantity always dwindling in a regularly diminishing ratio; it had recently barely enabled the men to sustain the usual guard duty, and they lay about the parade at other times, or at full length on the porches of the barracks, too feeble and dispirited to stir hand or foot without necessity. Corporal O'Flynn, one of the few officers fit for duty, with a shade of pallor on his face a trifle more ghastly than that of starvation, reported that five men had failed to respond to roll-call, and upon investigation it was found that they had burrowed out of the fort in the darkness, seeking to desert to the enemy, but their intentions being mistaken, or their overtures scorned, they had been stabbed and scalped at the edge of the forest, and there their bodies were visible in the early rays of the sun.

"May become unpleasant when the wind shifts," remarked Stuart easily, and without emotion apparently, "but we are spared the duties of punishing deserters according to their deserts."

Demeré's face had shown a sudden nervous contraction but resumed its fixed reserved expression, and he said nothing.

Corporal O'Flynn's report, however, was not yet exhausted. He hesitated, almost choked. The blood rushed so scarlet to his face that one might have wondered, at the show it made, that he had so much of that essential element in circulation in his whole thin body. He lifted his voice as if to urge the concentration of Stuart's attention which seemed so casual—he had it the next moment.

"I feel like a traitor in tellin' it, sor," said O'Flynn, "I'm just one of the men meself, an' it breaks me heart intirely to go agin 'em with the officers. But me duty as a soldier is to the commandant of the fort, an' as a man to the poor women an' childer."

He choked again, so reluctant was he in unfolding the fact that this was but the first step, providentially disastrous, of a plan by which the fort and the officers were to be abandoned, the rank and file determining to throw themselves on the mercy of the savages, since even to die at their hands was better than this long and futile waiting for succor. Through Choo-qualee-qualoo some negotiations with the enemy had been set on foot, of which O'Flynn was unaware hitherto, being excluded from their councils as a non-commissioned officer, but after the result of the desertion in the early hours before dawn, Daniel Eske, thoroughly dismayed, had once more reverted to his reliance on the superior wisdom of the commandant, and had seen fit to disclose the state of affairs to the corporal, whose loyalty to his superior officers was always marked.

O'Flynn was commended, cautioned to be silent, and the door closed.

The two captains looked blankly at one another.

"The catastrophe is upon us," said Stuart. "Fort Loudon must fall."

In this extremity a council of war was held. Yet there seemed no course open even to deliberation. On the one hand rose mutiny, starvation, and desertion; but to surrender to such an enemy as the Cherokees meant massacre. Their terrible fate held them in a remorseless clutch! At last, with some desperate hope, such as the unsubstantial illusion with which drowning men catch at straws, that the Indians might make and keep terms, it was agreed that Captain Stuart, at his earnest desire, should be the officer to treat with the enemy and secure such terms of capitulation as they could be induced to hold forth.

It might be imagined that the little band of officers, in their hard stress, had become incapable of any further vivid emotion, but in vicarious terror they watched Stuart step forth boldly and alone from the sally-port, a white flag in his hand, and arrayed, in deference to the Indians' love of ceremony and susceptibility to compliment, in full uniform.

He stood on the parapet of the covered way, motionless and distinct, in the clear light of the morning, against the background of the great red clay embankments. He was evidently seen, for through a spy-glass Demeré in the block-house tower noted the instant stillness that fell like a spell upon the Indian line; the figures of the warriors, crouching or erect, seemed petrified in the chance attitude of the moment. That he was instantly recognized by skulking scouts in the woods was as evident. His tall, sinewy figure; his long, dense, blond hair, with its heavy queue hanging on the shoulders of his red coat; a certain daring, martial insouciance of manner, sufficiently individualized him to the far-sighted Cherokees, and the white flag in his hand—a token which they understood, although they did not always respect it—intimated that developments of moment in the conduct of the siege impended.

There was no sudden shrill whistling of a rifle ball, and Demeré, thinking of the fate of Coytmore on the river-bank at Fort Prince George, began to breathe more freely. A vague sense of renewed confidence thrilled through the watching group. Stuart had stipulated that he should go alone—otherwise he would not make the essay. The presence of two or three armed men, officers of the fort, intimated suspicion and fear, incurred danger, and yet, helpless among such numbers, afforded no protection. The others had yielded to this argument, for he knew the Indian character by intuition, it would seem. He was relying now, too, upon a certain personal popularity. He had somehow engaged the admiration of the Indians, yet without disarming their prejudice—a sort of inimical friendship. They all realized that any other man would have now been lying dead on the glacis with a bullet through his brain, if but for the sheer temptation to pick him off neatly as a target of uncommon interest, whatever his mission might have betokened.

How to accomplish this mission became a problem of an essential solution, and on the instant. Not a figure stirred of the distant Cherokee braves; not one man would openly advance within range of the great guns that carried such terror to the Indian heart. Stuart stood in momentary indecision, his head thrown back, his chin up, his keen, far-seeing gray-blue eyes fixed on the motionless Indian line. Through the heated August air the leaves of the trees seemed to quiver; the ripples of the river scintillated in the sun; not a breath of wind stirred; on the horizon the solidities of the Great Smoky Mountains shimmered ethereal as a mirage.

Suddenly Stuart was running, lightly, yet at no great speed; he reached the river-bank, thrust a boat out from the gravel, and with the flag of truce waving from the prow he pushed off from the shore, and began to row with long, steady strokes straight up the river. He was going to Choté!

The observers at Fort Loudon, petrified, stared at one another in blank amazement. The observers at the Cherokee camp were freed from their spell. The whole line seemed in motion. All along the river-bank the braves were speeding, keeping abreast of the swift little craft in the middle of the stream. The clamors of the guttural voices with their unintelligible exclamations came across the water.

It was like the passing of a flight of swallows. In less than five minutes the boat, distinctly visible, with those salient points of color, the red coat and the white flag against the silver-gray water, had rounded the bend; every Indian runner was out of sight; and the line of warriors had relapsed into their silent staring at the fort, where the garrison dragged out three hours of such poignant suspense as seldom falls to the lot of even unhappy men.

The sun's rays deepened their intensity; the exhausted, half-famished sentries dripped with perspiration, the effects of extreme weakness as well as of the heat, as they stood shouldering their firelocks and anxiously watching from the loop-holes of the block-house towers, the roofs of which, blistering in the sun, smelled of the wood in a close, breathless, suffocating odor which their nerves, grown sensitive by suffering, discriminated like a pain. The men off duty lay in the shadow of the block-houses, for the rows of trees had vanished to furnish fuel for the kitchen, or on the porches of the barracks, and panted like lizards; the officers looked at one another with the significance of silent despair, and believed Stuart distraught. Demeré could not forgive himself that he had been persuaded to agree that Stuart should appear. Beyond the out-works, however, they had had no dream of his adventuring. To try the effect of a personal appearance and invitation to a conference was the extent of the maneuver as it was planned. There was scant expectation in Fort Loudon that he would be again seen alive.

When the tension of the sun began to slacken and the heat to abate; when the wind vaguely flapped the folds of the flag with a drowsing murmur, as if from out of sleep; when the chirr of the cicada from the woods grew vibratory and strident, suggestive of the passing of the day's meridian, and heralding the long, drowsy lengths of the afternoon to come, the little boat, with that bright touch of scarlet, shot out from behind the wooded bend of the river, and in a few minutes was beached on the gravel and Stuart was within the gates of Fort Loudon.

He came with a face of angry, puzzled excitement that surprised his brother officers, whose discrimination may have been blunted in the joy of his safe and unexpected return and the fair promises of the terms of capitulation he had secured. Never had a vanquished enemy been more considerately and cordially entreated than he at Choté. Oconostota and Cunigacatgoah had come down to the river-bank on the news of his approach and had welcomed him like a brother. To the great council-hall he was taken, and not one word would Oconostota hear of his mission till food was placed before him,—fish and fowl, bread, and a flask of wine!

"And when Oconostota saw that I had been so nearly starved that I could hardly eat—Lord!—how his eyes twinkled!" cried Stuart, angrily.

But Oconostota had permitted himself to comment on the fact. He said that it had grieved him to know of the sufferings from famine of his brother and the garrison—for were they not all the children of the same Great Father! But Captain Stuart must have heard of the hideous iniquities perpetrated by the British Colonel in burning the Cherokee towns in the southern region, where many of the inhabitants perished in the flames, and slaying their warriors who did naught but defend their own land from the invaders—the land which the Great Spirit had given to the Cherokees, and which was theirs. And, now that the terrible Colonel Montgomery had been driven out with his hordes, still reeking with Cherokee blood, it was but fit that the Cherokees should take possession of Fort Loudon, which was always theirs, built for them at their request, and paid for with their blood, shed in the English service, against the enemies of the English colonists, the French, who had always dealt fairly with the Cherokees.

Captain Stuart bluntly replied that it did not become him to listen to reflections upon the methods in which British commanders had seen fit to carry out the instructions of the British government. They had, doubtless, acted according to their orders, as was their duty. For his own mission, although Fort Loudon could be held some space longer, in which time reënforcements, which he had reason to think were on the march, might come to its relief, the officers had agreed that the sufferings of the garrison were such that they were not justified in prolonging their distress, provided such terms of capitulation could be had as would warrant the surrender of the fort.

As the interpreter, with the wooden voice, standing behind the chief, gabbled out this rebuke of the Cherokee king's aspersions on Montgomery, Stuart's ever quick eye noted an expression on the man's face, habitually so blank and wooden,—he remembered it afterward,—an expression almost applausive. Then his attention was concentrated on the circumlocutions of Oconostota, who, in winding phrase almost affectionate, intimated the tender truth that, without waiting for these reënforcements, the enfeebled garrison could be overpowered now and destroyed to the last man by a brisk onslaught, the Cherokees taking the place by storm.

Stuart shook his head, and his crafty candor strengthened the negation.

"Not so long as the great guns bark," he declared. "They are the dogs of war that make the havoc."

Then Oconostota, with that greed of the warlike Cherokee for the details concerning this great arm of the British service, the artillery, always coveted by the Indians, yet hardly understood, listened to a description of the process by which these guns could be rendered useless in a few minutes by a despairing garrison.

Their cannoneers could spike them after firing the last round. And of what value would the fort be to the Cherokees without them,—it would be mere intrenchments with a few dead men,—the most useless things under the sun. The English government would bring new guns, and level the works in a single day. The great chief knew the power of England. In the days when Moy Toy sent his delegation to London, of which he and Atta-Kulla-Kulla were members, to visit King George, they had seen the myriads of people and had heard many great guns fired in salute to the princely guests, and had assisted at the review of thousands and thousands of soldiers.

And with the reminder of all these overpowering military splendors of his great enemy, Oconostota began to feel that he would be glad to secure possession of these few of King George's great guns uninjured, fit to bark, and, if occasion should offer, to bite.

From that point the negotiation took a stable footing. With many a crafty recurrence on the part of Stuart to the coveted artillery at every balking doubt or denial, it was agreed that the stronghold should be evacuated;— "That the garrison of Fort Loudon march out with their arms and drums, each soldier having as much powder and ball as their officer shall think necessary for their march, and all the baggage they may chuse to carry: That the garrison be permitted to march to Virginia or Fort Prince George, as the commanding officer shall think proper, unmolested; and that a number of Indians be appointed to escort them and hunt for provisions during their march: That such soldiers as are lame or by sickness disabled from marching, be received into the Indian towns and kindly used until they recover, and then be allowed to return to Fort Prince George: That the Indians do provide for the garrison as many horses as they conveniently can for their march, agreeing with the officers and soldiers for payment: That the fort, great guns, powder, ball, and spare arms, be delivered to the Indians without fraud or further delay on the day appointed for the march of the troops."

These terms of capitulation were signed by Paul Demeré, Oconostota, and Cunigacatgoah, and great was the joy the news awoke among the garrison of Fort Loudon. The sick arose from their beds; the lame walked, and were ready to march; almost immediately, in the open space beneath the terrible great guns, were men,—settlers, soldiers, and Indians,—trying the paces of horses, and chaffering over the terms of sale. Provisions were brought in; every chimney sent up a savory reek. Women were getting together their little store of valuables in small compass for the journey. Children, recently good from feeble incapacity to be otherwise, were now healthily bad, fortified by a generous meal or two. And Fifine was stroking the cat's humped back, as the animal munched upon the ground bits of meat thrown prodigally away, and telling her that now she would not be eaten,—so had that terror preyed upon the motherly baby heart! Odalie had some smiling tears to shed for Hamish's sake, in the earnest hope that he might be as well off, and those whom she had consoled in affliction now in their prosperity sought to console her. The officers were hilarious. They could hardly credit their own good fortune—permitted to surrender Fort Loudon, after its gallant defense to the last extremity, to the savage Cherokees, upon just such terms as would have been dictated by a liberal and civilized enemy!

- 166 -

Demeré, after the first burst of reproach that Stuart should have so recklessly endangered himself, and of joy that his mission had been so successfully accomplished, was cheerfully absorbed in destroying such official papers as, falling into the hands of the French, might be detrimental to the British interest. Of them all, only Stuart was doubtful, angry, disconsolate. Perhaps because some fiber of sensitive pride, buried deep, had been touched to the quick by Oconostota's ill-disguised triumph; or he realized that he had labored long here, and suffered much uselessly, and but for the threatened desertion of the garrison felt that the fort might still be held till relief could reach it; or he was of the temperament that adorns success, or even stalwart effort, but is blighted by failure; or he was only staggered by the completeness of his prosperous negotiations with the Cherokees and doubtful of their good faith,—at all events he had lost his poise. He was gloomy, ruminative, and broke out now and again with futile manifestations of his disaffection.

Demeré, burning letter-books and other papers on the hearth of the great chimney-place of the hall, looked up from the table where he sorted them to remind Stuart, as he strode moodily to and fro, not to leave things of value to fall into the hands of the enemy. Stuart paused for a moment with a gloomy face. Then, "They shall not have this," he said angrily. The little red silk riding-mask, that was wont to look down from the wall, null and inexpressive, with no suggestion in its vacant, sightless orbs of the brightness of vanished eyes, with no faint trace of the fair face that it had once sheltered, save as memory might fill the blank contour, began to blaze humbly as he thrust it among the burning papers on the hearth. An odd interpretation of things of value, certainly—a flimsy memento of some bright day, long ago, and far away, when, not all unwelcome, he had ridden at a lady's bridle-rein. Demeré looked at him with sudden interest, seemed about to speak, checked himself and said nothing. And thus with this souvenir the romance of Stuart's life perished unstoried.

More characteristic thoughts possessed him later. He came to Demeré's bedside that night as he lay sleeping in quiet peace, even his somnolent nerves realizing the prospect of release. Stuart roused him with a new anxiety. There was a very considerable quantity of powder in the fort, far more than the Indians, unacquainted with the large charges required for cannon, suspected that they possessed. By surrendering this great supply of powder, Stuart argued, as well as the guns, they only postponed not precluded their destruction. Brought down with the guns to Fort Prince George in the hands of French cannoneers, this ample supply of artillery would easily level those works with the ground. The French officers, who they had reason to suspect were lurking in the Lower Towns, would be unlikely to have otherwise so large a store of ammunition in reach, capable of maintaining a siege, and before this could be procured for the service of the surrendered cannon some reënforcements to the commandant of Fort Prince George would arrive, or an aggressive expedition be sent out from South Carolina.

"At all events this quantity of powder in the hands of the Cherokees makes it certain that a siege of Fort Prince George will follow close on the fall of Fort Loudon," Stuart declared.

Demeré raised himself on his elbow to gaze at Stuart by the light of the flickering candle which the visitor held in his hand.

"I am afraid that you are right," Demeré said, after a grave pause. "But how can we help it?"

"Hide the powder,—hide it," said Stuart excitedly. "Bury it!"

"Contrary to the stipulations and our agreement," returned Demeré.

Stuart evidently struggled with himself. "If these fiends," he exclaimed,— the triumph of Oconostota had gone very hard with him,—"were like any other enemy we could afford to run the chance. But have we the right to submit the commandant of Fort Prince George and his garrison—to say nothing of ourselves and our garrison, hampered as we are with women and children, taking refuge with him,—to the risk of siege and massacre, fire and torture, compassed by materials practically furnished by us,—on a delicate question of military ethics?"

"If we do not keep our word, how can we expect Oconostota to keep his word?" asked Demeré.

"But do we really expect it? Have we any guarantee?"

Once more Stuart hesitated, then suddenly decided. "But if you have scruples"—he broke off with a shrug of the shoulders. "I should leave Oconostota enough powder to amuse him with the guns for a while, but not enough to undertake a siege. The government will surely occupy this place again. I expect to find the powder here when I come back to Fort Loudon."

His words were prophetic, although neither knew it. He cast a hasty glance at Demeré, who again objected, and Stuart went out of the door saying nothing further, the draught flickering, then extinguishing, the flame of the candle in his hand.

It was very dark about midnight when the whole place lay locked in slumber. The sentries, watchful as ever in the block-house towers and at the chained and barred gates, noted now and again shadowy figures about the region of the southeast bastion,—the old exhausted smoke-house had been in that locality,—and thence suppressed voices sounded occasionally in low-toned, earnest talk. No light showed save in glimpses for a while through the crevices in the walls of the building itself, and once or twice when the door opened and was suddenly shut. There Corporal O'Flynn and three soldiers and Captain Stuart himself, armed with mattocks, dug a deep trench in the tough red clay, carefully drawing to one side the dead ashes and cinders left by the fires of his earnest preparations against the siege. Then the lights were extinguished, and from the great traverse, in which was the powder magazine, they brought ten heavy bags of powder, and laid them in the trench, covering them over with the utmost caution, lest a mattock strike a spark from a stone here and there in the earth. At last, still observing great care, they tramped the clay hard and level as a floor, and spread again the ashes and cinders over the upturned ground, laying the chunks of wood together, as they had burnt half out after the last fire many weeks ago.

When Captain Stuart inveigled Captain Demeré thither the next morning, on some pretext concerning the removal of the troops, he was relieved to see that although Demeré was most familiar with the place he had not even the vaguest suspicion of what lay under his feet, for this was the best test as to whether the work had been well done. It was only at the moment of departure, of rendering up the spare arms, and serving out ammunition to the soldiers for the journey, that he was made aware how mysteriously the warlike stores had shrunken, but Oconostota's beadlike eyes glistened with rapture upon attaining the key of the magazine with its hoard of explosives, unwitting that it had ever contained more.

The soldiers went out of the gates in column, in heavy marching order, their flags and uniforms making a very pretty show for the last time on the broad open spaces about Fort Loudon. For the last time the craggy banks and heavily wooded hills of the Tennessee River echoed to the beat of the British drums. Behind, like a train of gypsies, were the horses purchased from the Indians, on which were mounted the women and little girls, with here and there a sick soldier, unable to keep his place in the ranks and guyed by his comrades with reviving jollity, in the face of hope and freedom, as "a squaw-man." The more active of the children, boys chiefly, ran alongside, and next in order came the settlers, now in column as "fencibles," and again one or two quitting the ranks to cuff into his proper place some irrepressible youngster disposed to wander. In the rear were the Indian safe-guards through the Cherokee nation, with their firelocks and feathers and scanty attire that suggested comfort this hot day. For the August sun shone from a sky of cloudless blue; a wind warm but fresh met them going the other way; the dew was soon dried and the temperature rose; the mountains glimmered ethereally azure toward the east with a silver haze amongst the domes and peaks, and toward the west they showed deeply and densely purple, as the summit lines stretched endlessly in long parallel levels.

And so these pioneers and the soldiers set forth on their way out of the land that is now Tennessee, to return no more; wending down among the sun-flooded cane-brakes, and anon following the trail through the dense, dark, grateful shades of the primeval woods. So they went to return no more,—not even in the flickering guise of spectral visitants to the scenes that knew them once,—scarcely as a vague and vagrant memory in the country where they first planted the home that cost them so dearly and that gave them but little.

Nevertheless, a hearty farewell it bestowed this morning,—for they sang presently as they went, so light and blithe of heart they were, and the crags and the hills, and the rocky banks of that lovely river, all cried out to them in varying tones of sweet echoes, and ever and again the boom of the drums beat the time.

CHAPTER XII

The definite ranks were soon broken; the soldiers marched at ease in and out amongst the Indians and the settlers, all in high good humor; jest and raillery were on every side. They ate their dinner, still on the march, the provisions for the purpose having been cooked with the morning meal. Thus they were enabled, despite the retarding presence of the women and children, and the enfeebling effects of the long siege, to make the progress of between fifteen and twenty miles that day. They encamped on a little plain near the Indian town of Taliquo. There, the supper having been cooked and eaten—a substantial meal of game shot during the day's march—and the shades of night descending thick in the surrounding woods, Captain Stuart observed the inexplicable phenomenon that every one of their Indian guards had suddenly deserted them.

The fact, however contemplated, boded no good. The officers, doubtless keenly sensitive to the renewal of anxiety after so slight a surcease of the sufferings of suspense, braced themselves to meet the emergency. A picket line was thrown out; sentinels were posted in the expectation of some imminent and startling development; the soldiers were ordered to sleep on their arms, to be in readiness for defense as well as to gain strength for the morrow's march and rest from the fatigues of the day. The little gypsy-looking groups of women and children, too, were soon hushed, and naught was left the anxious senior officers but to sleep if they might, or in default, as they lay upon the ground, to watch the great constellations come over the verge of the gigantic trees at the east of the open space, and deploy with infinite brilliance across the parade of the sky, and in glittering alignment pass over the verge of the western woods and out of sight. So came the great Archer, letting fly myriads of arrows of flakes of light in the stream near the camp. So came in slow, gliding majesty the Swan, with all the splendor of the Galaxy, like infinite unfoldings of white wings, in her wake. So came the Scorpio, with coil on coil of sidereal scintillations, and here and again the out-thrust dartings of a malign red star. And at last so came the morn.

Demeré, who had placed himself, wrapped in his military cloak, on the ground near Stuart, that they might quietly speak together in the night without alarming the little camp with the idea of precautions and danger and plotting and planning, noted first a roseate lace-like scroll unrolled upon the zenith amidst the vague, pervasive, gray suggestions of dawn. He turned his head and looked at his friend with a smile of banter as if to upbraid their fears;—for here was the day, and the night was past!

A sudden wild clamor smote upon the morning quiet. The outposts were rushing in with the cry that the woods on every side were full of Cherokees, with their faces painted, and swinging their tomahawks; the next moment the air resounded with the hideous din of the war-whoop. Demeré's voice rose above the tumult, calling to the men to fall in and stand to their arms. A volley of musketry poured in upon the little camp from every side.

"The men had been hastily formed into a square."

Demeré fell at the first fire with three other officers and twenty-seven soldiers. Again and again, from the unseen enemy masked by the forest, the women and children, the humble beasts of burden,—fleeing wildly from side to side of the space,—the soldiers and the backwoodsmen, all received this fusillade. The men had been hastily formed into a square and from each front fired volleys as best they might, unable to judge of the effect and conscious of the futility of their effort, surrounded as they were on every side. Now and again a few, impelled by despair, made a wild break for liberty, unrestrained by the officers who gave them what chance they might secure, and with five or six exceptions these were shot down by the Indians after reaching the woods. The devoted remnant, fighting until the last round of ammunition was exhausted, were taken prisoners by the triumphant savages. Stuart, his face covered with blood and his sword dripping, was pinioned before he could be disarmed, and then helpless, hopeless, with what feelings one may hardly imagine, he was constrained to set forth with his captor on the return march to Fort Loudon.

The Cherokees could hardly restrain their joy in thus taking him alive. So far-famed had he become among them, so high did they esteem his military rank, so autocratic seemed his power in the great stronghold of Fort Loudon, with his red-coated soldiers about him, obeying his words, even saluting his casual presence, that it afforded the most æsthetic zest of revenge, the most acute realization of triumph, to contemplate him as he stood bound, bloody, bareheaded in the sun, while the very meanest of the lowest grade of the tribesmen were free to gather round him with gibes and menacing taunts and buffets of derision. His hat had been snatched off in order to smite him with it in the face; his hair, always of special interest to the Indians because of its light brown color and dense growth, was again and again caught by its thick, fair plait with howls of delight, and if the grasp of the hand unaided could have rent the scalp from the head, those fierce derisive jerks would have compassed the feat; more than one whose rage against him was not to be gratified by these malevolently jocose manifestations of contempt, gave him such heavy and repeated blows over the head with the butt of their firelocks that they were near clubbing the prisoner to death, when this circumstance attracted the attention of his captor, Willinawaugh, who was fain to interfere. Stuart, regretting the intervention, realized that he was reserved to make sport for their betters in the fiercer and more dramatic agonies of the torture and the stake.

His fortitude might well have tempted them. In a sort of stoical pride he would not wince. Never did he cry out. He hardly staggered beneath the crushing blows of the muskets, delivered short hand and at close quarters, that one might have thought would have fractured his skull. That the interposition of Willinawaugh was not of the dictates of clemency might be inferred from the manner in which the return journey was accomplished. Forced to keep pace with his captor on horseback Stuart traveled the distance from Taliquo Town to Old Fort Loudon in double-quick time, bareheaded, pinioned, in the blazing meridian heat of a sultry August day. He hoped he would die of exhaustion. In the long-continued siege of Fort Loudon, necessitating much indoor life, to which he was little used, the texture of his skin had become delicate and tender, and now blistered and burned as if under the touch of actual cautery. With the previous inaction and the unaccustomed exposure the heat suggested the possibility of sunstroke to offer a prospect of release.

But he came at last to the great gates of Fort Loudon with no more immediate hurt than a biting grief deep in his heart, the stinging pain of cuts and bruises about his head and face, and a splitting, throbbing, blinding headache. Not so blinding that he did not see every detail of the profane occupancy of the place on which so long he had expended all his thought and every care, in the defense of which he had cheerfully starved, and would with hearty good-will have died. All the precise military decorum that characterized it had vanished in one short day. Garbage, filth, bones, broken bits of food lay about the parade, that was wont to be so carefully swept, with various litter from the plunder of the officers' quarters, for owing to the limited opportunity of transportation much baggage had been left. This was still in progress, as might be judged from the figures of women and men seen through the open doors and now again on the galleries, chaffering and bargaining over some trifle in process of sale or exchange. Indian children raced in and out of the white-washed interiors of the barracks which had been glaringly clean; already the spring branch was choked by various débris and, thus dammed, was overflowing its rocky precincts to convert the undulating ground about it into a slimy marsh. Myriads of flies had descended upon the place. Here and there horses were tethered and cows roamed aimlessly. Idle savages lay sprawling about over the ground, sleeping in the shade. In the block-houses and towers and along the parade, where other braves shouldered the firelocks, the surrendered spare arms, mimicking the drill of the soldiers with derisive cries of "Plesent Ahms!" "Shouldie Fa'lock!" "Ground Fa'lock!" only such injury as bootless folly might compass was to be deplored, but upon the terrepleine in the northeast bastion several Cherokees were working at one of the great cannons, among whom was no less a personage than Oconostota himself, striving to master the secrets of its service. The box of gunner's implements was open, and Stuart with a touch of returning professional consciousness wondered with that contempt for ignorance characteristic of the expert what wise project they had in progress now. For the gun had just been charged, but with that economy of powder, the most precious commodity in these far-away wilds, for which the Indians were always noted. The ball, skipping languidly out, had dropped down the embankment outside and rolled along the ground with hardly more force than if impelled down an alley by a passable player at bowls, barely reaching the glacis before coming to a full halt. Realizing the difficulty, the gun under the king's directions was shotted anew; erring now in the opposite extreme, it was charged so heavily that, perhaps from some weakness in the casting, or the failure to duly sponge and clean the bore, or simply from the expansive force of the inordinate quantity of powder, the piece exploded, killing two of the savages, serving as gunners, and wounding a third. The ball, for the cannon had been improperly pointed by some mischance, struck the side of the nearest block-house, and as its projectile force was partly spent by the explosion, the tough wood turned it; it ricochetted across the whole expanse of the enclosure, striking and killing an Indian lying asleep on the opposite rampart. A vast uproar ensued, and Stuart could have laughed aloud in bitter mirth to see Oconostota almost stunned alike by the surprise and the force of the concussion, timorously and dubiously eying the wreck. Then, with a subdued air of renunciation and finality, "Old Hop," as the soldiers called him, came limping carefully down the steep ramp from the terrepleine, evidently just enlightened as to the dangers lurking about the breech of the cannon, well as he had long been acquainted with the menace of its muzzle. The fury of the savages bore some similarity to the ricochet forces of the misdirected cannon-ball. Stuart plainly perceived himself destined to bear the brunt of the infuriating mishap in which, although he had no agency, he might be suspected of taking secret and extreme delight. It was for a moment a reversal of the red man's supremacy in the arts of war, that had been demonstrated by the results of the siege, the acquisition of the ordnance, the surprise and the massacre of the capitulated garrison. In the stress of the noisy moment, when the corpses had been carried off and the howling women and their friends had followed them to their assigned homes in the barracks, several braves, including Oconostota himself, had become aware of Stuart's return and gathered around him.

Nothing could have been more acutely malevolent than Oconostota's twinkling eyes; no words could have shown a keener edge of sarcasm than his greeting of the officer once more by the title of his dear brother. Stuart, impolitic for once, disdained to respond, and, grimly silent, eyed him with a sort of stoical defiance that struck the Indian's mummery dumb. There was a moment of inaction as they all contemplated him. His vigor, his fortitude, his rank, the consciousness how his proud spirit raged in his defeat and despair, all combined to render him a notable victim and promised a long and a keen extension of the pleasures of witnessing his torture.

And at that instant of crisis, as if to seal his doom, a great guttural clamor arose about the southeast bastion, and here was Willinawaugh, with wild turbulent gesticulations, and starting gleaming eyes, and a glancing upheaving tomahawk, for in the perspective a dozen hale fellows were dragging out of the pit beneath the old smoke-house the ten bags of powder that Stuart had concealed there—only two nights ago, was it?—it seemed a century! How had they the craft to find them, so securely, so impenetrably were they hidden! Stuart's store of Cherokee enabled him to gather the drift of the excited talk. One of the Indians, with the keen natural senses of the savage, had smelled the freshly turned clay—smelled it in that assortment of evil odors congregated in the parade!—and had sought to discover what this might be so recently buried. Fraud! Fraud! the cry went up on every side. Unmasked fraud, and Stuart should die the death! He had violated the solemn agreement by which the garrison was liberated; he had surrendered the spare arms and the cannon indeed, but only a fraction of the powder of the warlike stores—and he should die the death and at once. Stuart wondered that he was not torn to pieces by the infuriated savages, protesting their indignation because of his violation of the treaty,—while his garrison, under the Cherokees' solemn agreement of safe-conduct, lay in all their massacred horrors unburied on the plains of Taliquo. The cant of the Cherokees, their hypocrisy, and their vaunting clamor of conscience made them seem, if one were disposed to be cynical, almost civilized! Doubtless, but for Oconostota's statesmanlike determination to sift the matter first, Stuart could not have been torn from among the tribesmen and dragged to the seclusion of his own great mess-hall, where the door was closed and barred in their distorted faces as they followed with their howls. He was required to stand at one end of the grievously dismantled room and detail his reason for this reserve of the powder. Had he grounds to suspect any renewal of the English occupancy? Had he knowledge of forces now on the march in the expectation of raising the siege of Fort Loudon? Oconostota pointed out the desirability of telling the truth, with a feeling allusion to the Great Spirit, the folly of seeking to deceive the omniscient Indian, as the discovery of the powder sufficiently illustrated, and the discomforts that would ensue to Captain Stuart, should it be found necessary to punish him for lying, by burning him alive in his own chimney-place, admirably adapted for the purpose. Oconostota sat now with his back to it, with all his council of chiefs in a semicircle about him, on the buffalo rug on the broad hearth. The Indian interpreter Quoo-ran-be-qua, the great Oak, stood behind him and looked across the length of the room at Captain Stuart, the only other person standing, and clattered out his wooden sentences.

Stuart could make no further effort. His capacity to scheme seemed exhausted. He replied in his bluff, off-hand manner, his bloody head held erect, that they now had more powder than was good for them,—witness the bursting of that costly great gun! He had buried the powder in the hope of further English occupancy of the fort, which he had, however, no reason to expect; it was only his hope,—his earnest hope! He had left them spare arms, great guns, ball, powder,—much powder,—and if he had seen fit to reserve some store he could say, with a clear conscience, that it was done only in the interests of peace and humanity, and because of doubts of their good faith,—how well grounded the blood shed this day upon the plains of Taliquo might testify! His friends, his comrades, were treacherously murdered under the safe-conduct of the Cherokee nation. And if he were to die too, he was fully prepared to show with what courage he could do it.

His eyes flashed as he spoke; they seemed to transmit a spark across the room to the dull orbs of the interpreter. And what was this? Stuart's knowledge of the Cherokee language enabled him to discern the fact that after a moment's hesitation Quoo-ran-be-qua was clacking out a coherent statement to the effect that the concealment of the powder was Captain Demeré's work, and wrought unknown to Stuart during his absence on his mission to Choté, where, as the great chiefs well knew, he was detained several hours. Stuart stared in astonishment at the interpreter, who, blandly secure in the conviction that the prisoner did not comprehend the Cherokee language, maintained his usual stolid aspect. Whether Stuart's courage so enforced admiration, or whatever quality had secured for him the regard of the higher grade of Indians, the interpreter had sought, by an unrecognized, unrewarded effort, to save the officer's life by a sudden stroke of presence of mind,—a subterfuge which he supposed, in his simplicity, undiscoverable.

There were milder countenances now in the circle, and Stuart's attention was presently concentrated upon an eager controversy between Atta-Kulla-Kulla and Willinawaugh that was curiously enough, at this moment of gravest council, sitting in judgment on the disposal of a human life, a matter of chaffer, of bargain and sale. Willinawaugh had already refused a new rifle and a horse—and then two horses besides, and, still untempted, shook his head. And suddenly the interest in the concealment of the powder collapsed, and they were all looking at Willinawaugh, who gazed much perplexed down at the ground, all his wrinkles congregated around his eyes, eager to acquire yet loath to trade, while Atta-Kulla-Kulla, keen, astute, subtle, plied him with offers, and tempting modifications of offers, for the Cherokees of that date were discriminating jockeys and had some fine horses.

The wind came in at the loop-holes and stirred the blood-clotted hair on the prisoner's brow, and the suspension of the mental effort that the examination cost him was for a moment a relief; the shadowy dusk of the ill-lighted room was grateful to his eyes, the heavy, regular throbbing of his head grew less violent. He could even note the incongruity of the situation when he saw that Willinawaugh resisted upon the point that the matter was with him a question of character! The chief said he had lost his standing in public estimation because he had allowed the Englishman, MacLeod, and his brother, to deceive him on the pretense of being French,—for although he (Willinawaugh) spoke French himself, and that better than some people who had lost their front tooth, he could not understand such French as the two Scotchmen spoke, nor, indeed, as some Cherokees spoke, with their front tooth out.

Savanukah, seated on the rug an expression of poignant mortification on his face, his lips fast closed over the missing tooth, only muttered disconsolately, in his mingled French and Cherokee jargon, "C'est dommage! Sac-llé bleu! Noot-te![J] Ugh! en vérité—O-se-u!"[K]

Willinawaugh, pausing merely for effect, continued. He himself was not an interpreter, to be sure; he was a Cherokee war-captain, with a great reputation to sustain. He had captured the prisoner, and it ill accorded with his honor to yield him to another.

"Cho-eh!"[L] said Atta-Kulla-Kulla, softly.

And Stuart became aware, with a start that almost dislocated his pinioned arms, that it was the transfer of his custody, the purchase of himself, over which they were bargaining.

"Nankke—soutare,"[M] urged Atta-Kulla-Kulla.

Again Willinawaugh shook his head. Was he some slight thing,—seequa, cheefto, an opossum, a rabbit? "Sinnawah na wora!"[N] he cried sonorously. For months, he said, he had besieged that man in his great stronghold of Fort Loudon. Like a panther he had watched it; like a spider he had woven his webs about it; like a wolf by night he had assaulted it; like a hawk he had swooped down upon it and had taken it for the Cherokee nation; and it was a small matter if he, who spoke French so well, had not comprehended an Englishman who spoke French like an unknown tongue, and had let him pass, being deceived!

Would the great chief, whose words in whatever language were of paramount importance, accept a money price?

As several gold pieces rolled out on the buffalo rug, the wrinkles so gathered around Willinawaugh's eyes that those crafty orbs seemed totally eclipsed. He wagged his head to and fro till "him top-feathers" temporarily obliterated the squad of henchmen behind him, in woe that he could not take the money, yet not in indecision.

For lo, he said, who had done so much as he, whose prestige had been touched for a trifle, whose best-beloved brother, Savanukah, had maligned him—for the sake of an Englishman who could not speak French so that it could be understood. He had let that Englishman pass—it was a small matter, and if any had sustained harm it was he himself—for the English brother in the French squaw's dress had escaped through his lines, and came near raising the siege, perhaps—because of the French squaw's dress. But he was not there, and he gave the English boy no front tooth!

At this reiterated allusion, Savanukah's guttural grunt, O-se-u! was almost a groan.

"Rifle, six horses, seven pieces of gold in ransom," said Atta-Kulla-Kulla, slowly massing his wealth.

Once more Willinawaugh shook his head. His prestige had suffered because of aspersions. Yet he had besieged the fort and reduced the two captains and their splendid cannon—this for the Cherokee nation! He had followed hard on the march of the garrison, and with Oconostota and his force had surrounded them and killed many, and captured the great Captain Stuart alive!—this for the revenge of the Cherokee nation! But the scalp of the great Captain Stuart, with its long fair hair, like none others, was a

- 178 -

trophy for himself—this he should wear at his belt as long as he should live, that when he told how he had wrought for the Cherokee nation none should say him nay!

Oconostota suddenly showed a freshened interest. He turned to Atta-Kulla-Kulla, who sat on his right hand, and in an eager, low voice spoke for a moment; the half-king seeming anxious, doubtful, then nodded in slow and deliberative acquiescence. Meantime Willinawaugh's words flowed on.

And—he lifted his fierce eyes in triumph to the captive's face—for all those weary days of beleaguerment, for every puff of smoke from the shotted guns, for every blaze they belched, for every ball, death freighted, they vomited, for every firelock that spoke from the loop-holes in the midnight attack, would be meted out Captain Stuart's penalty—in pangs, with knives, with cords, with hot coals, with flames of fire! The time had come to reward his patience!

"You have done well," said Atta-Kulla-Kulla, "you should think well on your reward!"

And he laid before Willinawaugh a fine gold watch—an English hunting watch, with a double case, and the works were running; doubtless, it was another trophy from the slaughtered officers of Colonel Montgomery's harassed march. Willinawaugh was stricken dumb.

Stuart, in whose heart poor Hope, all bruised and bleeding, with wings broken but about to spread anew, astonished, overcome, with some poignant pang of gratitude that the semblance of kindness should be again extended to him by aught on earth, felt a stifling suffocation when Oconostota's voice broke in on his behalf, for naught from the crafty Cherokee king boded good. The "Great Warrior" declared that Willinawaugh's deeds spoke for themselves—not in French, not in English, but in the Cherokee tongue—in flame and in blood, in courage and in victory. The prisoner's scalp was no great matter in the face of the fact of Fort Loudon. The long fair hair of the English Captain to hang at his belt if he liked, but here was Fort Loudon to swing forever at the silver belt of the Tennessee River! He thought the great Willinawaugh had a right to choose his reward—the goods or the scalp. The scalp Atta-Kulla-Kulla could not wear, not having taken it. And the great Willinawaugh could be present and rejoice when Atta-Kulla-Kulla should choose to burn the captive; for whom he, himself, and Atta-Kulla-Kulla had devised a certain opportunity of usefulness to the Cherokee nation before Stuart should be called upon to expiate his crimes at the stake to satisfy the vengeance of his conqueror.

And who so glad as Willinawaugh to lose naught of his satisfaction— neither his material nor immaterial reward? who now so glad to protest that he would waive any personal gratification that stood in the way of utility to the Cherokee nation? He had the watch in his hand, dangling by the gold chain and seals; the ticking caught his ear. He held it up close, with an expression of childish delight that metamorphosed his fierce face and seemed actually to freshen the expression of "him top-feathers."

In obedience to a motion of Atta-Kulla-Kulla's hand, Stuart followed him out to the parade in the red rays of the sinking sun,—how often thence had he watched it go down behind the level ramparts of the Cumberland Mountains! They passed through the staring motley throng to Captain Demeré's house which the half-king had chosen for his own quarters. It was a log-cabin, floored, and of two rooms with a roofed but open passage between, not unlike the cabins of the region of the present day. Here the Cherokee paused, and with a pass or two of the scalping-knife cut the ropes that pinioned Stuart, opened the door of Demeré's bedroom and with an impassive face sternly motioned him to enter.

The door was closed and Stuart was alone in the quarters reserved for the chief. It had not yet been invaded by the filthy plundering gangs without, and its order and military neatness and decorum affected his quivering nerves as a sort of solace—as of a recurrence of the sane atmosphere of right reason after a period of turbulent mania. And suddenly his heart was all pierced by grief and a sense of bereavement. He had realized his friend was dead, and he felt that this might fairly be considered the better fate. But somehow the trivial personal belongings so bespoke the vanished presence that he yearned for Demeré in his happy release; the shaken nerves could respond to the echo of a voice forever silenced; he could look into vacancy upon a face he was destined to see never again. His jaded faculties, instead of reaching forward to the terrible future, began to turn back vaguely to the details of their long service together; as a reflex of the agitation he had endured he could not, in the surcease of turmoil, compass a quiet mind; he began to experience that poignant anguish of bereavement, self-reproach. He remembered trifling differences they had had in the life they lived here like brothers, and his own part in them gnawed in his consciousness like a grief; he repented him of words long ago forgiven; he thought of personal vexations that he might have sought to smooth away but carelessly left in disregard; and when he lay down in the darkness on the narrow camp-bed with his friend's pillow under his head, Demeré's look this morning, of affectionate banter, with which he had turned on the ground as they lay in the bivouac was so present to his mind that the tears which all his pains and griefs were powerless to summon, sprang to his eyes.

But the weary physical being sunk to rest, and then in the midst of his somnolent mental impressions was wrought a change. Demeré was with him still,—not in the guise of that white, stark face, upturned now to the stars on the plains of Taliquo,—but in his serene, staid presence as he lived; together they were at Fort Loudon, consulting, planning, as in its happier days; now it was the capacity of the spring which they wished to enlarge, and this they had done with blasting-powder; now it was the device to add to the comfort of the garrison by framing the little porches that stood before the doors of the barracks; now it was the erection of an out-work on the side exposed to assault by the river, and they were marking off the ravelin,—Corporal O'Flynn and a squad, with the tapes,—and directing the fashioning of the gabions, the Indians peacefully sitting by the while like some big, unintelligent, woodland animals, while the great, basket-like frames were woven of white oak splints and then filled with the solid earth. He was trying to tell Demeré that he was afraid something would happen to that second gun in the barbette battery on the northeast bastion, for the metal always rang with a queer vibration, and he had had a dream that Oconostota had overcharged and fired it, and it had exploded; and as Demeré was laughing at this folly Stuart realized suddenly the fact that the day was coming in to him again there in his friend's place, as it would come no more to Demeré, though dawning even now at Taliquo Plains where he lay. Instead of that essential presence, on which Stuart had leaned and relied, and which in turn had leaned and relied on him, there was in his mind but a memory, every day to grow dimmer.

Nevertheless, he rose, refreshed and strengthened with the stimulus of that unreal association, which was yet so like reality, with the comrade of his dreams. The orderly instincts of a soldier, as mechanical as the functions of respiration, enabled him, with the use of fresh linen from his friend's relinquished effects, to obliterate the traces of the experiences of the previous day, and fresh and trim, with that precise military neatness that was so imposing to the poor Indian, who could not compass its effect, he went out to meet the half-king with a gait assured and steady, a manner capable and confident, and an air of executive ability, that bade fair for the success of any scheme to which he might lend his aid.

Now and again he marked a glance of deep appreciation from the subtle Atta-Kulla-Kulla,[13] the result of much cogitation and effort at mental appraisement. He feared that important developments were to ensue, and after breakfast, at which meal he was treated like a guest and an equal, and not in the capacity of slave, as were most captives, his host notified him that his presence would be necessary at a council to be held at Choté.

Too acute, far too acute was Atta-Kulla-Kulla not to recognize and comment upon the different aspect of life at Fort Loudon. "The red man cannot, without use, become capable of handling the advantages of the white man," he said in excuse of the anarchy everywhere, with all the riot and grotesqueness and discomfort incident to being out of one's sphere. At

- 181 -

Choté the Cherokees would have seemed as easy, as appropriate, as graceful, as native as the deer.

And at Choté Oconostota seemed as native as the fox. There he sat on the great buffalo rugs, even his faculties much more at command in his wonted place, under the dusky red walls of the clay-daubed dome of the council-chamber. And there Captain Stuart learned the reason of the Cherokee king's interference yesterday to postpone his fate.

For Oconostota had evolved the bold project of the reduction of Fort Prince George. This would consummate the triumph of the fall of Fort Loudon, rid the greater portion of the Cherokee country of the presence of the English, and, with their strongholds in the hands of the Indians, reinforced by a few French gunners, prevent them from ever renewing foothold. The powder left by Stuart he had found, in experimenting with the guns, was not enough for a siege, but with the discovery of the ten extra bags, the supply would prove most ample. The ammunition, together with the guns, was to be at once removed and transported thither, laborious though it might prove.

Stuart attempted to set forth the great difficulties of the undertaking, but was met at every point by the foresight and ingenuity of Oconostota, who had considered evidently each detail. It was plain that the project was feasible, for the Indian, too lazy in peace to hoe a row of beans, is capable in war of prodigies of valorous industry. Stuart began to feel singularly placed, since he did not perceive in this his personal concern, to be thus admitted to a council of war with the enemy. The affability of Oconostota he knew was insincere, but being in the Cherokee king's power the fraud of his amiability was more acceptable than the ferocity of his candor.

"You will accompany the expedition," said the king of the Cherokees, suavely.

"In what capacity?" Stuart asked, also politic, seeking to disguise his anxiety, for any hesitation or refusal would renew his straits of yesterday, Atta-Kulla-Kulla being as eager, as capable, and even more subtle in planning the campaign than Oconostota.

"You will write the letters to the commandant of Fort Prince George, summoning him in our names to surrender, and"—with a twinkle of the eye—"advising him in your own name to comply."

Stuart bowed in bland acquiescence. "And the commandant will find it very easy reading between the lines of any letters I shall write him," he said to himself.

Nevertheless, he still sought to dissuade them. In ignorance of the state of the defenses at Fort Prince George, the strength of the works, the supply of ammunition and provisions, the difficulties that might have arisen in communicating with Charlestown, he sought to avert the dangers of a siege and a possible ultimate disaster such as had befallen Fort Loudon. But although he spoke with force and readiness it was very guardedly.

"If the great Cherokee kings would please to consider the experience which I have had in the management of cannon, I should like to represent that such an attack on Fort Prince George can but be a duel with artillery. I am not well acquainted with the armament of Fort Prince George," he declared, "but it may well chance that the cannon, captured by the Cherokees at so great a cost, may be disabled under a heavy fire and lost to Fort Loudon, which would then become mere intrenchments, to be leveled by a single brisk cannonade."

Atta-Kulla-Kulla, his quick, keen, fiery face aglow, informed him that they would leave a reserve of cannon at Fort Loudon, his advice having been to take with them only six of the great guns and two coehorns.

Stuart was baffled for a moment by the definiteness and the military coherence of these plans. He rallied, however, to say that the gunners of Fort Prince George were trained men, doubtless, and drilled with frequent target practice. And a commander of skill, such as theirs, was essential to the effectiveness of an aggressive demonstration.

A flicker of triumph illuminated Atta-Kulla-Kulla's spirited face. They were provided in this emergency also. He, the great Captain Stuart, would command the artillery of the expedition, the guns to be served by Indians as cannoneers under his direction; nicety of aim was not essential; a few days' practice would suffice, and at short range Fort Prince George was a large target.

For his life Stuart could not control his countenance; the color flared to the roots of his hair; his eyes flashed; his hand trembled; he could not find his voice; and yet angry as he was, he was both amazed and daunted.

Oconostota broke in upon his speechless agitation in a smooth, soothing voice to remind him of the clemency he enjoyed in that his life had been spared, and only yesterday, even at the supreme moment of the discovery of the treachery of his garrison in the concealment of the powder. They had not acquainted Willinawaugh with their designs, for Oconostota himself would lead the expedition. (Stuart as a military man realized a necessity, that sometimes supervenes in more sophisticated organizations, which they felt of curbing the power of a possibly too successful and a too aspiring subordinate.) How generous, declared Oconostota, had been the intercession of the noble Atta-Kulla-Kulla,—half-king of the Cherokees,—who had given in effect all his wealth to ransom him, a mere eeankke, a prisoner, from his warlike captor, the great Willinawaugh, that this military service might be rendered in exchange for his life.

Stuart's eyes turned away; he sought to veil their expression; he looked through the tall narrow door of the red clay walls at the waters of the Tennessee River, silver-shotted and blue as ever, still flowing down and down beyond the site of Fort Loudon—unmindful of its tragic fate, unmindful! The august domes of the Great Smoky Mountains showed now a dull velvet blue against the hard blue of the turquoise sky, and anon drew a silver shimmer of mists about them. Chilhowee Mountain, richly bronze and green, rose in the middle distance, and he was vaguely reminiscent of the day when he watched the young soldier rocking in his boat on the shallows close to the shore, the red coat giving a bright spot of color to the harmonious duller tones of the landscape, and wondered were it possible among these friendly people that the lad could be in danger of a stealthy rifle shot. Now there were no red coats,—nevermore were they to be seen here! Between himself and the water he watched only the white swaying of a tall cluster of the great ethereally delicate snowy blossoms, since known as the Chilhowee lily.

He kept his eyes still averted, his voice deepening with the seriousness of his sentiment as he replied that this was impossible—he could not undertake the command of the Cherokee artillery against Fort Prince George; he was bound by his oath of fidelity which he had sworn to the English government; he could not bear arms against it.

A choking chuckle recalled his gaze to the dusky red interior of the council-chamber. Oconostota's countenance was distorted with derision, and his twinkling eyes were swimming in the tears of the infrequent laughter of the grave Indian—even Atta-Kulla-Kulla's face wore a protesting smile of scorn as of a folly.

Twice Oconostota sought to speak, and he sputtered, and choked, and could not, for his relish of the thought in his mind. Then with a deep mock-seriousness he demanded slowly if it were fireproof. And relapsed into his shaking chuckle.

"What?" demanded Stuart, uncomprehending.

"This oath of yours—to the English government. Does this fidelity so clothe your body that it will not burn and crisp and crinkle in the anguish as of your hell? Does your oath harden your flesh as a rock, that arrows and knives shall not pierce it and sting and ache as they stick there waiting for the slow fires to do their work? Will your oath restore sight to your eyes when a red-hot iron has seared them?" He could say no more for the chuckling delight that shook and shook his lean old body.

Atta-Kulla-Kulla spoke in reproach. The Cherokee kings had offered Captain Stuart life and practically liberty in exchange for this service. If he denied it and talked of his oath, it was but just that vengeance should take its way. Many a Cherokee had fallen dead from the fire of his garrison of Loudon, both of great guns and small, and their blood called still from the ground. A wise man was Captain Stuart, and he would choose wisely.

He was a hearty man, still young, and in full vigor, and, although his life had been but little worth of late, he was loath to throw it away.

He began to temporize, to try to gain time. He sought to talk discontentedly of the project, as if he found it infeasible. The commandant, he said, as if he contemplated him only as the leader of an opposing force, would fight at an infinite advantage within the strong defenses of Fort Prince George, while he outside, without intrenchments except such hasty works as could be thrown up in a night, and beaten down by the enemy's cannonade in the morning, could but expect to have his guns soon silenced. A regular approach would be impracticable. The Indians were not used to fight unscreened. They would never open a parallel under fire, and a vigilant defense would make havoc among the working parties.

He noted the effect of the unfamiliar military theories upon the Indians, as they both seemed to anxiously canvass them.

"You cannot skulk behind a tree with cannon," he continued. "The artillery, to be able to command the fort with its fire, would be within range of the enemy's batteries, and without efficient cover it would be necessary, in serving each piece, for the gunners to be exposed to fire all the time."

An interval of deep, pondering silence ensued. At length Atta-Kulla-Kulla said he believed there would be little or no fight on account of the prisoners.

"What prisoners?" demanded Stuart, shortly.

Then Oconostota explained, with his blandest circumlocutions, that, partly as a check upon his dear brother's good faith, bound as he was by his oath of fidelity to the English government,—and he almost choked with the relish of his derision every time he mentioned it,—and to make sure that he should handle the guns properly, and fire them with due effect,—not aiming them wildly, so that the balls might fly over the fort, or fall short, not spiking the guns, or otherwise demolishing them, all of which his great knowledge of the arm rendered possible, and the ignorance of the poor red man unpreventable, they had determined to take with them the remnant of the garrison, their lives to be pledges of his good conduct and effective marksmanship; and if at last his earnest and sincere efforts should prove unavailing, and the commandant should continue to hold out and refuse to surrender when finally summoned, these, the countrymen and fellow-soldiers of that officer, should be singly tortured and burned before his eyes, within full sight and hearing of Fort Prince George.

As the fiendish ingenuity of this scheme was gradually unfolded, Stuart sat stunned. All the anguish he had suffered seemed naught to this prospect. He staggered under the weight of responsibility. The lives of the poor remnant of his garrison,—more, their death by fire and torture,—hung upon such discretion as he could summon to aid his exhausted powers in these repeated and tormented ordeals. He said nothing; he could not see and he did not care for the succession of chuckles in which Oconostota was resolved at the delightful spectacle of his dismay. The Cherokee had beaten this man of resource at his little game of war, and now had outmaneuvered him at his mastercraft of scheming!

FOOTNOTES:

[J] Tooth!

[K] Very excellent.

[L] Three.

[M] Four—six.

[N] The great hawk is at home!

CHAPTER XIII

Stuart seemed utterly vanquished—his spirit gone. In silence he was conducted back to his quarters in Demeré's house at Fort Loudon. And as there he sat in the spare, clean room, in the single chair it contained, with one elbow on the queer, rough little table, constructed according to a primitive scheme by the post carpenter, he stared forward blankly at the inevitable prospect so close before him. He had not now the solace of solitude in which he might have rallied his faculties. On the buffalo rug on the floor Atta-Kulla-Kulla reclined and smoked his long-stemmed pipe and watched him with impenetrable eyes. Once he spoke to him of the preparations making without, selecting the men for the gunners of the expedition. Stuart lifted his head abruptly.

"I will not go!" he cried in sudden passion. "So help me, God! I will die first!—a thousand deaths. So help me, God!" He lifted his clinched right hand in attestation and shook it wildly in the air.

"He stared forward blankly at the inevitable prospect."

He had a momentary shame in thus giving way to his surcharged feelings, but as he rose mechanically from his chair his restless eyes, glancing excitedly about the room, surprised an expression of sympathy in the face of the Cherokee as he lay coiled up on the rug.

"Atta-Kulla-Kulla!" Stuart exclaimed impulsively, holding out both arms, "feel for me! Think of me! The poor remnant of the garrison! My 'young men'! My own command! I will die first, myself, a thousand deaths!"

Atta-Kulla-Kulla began to argue, speaking partly in Cherokee and now and again in fragmentary English. Neither the one nor the other might be the victim. The commandant at Fort Prince George would yield under this strong coercion.

"Never! Never!" cried Stuart. "His duty is to hold the fort. He will defend it to the last man and the last round of ammunition and the last issuance of rations. For his countrymen to be tortured and burned in his sight and hearing would doubtless give him great pain. But his duty is to his own command, and he will do it."

Atta-Kulla-Kulla seemed doubtful. "And then," argued Stuart, "would such torturing and burning of the surrendered garrison of Fort Loudon before the eyes of the garrison of Fort Prince George be an inducement to them to surrender too, and perhaps meet the same fate? Be sure they will sell their lives more dearly! Be sure they will have heard of the massacre of the soldiers under the Cherokees' pledge of safe-conduct on the plains of Taliquo."

"To-e-u-hah!" Atta-Kulla-Kulla broke out furiously. "To-e-u-hah! It is most true!"

His countenance had changed to extreme anger. He launched out into a bitter protest that he had always contemned, and deprecated, and sought to prevent this continual violation of their plighted word and the obligations of their treaties on the part of the Cherokee nation. It invariably hampered their efforts afterward, as it was hampering them now. It took from their hand the tool of negotiation, the weapon of the head-men, and left only the tomahawk, the brute force of the tribe. Wahkane, wahkane! Was it not so when the treaty of Lyttleton was broken and Montgomery, the Terrible, came in his stead? And when the Cherokees had driven him out, and had taken their revenge on him for the blood which had been shed in his first foray, of what avail to massacre the garrison evacuating Fort Loudon, the possession of which had been for so long a coveted boon, and thus preclude a peaceful rendering of Fort Prince George and the expulsion of all English soldiery from Cherokee soil!

Stuart, cautiously reticent, let him dilate upon all the wrongs wrought in council by the disregard of his advice, only now and again dropping a word as fuel to the flame. Cautiously, too, he led to the topic of the regard and the admiration which the acute mind and the more enlightened moral sentiment of this chief had excited in the English authorities, and the

- 188 -

service this official esteem would have been to the headstrong nation if they had availed themselves of it. For was not Montgomery instructed to offer them terms on his account only? Their cruelty Atta-Kulla-Kulla was brought to perceive had despoiled them of the fruits of their victory; they might have, for all their patience and all their valor, and all their statecraft, only a few more scalps here and there; for presently the great English nation would be pressing again from the south, with Fort Prince George as a base, and the war would be to begin anew.

Deep into the night Atta-Kulla-Kulla dwelt on the treachery toward him,— for he had known naught of the enterprise of the massacre—that had so metamorphosed victory into disaster. The moonlight was coming in at the window, reminding Stuart of that night when he lay at length on the rug and consulted with Demeré and anxiously foreboded events, the news of Montgomery's departure from the country having fallen upon them like a crushing blow. How prescient of disaster they had felt—but how little they had appraised its force! Paler now was the moon, more melancholy, desolate to the last degree as it glimmered on the white-washed walls of the bare, sparely furnished room. His attention had relaxed with fatigue as he still sat with his elbow on the table, his head on his hand, vaguely hearing the Indian councillor droning out his griefs of disregarded statesmanship and of the preferable attitude of affairs, so rudely, so disastrously altered. Suddenly his tone changed to a personal note.

"But it was ill with you, starving with your young men, in this place—long days, heap hungry."

"They seem happy days, now," said Stuart drearily, rousing himself.

"And to-morrow—and yet next day?" asked Atta-Kulla-Kulla.

Stuart stirred uneasily. "I can only die with what grace and courage I can muster," he said reluctantly. He glanced about him with restless eyes, like a hunted creature. "I cannot escape."

He looked up in sudden surprise. The Indian was standing now, gazing down at him with a benignity of expression which warranted the character of bold and forceful mind, and broad and even humane disposition, which this Cherokee had won of his enemies in the midst of the bloodshed and the treachery and the hideous cruelty of the warfare in which he was so much concerned.

"John Stuart," he said, "have I not called you my friend? Have I not given all I possess of wealth to save your life? Do I not value it, and yet it is yours!"

Stuart had forgotten the chief's words that Christmas night at the great gates, but they came back to him as Atta-Kulla-Kulla repeated them, anew.

"I know your heart, and I do not always forget! I do not always forget!"

In Stuart's amazement, in the abrupt reaction, he could hardly master the details of the unfolded plan. The Cherokee declared he had made up his mind to a stratagem, such as might baffle even the designs of Oconostota. He doubted his own power to protect his prisoner, should the king learn that Stuart still refused his services in the expedition to Fort Prince George. Oconostota's heart was set upon the reduction of this stronghold, and so was that of all the Cherokee nation. And yet Atta-Kulla-Kulla could but perceive the flagrant futility of the expectation of the surrender of the garrison on the coercion that Oconostota had devised, especially as Fort Prince George was so much nearer than Fort Loudon to communication with the white settlements. "I contemplate the fact before it happens, they only afterward," he said.

On the pretext of diverting Stuart's mind after his glut of horrors, and in affording him this recreation to secure an influence over him, eminently in character with the wiles of the Cherokee statesman, he gave out that he intended to take his prisoner with him for a few days on a hunting expedition. The deer were now in prime condition, and Captain Stuart was known by the Indians to be specially fond of venison. In the old days at Fort Loudon they had often taken note of this preference, and stopped there to leave as a gift a choice haunch, or saddle, or to crave the privilege of nailing a gigantic pair of antlers to vie with the others on the walls of the great hall. Stuart himself was a famous shot, and was often called by them in compliment A-wah-ta-how-we, the "great deer-killer." The project created no surprise, and Stuart saw with amazement the door of his prison ajar. One might have thought in such a crisis of deliverance no other consideration could appeal to him. But his attachment to the British interest seems to have been like the marrow in his bones. He demanded of Atta-Kulla-Kulla the privilege of being accompanied by two men of the garrison of his own choice.

The chief cast upon him a look of deep reproach. Did he fear treachery? Had his friend, his brother, deserved this?

"I ask much of a friend—nothing of an enemy," declared Stuart, bluffly. "You know my heart—trust me."

Atta-Kulla-Kulla yielded. If he experienced curiosity, the names of the two men which Stuart gave him afforded no clue as to the reason for their selection; one was a gun-smith, an armorer of uncommon skill, and Stuart knew that he was capable of dismounting and removing the cannon,

- 190 -

without injury, through the tangled wilderness to Fort Prince George, should coercion overcome his resistance to the demands of the savages; the other, an artillery-man of long experience and much intelligence, himself adequately fitted to take command of the guns of the expedition, with a good chance of a successful issue. The massacre had swept away most of the cannoneers, and Stuart was aware that the infantrymen left of the garrison would be hardly more capable of dealing with the problems of gun service than was Oconostota, their careless and casual observation being worth little more than his earnest, but dense ignorance. Nevertheless, with his exacting insistence on the extreme limit of demand, he begged Atta-Kulla-Kulla, whose patience was wearing dangerously thin, to let him see them, speak to them for one moment.

"You can hear all I say—you who understand the English so well."

As he stepped into the old exhausted store-room, where the soldiers were herded together, squalid, heart-broken, ill, forlorn, Atta-Kulla-Kulla outside closing the door fast, a quavering cheer went up to greet Stuart. For one moment he stood silent while their eyes met—a moment fraught with feeling too deep for words. Then his voice rang out and he spoke to the point. He wanted to remind them, he said, how the action of the garrison had forced the surrender and left the officers no choice, no discretion; however the event would have fallen out, it would not have happened thus. "But I did not come here to mock your distress," he protested. "I wish to urge you to rely upon me now. I have hopes of securing the ransom of the garrison by the government,"—again a pitiful cheer,—"and as I may never be allowed to see you again this is my only chance. Be sure of this,—no man need hope for ransom who affords the Cherokees the slightest assistance in any enterprise against Fort Prince George, or takes up arms at their command."

He smiled, and waved his hat in courteous farewell, and stepped backward out of the door, apparently guarded by Atta-Kulla-Kulla, while that quavering huzza went up anew, the very sound almost breaking down his self-control.

The next day Stuart, accompanied by Atta-Kulla-Kulla, the warrior's wife, his brother, the armorer, and the artillery-man,—the supposititious hunting party,—set gayly and leisurely forth. But once out of reach of espionage they traveled in a northeastern direction with the utmost expedition night and day through the trackless wilderness, guided only by the sun and moon. What terrors of capture, what hardships of fatigue, what anxious doubt and anguish of hope they endured, but added wings to the flight of the unhappy fugitives. Nine days and nights they journeyed thus, hardly relaxing a muscle.

On the tenth day, having gained the frontiers of Virginia, they fortunately fell in with a party of three hundred men, a part of Bird's Virginia regiment, thrown out for the relief of any soldiers who might be escaping in the direction of that province from Fort Loudon, for through Hamish's dispatches its state of blockade and straits of starvation had become widely bruited abroad. With the succor thus afforded and the terror of capture overpast, the four days' further travel were accomplished in comparative ease, and brought the fugitives to Colonel Bird's camp, within the boundaries of Virginia.

Here Stuart parted from Atta-Kulla-Kulla, with many a protestation and many a regret, and many an urgent prayer that the chief would protect such of the unhappy garrison as were still imprisoned at Fort Loudon until they could be ransomed, measures for which Stuart intended to set on foot immediately. So the half-king of the Cherokees went his way back to his native wilds, loaded by Stuart with presents and commendations, and in no wise regretting the radical course he had taken.[14] Stuart had instantly sent off messengers to apprise the commandant of Fort Prince George of the threatened attack, and to acquaint the governor of South Carolina with the imminence of its danger and the fall of Fort Loudon, for Governor Bull had expected Virginia to raise the siege of Loudon, unaware that that province had dropped all thought of the attempt, finding its means utterly inadequate to march an army thither through those vast and tangled wildernesses carrying the necessary supplies for its own subsistence. Provisions for ten weeks were at once thrown into Fort Prince George, and a report was industriously circulated among the Indians that the ground about it on every side had been craftily mined to prevent approach.[15]

Stuart found that Hamish MacLeod, after performing his mission and setting out for his return to the beleaguered fort with the responsive dispatches, had succumbed to the extreme hardship of those continuous journeys throughout the wild fastnesses, many hundred miles of which were traversed on foot and at full speed under a blazing summer sun, and lay ill of brain-fever at one of the frontier settlements. There Stuart saw him—still so delirious that, although recognizing the officer in some sort, he talked wildly of pressing dispatches, of the inattention and callous hearts of officials in high station, of delays and long waitings for audience in official anterooms, of the prospect of any expedition of relief for the fort, of Odalie, and red calashes, and Savanukah, and rifle-shots, and Fifine, and "top-feathers," and Sandy—Sandy—Sandy; always Sandy!

Later, Stuart was apprised that the boy was on the way to recovery when he received a coherent letter from Hamish, who had learned that Stuart was using every endeavor—moving heaven and earth as the phrase went—to compass the ransom of the survivors of the garrison still at Fort Loudon or the Indian villages in its neighborhood. Hamish had heard of the fall of the fort and the massacre of the evacuating force, and still staggering under the weight of the blow, he reminded Stuart peremptorily enough of the services which Odalie had rendered in venturing forth from the walls under the officer's orders, when he dared not seek to induce a man to volunteer nor constrain one to the duty, and to urge upon his consideration the fact that she might be justly esteemed to have earned her ransom and that of her husband and child. Hamish had an immediate reply by a sure hand.

If it could avail aught to Mrs. MacLeod or any of her household, Stuart wrote with an uncharacteristic vehemence of protest, every influence he could exert, every half-penny he possessed, every drop of his blood would be cheerfully devoted to the service, so highly did he rate the lofty courage which had given to Fort Loudon its only chance of relief, and which under happier auspices would undoubtedly have resulted in raising the siege. Whatever might be forgotten, assuredly it would not be the intrepid devotion of the "forlorn hope" of Fort Loudon.

Hamish, left to his own not overwise devices, decided to return to the country where he had quitted all that was dear to him, dangerous though that return might be. And, indeed, those wild western woods included the boundaries of all the world to him—elsewhere he felt alone and an alien. It seemed strange to realize that there were other people, other interests, other happenings of moment. He long remembered the sensation, and was wont to tell of it afterward, with which he discovered, camping one night at the foot of a tree—for he journeyed now by easy stages, keeping sedulously from the main trail through the forest—the traces of a previous presence, a bit of writing cut on the bark of the tree. "Daniel Boon," it ran, "cilled a bar on tree in the year 1760."

That momentous year—that crucial time of endeavor and fluctuating hope and despair and death—a hunter here, all unaware of the maelstrom of mental and physical agony away there to the south in the shadow of the same mountain range, was pursuing his quiet sylvan craft, and slaughtering his "bar" and the alphabet with equal calm and aplomb.

Perhaps it was well for the future career of the adventurous young fellow that he fell in with some French traders, who were traveling with many packhorses well laden, and who designed to establish themselves with their goods at one of the Lower Towns of the Cherokees; they urged that he should attach himself to their march, whether from a humane sense of diminishing his danger, or because of the industry and usefulness and ever ready proffer of aid in the frank, bright, amiable boy, who showed a quality of good breeding quite beyond their custom, yet not unappreciated. They warned him that it would be certain death to him, and perhaps to his captive relatives, should he in a flimsy disguise, which he had fancied adequate, of dyeing his hair a singular yellow and walking with a limp, which he often alertly forgot, venture into the villages of those Cherokees by whom he had been so well known, and against whose interest he had been employed in such vigorous and bold aggression. The traders showed some genuine feeling of sympathy and a deep indignation, because of the treachery that had resulted in the massacre of the garrison of Fort Loudon,—although the English were always the sworn foe of the French. The leader of the party, elderly, of commercial instincts rather than sylvan, albeit a dead shot, and decorated with ear-rings, had a great proclivity toward snuff and tears, and often indulged in both as a luxury when Hamish with his simple art sought to portray the characters of the tragedy of the siege; and as the Frenchman heard of Fifine and Odalie, and Stuart and Demeré, and all their sufferings and courage and devices of despair— "Quelle barbarie!" he would burst forth, and Hamish would greet the phrase with a boyish delight of remembrance. Two or three of the party made an incursion into Choté when they reached its neighborhood, and returned with the news that the ransom of such of the garrison as were there had taken place, and they had been delivered to the commandant of Fort Prince George, but certain others had been removed to Huwhasee Town and among them were the French squaw, the pappoose, and the Scotchman. In his simplicity Hamish believed them, although Monsieur Galette sat late, with his delicate sentiments, over the camp-fire that night, and stared at it with red eyes, often suffused with tears, and took snuff after his slovenly fashion until he acquired the aspect of a blackened pointed muzzle, and looked in his elevated susceptibility like some queer unclassified baboon.

But at Huwhasee Town Hamish heard naught of those his memory cherished. He was greatly amazed at the courage with which Monsieur Galette urged upon the head-men that some measures should be taken to induce Oconostota to remove that fence, of which they had heard at Choté, which had been built of the bones of the massacred garrison, and give them burial from out the affronted gaze of Christian people. This was not pleasing, he said, not even to the French. He was evidently growing old and his heart was softening!

Lured by a vague rumor expressed among the party that those he sought had been removed to a remote Indian town on the Tsullakee River, Hamish broke away from Monsieur Galette, despite all remonstrances, to seek those he loved in the further west—if slaves, as Monsieur Galette suggested, he would rather share their slavery than without them enjoy the freedom of the king. And, constrained to receive two snuffy kisses on either cheek, he left Monsieur Galette shedding his frequent tears to mix with the snuff on his pointed muzzle.

And so in company with a French hunter in a canoe, Hamish went down the long reaches of the Tsullakee River, coming after many days to their destination, to find only disappointment and a gnawing doubt, and a strange, palsying numbness of despair. For the French traders here, reading Monsieur Galette's letter, looked at one another with grave faces and collogued together, and finally became of the opinion that the members of the family he sought were somewhere—oh, far away!—in the country where now dwelt the expatriated Shawnees, and that region, so great an Indian traveler as he was must know was inaccessible now in the winter season. It would be well for him to dismiss the matter from his mind, and stay with them for the present; he could engage in the fur trade; his society would be appreciated. With the well-meaning French flattery they protested that he spoke the French language so well—they made him upon his proficiency their felicitations. Poor Hamish ought to have known from this statement what value to attach to what they said otherwise, conscious as he was how his verbs and pronouns disagreed, and dislocated the sense of his remarks, and popped up and down out of place, like a lot of puppets on a disorganized system of wires. These traders were not snuffy nor lachrymose; they were of a gay disposition and also wore ear-rings—but they all looked sorrowfully at him when he left them, and he thought one was minded to disclose something withheld.

And so down and down the Tsullakee River he went, and after the junction of the great tributary with the Ohio, he plied his paddle against the strong current and with the French hunter came into the placid waters of the beautiful Sewanee, or Cumberland, flouted by the north wind, his way winding for many miles in densest wintry solitudes. For this was the great hunting-ground of the Cherokee nation and absolutely without population. His adventures were few and slight until he fell in with Daniel Boon, camping that year near the head waters of the Sewanee, who listened to his story with grave concern and a sane and effective sympathy. He, too, advised the cessation of these ceaseless wanderings, but he thought Stuart's letter evasive, somehow, and counseled the boy to write to him once more, detailing these long searches and their futility. Hamish had always realized that Stuart's sentiments, although by no means shallow, for he was warmly attached to his friends, were simple, direct, devoid of the subtlety that sometimes characterized his mental processes. Life to him was precious, a privilege, and its environment the mere incident.

He now replied that he had not dared divulge all the truth while Hamish MacLeod was in the enfeebled condition that follows brain-fever, and had been loath, too, to rob him of hope, only that he might forlornly mourn his nearest and dearest. But since the fact must needs be revealed he could yet say their sorrows were brief. In that drear dawn on the plains of Taliquo the mother and child were killed in the same volley of musketry, and afterward, as he ordered from time to time the ranks to close up, he saw Sandy, who had been fighting in line with the troops, lying on the ground, quite dead. "You may be sure of this," Stuart added; "I took especial note of their fate, having from the first cared much for them all."

The terrible certainty wrought a radical change in Hamish. From the moment he seemed, instead of the wild, impulsive, affectionate boy, a stern reserved man. In the following year he enlisted in a provincial regiment mustered to join the British regulars sent again by General Amherst to the relief of the Carolina frontier; for the difficulties in Canada being set at rest, troops could be put in the field in the south, and vengeance for the tragedy of Fort Loudon became a menace to the Cherokees, who had grown arrogant and aggressive, stimulated to further cruelties by their triumphs and immunity. Nevertheless, Atta-Kulla-Kulla went forth to meet the invaders, and earnestly attempted to negotiate a treaty. It was well understood now, however, that he was in no sense a representative man of his nation, and his mission failed. Lieutenant-Colonel James Grant, on whom Colonel Montgomery's command had now devolved, at the head of this little army of British regulars and provincials, preceded by a vanguard of ninety Indian allies and thirty white settlers, painted and dressed like Indians, under command of Captain Quentin Kennedy,—in all about twenty-six hundred men,—continued to advance into the Cherokee country. At Etchoee, the scene of the final battle of Colonel Montgomery's campaign in the previous year, they encountered the Cherokees in their whole force—the united warriors of all the towns. A furious battle ensued, both sides fighting with prodigies of valor and persistence, that resulted in breaking forever the power of the Cherokee nation. Three hours the rage of the fight lasted, and then the troops, pushing forward into the country, burned and slew on every side, wasting the growing crops all over the face of the land, and driving the inhabitants from the embers of their towns to the refuge of caves and dens of wild beasts in the mountains. They stayed not their hand till Atta-Kulla-Kulla came again, now to humbly sue for peace and for the preservation of such poor remnant as was left of his people.

After this the colonists came more rapidly into the region. A settlement sprang up at Watauga, the site of one of Hamish's old camps as he had journeyed on his fruitless search for those who had made his home and the wilderness a sort of paradise. But the place, far away from Loudon though it was, seemed sad to him. The austere range of mountain domes on the eastern horizon looked down on him with suggestions which they imparted to none others who beheld them. He and they had confidences and a drear interchange of memories and a knowledge of a past that broke the heart already of the future. He was glad to look upon them no more! His mind had turned often to the trivial scenes, the happier times, when, unbereaved of hope, he had hunted with the Frenchman on the banks of the beautiful Sewanee River. And he welcomed the project of a number of the pioneers to carry their settlement on to the region of the French Salt Lick, which other hunters had already rendered famous, and with a few of these he made his way thither by land while the rest traveled by water, the way of his old journey in search of his lost happiness. And here he lived and passed his days.

He heard from Stuart from time to time afterward, but not always with pleasure. It is true that it afforded him a sentiment of deep gratification to learn that the Assembly of South Carolina had given Stuart a vote of thanks for his "courage, good conduct and long perseverance at Fort Loudon," with a testimonial of fifteen hundred pounds currency, and earnestly recommended him to the royal governor for a position of honor and profit in the service of the province; the office of Superintendent of Indian Affairs for the South having been created, Stuart's appointment thereto by the Crown was received with the liveliest public satisfaction, it being a position that he was pronounced in every way qualified to fill.[16] For some years this satisfaction continued, failing only when, in the growing differences between the colonists and Great Britain, Stuart, wholly devoted to the royal cause, conceived himself under obligations to carry out the instructions which the British War Department sent to him and the four royal governors of the southern provinces to use every endeavor to continue the Indians in their adherence to the British standard as allies against all its enemies; even concocting a plan with General Gage, Governor Tonyn, Lord William Campbell, and other royalists,—which plan happily failed,—to land a British army on the western coast of Florida, whence, joined by tories and Indians, the united force should fall upon the western frontiers of Carolina at the moment of attack on the eastern coast by a British fleet, in the hope that the province thus surrounded would be obliged to sue the royal government for peace.

Hamish had had some opportunity at Fort Loudon to observe the tenacity with which Stuart at all hazards adhered to his "instructions and the interest of the government," but in this crisis it ceased to appear in the guise of duty. In such a time it seemed to Hamish an independent, enlightened judgment partook of the values of a pious patriotism. A permanent breach in their friendship was made when Stuart wrote to Hamish to call his attention to the fact that the MacDonalds of Kingsburgh and the MacLeods and other leal Scotch hearts in the southern provinces were fighting under the royal banner. Hamish replied succinctly that "on whatever side the MacLeods fought, with whatever result, be sure the thing would be well done." As if to illustrate the fact, he himself some time afterward set forth with the "mountain men" to march against the royalists under Ferguson, and was among the victors in the battle of King's Mountain.

In the earlier times of the settlement of the State, fraught with troubles with the Indians, who, more timorous than formerly, were yet more skulking, Hamish was wont to take with hearty good-will to the rifle, the knife, the pistol, and the firebrand. He was with Sevier on more than one of those furious forays, when vengeance nerved the hand and hardened the heart, for many of the pioneers avenged the slain of their own household. But as he grew old, the affinity of his hand for the trigger slackened, and he liked only the blaze of the benignant fireside; sometimes he would laugh and shake his gray head and declare that he reminded himself of Monsieur Galette, with his theories of sweet peace in that fierce land, and his soft heart and his sinewy old hand that could send a bullet so straight from the bore of his flintlock rifle. And so great a favorite did Monsieur Galette become in Hamish's fireside stories, so often clamored for, that he would ask his grandchildren, clustering about him, if they would like him better with a muzzle of snuff and a pair of ear-rings and a tear-discoursing eye, and declare that he must take measures to secure these embellishments.

And so, gradually, by slow degrees, he was led on to talk of the past,—of the beautiful Carolina girl who had been his brother's wife, of the quaint babble of Fifine, of Stuart and Demeré, of Corporal O'Flynn, and the big drum-major, and the queer old African cook, and the cat that had been so cherished—but he never, never ventured a word of Sandy, to the last day of his life; Sandy!—for whom he had had almost a filial veneration blended with the admiring applausive affection of the younger brother for the elder.

When he had grown very old—for he died only in 1813—he had a beneficent illusion that might come but to one standing, as could be said, on the borderland of the two worlds. It came in dreams, such perhaps as old men often dream, but his experiences made it the tenderer. Sometimes in the golden afternoon of summer, as he sat in placid sleep, with his long, white hair falling about his shoulders, one of his wrinkled, veinous hands lying on the arm of his chair would tremble suddenly and contract with a strong grasp, and he would look up, at naught, with a face of such joyous recognition and tender appeal, that the children, playing about, would pause in their mirth and ask, with awe, what had he seen.

And it seemed that he had felt his hand caught with a certain playful clasp such as years ago—more than half a century—Odalie was wont to give it, when she had been waiting for him long, and would wait no longer. And looking up, he could see her standing there, waiting still, smiling serenely, joyously as of yore; and so she would stand till the dream vanished in the reality of the children clustering around his knees, besieging him once more for the story of Old Fort Loudon.

NOTES

1 Page 8. In addition to luring an enemy within shot by the mimicry of the voice of bird or beast the Indians' consummate art of ambuscade enabled them to imitate the footprints of game by affixing the hoofs of deer or buffalo or the paws of bear to their own feet and hands, and thus duplicate the winding progress of these animals for miles with such skill as to deceive not merely the white settlers, new to the country, but Indian enemies of other tribes, expert woodmen like themselves.

2 Page 18. The name of this famous town is variously given. Adair spells it as Choàte. Bancroft inclines to Chotee. Bartram has it as Chote-Great. Some of the old maps show it as Chotte. Modern historians of Tennessee, Hayward, J. G. M. Ramsey, Putnam, and others make it Chota, but most of the earlier writers concerning this region adopt the French rendering and call it Choté; Hewatt, however, David Ramsey, and others use the accent grave, Chotè. This town, seldom alluded to without the phrase "old town" or "beloved town," to distinguish it from another Indian village of the same name among the Lower Towns, was a veritable "city of refuge," and the only one of the Cherokee nation. A murderer, even if a white man and the victim a Cherokee, might live for years here secure from vengeance. Although there is an instance known of a malefactor, who sought an asylum here and was prevented from landing, being held down in the Tennessee River until drowned, still the rule was inviolable that if the refugee could but gain a footing on the ever-sacred soil, he was as safe as if clinging to the horns of an altar. This fact contributed, with other confirmatory circumstances of usage and tradition, to continue the speculations touching the identity of the American Indians with the lost tribes of Israel. Humboldt says that from the most remote times of the Missions the opinion has been entertained that the languages of the American Indians and the Hebrew display extraordinary analogies. He ascribes this fact to the position of the personal and possessive pronouns at the end of the nouns and verbs, and the numerous tenses of the latter, a characteristic of both the Indian and Hebrew tongues which naturally struck the attention of the monks. An analogy, however, does not go far to prove an identity of origin. He refers to Adair as among travelers "somewhat credulous who have heard the strains of the Hebrew Hallelujah among the Chickasaws and Choctaws of North America,"—and he might have added the Cherokees also. James Adair, however, could hardly be called a traveler. He published in London in 1775 the results of his observation during a residence of forty years as a trader among the

Chickasaws and neighboring tribes. He adduces many analogies of their languages with the Hebrew, and calls attention to many customs for which he seeks to discern precedent in the Mosaic dispensation. How much he had read of previous speculations it is impossible to say. He protests that he is but a trader and not "a skillful Hebraist," by his vocation obliged to write far from all libraries, literary associations, and conversation with the learned, compelled even to keep his papers secret from the observation of the Indians, always very jealous of the enigmatical "black marks" of the traders' correspondence, but he quotes largely from many writers both English and foreign—the Reverend Mr. Thorowgood, Don Antonio de Ulloa, Acosta, Benzo, etc., and shows considerable aptness of logic in adapting his theories to his investigations into the structure of the Indian languages. Such nice verbal distinctions, such order and symmetry, such a train of subtle and exact religious terms, he argues, could not be invented by a people so ignorant and illiterate as the modern Indian, and contends that they obviously bear all the distinctive marks of a language of culture. He further declares that one of the Chickasaw prophets, the Loache, assured him that they had once had an "old beloved speech," which in the course of time and national degeneration they had lost. In this connection, but entirely apart from all Hebraic analogies, one is moved to wonder if there were also among them a reminiscence of an "old beloved character," and if the extraordinary invention of the Cherokee character of the "syllabic alphabet" by the Indian, Guest, early in the present century, partly partakes of the nature of tradition.

3 Page 22. The high value which the French government placed on the services of these allies may be inferred from a remark which has come down from a council of state, in reference to their conduct in this battle: "Quoique je n'approuve pas qu'on mange les morts, cependant il ne faut pas quereller avec ces bonnêtes gens pour des bagatelles."

4 Page 38. Among others bearing witness to these strange relics, Timothy Flint says, in his History and Geography of the Mississippi Valley: "In this state [Tennessee] burying grounds have been found where the skeletons seem all to have been pigmies. The graves in which the bodies were deposited are seldom more than two feet or two feet and a half in length. To obviate the objection that these are all the bodies of children, it is affirmed that the skulls are found to have possessed the dentes sapientiæ and must have belonged to persons of mature age. The two bodies that were found in the vast limestone cavern in Tennessee, one of which I saw at Lexington, were neither of them more than four feet high; the hair seemed to have been sandy, or inclining to yellow. It is well known that nothing is so uniform in the present Indian as his lank, black hair. From the pains taken to preserve the bodies, and the great labor of making the

funeral robes in which they were folded, they must have been of the 'blood royal' or personages of consideration in their day." (Hayward, in his quaint and rare Natural and Aboriginal History of Tennessee, referring to the curious method of interment, in a copperas cave, of two mummies, both of full size, however, arrayed in fabrics of great beauty, evincing much mechanical skill in manufacture, also mentions the hair on the heads of both as long, and of a yellow cast and a fine texture.) Webber, in his Romance of Natural History, gives the size of the diminutive sarcophagi of the supposed pygmies found in Tennessee as three feet in length by eighteen inches in depth. Hayward also mentions the pygmy dwellers of Tennessee, and another writer still, describing one of these singular graveyards of the "little people," states that the bones were strong and well formed, and that one of the skeletons had about its neck ninety-four pearls. The painfully prosaic hypothesis of certain craniologists that such relics were only those of children is, of course, rejected by any person possessed of the resources of imagination.

5 Page 40. This name is also given in one or two instances as Dejean, and several dates both earlier and later have been assigned to the disastrous visit to Choté to which reference is here made.

6 Page 82. Washington readily recognized the futility of the cumbrous regular military methods in a rough, unsettled country. On the Forbes expedition, to counteract the French and their Indian allies, Washington continually sent out small parties of the Cherokees under his command. "Small parties of Indians," said he, "will more effectually harass the enemy by keeping them under continual alarms than any parties of white men can do." However, "with all his efforts," says Irving, "he was never able to make the officers of the regular army appreciate the importance of Indian allies in these campaigns in the wilderness." But the fact has been taught elsewhere, both earlier and later than Washington's day. General Gordon, in his journal, says of the Soudan: "A heavy lumbering column is nowhere in this land. Parties of forty or sixty men moving swiftly about will do more than any column. Native allies, above all things, at whatever cost. It is the country of the irregular, not of the regular. I can say I owe the defeats in this country to having artillery with me, which delayed me much, and it was the artillery with Hicks which in my opinion did for him." And as if he himself merely turned back a leaf instead of the pages of centuries, he here inserts an extract from Herodotus: "Cambyses marched against the Ethiopians without making any provision for the subsistence of his army or once considering that he was going to carry his arms to the remotest parts of the world, but as a madman ... before the army had passed over a fifth of the way all the provisions were exhausted, and the beasts of burden were eaten.... Now if Cambyses had then led his army back he would have

proved himself a wise man. He, however, went on ... the report was that heaps of sand covered them over, and they disappeared." Gordon comments, "Hicks' army disappeared. The expedition was made into these lands."

7 Page 137. This pride flourished probably too far on the frontier to be deteriorated by the knowledge of the gradual decline in the popularity of the periwig then in progress, for only a few years later the wig-makers of London found it necessary to petition the king, setting forth their distresses occasioned by the perversity of the men of his realm in persisting in wearing their own hair. The most definite outcome of this proceeding was the sprightly travesty of the petition, appearing in the Gentleman's Magazine on behalf of the carpenters, entreating his majesty to wear a wooden leg himself, and to require this of all his subjects, since otherwise the advent of peace bade fair to ruin the joiner's trade in wooden legs.

8 Page 148. The Duke of Cumberland has never been considered what is prettily called a "lovely character." His temperament, which would not even brook that certain gentlemen, whom he denominated with a profane adjective "old women," should talk to him "about humanity" (and it may be said in passing that these hopeful "old women" were most obviously condemned to disappointment at least), his rigid discipline of his own troops, and his unparalleled brutality to the enemy, leave the devotion exhibited for him by his soldiers to be accounted for only by the admiration which they felt for his personal courage, which was very great, and of which Walpole tells a good story about this time,—of course before the days of anæsthetics: "The Duke of Cumberland is quite recovered after an incision of many inches into his knee. Ranby [the surgeon] did not dare to propose that a hero should be tied, but was frightened out of his senses when the hero would hold the candle himself, which none of his generals could bear to do: in the middle of the operation the Duke said 'Hold!' Ranby said, 'For God's sake, Sir, let me proceed now—it will be worse to renew it.' The Duke repeated, 'I say, hold!' and then calmly bade them give Ranby a clean waistcoat and cap; 'for,' said he, 'the poor man has sweated through these.' It was true; but the Duke did not utter a groan."

9 Page 168. It is with a renewal of confidence in the better aspects of human nature, and the genuineness of such sanctions as control civilized war that we realize that the French and English officers encountering dangers so far transcending legitimate perils as those pervading Indian fighting manifested individually, now and again, a true and soldierly sympathy with one another, and sought to protect the helpless in their power, often liberating those exposed to torture at the hands of their savage allies. For the methods of the Indians were by no means ameliorated by association with their civilized comrades, and they could scarcely be held

- 203 -

subject to any control. Washington himself, whose capacity in authority amounted to a special genius, even when only a young provincial officer, could not restrain his Indian allies from scalping the slain, and in several instances it required his utmost exertions to prevent a like fate from befalling his own living prisoners.

10 Page 217. Governor Lyttleton on the request of Atta-Kulla-Kulla released Oconostota, Fiftoe, the chief warrior of Keowee Town, and the head warrior of Estatoe, who the next day surrendered two other Indians to be held as substitutes. Although it has been generally said that there were twenty-two hostages, only twenty-one seem to have been detained, and it is therefore possible that Oconostota was liberated without exchange, on account of his position and influence in the tribe, being always known as the "Great Warrior." The names of the hostages detained are as follows: Chenohe, Ousanatanah, Tallichama, Tallitahe, Quarrasatahe, Connasaratah, Kataetoi, Otassite of Watogo, Ousanoletah of Jore, Kataletah of Cowetche, Chisquatalone, Skiagusta of Sticoe, Tanaesto, Wohatche, Wyejah, Oucachistanah, Nicolche, Tony, Toatiahoi, Shallisloske, and Chistie.

11 Page 236. Bancroft says this detached force comprised six hundred Highlanders and six hundred Royal Americans. Adair says it consisted of twelve hundred Highlanders. Other historians add to this number a body of grenadiers. Hewatt, who writes almost contemporaneously, publishing in 1779, and who was a resident of Charlestown, where the force landed and whence it departed, states that it consisted of a battalion of Highlanders and four companies of the Royal Scots, and it was there joined by a company of South Carolina Volunteers. He further mentions that upon Colonel Montgomery's return to New York he left four companies of his force in Charlestown, upon the urgent request of the governor and assembly, to aid the defense of the Carolina frontier, and that these were of the royal regiment under the command of Major Frederick Hamilton. The Royal Scots, being one of the oldest and most celebrated of military organizations, has the peculiar claim on the consideration of all the world, that having been the body-guard of King Louis XI. of France, the renowned Scottish Archers, it must surely bear on the ancient and illustrious rolls the ever-cherished name of Quentin Durward, for are we not told that the venerable commander of the guard, Lord Crawford, entered it there himself? And if it is not now to be seen, why—so much the worse for the ancient and illustrious rolls!

12 Page 261. The personal vanity of the Cherokees was so great that after discovering the functions of a mirror the men were never without one. Even in their most unimpeded war-trim they carried a mirror slung over one shoulder and consulted it from time to time with pleasure doubtless. When the small-pox broke out among them, those whose appearance had

suffered from that disease could not endure to survive their disfigurement, and promptly took their own lives, although suicides were buried without the highly esteemed honors usually paid to the dead.

13 Page 366. The temperament of Atta-Kulla-Kulla seems far more complex than the simple traits attributed usually to untrained character. Apart from his savage craft, courage, and a sort of natural eloquence which he shared with his tribe, the close discernment shown in some of his speeches still extant, his magnanimity, his capacity to receive and assimilate new impressions, his diplomatic talents, all suggest a versatile mind, and he also possessed a caustic wit to which he was wont to give rein touching the oft-broken promises of one of the governors of South Carolina, from whom it is related he had received many letters which he said "were not agreeable to the old beloved speech." He kept them regularly piled in a bundle in the order in which he had received them, and often showed them. "'The first,' he used to say, 'contained a little truth,' and he would devise fantastic excuses for the failure of the rest of it, urging the governor's perplexing rush of official business which had occasioned him to forget his strong promises. 'But count,' said he, 'the lying black marks of this one'—and he would descant minutely on every circumstance of it." His patience, he would declare, was exhausted, and he felt that the letters were "nothing but an heap of broad black papers and ought to be burnt in the old year's fire." The old year's fire was a symbol of departed values, the new year's fire being kindled with great ceremony by the Cheera-taghe, or prophets, "men of the divine fire."

14 Page 386. It is pleasant to know that this strong friendship suffered no diminution by reason of time and distance. Bartram relates that when he traveled in the Cherokee country in 1773 he met descending the heights a company of Indians all well mounted on horses. "I observed a chief at the head of the caravan, and as they came up I turned off from the path to make way in token of respect, which compliment was accepted and gracefully and magnanimously returned, for his highness, with a gracious and cheerful smile, came up to me and clapping his hand on his breast offered it to me, saying, 'I am Ata-Cul-Culla,' and heartily shook hands with me, and asked me if I knew it. I answered that the good spirit who goes before me spoke to me and said 'that is the great Ata-Cul-Culla.'" The chief then asked him if he came direct from Charlestown, and if his friend John Stuart were well. Mr. Bartram was able to his great pleasure to reply that he had seen John Stuart very recently, and that he was well.

15 Page 386. French emissaries were shortly in the vicinity of this fort. At a great meeting of the Cherokee nation the indefatigable Louis Latinac struck a hatchet into a log, crying out, "Who will take up this for the king of France?" Saloué, the young warrior of Estatoe, instantly laid hold of it,

exclaiming, "I am for war!" And in indorsement of this compact many tomahawks were brandished, already red with British blood.

16 Page 397. As an interesting example of the appropriate and successful method to address barbarous peoples, the historian Hewatt gives entire the text of a speech to several tribes of Indians which Stuart, in his capacity of superintendent of Indian affairs for the South, delivered at a general congress at Mobile, attended by Governor Johnstone and many British officers and soldiers. It is strikingly apt, and despite the figurative language for which the Indians had so strong a preference, it is direct and simple, bold yet conciliatory, dignified in tone, but with a very engaging air of extreme candor, and it may be that Stuart's influence over them lay chiefly in fair and impartial measures and the faithful performance of promises. Among the writers of that date he is rarely mentioned without some reference to his mental ability, which seems to have been very marked, or to the exact and strict fidelity with which he followed the letter and spirit of his instructions. A certain fling, however, by one who had wanted the office to which Stuart was afterward appointed is so deft a bit of character-drawing in few words that, regardless of its obvious spite, it is worth repeating,—"a haughty person, devoted to parade, and a proud uniform."

Milton Keynes UK
Ingram Content Group UK Ltd.
UKHW030848141124
451205UK00005B/405